Praise for *Checkmate, My Lord*

"Spies, adventure, risk, high stakes attraction—*Checkmate, My Lord* is a compelling read that will keep you turning pages way past midnight."

—Anna Campbell, author of
Seven Nights in a Rogue's Bed

"Devlyn's seamless writing will entice readers and keep them eager for the next installment."

—*Publishers Weekly* Starred Review

"Devlyn's edgy and sexy series is gaining momentum, and historical-romantic suspense fans, particularly those who enjoy Brenda Joyce, will delight in this."

—*Booklist*

"If spies, danger, murder, suspense, sexual tension, and a fast pace are what a reader craves, then Devlyn's second Nexus novel is the perfect read. Devlyn delivers an emotional, powerful read."

—*RT Book Reviews*

"*Checkmate, My Lord* is an edge-of-your-seat-exciting read!"

—*Fresh Fiction*

"Very fast-paced...had me on the edge of my seat. I strongly recommend reading *Checkmate, My Lord* for its steamy romance and thrilling espionage from a promising new author."

—*Night Owl Reviews* Reviewer Top Pick, 4.5 Stars

A Lady's Secret Weapon

TRACEY DEVLYN

sourcebooks
casablanca

Published by Sourcebooks Casablanca, an imprint of Sourcebooks,
Inc.
P.O. Box 4410, Naperville, Illinois 60567-4410
(630) 961-3900
Fax: (630) 961-2168
www.sourcebooks.com

Printed and bound in the United States of America.
VG 10 9 8 7 6 5 4 3 2 1

To all the silent, unsung heroes… Thank you.

Prologue

PAIN SPLINTERED INSIDE ETHAN'S SKULL THE MOMENT his head slammed against the cold surface. Against his will, a moan ripped from his throat, and his body curled into a tight, protective knot.

"*Dammit.*" His breath huffed against the floor, forcing a cloud of ancient dust into his face.

"Careful, my lord," a voice rasped, a moment before something soft slid beneath Ethan's head.

He tried to open his eyes but managed only a small slit, barely enough to discern the broken crate to his left and the hooded figure kneeling at his side.

"Where am I?" Ethan made another attempt to open his eyes, to no avail.

"In a warehouse near the London Docks."

Docks. Images flashed through his mind like the blast of a firing squad. Three Goliaths, an uncomfortable carriage ride, a sound beating in a dockside alleyway. A cool hand pressed against his throbbing forehead.

Ethan's jaw clenched. He'd been so close to locating the Frenchman who had brutalized his sister. The anticipation of snapping the man's neck had made him lose sight of his surroundings, for which he'd paid dearly.

"How did I get here?" He struggled to a sitting position. "Who are you?"

The cloaked figure's gloved hands halted his clumsy attempt. "You were carried, and my identity is of no consequence."

Unable to resist, Ethan eased back down. Even though the cloak's hood hid his savior's features, Ethan felt the stranger's intense scrutiny. "Why do you protect your face? You have nothing to fear from me."

"What makes you think fear is the reason behind my need for privacy?"

Ethan sensed, more than saw, his savior retreating. An unfamiliar terror gripped his gut. "Wait."

"Rest, Lord Danforth. You are safe here."

Quiet confidence laced the stranger's raspy voice, soothing the edges of Ethan's fear. Never had he felt so helpless, or so tired. He fought the pull of oblivion for all of ten seconds. Before he slipped into darkness, a single thought registered.

How did the stranger know my name?

❦

Sydney paused to give her eyes time to adjust to the large, gloom-filled room. The moment the makeshift bed against the far wall took shape, she moved quietly to the viscount's side.

The low light hid most of the destruction to his handsome face, as did the cold compress over his swollen eyes. However, she could still see the darkened flesh across his jaw. The apothecary she brought in to assess the damage had discovered severe bruises covering his torso and lacerations dotting his face and body. Thankfully, she had detected no broken bones, though the woman had cautioned her that he might have sustained injuries inside his body. Only time would reveal what's hidden beneath the flesh.

Rest, cold compresses, and beef tea would see him through the worst of it, the apothecary had said. Sydney had no doubt. His lordship had youth, strength, and sheer stubbornness on his side. Besides, he'd likely survived far worse. Still, she didn't want to wake him from his healing slumber. He'd hardly moved an inch since they placed him on the narrow cot hours ago. Every so often, she would hold her fingers below his nose to make sure Death had not visited while she'd been away.

Sydney sighed. No matter how difficult, she would follow the apothecary's prescribed orders. The quicker his lordship healed, the quicker she could send him on his way. She set the tray containing a bowl of beef tea, a linen filled with ice chips, a glass of water, and a bottle of laudanum on the floor and then perched on the edge of his bed. The frame creaked, and his lordship shot upright, his steel-like fingers clamped around her arm, digging deep. The spent compress covering his eyes dropped to the floor with a *splat!*

"What are you doing?" he asked between gritted teeth. He angled his head back to better see her, blinking several times for focus.

Sydney hunched her shoulders and tucked her chin to protect her features, even though she'd already rubbed coal dust on her face and pinned a large, frilly maid's cap on her head to protect her identity. "I've brought you food and something to relieve your pain, m'lord." She prayed her tone carried the right amount of submissiveness. "How are you feeling?"

His harsh breaths penetrated the short space between them. Finally, his grip slowly eased, though he did not release her. As he lowered himself back down to his mound of pillows, his hand slid along her arm until his fingers bracketed her wrist.

"Like a ballroom full of drunken lords trampled my body."

"Better then."

He squeezed her wrist. "How long was I out?"

"All of a day and most of a night."

"So long?"

"The apothecary gave you something to help you rest."

A long pause. "I don't remember."

"You were fighting a fever." Sydney pressed her palm to his forehead. "Much better now."

"I have to get out of here. My sister—" He sent her a wary glance. "She'll be worried."

"You mustn't move for a few more days." She smoothed her hand over her rough, threadbare skirts. "If you'd like to give me her address, I'll have a note sent around."

An emotion Sydney didn't understand hardened his jaw a moment before he shifted his attention away.

She bent to collect the tray but was unable to balance it with one hand. Pausing, she slanted a meaningful glance at her wrist.

He opened his fingers.

"Thank you." When she reached for the tray again, his hand moved to her leg. She whipped her head around to peer at him, jarring a lock of hair free. "Kindly remove your hand, m'lord."

His lips quirked into a spare smile. "I'm hardly in a position to ravish you."

Sydney could barely think above the hammering of her heart. The heat from his palm penetrated the rough layers of her skirts, directing her attention to that small four-inch-by-four-inch area. Setting her jaw, she lifted the tray to her lap and tucked the loose skein of hair behind her ear. Then she laid the icy compress across his eyes.

He sucked in a startled breath. "Perhaps a little warning next time," he said through gritted teeth.

"The same could be said to you, sir." She opened a small bottle and tapped several drops of the reddish-brown liquid in the glass. She swirled the water around before removing the compress from his eyes. "Drink this."

"What is it?"

"Water laced with laudanum."

His lips firmed into a thin line before raising the shaking drink to his lips. Liquid splashed over the rim. "Damn me!"

"Here, m'lord." She wrapped her hands around his, steadying the glass. "All of it," she commanded when he tried to stop halfway.

When he finished, he shoved the glass away, scrunching his face at the bitter taste. "Next time, dribble your poison into some brandy. Might be a little more palatable that way."

Ignoring his surly remark, she retrieved a bowl of broth and raised a brimming spoonful to his mouth.

"You're not feeding me like a greenling cub."

She returned the spoon to the bowl. "Then you'll go hungry."

"How do you figure, Miss—?" When she did not fill in the blank, he continued, "I've been feeding myself for a rather long time."

"Not with those trembling hands." She ventured another spoonful up to his lips. He waited a belligerent three seconds before opening his mouth.

Relief spread through Sydney. She didn't know what she would have done if he'd refused the beef tea. For some men, pride forced them into making poor decisions that had terrible consequences. She was glad Ethan deBeau was not one of them.

Her relief quickly faded into agitation. She could feel the intensity of his stare all the way to her bones. An insistent quiver started at the base of her spine and worked its way up. The darkened chamber and his swollen eyes would limit his visibility. She knew this, believed it. But she could not shake her sudden, desperate sense of urgency.

"Where's the cloaked chap that dragged my carcass in here?" Fatigue laced his words.

"I couldn't say, m'lord."

"I owe him my thanks."

She quickened her pace, refusing any further attempts at conversation. The less he knew, the less likely their paths would ever cross again.

"Rest your head on the pillow again, please."

"You're leaving." His voice was hollow, resigned.

Empathy gripped her heart. She glanced around the desolate chamber, hating that she had to keep him here. "Would you like a candle? A book? Perhaps another blanket?"

He grasped the ice-filled linen and placed it over his eyes. "No."

Dismissed.

Sydney gathered everything onto her tray and made her way to the door. An odd reluctance to leave him held her immobile. She chanced a glance over her shoulder at the same time he delivered a low, unmistakable warning.

"I won't be this helpless forever, little maid."

One

ETHAN DEBEAU, VISCOUNT DANFORTH, HATED BEING a drunkard.

The occupation enjoyed none of the creature comforts to which he was accustomed. Indeed, for the past hour, he had been forced to lounge on the hard ground, propped against a gnarled tree, in too-tight clothes that reeked of unwashed flesh and stale liquor. And if that weren't enough, his surveillance position was directly above a rather active anthill.

Once Lord Somerton appointed him Chief of the Nexus, Ethan would never again have to fend off insects, sit on the hard ground, or warm a woman's bed for the sole purpose of coaxing information from her. Of course, not being in the field meant long hours behind a desk, reading mounds of reports, and attending meeting after meeting. He wasn't sure which would be worse—the ants or the paperwork.

One niggling thought caused his pulse to jump. He didn't know his competition for the job. The Nexus was so shrouded in secrecy that one agent could be dancing with another and not even know it. He knew the identities of only two agents. Others he suspected, but it wasn't as though he could work the question into a conversation. What would he say? *Hello, I'm an agent with the Nexus. My specialty is seducing information from women and retrieving prisoners of war. What's yours?* And when the person looked at him with a blank stare, it's not as if he could enlighten them. *Never heard of the Nexus? We're a secret section of the Foreign Office attempting to prevent Napoleon from taking over the world. Like to join us?*

At that precise moment, a larger, more inquisitive ant raced along his inner thigh, heading straight for his groin. He flicked it off, the movement jarring his too-large pilfered hat, so that it now blocked his view of the boys' home. He swiped his hand across his forehead, pushing his hat back into position. The moment he could see again, he noticed a child emerging from the lower-level servant's entrance of the Abbingale Home for Displaced and Gifted Boys, also known as the Home or Abbingale. The boy, perhaps seven or eight years old, scrambled up the stairs to street level, then took off.

Ethan raised a half-empty bottle of gin to his lips while he followed the boy's zigzag progress down White Horse Lane. Once the child disappeared into the crowd, Ethan turned back to the boys' home and continued to mentally catalog every rippling curtain, passing silhouette, inquiring vendor. He noted anything and everything of possible interest and would sort through the morass tonight.

As soon as he understood Abbingale's daily operation, he would make plans to penetrate the home, search for Giles Clarke, and extract him. He had never heard of the boy until a sennight ago, when his dying mother had begged the Nexus to rescue her son. And so they would, even though settling domestic issues was not one of the agency's objectives.

The Nexus's main purpose was more far-reaching. Some would say far more important than saving a single child. Operating under the auspice of the Alien Office, a little-known section of the Foreign Office, Nexus secret service agents worked tirelessly to prevent Napoleon Bonaparte from breaching England's shores.

He would see to the boy's safety—assuming he was inside Abbingale—and then return to discover why a murdered Nexus agent mentioned Abbingale Home in one of his last coded messages.

A black carriage, with a driver in front and two footmen hanging onto the back, rolled to a halt outside Abbingale. Ethan's senses perked up, even while his body slouched farther into its uncomfortable pose. The footmen jumped down, one running to help his employer alight and the other to rap on the door.

Through the carriage window, Ethan glimpsed two feminine profiles before their shadowy figures slipped out of sight. They reappeared a few seconds later, ascending the front steps. The women were opposites in every way. One stood several inches above the other, with dark hair, square shoulders, and clothes stylish enough to grace any *ton* drawing room, while the shorter blond wore more sedate clothing and clutched a notebook to her chest.

The door swung open, and the women strode inside. Ethan's gaze shifted to the bewigged footmen, who appeared, from this distance, to be a perfectly matched pair. Handsome, too. *Bravo*, he thought. Accomplishing such a difficult feat assured their mistress a place of envy amongst the hostesses of her set. Why the wealthy put so much stock into something of so little consequence, Ethan didn't know. But then again, he had once spent

an entire sennight searching for a matching pair of bays
to complement his new phaeton.

When the footmen put their heads together in
conversation, Ethan slung his knapsack over his shoulder
and rolled to his feet. He paused to draw hard on his gin
bottle before toddling across the cobbles toward them
in an uneven line. The more clean-shaven of the two
footmen noticed his approach and eyed him like one
would a rabid animal.

Ethan stubbed his toe on a nonexistent stone, making
a big show of catching his balance. "Damn me, who
put that there?" He glanced around while grumbling to
himself and scratching the back of his head.

The eagle-eyed footman finally decided he posed no
threat and rejoined his companion. After a couple more
tottering steps, Ethan came within hearing distance.

"My bones hurt," the stubble-faced footman said.

His partner sent him a sharp glance. "How long?"

"Not quite sure," stubble man said. "You know how
it is."

"Perhaps you could make a guess."

"No need to get testy, Mac. The pain started gradual-
like. Sometimes it's there for a while before my brain
registers the discomfort."

Eagle-eyed Mac sighed. "When did you first notice
your bones, Mick?"

"When we were leaving the agency."

Mac glanced up at the Abbingale's facade. "You
should have told me before now, dammit."

Ethan veered around the two men and stumbled
up onto the foot pavement, belting back a drink and
swaying to the side.

"What?" Mick asked. "You think you could have
stopped her?"

"That's not the point. I could have warned her to stay alert."

"Do you even realize what you're saying?" Mick asked. "Have you ever known Miss Hunt—"

A *shhh*-ing sound stopped stubble man mid-sentence.

"Right." Mick glanced around. "Have you ever known *her* to go into a situation with blinders on? Get your head out of your heart, brother."

"My head is exactly where it needs to be," Mac said in a lethal tone. "As will be my fist, if you don't shut your trap."

"There's nothing that can come of it. You'd be better off paying more attention to the looks Amelia keeps giving you."

"Amelia, is it?"

Mick's mouth curled into a roguish smile. "Since you weren't interested, I've become quite friendly with the wee assistant. Sweet thing."

Mac stepped forward. "Keep your filthy hands off Mrs. Cartwright."

"You can't have them both."

Hoping the footmen would continue their conversation, Ethan plopped down on Abbingale's steps and curled up in a nap-worthy ball. His new position shook things up a bit, causing him to burp loudly. Gin fumes stung his nostrils. The two brothers on the verge of a nice bout of fisticuffs turned to him. Both had the same rugged features highlighted by the lightest blue eyes he'd ever seen. They were indeed perfectly matched. Twins.

"Here now." Mick grabbed Ethan's arm. "You can't bed down there."

Ethan knocked his hand away. "I'll cut ye heart out if ye try to steal me medicine again."

"Medicine." Mac snorted in disgust. "We don't want your damned gin." He moved to the other side.

Strong hands clasped Ethan by his upper arms and yanked him into a standing position.

"Good God, man," Mick said. "Are you drinking your spirits or bathing in them?"

"Let me go, ye bleeders. Ye got no cause to send me on me way."

"That's where you're wrong," Mac said.

"Can't have you blocking our mistress's way when she comes out," Mick said. "Besides, don't want you scaring any of the children."

They half dragged, half carried him several feet away before propping him up against the building next door. "Too fine a lady to walk around?" Ethan mumbled, checking to make sure he still had his knapsack.

"The very finest," Mac said.

Mick tugged on Ethan's coat at various places, presumably to make him more presentable. "Sober up first, my friend," he said with a pat to Ethan's shoulder.

Ethan frowned, not understanding the footman's advice. "First for what?"

But the stubble-faced footman only winked at him before they resumed their positions near the carriage. Beneath the rim of his hat, Ethan studied the footmen, marveling at their firm, yet respectful care of him. They obviously held their mistress—Miss Hunt—in high regard. Every time they spoke of her, their voices took on a reverent tone.

Abbingale's entrance door opened and the estimable Miss Hunt and her assistant swept through the opening. Halfway down the steps, Miss Hunt's gaze found her footmen, and she sent them one hard shake of her pretty head. The action struck a discordant note with Ethan, but he was at a loss as to say why.

From his new vantage point, Ethan affirmed his earlier

assessment of the lady and developed some new ones. High cheekbones, black eyebrows above emerald eyes, and a strong, yet feminine jawline made her an intriguing contrast to many of England's delicate, oval-faced beauties. Even though she wore a high-necked gown and pelisse, one could not miss the elegant quality of her statuesque frame. She not only walked with a confident stride, she gazed into a man's eye with absolutely no timidity. Like she was doing with him right now.

Recognition struck Ethan sharply in the chest. His path had crossed with hers once before. But where? The answer danced just out of range, then disappeared altogether.

The woman raised a brow, and Ethan realized he'd been staring. Cursing beneath his breath, he blinked owlishly. "Ye gents didn't tell me yer lady was so buxom. I wouldn't have been so easily removed." He produced another belch for good measure.

She slashed another glance at her eagle-eyed footman, who shrugged his shoulders. "Come along, Mrs. Cartwright."

The assistant nodded, and the women started down the steps.

"Mrs. Henshaw, your gloves." An older woman emerged from Abbingale's entrance door, holding out a pair of kidskin gloves to... Miss Hunt.

Ethan's gaze sharpened and he saw Miss Hunt's hard features transform into a vapid expression he'd seen a hundred times in ballrooms across London.

"Oh, dear me," Miss Hunt tittered. "I would have been quite distraught without my favorite pair of kids."

Ethan cast a brief glance to the footmen standing at the bottom of the steps. Mac's stony expression revealed nothing, as usual; however, his brother seemed to be holding back a smile.

"Thank you, Mrs. Drummond." Miss Hunt's assistant accepted the gloves from the older woman and handed them to her mistress.

Miss Hunt clasped her kids to her chest and flashed a brilliant smile at the older woman. "Good day, Mrs. Drummond. I shall see you again soon."

"We look forward to your return, Mrs. Henshaw."

Twirling about, Miss Hunt led the way to the carriage. Once the women were settled inside, Mac secured the steps and closed the door. Within seconds, the carriage lurched forward and the footmen jumped onto the rear. As they passed, Mick gave Ethan a jaunty salute.

Ethan swiped his nose.

Mick laughed.

After following the carriage's progress for a while, Ethan glanced back at the Home. What he saw there surprised him. The older woman—Mrs. Drummond—watched Miss Hunt's conveyance roll away with something akin to hatred sparkling in her eyes.

What exactly was going on? A footman in love with two women, a well-dressed lady whose business at the boys' home upset the staff? A lady who also answered to two names? What did her footmen need to warn her about?

Any other mission, Ethan would dismiss the incident and refocus on his original assignment. But his ultimate target was more than likely linked to this place, which meant Ethan had to follow every possible trail. Besides, he wanted to know where he'd come across Miss Hunt before. Her name—or names—wasn't at all familiar. Something about her features had sparked an air of familiarity, one he would attempt to connect with again.

Ethan turned to gauge the carriage's location and cringed at how far it had traveled. Time to go. He would return to Abbingale tomorrow.

Careful not to break his cover, he took another drink of his gin and got to his feet, readjusting his knapsack over his shoulder. The older woman's malevolent gaze shot to his location, and Ethan raised his near-empty bottle in her direction.

The woman squared her shoulders and sniffed the air as if she'd caught scent of something offensive before pivoting to reenter Abbingale. She shut the door with ominous finality.

Feeling a sense of urgency now, Ethan wove his way down the foot pavement, stopping occasionally to scratch an inappropriate area or to cough up a disturbing amount of phlegm. A few minutes later, he straightened his spine, tossed his bottle in a bush, and laid his coat across a bedraggled woman curled up beneath a lamppost.

He quickened his step. When Miss Hunt's carriage turned a corner, he changed his stride to a full-out run. His hat flew off, and he tightened his grip on his knapsack's strap. Rounding the corner, he came to an abrupt and jarring halt. Miss Hunt's carriage sat idle in the lane, waiting for traffic to clear.

Ethan searched for a doorway, a cart, a building, anything large enough to hide his big frame. He started for a nearby alleyway when the sound of his name stopped him cold.

"Danforth," an incredulous voice said, "is that you, old boy?"

Equal parts relieved and frustrated, Ethan considered ignoring the Marquess of Shevington. The gentleman's slurred words were a testament to too much drink and not enough sleep. Knowing Shev, he probably hadn't slept at all and would likely not even recall hailing Ethan ten minutes from now.

Ethan chanced a look at Miss Hunt's conveyance, and

thankfully found her footmen's attention on the clog of carriages ahead and not the scene unfolding behind. Decision made, he finger-combed his hair before facing the marquess's squinting countenance.

"Good God, it is you," the marquess said, hanging his head out the open carriage window. "What in blazes are you doing here, dressed like that?"

Striding forward, Ethan opened the carriage door and bounded inside. "Morning, Shev." Instead of taking the open, back-facing seat, Ethan squeezed in next to his old school chum. "Be a good man and tell your driver to follow the carriage with the green livery."

Instead of complying, the marquess dug out his handkerchief, flicked it open, and used it to cover his nose. "My word," he said, the linen muffling his words. "Someone must have tried to drown your aristocratic hide in a vat of Blue Ruin. Either that, or you're harboring a dead animal upon your person." He moved to sit on the opposite side of the carriage. "Tell me you did not leave the lush confines of Madame Rousseau's last night for," he waved a hand toward Ethan's attire, "this."

Ethan began digging items out of his knapsack and tossing them onto the bench next to his friend. "You had disappeared into the depths of the Pearl and Ruby Room, so I had to make my own way home."

"You're blaming me for your current dishabille?"

"In a word, yes." Opening the door, Ethan checked Miss Hunt's location and gave Shev's driver instructions to follow. Before sitting back, he drew the window curtain closed, leaving a small opening.

"Are you absconding with my carriage?" Shev asked, sounding more intrigued than put out.

The vehicle lurched into motion. "For a little while."

He and the marquess had been in each other's pockets

since before either could speak an intelligible word. Shev knew nothing of Ethan's life with the Nexus, and Ethan went to great pains to keep it that way. Even though Shev had come across his friend in some odd situations—such as now—the marquess seemed content with his less-than-descriptive explanations.

Lifting the tail end of his shirtsleeve, Ethan ripped off the foul-smelling coarse garment and rubbed his hands over his chafed skin.

"What, may I ask, are you doing?" Shev drawled.

Ethan grabbed a clean shirt from the stash of clothes he'd pulled from his knapsack. "Your eyesight can't be that bad, old man." Soft linen cascaded over his bare torso, soothing his abraded flesh. He began working on the fastenings of his filthy breeches.

"Really, Danforth, must you do that now?" The marquess peeled back the curtain to peer outside. "What if we're set upon by highwaymen and they thrust open the door to find you in your smalls? Do you know what that will do to my reputation *and* my chances to continue on with my dissolute existence?"

Ethan pushed his breeches down and removed his stockings. "Have you always had such dramatic inclinations?"

The marquess sniffed and turned away from the window. "Protecting one's reputation is a constant struggle."

"You must be very busy." Ethan drew on fresh stockings.

"I suppose if I ask about your activities," Shev said, "you'll tell me to get buggered."

"You suppose correctly."

"Why do I bother being your friend if *everything* is a secret?"

"Because of my charming wit?"

Shev snorted. "Please alert me when either your charm or your wit appears. I'd like to make a note of the occasion."

"Continue along this same vein and I'll be forced to remove my smalls, too."

"Good God, Danforth." Shev leaned away. "No need to threaten me with blindness."

Ethan sent his friend a quelling glance while he jabbed his feet into the legs of his breeches. Once they were secure about his waist, he fastened the front placard. Then he tackled his neckcloth, tying it into a simple knot, before pulling on a buff-colored waistcoat shot with silver thread. His exertions left a fine line of moisture along his hairline, which he used to help bring some order to his tousled hair.

Spreading his arms wide, Ethan asked, "How do I look?"

The marquess appraised his appearance with a discerning eye. "Like a degenerate viscount?"

"Perfect."

The carriage jolted to a halt, and a liveried footman approached the window. "What would you like the coachman to do, my lord?" he asked. "The carriage stopped outside 57 Mansell."

Shev sent Ethan a this-is-your-adventure-not-mine look.

Ethan said, "Drive by slowly, but not so slow as to draw attention."

Nodding, the footman said, "Yes, sir."

Seconds later, the slap of reins and the jangle of tack reached Ethan's ears before the carriage rolled forward at a sedate pace. Anticipation curled around his insides, gliding over each organ with aching slowness, squeezing gently, inexorably.

Number 57 stood at the edge of a long row of town houses. The building's edifice looked as though it had received special care in the last few years, with new windows and a refurbished limestone portico supported by Ionic pillars. Flowers flourished in tall earthenware urns placed on each side of the entrance. Above the door swung a sign. Ethan squinted to make out the words.

"Hunt Agency," Shev said near his ear before plopping back in his seat. "Charming. Are you going to finally hire a valet instead of depending on your poor butler for such a position?"

Once they had passed, Ethan sat back. "You're familiar with the agency?"

"Most households are," Shev said, with a pointed look. "The Hunt Agency is only one of the most prominent staffing agencies in London. Operated by the iron will and hand of Miss Sydney Hunt. I'm sure your housekeeper can provide more detail." His eyes narrowed. "What is your interest in the proprietress of the Hunt Agency?"

"Curiosity, nothing more."

The marquess released a long sigh. "There's *always* something more with you, Danforth. Are you quite finished with your clandestine activities? I need to be rid of you, so that I might go home and sleep the day away." He glanced out the carriage window, his head tilted in a way to suggest he was noting the blue sky and bright sunshine. "It's far too cheerful-looking for one of my disposition."

Chuckling, Ethan said, "I don't recall you being so querulous in the morning."

"And I don't recall ever having my carriage and person seized before."

"Then I am glad to be your first." Ethan draped an arm over the back of the seat and propped a booted foot next to the marquess. He waved his hand in the air. "You may proceed in getting rid of me."

Ethan thought his friend mumbled "Thank God" beneath his breath before barking out orders to his driver.

Would Miss Hunt complicate his mission to find Giles Clarke? Why was she poking around *his* boys' home, using an alias and acting the featherbrain? Once he figured out their former connection, he would coax the answers to his questions from the lovely Miss Hunt. Of this, he had no doubt. Because that's what the Nexus paid him to do.

Seduce information from the most beautiful women in the world.

Anticipation unfurled in his chest, the sensation shocking due to its scarcity. How long had it been since he'd looked forward to such an assignment? *Years.* He rubbed the palm of his hand over his tight chest, his thundering heart.

The corners of his mouth lifted into a predatory smile.

Two

"LAST ONE."

Sydney Hunt accepted the final contract from her assistant. "Five new placements in two days." She dipped her quill pen into the inkwell. "Is that our best yet?"

"A month ago, we placed six in one day," Amelia Cartwright said. "Five is a great accomplishment."

Sydney scratched the pen's nib across the page. "How is Fanny Talbot adjusting to her new position?"

"Quite well," Amelia said. "As you predicted, the housekeeper is the mothering sort and has taken little Fanny under her wing."

She handed the signed contract back. "I'm glad to hear someone else could look beyond Fanny's infirmity to see all that beautiful eagerness beneath."

While working as a scullery maid, the thirteen-year-old girl had been brutalized by one of her master's vicious friends. Shocked by the extent of her injuries, the young earl had ordered Fanny be taken to a surgeon as far away from Mayfair as possible. There, the incompetent surgeon set the bone incorrectly, causing a deformity of the girl's left arm.

Mac had found the bedraggled, starving girl a few

weeks later, trudging down the middle of White Chapel Road, begging for assistance from passersby. Sydney would never forget the day Mac carried the girl into her study. Her chest still ached from the impact, and that was over four months ago.

"Do I have any reference letters to write?" Sydney asked.

"We do have a new request."

She noted the neutral set to her assistant's features. After working with Amelia for four years, Sydney had perfected her ability to divine the young woman's thoughts with nothing more than a glance. But that didn't stop her from going through her list of questions. She had learned through experience that no one was infallible, not even those she trusted most.

"Male or female?" Sydney asked.

"Male."

"Position requested?"

Amelia pulled out a sheet of paper from the stack in her arms. "Valet."

"Previous post?"

"Valet."

"Reason for leaving?"

"Theft."

"Did our sources confirm the charge?"

"Yes."

"No extenuating circumstances?" Sydney asked. "A refusal to pay his wages, perhaps?"

Amelia shook her head. "Mr. Patterson's been released for the same reason on two other occasions. He does not purloin anything of great value, only small articles he can sell and that are not quickly missed."

Sydney nodded, expecting as much. "I will not jeopardize the agency's reputation by providing a letter of recommendation for a sneak. Please inform Mr.

Patterson's sponsor that I am unable to accommodate the request."

"Of course, Miss Hunt."

"Good work, Amelia," Sydney said. "Uncovering damaging information from our potential clients' backgrounds is time-consuming, but so necessary. Thank you for your vigilance."

Although Sydney was never miserly with her praise, Amelia's cheeks flushed. "Thank you, Miss Hunt. I cannot take full credit, though. Mick helped."

Leave it to Amelia to avert attention away from herself. "I will be sure to thank him as well."

With her father's assistance, Sydney had established the Hunt Agency in an effort to improve deplorable working conditions for servants across the city. Many worked from before sunrise to nearly midnight every day, with no time—or only a half day—off during the week. And if that wasn't difficult enough, the female servants found themselves consistently under attack from not only the masters of the house, but the male servants as well.

Drawing from her father's keen business sense, Sydney had managed to build a good reputation with her service clients and her hiring clients, a reputation and level of success she protected with her mother's tenacity.

"When am I—or shall I say, the featherbrained benefactress Mrs. Henshaw—scheduled to resume touring Abbingale Home?" Sydney asked.

"Friday morning."

"Good," Sydney said. "We saw so little of the facility on Wednesday and nothing of the boys before the matron was called away."

"Forgive me, Miss Hunt," Amelia said. "But I'm still unclear as to how visiting the boys' home will help us locate the baron."

"My contact with the Nexus believes there might be a connection between Abbingale Home and Lord Latymer, and I tend to agree, though I'm not sure how as of yet." Latymer had once been the Under Superintendent of the Alien Office until his too-friendly relationship with the French was uncovered. Now he was a hunted man, with no country, no friends, and soon, nowhere to hide.

A little over two years ago, Sydney had begun sharing intelligence with a Nexus agent. In that time, she had managed to identify a few more of the secret organization's members. She admired every single one of them, for very different reasons. Ethan deBeau's image wavered before her eyes. Regret clamped around her throat, making it difficult to swallow. She forced the past away and focused her attention on finding the elusive baron.

"Since we have no one familiar with the inner workings of Abbingale Home, I thought it best to root about myself," Sydney said. "I'm hoping that I'll see or hear something that will lead us to Lord Latymer."

"Miss Hunt, I—"

"I know, Amelia," Sydney said in a low voice. Even though she had given her assistant leave to use her Christian name years ago, Amelia refused to do so, claiming she could never be so informal with her employer. Sydney suspected her persistence had more to do with maintaining an emotional shield against those around her. "Our involvement in this situation has gone beyond what is comfortable. The more we help the Nexus, the closer we come to their enemies. However, if a child is involved—"

One of Amelia's rare smiles appeared, interrupting her. "What is it?"

"Would there were more people like you," Amelia said, with a sincerity that made Sydney's chest tighten.

"Like me?" Sydney released an embarrassed chuckle. "Willful? Too obliging? Impetuous? Those are my dear mother's favorites."

Amelia raised a brow, as if challenging the woman's assessment. "Resolute, kindhearted, courageous, intelligent, resourceful, selfless."

Sydney squeezed her assistant's hand. "I shall have to invite you to my family's next get-together so you can defend my honor." In truth, Sydney's mother was quite supportive of her efforts at the Hunt Agency. Sydney cringed to think of what drastic measures her protective mother would take if she ever learned of Sydney's clandestine activities.

Amelia's lips twitched. "I look forward to the opportunity."

A knock sounded at the study door. "Come in," Sydney called.

Mac O'Donnell entered, closing the door behind him. "A gentleman's here to see you." He kept his voice low, and his gaze, always serious, could have sliced through steel.

Sensing unwanted news looming at her doorstep, Sydney released the stiffness from her spine and settled back into her chair. Relaxing her muscles always helped her assess a situation more clearly. "Who has come, Mac?"

"Viscount Danforth."

A wave of dread burned over every inch of her flesh, then a second wave, frigid and slow, crept along in its wake.

Amelia sucked in a sharp breath.

Mac's gaze flicked to her assistant before swinging back to Sydney. "Should I get rid of him?"

"Did his lordship provide a reason for his visit?"

"He's in need of a butler," Mac said. "His current one is on the verge of retirement."

Sydney sent her assistant a glance. "See what you can find out."

"Yes, Miss Hunt."

Amelia gathered her materials and skirted around Mac's large form; he followed her progress out of the corner of his eye.

"Where is he now?" Sydney asked.

"In the drawing room."

"Very well." For what seemed the hundredth time, she tucked a stubborn lock of hair behind her ear. "Let us adjourn to my study below."

"You're certain?"

"Yes," she said. "I don't believe in coincidences. It's best to determine what his lordship is about."

"What if he recognizes you?"

On unsteady legs, Sydney rose and strode around her desk, laying a hand on her bodyguard's arm. "That's a very good question, Mac. Let's see what we can find out."

Keeping her pace even, she led the way to the first floor. At the end of the stairs, Mac continued down a flight and Sydney veered right to a smaller study she used to meet with clients, or potential clients. Unlike her private study upstairs, everything was in order in this room, tidy and clean. Nothing sat around that could reveal the full extent of the Hunt Agency's activities. Activities that some might construe as unscrupulous.

Too many people relied on her agency, and she could not afford to make even the tiniest mistake, or many would lose their livelihoods, including her. For those reasons and more, Sydney conducted her day-to-day operations out of a bedchamber-turned-study up on the second floor. The only staff she allowed in her haven were Amelia, Mac, and Mick. When dust balls threatened to overcome the chamber, she would take a break from her paperwork and tackle the cleaning herself.

Sydney pulled papers from the upper drawer of her desk and placed them on the top, scattering them the slightest bit. Then she retrieved some ledgers and laid them on the opposite side. The last item she extracted was a tiny silver bell; this she set in the middle of the desk, just above the ink blotter.

Opening one of the ledgers, she dipped a pen into the inkwell and waited. Before long, she heard her housekeeper's familiar rapid approach followed by the more solid *thunk* of a gentleman's step. She began writing.

Her housekeeper rapped twice on the door before entering. "Miss Hunt, Lord Danforth to see you."

"Thank you, Wells."

She took her time replacing her pen in its holder before plastering a welcoming smile on her face. Sydney rose to greet one of the few people in all of London who could ruin everything she'd worked for. "Good morning, my lord."

"Miss Hunt," he said, with an abbreviated bow, "thank you for seeing me."

He lifted his gaze to meet hers, and Sydney's breath caught. Never before had she seen such a riveting shade of blue swirled with an equally captivating green. Sound narrowed to a pulse beat. Thump. Thump. *Thump, thump, thump, thump.* With bruises, scrapes, and swollen flesh marring his handsome features, he had been compelling. Without them, he was mesmerizing.

She braced her fingertips on the top of her desk, struggling to regain her composure. But she could not stop making comparisons to the last time she saw him, sprawled on a narrow cot in an abandoned building.

Today, broad shoulders tapered down to solid hips. Fawn-colored breeches strained against the musculature of his thighs, and his midnight blue superfine coat set off his wavy sable locks to godlike splendor.

Many a lady had sold her soul for one night in his bed. He made them feel like heavenly goddesses, unearthly creatures made for his love, and the most important woman in his life… at that moment in time. Or so she'd been told. The fingers that were only moments ago supporting her unsteady legs curled into a fist.

Even though she understood the reasons motivating his actions, he still represented everything she despised in a man. Gentlemen such as he walked the upper echelons of society, with money and power at their disposal, and laws at their mercy. They discarded women like they discarded a spent cheroot, while honorable men like Mac and Mick scraped by, day after day.

Sydney would make sure she did not become one of Ethan deBeau's golden deities.

"Of course." She slipped a stray curl behind her ear before indicating the lone chair in front of her desk. "Please make yourself comfortable."

Instead of complying, his lordship cocked his head at a curious angle and his mesmerizing blue-green eyes studied her face.

The very last thing she wanted him to do. She lowered her chin a bit while she took her seat, hoping to break his concentration on her face. Once she was settled, she waved her hand toward his chair again. "My lord?"

"Forgive me," he said, taking his seat. "You reminded me of someone."

Sydney forced back a burst of anxiety. "You are not

the first to think so," she improvised. "I seem to have one of those faces."

He said nothing, though he continued to scrutinize her features with maddening thoroughness.

Releasing a long, slow breath, she settled back in her chair. "Now then, how may I help you?"

The intensity hardening his expression dissipated, and something altogether more dangerous took its place. Something predatory. "As I mentioned to your housekeeper," he said. "I'm in need of a butler."

"What is your time frame?"

"Tanner is retiring at the end of the month."

"Why so little notice?" she asked. "That barely gives you a fortnight to react."

Glancing down at his coat sleeve, he brushed his fingers over it twice as if removing an annoying speck of dirt. "According to Tanner, his heart can't take the constant strain."

"Oh, that is unfortunate," she said. "I take it you'd like Tanner's replacement to be in his prime?"

"Not necessarily," he said. "As long as he knows his duties, I have no care for his age."

"But what of the strain?"

He stared at her curiously, then the area around his eyes crinkled. "The *strain* Tanner referred to was not in reference to his onerous duties."

When he did not bother to explain further, she asked, "If not his duties, then what?"

"Me."

"You?"

"Yes," he said as if the notion of torturing his butler brought him great enjoyment. "It's nothing you need to be concerned about for the new butler."

"I see." Though she didn't. She experienced a wave

of empathy for his lordship's old retainer. "So, age is not a concern, but you want Tanner's replacement to be an experienced butler. Do I have that correct?"

"You do, indeed."

"What about hair color?" she asked. "Do you wish it to match the other servants?"

He barked out a laugh. When she did not join in, he said, "Please tell me you're not serious."

"Some of my clients have very exacting criteria when it comes to their servants."

"Even if the manservants are powdering their hair or wearing wigs?"

"Even so."

Shaking his head, he said, "I will save you the trouble of fulfilling a particular hue, Miss Hunt."

"As you wish." She glanced down at her list. "With or without a family?"

"Without."

"How tall?"

A heavy-lidded smile replaced his consternation, and he slouched back in his chair in the same manner she did when under pressure. "My height or a few inches less," he said. "I prefer to be the tallest man in my castle."

Ah, the charming rogue fully emerges. She understood why the ladies fell under his spell. No gentleman should be equipped with so much disarming weaponry. Even Ares, the mythical god of war, would not hold a lady's attention long if Lord Danforth strolled into the same room, wearing his gorgeous smile.

Much to Sydney's consternation, she was not immune to the raw power pulsing beneath his fine clothes and devil-may-care manner. He fairly reeked of the boudoir, so potent was his sensuality. An image of his sun-kissed flesh writhing amidst white silken sheets captivated her mind's eye. With every rustle of his legs, the sheet shifted to reveal another glorious inch of his well-toned bottom.

Sydney's insides clenched violently, jerking her back to the flesh-and-blood viscount, who stared at her with a knowing smile. She halted her body's mad spiral into the chasm of desire with a ruthlessness that surprised even her. She *hated* that I've-got-you-now curve of a gentleman's lips. Hated it with a dedication that guided her efforts at the Hunt Agency every day.

"Indeed," she said. "Your requirements are not complicated, my lord, but I don't believe the Hunt Agency can help you in so short a time."

That wiped the seductive smile off his face. He straightened. "I have it on good authority that your agency has built its reputation on finding good matches under difficult circumstances."

"Whose good authority would that be?"

His eyes narrowed. "A number of acquaintances have conveyed as much to me."

Why was he resistant to sharing the name of his referrals? If she knew who he was conferring with about her agency, she could use the connection to find out if his request was a legitimate one or not. "Have you no one among your staff whom you could promote?"

"No. I keep a modest number of servants, and my only footman is not suitable for the position."

"That is too bad," she mused. "Promoting from within your own household reduces the amount of learning a new servant must undertake."

"True," he said. "However, I'm looking forward to introducing a new perspective. Bring someone in who can look at the running of my household with an objective eye. One thing I cannot abide in my staff is complacency."

An interesting observation from a bachelor with a modest number of servants.

"Won't you reconsider, Miss Hunt?" he asked. "I have every faith that you will find an appropriate replacement butler in time."

Could his lordship's visit simply be a coincidence? Every instinct told her no, but outside his initial reaction to seeing her, she had detected no ulterior motive. Perhaps the old saying about keeping one's enemy close at hand might be excellent counsel in this situation. Though she did not precisely view him as an enemy. Not yet, at least. If his suppressed knowledge of her identity ever surfaced and he threatened her business and all that entailed, he would become not only her enemy, but her mortal enemy.

Making her decision, she said, "Give me a day or two to review whom we have available, my lord. Tomorrow, I will tour your residence and interview your butler, so that I might better understand the scope of your needs."

His eyes widened. "You wish to visit my home?"

"If that is convenient for you, of course."

Although he made a gallant attempt, the viscount could not completely mask the caged look in his eyes. "Tomorrow?"

"Yes," she said. "I prefer not to tarry long over a new assignment."

"Good to know, but I don't understand why you feel the need to visit my home. Did I not give you enough information to conduct your search?"

No servant placed through the Hunt Agency ever went to a new situation without either Sydney or Amelia visiting the household first. Much could be derived by a few well-placed questions to the other servants and viewing the living conditions of the home.

Amelia's ability to detect malevolence beneath a pleasant mask was one of the many reasons why she was so valuable to Sydney. Sydney would never forgive herself if she inadvertently sent one of her people into a bad situation like the hell her mother had endured. But her wealthy clients did not need to know that she was interviewing them as much as they were interviewing their new servant.

"Of course you did, my lord," she said, with practiced finesse. "I simply like to get a firsthand feel of my clients' needs before placement. The last thing I want to do is send you an incompatible butler if a thirty-minute visit could have prevented such a waste of everyone's time."

"You have put a great deal of thought into this process."

"It is my livelihood, sir," she said. "Word of mouth has proven to be my best advertisement. If I become too complacent, my clients will become dissatisfied. Dissatisfied customers are the death of any vocation."

"A valuable motto."

"The credit must go to my father," she said. "He taught me everything I know about business matters."

"Then you were lucky in your mother's choice of husband."

Indeed, she was. However, luck was but one component in her good fortune. "I have much for which to be thankful."

The viscount's charming smile slowly reemerged, softening the square angles of his face and making him intolerably handsome. Lethal, even. "As much as I would like to accommodate your in-person observation, I'm afraid tomorrow's not possible. Another appointment, you understand."

Sydney had battled charmers, bullies, vacillators, and evil all her life. She knew how to handle each set with barely a flicker of forethought. Dealing with Ethan deBeau was no exception, though her adjustments to his moods came much more slowly than normal.

"Please do not concern yourself, my lord," she said. "There is no reason for you to be present. I have your requirements—unless you have something more you'd like to add?"

A new intensity entered his study of her. "No, Miss Hunt. I have nothing more." He lowered his voice. "At the moment."

The promise behind his words raised the soft hairs running along the back of her neck. She pushed out of her chair. "Very good, then," she said. "If you could let your staff know of my visit, I would be grateful."

Rather than heeding her dismissal, he crossed one leg over the other and his body shifted to the left. He propped his elbow on the chair's arm, smoothing his forefinger and thumb over his freshly shaven chin. The idleness in his action bespoke of contemplation and of quiet challenge.

Sydney's gaze was riveted on the slow glide of his fingers, waiting with an embarrassing amount of anticipation for the soft pads to trail across his full bottom lip.

"Tell me, Miss Hunt. How long has your agency been in existence?"

She forced her attention up, away from temptation. "A little over four years."

His fingers slowed to a provocative crawl. "Quite an accomplishment for an unmarried woman."

Ah, familiar ground. The first ten minutes of their meeting had been nothing more than reconnaissance. Now that he knew the lay of the land, so to speak, Sydney suspected she would soon learn the real reason behind his visit.

She raised a brow. "Perhaps you would like a refreshment?"

The corner of his mouth quirked up at her disgruntled tone, and he stopped caressing his chin. Sydney experienced a stab of disappointment.

"Thank you, no." He rested his cheek between his L-shaped fingers. "I'm intrigued by your story. How did you construct such a thriving enterprise?"

After exhaling a careful breath, Sydney resumed her seat. "I could not have accomplished half so much without the generous support of my parents and staff."

"You must have a small army running around behind the scenes."

She smiled at his probing question. "Hardly an army, sir. We are most fortunate in the number of clients seeking our assistance, but, like you, I am able to manage things with a modest number of well-qualified staff."

"I wonder if perhaps I know your father. I'm acquainted with an Orson Hunt. Any relation, by chance?"

"Afraid not. Hunt was my mother's family name."

"What of your father? Did you not mention him earlier?"

Despite all of her bravado, Sydney did not enjoy sharing this part of her life, though she had never tried to hide the details of her parentage. But divulging the sordid facts of her upbringing to the viscount made her stomach turn queasy. "Jonathan Pratt is my stepfather. He raised me from an early age and is the only father I've ever known."

She watched him sift through her explanation, bracing for the moment when he discerned he was about to contract the services of a bastard spinster.

"Why did your parents not change your surname to Pratt?"

"Do you always inquire into such personal matters?"

"Always."

She leveled her gaze on him. "They discussed the notion with me, but I declined."

"Why would you not accept such a generous offer?"

Generous, because not every gentleman would take on the responsibility of another man's illegitimate child and have that base fact dangled before him every day by way of a surname.

"To remember."

He waited for her to expound. She did not. Would not. Ever.

"You are becoming more intriguing by the second, Miss Hunt."

Blood pounded in her ears. Instead of censure, his lordship's countenance heightened with peculiar interest. Why hadn't she realized feeding bits of information to this man would only provoke his curiosity? She should have devised a bland background that would have induced sleep rather than intrigue.

A wave of vulnerability washed over her. *Always have a means of escape, Sydney. Always.* Her mother's warning filled her mind, and a flush of panicked heat dampened her skin. Sydney's gaze shot to the closed door.

"Is anything amiss?" he asked.

She was overreacting to their byplay and knew it. But too many worries were converging in a short amount of time, heightening her deep-seated fears. *Escape route.* She had one. She always had one.

She blinked to clear her vision. There, precisely where she had placed it at the edge of the ink blotter, sat her silver bell. Her means of escape. The welcome sight acted like a balm for her overreactive nerves. She ached to wrap her palm around the cool metal, but could not devise a way of doing so without snagging the viscount's attention. Instead, she drew in a soothing breath. As quickly as her anxiety had manifested, the debilitating emotion ebbed away on a long exhalation.

"Everything is fine, my lord." She tilted her lips up into what she hoped was a convincing smile, while taming her hair once again. "In light of my revelations, I will, of course, understand if you wish to retract your request for my agency's services."

"I have no concern for your parentage, Miss Hunt," he said. "Only your ability to find me a competent butler."

"Then I had best get started."

He unfurled his big body and moved closer to the front of her desk. Leaning forward, he planted his fingertips on the smooth surface. "Are you sure we have not met before?"

Sydney forced herself to hold her position, even though everything inside her sought the cloak of darkness. Darkness had always protected her, but no such protector could be found in the middle of the day.

She rose to her full height, meeting him eye to eye. "I believe we have already established that I have one of those faces that can be familiar to many."

He angled his big body over her desk and lifted his hand. "No, Miss Hunt. *We* did not." His attention shifted to where his fingers brushed the hollow of her cheek. "No man could ever mistake these contours for another's."

His featherlight touch should have repelled her, should have been a reminder. But it did not, was not. Instead, his aching gentleness compelled her to block all rational thought and to revel in the moment. Who would have thought such a large man could be so tender? By slow degrees, she relaxed the muscles in her neck and, by doing so, she leaned—the slightest bit—into his awaiting palm. Strength, warmth, comfort surrounded her cheek, and Sydney nearly groaned in response to the unexpected pleasure, closing her eyes. She had missed this, though Philip's touch had never made her insides quiver with embers of desire.

His breathing roughened, making the embers spark into flame. Yet something nagged at the edge of her awareness. *Too close. He was far too close.* But she could not heed her mind's warning, begging her to back away.

His warm breath fanned across her mouth. Her eyes flew open, and she found his face barely an inch away. In that instant, she knew she was not strong enough to prevent the kiss. Knew she would sink into it with a passion that would compromise everything. Already regretting her actions, but helpless to do otherwise, her hand fumbled on the desk between them.

A bell trilled out three times, rending the precious moment.

Startled, he glanced down. She followed his gaze to the tiny silver bell dangling from her fingers.

The door burst open, crashing against the wall. Mac and Mick stormed into her study, their hard gazes centered on his lordship.

Setting the bell down, she clasped her shaking hands before her and swallowed hard to control the erratic fluttering in her chest. The second she felt her voice would not betray her, she said, "Gentlemen, I believe Lord Danforth is ready to depart."

Mac swept his hand toward the door. "My lord."

His lordship didn't move. Those piercing, blue-rimmed eyes of his studied her with an odd mixture of primal need and empathy. She must never again allow herself the pleasure of his well-honed caress. She knew better this time but had been unable to resist his touch. A touch that had ruined scores of women or, more accurately, their men. For a perilous moment, she had allowed herself to forget. Forget his caress was nothing more than the razor edge of a warrior's blade.

"Good day, Miss Hunt," he said finally. "My staff will be ready for your visit tomorrow."

"Of course, my lord."

The twins followed Lord Danforth out, leaving Sydney alone to deal with her humiliating weakness. Covering her nose and mouth with her cupped hands, she strode to the window overlooking the street below and waited for his crown of sable-colored waves to appear. When she realized what she was doing, she whirled away and leaned against the wall near the window. She dropped her arms to her sides and tilted her head back, knocking it twice against the wallpapered surface, thankful no portraits hung above.

What had she almost done? Fallen prey to a man who consumes women like one feasts upon a favorite treacle tart? On what was, for all intents and purposes, their first meeting? She let out a derisive laugh. What had she been thinking? He was not interested in her in that way. His lordship choreographed the entire scene to loosen her reserve and draw out her weaknesses.

She recalled the day Mac had given her the beautiful silver bell, the day after a rather frightening encounter with an angry groomsman. Mac had given her the thoughtful gift along with strict instructions to keep it within reach anytime she was alone with a man. Any man. It didn't matter if the gentleman was young enough to be her son or old enough to be her grandfather.

She had given in to Mac's demand because she trusted him in the same way she trusted Jonathan Pratt. Mac had never let her down, and if her keeping a bell within reach brought him comfort, she would gladly do so.

The area between her eyes pounded with tension. She pressed the pads of her fingers against the throbbing flesh and rubbed in a circular motion. But the action had little effect; the pain had advanced too far. Her fingers curled into balls of frustration. She couldn't afford this distraction now. With his lordship sniffing around her heels, she needed all of her wits to stay two steps ahead of him.

She pushed away from the wall, leaving thoughts of Lord Danforth behind, and made her way to her bedchamber. After many bouts of stubbornness that only resulted in prolonging her misery, she had finally learned not to fight the megrim and to take the laudanum sooner, rather than later. She despised the sluggish effects of laudanum almost as much as she hated the megrims themselves, but she knew no other way to reduce the fury in her brain.

When she rose from her bed, Sydney would have to face a new fury. One that, if she did not handle in the correct fashion, could cripple a nation. She had to find Lord Latymer. After his recent failure, he must be desperate now, and desperate people do desperate things. She refused to dwell on the possibility of her own failure. The last few years, she had navigated through worse odds and had emerged the victor.

She would do so again.

If she could keep one handsome viscount at bay.

Three

"TANNER." ETHAN STORMED INTO THE ENTRANCE HALL of his Hill Street town house in Mayfair. "As of this afternoon you're retiring."

His butler blinked. "I am, sir?"

"Yes." Ethan handed over his hat and gloves. "Can you pull it off?"

"Of course. Am I to retire in conversation only or must I make myself scarce?"

"Conversation only." Ethan led the way to his study. "See that Mrs. Tanner understands the situation, would you?"

"She would serve me up boiled toast every day if I didn't." Tanner stopped just inside the study door. "Might I ask for how long and for whom?"

"A sennight and Miss Hunt." Ethan poured himself a fortifying glass of brandy. "For reasons I can't explain, I've hired her agency to find a replacement butler. Unfortunately, she feels the need to visit here and ask you some questions. She wants to prepare the new chap, or some such."

A fleeting image of Miss Hunt wavered before his eyes. He had wanted desperately to break through the iron casing surrounding the proprietress and had resorted to what he did best: flirtation. The result had both amazed and dismayed him. Passion had softened her pretty green eyes moments before the panic had set in. That alarm had haunted his thoughts all the way home. He stared at the drop of brandy rolling around at the bottom of his glass. Still haunted him.

"Quite understandable, sir," Tanner replied.

Ethan glanced up from his brandy-induced contemplations. His butler was a marvel, as was Mrs. Tanner. The couple had come with the estate when he'd inherited his title over a decade ago. Of course, his old retainer didn't understand the reasons behind such secrecy and would never ask. While under the protection of Ethan's father—the former Lord Danforth and Chief of the Nexus—Tanner had learned it was better to simply follow along.

When the former Viscount Danforth was murdered, Ethan had been too young to take his father's place as chief. Not so now. Ethan had spent the intervening years preparing for this moment. Had taken on some of the most dangerous missions, like stealing behind enemy lines to rescue prisoners of war, to show Somerton his mettle. Somerton had taught him everything he knew about protecting England and himself from their ancient enemy, France. Moreover, as his legal guardian, the man had raised him from the age of fourteen, the year his parents were murdered, the year he became the next Viscount Danforth.

Some might think Ethan's efforts heroic, brave, and noble. But he would never give so honorable a label to the savagery he'd had to commit. In order to save English prisoners, he'd been forced, at times, to sacrifice the lives of others. Some had been innocents or, at least, ignorant of what went on right beneath their noses. Others had likely been aware and simply not cared. He had killed for the greater good, as they say. Who could ever call that heroic? Ethan couldn't.

Rotating his left hand, palm up, he splayed his fingers wide, revealing the cobweb of small and large creases marking his flesh, the fine scars and building calluses. So many times he had done this exact same exercise, hoping—no, praying—he would no longer see the blood of his victims stained within the deep recesses of his skin. He set his empty glass down. Out of habit, he rubbed his hands together, desiring soap and water to help cleanse away his sins. The stain gleamed brighter.

"Do I have any plans after my retirement, my lord?"

Ethan poured himself another drink and belted it back. The slow burn down his throat helped take his mind off the heinous images flooding his sight. "How the devil should I know? It's my job to come up with a far-fetched plan, and yours to execute it."

"Quite right, sir. That particular nuance slipped my mind."

Ignoring his butler's gibe, Ethan said, "You can expect an appearance from Miss Hunt sometime tomorrow."

"Are you speaking of Miss Hunt from the Hunt Agency?"

Shev was right. "Yes, you know it?"

"The agency is known for providing hardworking and trustworthy servants in exchange for a few concessions from their potential employer."

"Such as?"

"An adequate wage—based on the individual's experience and prior performance—and one and a half days off each week."

Ethan blinked. "One and a half days off?" The extra day seemed rather generous, to his mind. What would the servants do with all that extra time on their hands? He made a mental note to discuss the issue with Miss Hunt.

"That's what I've heard, sir. They're limited to a twelve-hour day, too."

"How many hours a day does my staff work?"

Tanner's chin rose. "As many as it takes, my lord."

Guilt wrapped around Ethan's chest and squeezed.

"Do you need anything more at the moment, sir?"

"No, Tanner. I suspect I've inconvenienced you enough."

The study door closed softly, and the quiet that followed felt like the death knell of a judge's gavel. He knew the life of a servant was difficult, but until this moment he never considered they might wish for something more than serving their master. An image of Miss Hunt's disappointed countenance surfaced, and the band of guilt around his chest tightened.

Thoughts of the proprietress drew forth their earlier conversation. The memory picked at his mind like a surgeon removing splinters from a festering wound. Raw and painful.

No matter how hard he tried to woo information from her, she hadn't yielded. In fact, she seemed to anticipate his probing questions. But the most frustrating part was his inability to place her. Her unusual height, voluptuous build, and dark hair created a memorable image, one not easily cast aside like that of so many other ordinary women.

And then there was the issue of the alias she used while visiting Abbingale Home. Why? Why would a respectable businesswoman feel the need to shield her identity? What possible reason could she have for visiting the boys' home under such pretense?

He glanced at the clock. His appointment with Somerton wasn't for another forty minutes. Even though he had arrived home only a quarter hour ago, he felt a restless need to be off again. Perhaps Somerton would be available to see him early. If not, he would make his way up to Somerton House's attic. His sister Cora had mentioned that their old target area, where they used to practice throwing their knives, was still there. He had never mastered the skill like Cora, but he could hit any target he aimed at and achieve the desired result.

His palms tingled, though he refused to fall prey to their call. Focusing his mind on the tight rings of a target might be just what he needed, especially if he wanted to be at his best during his audience with Somerton. The course of his life would likely change in the next hour, and he wanted to be prepared for the arrival of his dream.

Whirling about, he left the study and, when he gained his butler at the entrance, he plucked his gloves and hat from Tanner's grip. "I'll be at Somerton House if you should need me."

"Will we see you for dinner, my lord?"

"Tonight's sugar puff night, isn't it?"

"Yes, indeed."

"I'll be here, unless someone carts me off." *Again.*

"Pardon, sir?"

Ethan closed the door, warding off further questions. He jogged down the few steps to the pavement and then turned toward Charles Street.

Not long ago, he had attempted to hunt down the French bastard who had kidnapped his sister Cora and tortured her for information about the Nexus. He'd followed a trail of information to the London Docks, where he met up with three bears of men. The hired footpads had grabbed him in broad daylight and then hauled him to a deserted area near the docks and proceeded to beat him senseless.

But sometime during the night, a cloaked figure had moved him from the wretched, damp alleyway to an abandoned warehouse, where a dark-haired maid had looked after Ethan for several days. She had kept him in a laudanum-induced fog so he could sleep and heal. A state he appreciated at the time. Now, though, he had trouble recalling anything of significance of his stay in the warehouse, including a clear picture of either of his saviors.

Once the threat to Cora had passed, he'd returned to the docks and made inquiries about the two strangers who had helped him, to no avail. Why had they disappeared? He wanted to thank them and possibly return the favor in some way.

The more time that slipped by, the more Ethan's agitation grew. Their avoidance only made him more driven to track them down. When he found them—and he would—it would be a toss-up as to whether he would express his gratitude or hang them up by their big toes.

Ethan rapped on the door at 35 Charles Street. A distinguished man in his early fifties answered.

"Hello, Rucker," Ethan said. "I'm a little early for my appointment with Somerton."

The butler stepped back. "His lordship has not yet returned. Shall I see if Mrs. Ashcroft and her mother are available?"

He glanced up toward the attic and wondered if he could indulge in a few rounds of target practice before imposing upon Somerton's almost-betrothed, Catherine Ashcroft. "No need to disturb the ladies. I'm going up to the attic to throw a few rounds first."

Rucker, who was even more accustomed to looking the other way than Tanner, didn't miss a beat. "As you wish, my lord."

Ethan had ascended no more than two stairs when Catherine Ashcroft appeared on the landing above him. Still dressed in mourning black for the death of her father and husband, she carried the quintessential features of many English women. Average height, blond hair, oval face, creamy complexion, slim figure. The only fissure in her classical landscape was a pair of piercing brown eyes that saw far too much for a country miss.

Her face brightened, and she held out her hand while giving him a warm, welcoming smile. "Ethan, how nice to see you."

Her genuine pleasure helped assuage the sharp edge of anticipation gliding across his nerves. "Catherine." He climbed the remaining stairs, kissing her cheeks. "I'm sorry to have disturbed you. I thought to keep myself busy in the attic until Somerton arrived."

"The attic?" Her smile widened. "Whatever for?"

The widow's run-in with a traitorous Foreign Office official gave her access to knowledge about the Nexus few outside the Alien Office had. Ethan had no way of knowing if Somerton had revealed details about their covert activities beyond that one incident, nor did he know if Somerton had discussed his role in Ethan and Cora's unusual upbringing. Not everyone would understand why the young deBeaus were shown how to pick locks, lift goods from pockets, and use their bodies as weapons.

He decided to take the careful route. "Something Cora and I used to do as children. Perhaps you will allow me to keep you company until Somerton arrives."

"Of course," she said. "Rucker, will you ask Marston to send around a tea tray?"

"Of course, madam."

She led Ethan to a small sitting room that appeared

to double as a workspace. The writing desk near the window held a number of ledgers, and a low table in front of the sofa had an assortment of papers strewn across its surface.

The widow's skill at developing task lists and charting out work schedules had brought her to Somerton's attention, and Ethan doubted she would ever be free of the earl again, especially once her mourning period was over. Catherine appeared quite content with the arrangement.

"How goes your search for Giles Clarke?" she asked.

Out of habit, Ethan hesitated to reveal the details of his current mission. So much of what he and the Nexus did hinged on absolute secrecy. But, in this case, Catherine had been drawn into the situation from the beginning and deserved an update.

"I'm afraid I can report little progress. Right now, I'm trying to get a sense of the Abbingale's operation and hopefully gain a visual on the boy. But you must trust that I will find him, Catherine," he said. "I am very good at locating missing persons and retrieving them."

She nodded. "Sebastian said as much. I don't mean to imply otherwise. It's just that—the woman obviously loved her son and would have done anything to keep him safe."

Time for a change in topic, but Ethan was damned if he knew what. He still had another twenty minutes before his meeting with Somerton. What the devil was he going to discuss with Catherine in the meantime?

Then it struck him. "When we were all last together, Somerton had mentioned you'd noticed an unfamiliar maid at Sophie's birthday celebration," he said. "I'd like to know more about her."

One delicate eyebrow arched high. "I wondered when you would get around to inquiring. You seemed inordinately curious about her at the time. Something to do with the warehouse incident?"

"Yes," he said. "Can you provide more of a description? Her height, her build, any distinguishing features that might set her apart from other women? A scar, perhaps?"

Catherine's expression turned thoughtful. "I recall her being tall, with a full figure. Not robust, mind you. Ladies would envy such curves and men would worship them." Realizing what she'd said, the widow's cheeks flushed scarlet. "Pardon, my lord. I doubt those were the types of distinguishing features you were inquiring about."

"Actually, those are exactly the types of observations I'm interested in. Please go on."

"She wore a pair of gold-rimmed spectacles. In her early twenties, I'd say. Very dark hair." The widow's forehead knitted together. "I'm afraid that's all I remember at the moment. She was some distance away when I noticed her."

"Did you see her engaged in conversation with any of the guests?"

"Not that I saw," Catherine said. "She appeared to be absorbed with clearing away the dirty dishes and eyeing the guests."

"Eyeing the guests?"

She smiled. "It seems I have a knack for identifying such insignificant details. Sebastian learned early on the futility of keeping secrets from me."

"Any thoughts on what the maid might have been searching for in the crowd?"

"No, sorry. Most of my attention was focused on my daughter's whereabouts."

"Quite understandable. She spoke to no one during the party?"

"Of course she spoke to the guests," Catherine said.

"But she did not engage any of them in conversation. At least, not that I noticed."

Disappointment curled in Ethan's chest. There had to be thousands of tall, dark-haired maids in England. Why he thought his dockside nurse and Catherine's mysterious servant might be one and the same, he didn't know. He would blame it on this seething desperation to bring the warehouse incident to an end. His family had always accused him of being rather bullheaded when it came to resolving matters or protecting loved ones. For the first time, he could clearly see what they meant.

"Thank you, Catherine." He braced his hand against the windowsill and peered down at the garden. "Seems I have more missing persons to find. But do not fear. Giles takes priority over my personal needs."

"Sebastian remarked that the people who saved you are avoiding you. Why do you think that is?"

"They're not avoiding me, per se," he said through tight lips, turning back to her. "More like, they do not wish to be found." Her eyebrow arched again, so he clarified. "By anyone."

"When you find them, what will you do?"

Ethan did not miss her reference to "when," rather than "if," he would find the cloaked figure and the maid. "Initially, I wanted to thank them and be done with the whole thing. Now that they've caused me a great deal of inconvenience, I have other, less pure thoughts traveling around in my mind."

"I don't blame you." She canted her blond head to the side. "Are you sure your interest does not go beyond gratitude?"

"To what?" Ethan shook his head and began to pace. "No, there is nothing brewing beneath the surface of my interest. It's unfinished business, that's all."

"No desire to uncover the individual beneath the cloak?" she pressed.

His eyes narrowed. "How much time have you been spending with Cora?"

"Is that a polite way of saying 'mind your own affairs'?" She grinned. "I suppose you're right, but your curiosity has roused my own."

"Perhaps," he said in a menacing tone, "I should continue my march up to Somerton's attic and remove such temptation from your presence."

She rose, her lips fixed in a knowing smile. "If you insist, my lord."

The door burst open. "Mama!" A mop of blond and red curls streaming behind a miniature body ran into the room. Then the girl spotted him, and her pixie face lit up much the same as her mother's had. "Ethan!"

Sophie Ashcroft's little body plowed into his midsection. She had changed directions so swiftly and with such force that the assault caught him off-guard. The impact of her enthusiasm forced out a whoosh of air between his lips.

"Where have you been?" his assailant asked.

After catching his breath, he looked down at the newly minted seven-year-old clinging to his waist. Her sparkling blue eyes danced up at him. They had only been acquainted a few weeks, but she had taken a distinct liking to him on sight. When it came to him, she respected nothing. Not his clothing, his space, or his time. She had an affinity for his lap and putting her grubby hands on his face while speaking to him from a mere three inches away. Ethan had no notion of what to do with her or her overabundance of affection. In this instance, he patted her shoulder.

"Hello, banshee. Did you escape your grandmama again?"

Her grin broadened. "Have you come to take me for a ride in the park?"

"And have Teddy rip out my guts?" Ethan asked, recalling the stable lad who had been instrumental in thwarting a kidnapping attempt on his playmate. "I don't think so."

She bent back to see him better. "Don't be a silly goose," she said. "Teddy's in Showbury. He'll never know."

"Sophie," her grandmama said, coming into the room. "Do not call Lord Danforth a silly goose. It's bad enough that you use his Christian name."

"Yes, Grandmama." The girl's blue eyes gazed up at him with an eagerness that did strange things to his chest. "May we go for a ride in the park?"

Ethan grasped her narrow shoulders and stepped back at the same time, exerting pressure until her vine-like arms released their hold. "Just because your young man is miles away and will likely not hear of our escapades in the park doesn't mean we should. Send him a letter and ask if he minds. If he gives you the nod, I will be happy to escort you about the park."

She folded her arms over her chest. "Why should I ask him for permission? He's not a relative."

He inched toward the door. "A courtesy for saving your life."

"But I've already thanked him, plus Bastian hired someone to fix his sick mama."

Ethan glanced up to find *Bastian*, or Sebastian Danvers, Lord Somerton, in the doorway, looking upon the girl with fatherly affection. "All the same," he said, feeling safer with another male nearby. "Get Teddy's consent and then send me a note."

Sophie huffed a discontented breath. "That'll take days."

Why, yes, it will. "Doing the right thing is not always

the easiest path." The sage advice sounded pompous, even to his ears. "Somerton, shall we begin our meeting?" He widened his eyes in a "help me" gesture, hoping his mentor would take the hint.

"By all means," Somerton said, though he did not look pleased. "Sophie, I will take you for a ride in the park once my business is done with Lord Danforth. Will that suit?"

"Oh, yes, Bastian." She lifted up onto her toes and clasped her hands together. "That would suit very well." Her happiness dimmed a bit when she glanced at Ethan.

To Catherine, Sebastian said, "I'll be back in a half hour."

"Take your time," she said. "Good day, Ethan."

He nodded to the women and followed Somerton to the study, trying desperately to put Sophie's miserable little face from his mind. She was not the first female he had made unhappy today. When had he shifted from charmer to destroyer of happiness? He shrugged off the unpleasant realization. With all his other responsibilities, he had no time left to play nursemaid to a child, especially one with so much zest for life. Not only was he on a personal quest to uncover the identities of his saviors, but he also had a mission to complete. He had to verify Giles Clarke's presence in Abbingale Home and then extract the boy.

What Somerton planned to do with the Clarke boy after extraction, Ethan didn't know. With the mother dead and no other living relative to contact—at least, none they knew of—the boy would likely wind up in another home, but one of Somerton's choosing.

First things first. Right now, he had to mentally prepare himself for one of the most important meetings of his life.

⁓⁓

While Somerton closed the study door, Ethan moved to stand before the earl's desk and did his best to settle his nerves. All his preparation and dedication to the Nexus—and to Somerton—had led him to this moment. He was ready, both in mind and body. Stepping into the chief's position would validate all his hard work and sacrifices.

He would finally be a greater asset to the Nexus than a boudoir spy. Although he'd ventured outside that role in recent years, seducing information from women was the one that had defined his career and the one he had come to dread. In the early days, bedding beautiful women and coaxing away their secrets had been a young agent's ideal mission. The assignments had brought him great physical pleasure without all the emotional aftermath. But, within a few short years, his expertise had felt more like a burden than a gift.

Somerton drew up a chair. "Have a seat, Danforth."

"I hope I did not offend Catherine by my desire to make a hasty exit," Ethan said. "She was kind enough to answer some questions, and the last thing I wanted to do was upset her."

"You'll find Cat's skin to be thicker than most women's. Besides, she's fully aware of Sophie's impact on others."

"She's a sweet girl, but I've no notion what to do with her."

"You don't have to do anything with her. Next time, bring up the subject of horses and she'll take it from there."

Ethan nodded, even though he thought there must be more to dealing with children than talking about four-legged animals with manes.

"What questions did you have for Catherine?"

"I took the opportunity to ask her about the unknown servant at Sophie's birthday celebration."

"Still trying to make the connection between Cat's maid and your benevolent stranger?"

There were times, such as this, when Somerton's questions made Ethan feel lacking in the intelligence arena. In this instance, the feeling trebled, because Ethan knew it was a stretch to connect a maid from the country to one in the city, especially one who moved about the docks with no care to her personal safety. He wondered what the spymaster would say if he knew Ethan's thoughts had even wandered to Hunt Agency's proprietress.

"Conducting my due diligence, sir. Even though my mind finds little logic connecting the two, my gut is guiding me at the moment."

"Very well. Do not allow this issue to take priority over retrieving Giles Clarke, though."

This wasn't the first time Somerton felt the need to deliver an unnecessary warning or command. Ethan refused to believe that the one mistake he'd made a few weeks ago warranted such greenling treatment. Outside a handful of missions with his friend Helsford, he had operated alone and had done so quite successfully. If Ethan wasn't determined to remain on his best behavior today, he would tell Somerton what he could do with his advice. "Of course. As I told you before, I learned my lesson well and won't veer from protocol again."

He studied Somerton, trying to gauge the man's mood. But, as always, his mentor's expression revealed nothing.

"I think you know why I've asked to meet with you today," Somerton said.

"Yes, sir. I have an idea of the reason."

"I don't think I have to tell you what a good and valued agent of the Nexus you've become."

Somerton did not dole out praise often, so hearing his mentor's thoughts now made his chest swell and his back straighten. "Thank you," Ethan said, swallowing back his emotion. "I am honored to be part of such a worthy cause."

"Now that I've assumed my new duties as Under Superintendent of the Alien Office, Superintendent Reeves has asked for a recommendation for the chief's position."

Ethan's breaths were coming harder, and he found it difficult to maintain his calm mask. "Of course."

"The candidate I'm considering is someone I've known for many years and someone whose career I helped mold."

"Someone you trust."

"Implicitly. His integrity is above reproach, and he has the intelligence and strength to coordinate an international operation."

"Who have you chosen, sir?"

"Helsford."

Ethan's vision blurred. An image of his best friend hovered between them, blocking thought, arresting sight, and stealing every snatch of sound. He shook his head to clear the confusion. "Helsford?"

"Yes. I had considered your sister, Cora, but after all that's happened in the last few months, I don't believe she's ready to take on such an onerous position."

Blood pumped through Ethan's veins like thick, black sludge. It oozed from one extremity to the other, slow and deliberate. He closed his eyes as the meaning behind Somerton's announcement struck him full force in the chest.

He wouldn't be chief, after all. He'd lost his one true goal in life.

Somerton had chosen Cora and Guy over him. Two

people who had joined the group for reasons other than a belief in the Nexus's core mission—to stop Napoleon. Cora had learned what she could from Somerton in order to track down the French assassin responsible for their parents' murders. And Guy had joined only to watch over Cora. Both were noble reasons, but neither had devoted their life to the advancement of the Nexus's cause.

Ethan had. Every decision he'd ever made had been in support of this organization. An organization that was now kicking up its nose at over a decade's worth of dedicated service. Anger like nothing he had ever experienced slashed against the thin thread of his control.

He would not give Somerton reason to believe he'd made the right decision. Through his nose, he forced his breathing into an even rhythm. He focused his entire concentration on the smooth, slow glide of air. In, out. In, out. Over and over until the anger building in his heart tempered into something manageable. In a low voice, he asked, "Has Helsford accepted?"

Somerton's gaze sharpened. "I haven't approached him yet. Before I did, I wanted to hear your opinion on my decision."

"Why?"

Somerton paused, studying him. "Because you know Helsford better than anyone. Do you think his concern over Cora will distract him too badly from doing his duties as chief?"

A dozen answers swirled around Ethan's mind, each one confirming Somerton's fears about Helsford's inability to lead the Nexus. All he had to do was voice one—just one—and he knew Somerton would bypass his best friend and move on to the next candidate. But who would that be? Him? Somehow Ethan didn't think so.

He thought back to the mission before last, when he

had gone off on his own in search of his sister's abuser. He had wanted to remove the threat against her. Kill Valère before the French bastard had an opportunity to settle on English soil. But someone had known what he was about and had him attacked and left him to rot. What followed after had caused his family great distress when no one knew whether he was alive or dead. That incident had secured him the epithet *King of Rogues*, and not because of his prowess in bed.

No, he had earned that ignominious title by ignoring protocol. One mistake. That's all it took to lose the one thing that mattered to him most. He lifted his gaze to Somerton's. "If Helsford accepts the position, he will not disappoint you." Ethan rose to his feet; his head and arms felt as though they weighed twenty stone. "If you have nothing more, I have an appointment to keep."

Somerton unwound his tall frame. "That's all you have to say?"

"What else is there? I'm sure you've put a lot of thought into your selection and your mind is set, no matter my input."

"Your opinion matters a great deal, Danforth."

Ethan clenched his teeth. "Helsford will lead the Nexus well."

Silence darkened the chamber. Then Somerton asked, "How is the investigation going? Have you managed to catch sight of Giles Clarke?"

"Not yet, sir, but I expect to soon."

"Keep me updated. I want to know if there is a link between the boys' home and Latymer."

Latymer. The disgraced former Superintendent of the Alien Office had plagued them for weeks. Not only had he sold his soul to the French, but he had also betrayed and tried to kill Somerton, his friend.

"You'll be the first." Ethan pivoted on his heel. "Good day."

"Danforth."

He drew in an unsteady breath and released it. Glancing over his shoulder, he lifted an inquiring eyebrow.

"Is there anything more you wish to say to me?"

You made a damn mistake? What's the point? "No, sir."

"You're sure?" Somerton pressed. "No concerns about taking direction from your friend?"

His jaw hurt from the pressure of keeping damaging words behind his teeth.

"If so, I can make special arrangements—"

"There's no problem, sir," Ethan cut in before the man could eviscerate him further. "I'll report back in a few days."

Not waiting for a proper dismissal, Ethan strode from Somerton's presence, praying he would not come across Sophie or Catherine. His long stride did not falter all the way home. It wasn't until he closed the door to his bedchamber that he allowed his rage its freedom. He tore off his coat and wrenched the cravat from around his neck. Breathless, he raked his fingers through his hair and grabbed onto his skull as if the pressure alone would stop the insidious voice of failure.

Dropping his hands to his side, he searched the chamber. He searched for nothing in particular. Just something, anything, to relieve the pain of Somerton's words. Alcohol. He needed alcohol to dull his senses. And sex. A vision of Miss Hunt glommed on to his thoughts. *No. Dear God, no.*

He needed mindless sex with a woman who would not make him think about every damn word coming out of his mouth. Better yet, he would speak to Madame Rousseau to make sure the woman she sent to his bed did not utter a single syllable—unless it was to beg for more. All he needed was a quick release and maybe, just maybe, the tension cramping his muscles would ease enough for him to breathe normally again.

Four

SYDNEY CLASPED HER GLOVED HANDS BEFORE HER while the stern-faced Mrs. Drummond closed the door. She performed a thorough sweep of Abbingale's entrance hall, taking in the restrained interior that bespoke of both functionality and a care for cleanliness.

"No companion today?" Mrs. Drummond asked.

Shaking her head, Sydney replied in her silliest voice. "I'm afraid not. Poor Mrs. Cartwright wasn't feeling quite the thing, so I insisted she stay behind." Sydney wrinkled her nose. "No one wants to be around a dribbler. So, you have me all to yourselves!"

In truth, Sydney had asked Amelia, along with the O'Donnell brothers, to spend the day meeting with the agency's many service clients to see if anyone could provide information on Lord Latymer's whereabouts. Instinct urged her to use every resource at her disposal to find the gentleman before he caused any more harm.

Unfortunately, when Amelia realized that Sydney planned to visit Abbingale alone, her assistant had made her promise to take Mac and Mick. Sydney reluctantly agreed but insisted Amelia return to the agency in two hours to retrieve Mick for the rest of her interviews. All in all, their debate ended quite equitably, which was why they all worked so well together.

Mrs. Drummond continued, "Matron is settling in a new unfortunate. She asked me to take you about the facility, then she'll meet us on the third floor, where the fortunates sleep."

In the midst of surveying her surroundings, Sydney paused. "So the children are considered unfortunate when they arrive and fortunate once they become residents?"

"Yes, ma'am. Matron likes symbolizing each child's turning point with a descriptive word. It gives them something they can aspire to, or some such thing. I'm afraid most of it's lost on me. And if it's lost on me, these ignorant boys aren't likely to understand."

For a woman who worked with children all day, Mrs. Drummond had no idea how intelligent and perceptive they could be. Drawing forth her most grating feminine voice, Sydney asked, "Oh, la. Such things are so tiresome. I have a dear friend who insists that I should read poetry to expand my mind. Honestly, who can follow such wandering, nonsensical thoughts? It's as if the poet spent time searching for the words at the bottom of a bottle before applying them to paper." She let out a sigh and then started walking. "What do you do here, Mrs. Drummond?"

The woman took a moment to respond, no doubt stunned into speechlessness by the seemingly unending stream of words, followed by an abrupt change of topic. Mrs. Drummond cleared her throat. "I'm one of two nurses employed here. When it comes to the boys, whatever needs done, I do." Her back straightened into a proud line. "I make sure the children rise at six, wash their faces, eat their meals, attend the schoolroom, complete their chores, and then I send them to bed by eight."

Halting, Sydney asked, "You do all that in a single day?"

Mrs. Drummond's barely contained disgust was something to behold. "I do all that every day, Mrs. Henshaw."

Hearing the name of her old, beloved schoolmistress sent a wave of nostalgia through Sydney. Word of Agnes Henshaw's sudden death had reached Sydney only a month ago. When she'd decided to assume another identity for her observation of Abbingale, it seemed fitting to use the name of the woman she had admired so much.

Sydney flipped open her frilly pink fan and worked it enthusiastically. "Goodness, I feel faint just listening to you."

The nurse pursed her lips. She motioned up the stairs. "Shall we?"

Sydney nodded and preceded the scrawny woman up two flights of stairs, even though she had the distinct and uncomfortable feeling that the nurse was studying her figure. Mrs. Drummond barely came to Sydney's shoulder and weighed little more than a candelabrum—and was about as wide as one, too.

Over the years, Sydney had grown comfortable with her height and more robust frame. As a matter of fact, she had used it to her advantage on more than one occasion. But there were still times when her height felt like a lodestone hanging around her neck, taunting her to drop her shoulders and curve her spine. Anything to make her appear smaller, more feminine. More accepted amongst her female counterparts.

At five-foot-nine, she towered over most women and some men, especially when wearing her walking boots, with their two-inch heels. Mac had never minded her size, probably because he stood several inches taller. Then his scapegrace brother Mick came onto the scene a little over a year ago. The first time he saw her, he murmured, "My, aren't you a Long Meg," in his soft Irish bur. He followed the comment with a devilish wink, and no more was said on the subject. She wished all her encounters could be so painless.

All the same, she was thankful for this chance to speak with another one of Abbingale's staff. The opportunity allowed her to crosscheck the matron's facts. "How many children are living here now?"

"The new unfortunate makes twenty-eight boys."

"No girls?"

"Thankfully, no," Mrs. Drummond said, with an ugly twist to her mouth. "I shudder to think of the problems we would have with boys and girls under the same roof."

"What are the boys' ages?"

"Most of them are between five and thirteen."

"What happens at the age of thirteen?"

"Mrs. Kingston finds them a situation where they'll spend the next five years apprenticing."

"How wonderful that you prepare the children for a life beyond Abbingale."

"It's too bad, however, that our funding only provides for a change of ill-fitting clothes, a hat and coat, and a coach ride to their destination."

"What a dreadful way to begin a new life." Sydney produced a tittering laugh. "I suppose you're going to tell me the boys are dropped off with little or no under-standing of what they'll be doing for the next five years."

The nurse's back went rigid. So much so, that if a strong wind blew against her, she would likely snap in half. "There's simply not enough time or money for such things, Mrs. Henshaw."

Sydney sighed. "Poor little dears. Their fates are not unlike a new bride's. No one dares to explain The Act to her, so she goes to her husband's bed ignorant and frightened and makes quite a mess of it."

"My word, Mrs. Henshaw," the nurse said. "There are children about."

Whirling, Sydney exclaimed, "Brilliant. Where are the little darlings?"

Mrs. Drummond sputtered, "They're not here in this room, but they could pass by at any moment. It wouldn't do for them to hear such scandalous talk."

"Do not tease me so, Mrs. Drummond." Sydney infused disappointment into her voice. "I am ever so anxious to meet the boys."

"I was not trying to tease you, ma'am—"

Sydney sailed away, scanning the next room with an intent eye masked behind airy nonchalance. The more she played the role of twit, the more she liked it. There was something oddly liberating about hiding one's identity in full view of others—and saying whatever came to mind. "How are their apprenticeships chosen if they're not exposed to the various crafts ahead of time?"

"Matron decides where the boys go."

"Do their new masters expect them to be at least peripherally aware of their livelihood?"

"They have only two expectations of our boys—learn quickly and work hard."

Anger simmered beneath Sydney's thin facade. She had heard many tales of abusive masters. Last year, a shipwright beat an eight-year-old boy to death for losing his draw-knife. The only punishment served was to force the shipwright to pay the boy's annual wage of five pounds to his parents. "How does Mrs. Kingston ensure the boys are being sent to a good situation?"

"If the craftsman or merchant is unkind, the boys

choose the streets rather than endure years of abuse. I don't blame them their choice. However, I'm not sure they would fare any better living hand to mouth and thieving their way through life."

"How horrible," Sydney said. "Mrs. Kingston knows all this and does nothing about it?"

"Matron knows everything concerning the boys." Mrs. Drummond paused in the massive dining hall. "Thankfully, the poor situations do not occur often."

"Why don't the boys return to Abbingale, rather than live on the streets? Surely, Mrs. Kingston could find another apprenticeship for them."

"Who's to say? Children are beggars at heart. Perhaps, pickpocketing is a truer vocation for them at that age."

After an arrested moment of silence, Sydney dug deep into her repertoire of acting skills, rather than doing what she really wanted—wrap her hands around the woman's scrawny neck and finish her off with a rather zealous bout of squeezing and shaking. "Dear Mrs. Drummond, you quite had me under your spell for a second. 'Beggars at heart,' indeed."

Sydney linked her arm with the nurse's and gave it a small jerk as she sailed onward once again. Being in such close proximity to the woman made her muscles bunch and her nose quiver over the abundance of starch the woman used. "Come, Mrs. Drummond. Tell me what the boys are doing when they are not at their studies."

She didn't think it was possible for the older woman's back to get any straighter or her lips to get any firmer. But Mrs. Drummond managed it with great aplomb. "Each child has a task he must complete before the sun sets."

"Intriguing," Sydney said. "Do these tasks ever take them outside of Abbingale?"

The woman's gaze shifted to the floor above. "I'm afraid you'll have to ask Mrs. Kingston your question. She develops the task schedule each week."

They made their way down the long corridor, and Mrs. Drummond continued highlighting the different aspects of Abbingale Home. This floor held three large, rectangular sleeping chambers, each one holding ten narrow beds and little else. The beds lined each side of the room, with a corridor of empty space down the middle. Trunks rested at the foot of each bed, holding the boys' meager belongings. Everything was uniformly in its proper place, much like what she would expect from a rigid military installation. Outside of the single portrait on the far wall, the room held not a speck of color.

"Who's the stern-looking gentleman with the odd-looking creature sitting on his lap?"

"Sir Francis Abbingale and Zeus."

Sydney's eyes narrowed. "Is that a feline?"

"Matron calls the abomination a scant-haired cat."

"I've never heard of anyone making a mouser into a pet." Sydney wondered if the cat's lack of hair was one of those unusual birth defects that occur not only in the animal world but with humans as well.

"And you'll likely not hear of it again. Sir Francis has a penchant for finding the unusual."

"Obviously, Sir Francis is one of the founders. Who else sits on the Board of Trustees?"

"There are five trustees, including Sir Francis, Lady Kipland, and Mr. Livingston."

Sydney ticked off the names on her fingers. "Francis, Kipland, and Livingston. What about the last two?"

"They prefer to keep their involvement anonymous."

"Anonymous?" Sydney repeated, confused. "Is that even possible?"

The nurse snorted. "Anything is possible when one waves money around."

"Yes, well, look at these beds," Sydney said brightly, redirecting their attention. She made a mental note to have Amelia ferret out the names of the final two trustees. "So crisp."

The nurse glanced around. "As always."

"Do the boys make their own beds?"

"Of course. We do not tolerate any of the seven deadly sins, especially sloth. If left alone, the little beasts would do nothing all day except play dice and cause mischief."

"Your diligence is so refreshing." Sydney wondered if laughter ever echoed off these walls.

Mrs. Drummond insisted Sydney view the other two sleeping chambers, and Sydney found them both depressingly similar to the first, right down to the portrait of Sir Francis Abbingale. In the other two paintings, the gentleman held an incredibly small monkey in one and a masked rodent with black bands on its back in the other.

"What happens to the boys if they don't complete their task by sunset?"

"They are persuaded not to have it happen again."

"Oh?" Sydney paused to swipe her gloved finger along the bed frame. Spotless. "In what way? Do you force them to darn all the stockings in the laundry?"

"I couldn't say."

"Because you don't know?"

The older woman's lips clamped together.

"Would the other nurse? Or, perhaps, Mrs. Kingston?"

"What is the point of these questions? As you can see, the boys are well-attended."

"On the contrary, Mrs. Drummond. I see only empty

beds. How is it that I am in a home for orphan boys and it has no orphans?"

"You will see them soon enough."

Sydney forced a sparkling smile. "Splendid!"

"Good morning, Mrs. Henshaw," a new voice called. "I see Mrs. Drummond is taking good care of you."

Sydney glanced up to find Abbingale's matron standing in the doorway. "Indeed, she is, Mrs. Kingston."

"Mrs. Henshaw would like to know where we're keeping the orphans, ma'am."

For some unknown reason, Sydney's first inclination was to smile in response to the nurse's snide statement. The woman had such a sour attitude that Sydney did not think sucking on a lemon would pucker her up any more. Why would anyone ever think it a good idea to place someone like her in an authoritative position over impressionable young children? A shudder ripped down the length of her spine just thinking about the lasting impact of this mean-spirited nurse.

Sydney's second inclination—and the one she settled on—was to give Mrs. Drummond a taste of her own intimidation. She straightened her spine, lifted her chin, and leveled her gaze on her nemesis. She topped it off with a beguiling smile so as not to be too obvious. The small shift in position gave her hulking frame even more height and the illusion of immense strength. When her sharp-tongued guide took a step closer to the matron, Sydney suppressed a knowing smirk. Her victory over the unkind nurse should not have pleased her quite so much. But it did. Oh, how it did.

"During my last visit," Sydney said, "I assumed the quiet meant the children were either outside playing or upstairs napping." She swept her hand over the empty beds. "That does not seem to be the case today."

The matron's smile was gentle. "We prefer to keep the boys' minds occupied much of the day. Too much idleness can lead to wickedness."

"Is it not normal for young boys to be wicked?"

"To a degree," Matron said. "But with so many boys occupying a small space like Abbingale, we curtail their natural tendencies as much as possible."

"What occupies them so thoroughly that I do not even hear the hum of low voices?"

"Walk with me, won't you, Mrs. Henshaw?"

"Of course." Sydney followed the matron down a long, narrow corridor, which led to an even narrower staircase. They ascended the stairs, with Mrs. Kingston leading the way and Mrs. Drummond following behind Sydney.

Shadows thickened and the air turned stale, as if fresh air had not entered the upper floors for months. Years, even.

"Watch your step," Mrs. Kingston warned, when they approached a small landing that led to another set of stairs. "Cassie has not made it up here yet to light a lamp."

Had Sydney not been looking ahead, she would have missed the faint halo of light spilling out onto the landing's floor. No sooner had she squinted her eyes for a better look, then the light disappeared.

Once she reached the landing, she could not locate a door or an opening of any kind. She saw nothing but a shadow-drenched wall. She hesitated, fighting a sudden urge to drop to her hands and knees and investigate the source of light.

"Is something the matter, Mrs. Henshaw?"

Tearing her gaze away, Sydney glanced up to find Mrs. Kingston studying her with an open yet slightly bewildered expression. She cursed beneath her breath. She knew better than to be so careless. If something was going on at Abbingale, one of these two women could be involved. Anything she saw here that was out of the ordinary, she had to be more circumspect in her interest. Now she would have to redouble her efforts as the wealthy twit.

Ducking her head, she molded her features into a look of chagrin. "You will think me a silly goose."

"Not at all, ma'am. Did you see something of concern?"

Sydney let out a nervous laugh. "Not really." She waved her hand around. "I daresay if this landing had been properly lit, I would not have been reminded of my elderly Aunt Lucille's house."

Matron stared at her for several silent seconds. Then she ventured, "Aunt Lucille's house?"

"My aunt was quite frugal, so any chambers not in use were closed off. On occasion, this meant shutting off entire floors."

A large sigh sounded from behind Sydney.

"Go on, please, Mrs. Henshaw."

"As you know, when an adult forbids a child from going into a particular place, that's where she most wants to be." Sydney shared a smile with the matron. "So I tiptoed my way up to the third floor and came across a landing very similar to this one. And that's when I found it."

"Found what?"

"The secret chamber." She paused to allow her words to sink in and watched the matron's face for any telltale sign of guilt. "So, you see why I hesitated on your landing."

The woman's expression did not falter. "I'm not altogether sure I do."

Sydney clasped her hands together and released an excited laugh. "I was looking for the door to your secret chamber." She whirled around to see the nurse's reaction. "Is that not the most gothic notion?"

Mrs. Drummond swallowed hard, and Sydney noticed the woman's face was recovering from having lost every ounce of blood. "It sounds a bit far-fetched, if you ask me."

"Your tale is quite intriguing, Mrs. Henshaw," Matron said, pulling Sydney's attention forward again. "But, I assure you, we have no secret chambers or skulking villains at Abbingale. Just a group of boys in need of care and a small, dedicated staff."

Sydney nodded. "I did warn you about thinking me a silly goose."

Mrs. Kingston started up the stairs again. "No one here thinks that of you. It's a lovely story, but you do not need to worry about the boys. They're in good hands."

Had the matron hoped to steer the conversation away from a sensitive subject by not addressing the possibility of a hidden chamber? Sydney had detected no artifice in the woman, nor condescension. Every word the matron had uttered was kind and gave the appearance of being genuine. Quite unlike her counterpart. Could the matron's calm solicitude and caring nature be nothing more than a convincing ruse?

Maybe the woman simply thought Sydney's story was so unbelievable as to not warrant more discussion. Entirely possible. As for herself, Sydney was rather proud of the tale. Who knew she had the ability to string together several nonsensical thoughts on cue *and* make them relevant to the situation?

Sydney smiled at the matron. "I will try to keep your words of reassurance in mind." Falling in behind Mrs. Kingston, she ascended the staircase. They had ventured no more than a half dozen stairs when the press of gloom settled on her shoulders and prodded at her mind.

Had Sydney's purpose been anything other than gathering information on the inner workings of Abbingale

Home and search for links to Latymer, she would have still been shaken by the realization that something was wrong here. Everything seemed too perfect and yet off-balance.

"Here we are." Mrs. Kingston pushed open a door and gestured Sydney forward. "The boys should be finishing their writing lesson."

Inside, six rows of five desks filled the schoolroom, most containing a uniformed child. In front of the individual desks stood a long bench, seating a handful of the youngest boys. Another bench, about a foot higher and with a raised edge, stood before them. Although Sydney could not see the surface of the higher bench, she knew it was likely painted black and covered with sand. Such was a common practice for children learning their alphabet. When their stubby, uncoordinated fingers sketched letters in the white sand, the black background would reveal their efforts to greater advantage.

At Sydney's entrance, little heads swung her way, the boys' features impassive and pale. Varying in ages between five and thirteen, they appeared terribly innocent, with their hair combed back and controlled by some type of taming agent and their hands clasped before them.

"Mrs. Henshaw," Matron said, "may I introduce you to Abbingale's schoolmaster, Monsieur LaRouche. Monsieur, Mrs. Henshaw, a potential benefactress."

"Welcome to Abbingale, *madame*," he said with a nod. "I hope you are finding everything satisfactory."

The schoolmaster was a handsome man, with thick blond hair that curled at the tips and eyes a piercing deep blue. Though he stood at a level with her, his square shoulders and erect stance gave him an air of confidence normally reserved for gentlemen of greater height. She found herself staring at his mouth, not because of the fullness of his lips, though. No, her gaze remained riveted on his mouth, hoping to hear more melodic words slip between the seam of his lips.

Though his surname was French, his voice carried a trace of Italian and he spoke perfect, unbroken English. The combination was hypnotic and soothing. Rich and sensual. Dark and dangerous. They were all there, entwined between each syllable and flowing beneath the surface. Mesmerizing in a disturbingly intimate way.

Sydney shook herself free from her odd trance and sent the schoolmaster her most beatific smile. "It's a pleasure to meet you, monsieur."

"Gentlemen," LaRouche intoned. "Say hello to our guest, Mrs. Henshaw."

As one, the boys scooted off their seats and bowed toward Sydney. "Good morning, Mrs. Henshaw."

Their flawless greeting felt more like a monastic chant, one they'd performed countless times until every note was a symphony unto itself. Rather than be inspired by the work involved in perfecting their greeting, Sydney shivered. Trepidation, cold and seeping, settled into her bones.

"Good morning," she said. "Please sit. I did not mean to disturb your studies."

They faced forward and slid back into their seats. No one spared her a glance, no one made a sound. They sat there, waiting, with patience unnatural to children their age. Sydney's gaze scanned their faces, seeking some indication life existed behind their porcelain masks. Not a single glimmer. Not one.

Heartsick, she started to turn away and collect what information she could from this section of the facility. That's when she caught the lightning shift of another's gaze. She moved forward, her back to the women and schoolmaster, feigning interest in their lesson by stopping beside each student. Between one boy and the next, she glanced up in time to catch the shift again. Clear green eyes latched onto hers, and Sydney's stride faltered.

For no more than a second, a mere spit of time, she was pulled into the boy's desolate existence. Fear and helplessness swirled around her in layers of impenetrable black and wisps of blood red. Then he blinked, and the disturbing veil disappeared, jarring Sydney.

She stared at the green-eyed boy, desperate to read something besides bleakness in his expression. But he refused to meet her gaze again, as did all the others. Her attention drifted down to the sheet of paper resting on each of their desks, perfectly positioned in its center. Depending on the boy's age, the sheet reflected an appropriate level of learning. A child of five practiced his uppercase and lowercase letters, where a child of nine prepared short essays.

Sydney made a full circle before halting near the matron and schoolmaster. Knowing they expected her to remark upon the boys' studies, she said, "Quite impressive. They are taught reading, writing, and their numbers, I take it."

"Yes, *madame*," LaRouche said. "As well as history and geography."

She turned to the schoolmaster. "Any languages?"

Even though she knew her airy mask was in place, the schoolmaster studied her as if he saw not her guise of empty-headedness, but the intelligence-seeker beneath.

"A smattering of Latin and French," he said finally.

"Truly?" she asked. "I should like to come up and practice with them sometime. I'm afraid my French is quite abysmal."

He inclined his head. "It would be our pleasure to have you join us."

"Shall we proceed, Mrs. Henshaw?" Matron asked.

She did not want to leave the boys, yet she itched to be quit of this place. If she had such a strong aversion to what was going on here—whatever that was—how must these innocents feel? "I am ready when you are, Mrs. Kingston."

"Gentlemen," LaRouche said. "Say your good-byes."

Like a faithful cuckoo clock, the boys scooted out of their seats, bowed, and chimed, "Good day, Mrs. Henshaw."

Amidst the chant, Sydney caught a muffled cry of pain. She searched their young faces, trying to locate the source, but they all looked on without expression. Her attention settled on the green-eyed boy and noticed a flush of red carpeting his cheeks that wasn't there a minute ago. She tried to catch his eye again, but he focused on something beyond her shoulder.

"Good day, gentlemen," she said.

Mrs. Drummond filled her vision. "After you, ma'am."

The moment she stepped across the threshold, Sydney lifted her hand to say farewell to the schoolmaster, but he was not where he had been. She located him striding slowly along the rows of small chairs. When she made to say good-bye, Mrs. Drummond's countenance once again filled her vision and the doorway.

The nurse's thin lips slanted up into a poor excuse for a smile. "Enjoy your tour." She closed the door in Sydney's face, but not before Sydney saw the schoolmaster stop near the green-eyed boy.

Heart pounding, Sydney stood staring at the wood panels, trying to make sense of the last ten minutes. In her bones, she knew something was amiss. But what exactly? The young boy was clearly miserable, but perhaps he had only just arrived and had not yet settled into his new life. He might even be the unfortunate Mrs.

Drummond spoke of earlier. If that's the case, everything must seem frightening to one so young.

"Mrs. Henshaw," Matron called. "Are you coming?"

Sydney pressed her fist against her mouth and drew in a deep breath before whirling around. "If you don't mind, Mrs. Kingston, I should like to finish the tour another day."

"My apologies," Matron said. "Have we taken up too much of your time?"

"Not at all." She rubbed her temples. "An annoying headache is coming on, I'm afraid."

"Then let me see you to your carriage."

"Thank you." It wasn't until Sydney reached the bottom of the stairway that the niggling voice in the back of her mind, the one that had been there since the moment she had stepped foot inside the schoolroom, finally calmed. The calm did not last long, though, for it opened the door to her instincts.

And they were screaming.

Five

THE ONLY THING ETHAN HATED MORE THAN BEING A drunkard was being a flower girl. Especially one wearing a long, tattered cloak over a decades-old dress and scratchy petticoats that made him itch in inconvenient places. His shoes were no better. They were made from a scrap of thin, worn leather that did nothing to repel sharp, painful objects.

With excruciating care, he wheeled his rickety cart, filled with half-dead posies, along the side of the street near Abbingale. All morning, he had wandered up and down the street, viewing the boys' home from different vantage points. Though he was no closer to identifying Giles Clarke's whereabouts, he now held one valuable piece of information: Abbingale was more than a home for orphan boys.

During his three days of observation, he had caught sight of no fewer than four boys emerging from the lower level of the house and three entering the lower level, and they had all taken the same circuitous path down White Horse Lane, coming and going. Where did they go? And from whence did they arrive? He had made two attempts to follow the boys, but both times they had buried their wee bodies in thick market crowds and disappeared. Though he had stayed with them long enough to realize their destinations had not been the same. Interesting.

Pushing his cart, Ethan continued to make his way toward Miss Hunt's idling carriage, where her two footmen conversed while awaiting their mistress's arrival. He hunched his shoulders into a severe curve, made sure the cloak covered his big hands, and then added a ponderous limp. When he was within hearing distance, but not so close as to draw their suspicion, Ethan set his cart down and listened.

"Any more from his lordship?" Mick asked.

"Not yet."

"Do you think he's toying with Miss Hunt, or is it all just a coincidence?"

"We'll find out soon enough."

"How's she holding up?"

"As well as can be expected." Mac stared at the stone edifice of Abbingale Home. "This scheme concerns me."

"What is she going to do if things aren't what they seem?"

"Fix it, of course."

Mick groaned. "She can't put all the wrongs in London to rights."

A short silence followed. "Don't be so sure," Mac said. "She's an extraordinary and determined woman."

The servant's praise of Miss Hunt created an uncomfortable pressure in Ethan's chest. The man's belief in the proprietress went much deeper than a mere employment arrangement. His kind of loyalty stemmed from years of witnessing one victory after another, of following her into the bowels of hell and emerging unscathed. Of never experiencing profound disappointment. The kind of disappointment that taints one's opinion after a single act of impulsive independence. An opinion that can't be changed no matter how hard one tries. And tries.

Ethan blinked back the barrage of self-pity, disgusted by his lack of focus. He cast a sidelong glance at Miss Hunt's footmen. Their conversation stirred his troublesome curiosity. He wanted to know more about this gentleman toying with the proprietress and what business she had at Abbingale that would cause her servants concern.

Mick caught his eye and winked. The unexpected action startled Ethan, causing his skin to flush with heat like a damned schoolgirl. He cursed and hunched shoulders.

"How's business today?" Mick asked, strolling forward.

Pretending to fuss over his flower cart, Ethan turned his back on the footman. He hoped the long hairpiece and kerchief he'd secured around the crown of his head would hold up to close scrutiny. "Not so good, sir," Ethan said in his best crone's voice. "Best ye buy yer lady a couple posies to help out an old woman."

The footman stopped near the cart. Ethan felt the man's gaze, inspecting him from head to toe.

"You're a big girl, aren't you—?"

"Gabby," Ethan said with a huff. "So I've been told before. Do ye want a posy or not, sir?" He braced himself.

"My apologies, old girl," Mick said, his voice softer. "I didn't mean to scrape an old wound. Do you have a pretty bunch that will put a smile on my lady's face?"

"They all will, sir," Ethan scratched his oversized midsection. "Though them yellow ones ought to make her swoon."

"You're sure?" Mick asked, clearly not impressed with the bundle's drooping heads.

"A bit of water will snap 'em right out of their wee nap." Ethan grabbed the pathetic bunch and thrust them at the footman, careful to keep his hands hidden. "Ye have Old Gabby's word on it."

"Tell me, Gabby." Mick accepted the posy and tossed a shilling onto the cart's bed. "Hear much about the goings-on in the boys' home?"

Ethan snatched up the coin, a generous sum for a half-dead bundle of flowers. The footman had much to learn about wooing information from women, or from anyone for that matter. One should never give up the coin before receiving the desired details. Otherwise, the informant has no real incentive for helping. Ethan had learned that a long look, full of promise, topped with the flash of a shiny coin was the most effective combination in intelligence gathering.

"One hears all sorts of things," Ethan replied.

Another shilling clattered onto the cart. "What kinds of things?"

Scrunching up his face, Ethan said, "Boys coming and going at all hours of the day."

"Anything else?"

"Some say there's more going on than taking care of orphans in that big old building."

"Any guesses as to whom or what they're talking about?"

Ethan narrowed his eyes. "What business does your lady have in there?"

The footman's gaze shifted to his brother before answering. "She's considering making a donation. But my gut tells me you're right about that big old building."

"Could be nothing but a bout of indigestion."

Mick grinned. "Ever come across the name of Latymer in your travels?"

Ethan's mind froze around the name. Could Latymer be that common? Was this nothing more than an unlikely coincidence? He didn't think so on either account. So, what possible reason could this footman have for inquiring about Lord Latymer, the same man the Nexus were hunting?

"Latymer?" Ethan said in his crone voice. "What's that? A quack's potion?"

Chuckling, Mick said, "Not quite, Gabby, my girl." He pulled out a card. "If the name comes up, let me know. I'll buy a whole cart full of your posies."

"That important, is he?"

"Oh, yes. Hear anything else interesting?"

"How many more coins you got?"

"That was my last one."

"Then I ain't got nothing else."

Instead of being irritated by Ethan's surly response, Mick's eyes twinkled. "Gabby, old girl, I'll be right over there," he pointed to a spot near his brother, "if you think of anything else."

"Ye come up with some more silver, ye Irish rogue, and I'll think about taxing my poor memory."

Using the wilted posies, Mick saluted Ethan-the-flower-girl and sauntered away.

Not wanting to press his luck, Ethan grabbed the cart's handles and set off in the opposite direction, grumbling under his breath about cheap scapegraces who were too handsome for their own good. His comments were met with a bark of laughter.

Beneath his grousing, Ethan's mind was aflame with possibilities. The one that surfaced again and again was the idea that Miss Hunt was one of them. One of the Nexus. Why else would she be using an assumed name and looking for Latymer? Only one person would know for certain, and Ethan refused to ask Somerton for anything at the moment. Even if he weren't seething with rage over his loss, Ethan doubted the former chief would confirm the identity of one of his operatives. He protected them all like a lion protected his pride. And like a lion, he found it was sometimes necessary to safeguard the pride from one of their own.

Abbingale's front door bolted open, drawing Ethan from his extraordinary train of thought. Glancing back, he saw Miss Hunt storm through the opening and fairly run down the front steps. Her face was pale and frozen, as if a sudden movement would shatter her countenance into a thousand tiny shards.

Dropping the cart, he took several long, swift strides in her direction. Realization slammed into him, and he jerked to a halt. The violent action jarred his bones and rattled his brain. Like a greenling agent, he'd broken cover to comfort a woman in distress. The oldest, most deadliest tool one enemy could use against another. Ethan's straight back melted into an uncomfortable curve and he bent low, as if plucking a coin from the street.

Straightening, his gaze sought out Miss Hunt, and he felt a measure of relief to see the proud lines of her proprietress's mask shoving their way to the fore. What had she come across inside Abbingale to illicit such a response? He contemplated the reasons why while he ambled back to his cart, thankful the footmen had been focused on huddling their mistress into the carriage and not on the deranged flower girl barreling toward them.

Six

FRANÇOIS LAROUCHE LEANED CLOSER TO THE WINDOW, absently tracing his forefinger over his lower lip while he watched Mrs. Henshaw's footmen bundle her into a well-equipped carriage. Their actions appeared rushed, protective, as if they were guarding her from an unseen threat. Movement to his left caught his eye, drawing his attention away from the benefactress. A flower girl, one who had peddled her wares long past her prime, waddled toward her cart, glancing back at Mrs. Henshaw's disappearing carriage several times. Interesting.

Shuffling sounds behind reminded him of the unfinished business he left. Turning back to the classroom, LaRouche studied the group of boys, touching on each of their faces and allowing the silence to lengthen. He said nothing until the air vibrated with the panicked beats of their hearts. "All but the five gifted boys may leave." He nodded to Mrs. Drummond, and she opened the door.

Without a word, two dozen boys stood. Backs erect, chins high, eyes forward. One by one, they filed out of the room, closing the door softly behind the last child. Their obedience pleased him.

LaRouche glanced down at the trembling child, whose hair carried the same mahogany tint as his mother's. He lowered his hand onto the boy's shoulder. "You should not have done that, *mon petit.*"

The boy flinched and tried to evade his touch. LaRouche shook his head with regret. The boy knew better than to defy him, they all did. He had warned the boys against such independent thought, for it led to rash action and disagreeable outcomes.

With brutal slowness, LaRouche curled his fingers into the boy's narrow shoulder. The child's whimper disturbed him not at all. He continued exerting pressure until he was assured a dark reminder of his power was left behind.

"Kindly remember what I told you when you first arrived at Abbingale," LaRouche said, addressing the schoolroom. "As long as you do everything you are told, no harm will come to your families. That includes your silence, both within and without Abbingale."

He tucked his finger beneath the boy's chin, lifting until their gazes met. "Silence includes no speaking with any part of your body, including your eyes. Understood?"

Swallowing, the boy nodded.

"Do you have anything to say?"

"Sorry, sir."

LaRouche released him, and the boy lowered his head. The small act of obeisance mollified his anger somewhat, thereby lessening the boy's punishment... by a degree. He turned his attention one row over, to an older boy, whose countenance could only be described as tragic. Severe pockmarks scored the entire lower half of his face, whereas the upper half remained blemish free. One could detect a promise of beauty in his wide-set eyes and strong forehead, but the pockmarks and the cap of straw-straight, dull brown hair ruined his potential for handsomeness.

"Come here," LaRouche said.

The older boy stood. "Yes, monsieur."

"Am I wrong in thinking you were the one who disciplined young Giles for trying to communicate with our guest?"

As if the scars were not hideous enough, the boy's face flushed a ghastly red, making the pockmarks stand out even more. "M-my apologies, monsieur. I hit him on the shoulder harder than I'd intended. I only meant to give him a good sting on the arm, not to make him cry out."

LaRouche curled his mouth into a conciliatory smile. "Of course, you didn't. Join me over here, would you?" The older boy weaved his way around the desks and came to stand beside LaRouche. "What do you think we should do about young Giles defying my order?"

The pockmarked boy fidgeted. "He could go without supper tonight, sir, and then sort and mend all the stockings tomorrow."

Giles did not lift his head, though LaRouche could see his terror in the tight clasp of his hands. "Yes, those punishments will do nicely, don't you agree, Giles?" He reached toward his coat pocket and slid his fingers inside.

Nodding, Giles said, "Yes, monsieur."

"Giles, look at me."

When the boy lifted his fearful green eyes, LaRouche said, "I have one more punishment for you, but you must be brave or you will only prolong the pain. Understood?"

Tears welled in the boy's eyes. "Yes."

LaRouche pulled the leather gloves from his pocket and slashed them across the older boy's pocked left cheek and then his right. He repeated the action twice more before tucking the gloves away again. Their harsh breaths sliced into the shocked silence. LaRouche applauded the older boy's control, for if he had cried out or raised his hands in defense, he would have been forced to beat the boy senseless. No one defied him. No one.

Giles scrubbed at his wet cheeks while staring at his schoolmate with remorseful eyes.

"Do you see what happens when you disobey me?" LaRouche asked.

Anger replaced the boy's remorse. "*Yes*, monsieur."

"Your tone displeases me." LaRouche slipped his hand back into his pocket. "Do I need to bring another boy up here to discipline for your sins?"

Panic flared in the boy's green eyes. He shook his head and dropped his gaze. "No, Monsieur LaRouche. Please don't punish anyone else. I'll do as you say."

To the older boy, LaRouche said, "Go to Mrs. Drummond. She will tend to you." He glanced at the other boys. Their pale faces displayed varying degrees of trepidation. The boys who had been at Abbingale for a while were familiar with LaRouche's swift discipline. Because of this, they had learned how to school their features into impassivity. Good little soldiers.

"Gentlemen," LaRouche said. "Do not forget what you saw here today. It is best that no one repeat the same infraction as your schoolmate, Giles. You may return to your dormitory to clean your hands and faces before going down for your midday meal."

"Thank you, monsieur," they chimed as one.

While the boys filed out, LaRouche strode back to the window, his thoughts returning to Mrs. Henshaw and the odd circumstances surrounding her visit. During his brief conversation with the benefactress, he had detected moments of keen intelligence flowing beneath the surface of her empty-headed mien. Many young women of wealth and privilege were taught at an early age to suppress their leanings toward academia so as not to bore potential suitors. Many gentlemen welcomed such shallow creatures into their marital beds and then they found more engaging bedmates in their mistresses.

But LaRouche had not reached his level of importance in Emperor Bonaparte's government by ignoring small, incongruent elements. No, his attention to detail had saved the Emperor embarrassment more than once—and LaRouche had been lavishly rewarded for his efforts. Soon, he would hand the Emperor the key to controlling the British Navy, the last barrier to Absolute Rule.

One leader, under God. Napoleon Bonaparte.

LaRouche would be the man who handed the world to the Corsican. Power, like nothing he'd ever imagined, would be his.

Not bothering to turn around, he spoke to the nurse, who stood quietly near the door, awaiting his instructions. "I want to know everything the benefactress said today and during her previous visit. Leave nothing out."

Seven

MAC YANKED THE CARRIAGE DOOR OPEN AND CLIMBED inside. "What happened?" he asked once they were in motion again.

"I haven't the faintest idea." Sydney shook her head. "Everything about Abbingale feels wrong, yet I have little to report that would affirm such feelings."

"Trust your instincts, Sydney. They have yet to let you down. Tell me what you saw."

Sydney curled her arm around her middle and propped her elbow against it. Using the pads of her fingers, she rubbed her forehead in a circular motion, as if that small action would make sense of all she had witnessed inside Abbingale. "Boys sitting in the schoolroom, with their written assignments in front of them."

"I'm not following. What makes the scene unusual?"

"It was nothing more than a well-choreographed display for my benefit, I daresay." She lifted her head and tapped the side of her forefinger against her lips. "The only thing missing from their writing lessons was writing instruments."

Mac frowned. "You came upon a lesson in progress?"

"So they would have me believe." She recalled the

sick feeling in her stomach when she realized the staff's perfidy. "Their lessons were proudly displayed on the desks, yet not one quill pen, inkwell, or pencil was in sight."

"What would be the point of such an elaborate scheme?"

"That's what we need to find out, my friend."

"Are you sure you want to get involved in this?"

"The choice is no longer mine to make. I must dig until I know if the children are safe or not." She blew out a tired sigh. "This could not be any worse than tracking down Lord Latymer. The baron attracts evil men like a dog attracts pesky fleas."

"I'm not so sure," he said. "Mick's bones were aching. That's never a good sign."

No, it wasn't. Sydney dug her fingers into her waist. Mick's bones forecasted impending danger. He never really knew when or where, only that it was imminent.

"Do me a favor and work with Amelia on learning as much as you can about the nurse, Mrs. Drummond, and the schoolmaster, LaRouche," Sydney said. "Those two forced me to keep my guard up the entire time I was in their presence. I suppose it wouldn't hurt to include the matron, Mrs. Kingston, though I could detect no ill intent from her."

Mac's jaw tightened. "I'll have Mick sort through their backgrounds with your assistant."

Sydney shook her head. "I'd prefer you to take care of it. Mick can continue with the interviews and keep an eye on Lord Danforth for me."

"I'll do that—"

She held up a staying hand. "I know you do not approve of Amelia, and I have tried to keep the two of you separated. But, in this, I need your level head combined with Amelia's eye for detail."

The hand resting on his leg curled into a fist, and he glared at the coach door for several long seconds.

"Can you do this for me, Mac?"

He gave her a short nod, and they lapsed into silence the rest of the way home. Not for the first time, Sydney wondered what had happened between her two most trusted friends. When she had selected Amelia for the assistant's position, Mac had supported her choice. But something had shown up in the young woman's background that had transformed Mac's approval into barely masked disgust.

Contrarily, he would not share with her his findings. When she questioned why, he would only say that the issue would not affect Amelia's ability to perform the assistant's duties. Despite Mac's obvious about-face, Sydney decided to give the young woman a chance, and Amelia had never given her a moment's regret over her decision.

The only black mark on the situation was Mac's almost obsessive desire to avoid her assistant. Though Sydney had not missed the way her bodyguard's gaze tracked Amelia's movements. Any time the two were in the same room, the air fairly crackled with tension.

Perhaps she should find other ways to force them to spend more time together. They would never be able to mend the rift if they're constantly at opposing ends. Yes, a few pushes in the right direction should do it.

❧

A few hours later, Sydney found herself standing in the entrance hall of Lord Danforth's town house, trying desperately to focus on his butler's words. But the disturbing hour she'd spent in Abbingale Home continued to overpower her concentration.

Everything had been too perfect, too quiet and organized for a house full of excitable boys. If not for her brief communication with the green-eyed boy, she might have left there thinking the home nothing more than a gloomy place, despite its possible link to Latymer. Then again, she would not have been able to ignore the call of the secret chamber.

As it was, the staff's odd behavior had only succeeded in sparking Sydney's protective instincts. What she needed to protect the boys from, she didn't yet know. But something inside that house licked at a dark shadow hovering on the edge of her consciousness, a raw, ugly place she had locked away many, many years ago, without looking back.

Nor would she now.

"I'm sorry, Tanner," Sydney said to the butler. "When is your last day again?"

"End of the month, miss."

Amelia chimed in. "How many footmen do you oversee?"

"Only one, ma'am. His lordship prefers keeping a small staff."

"Oh?" Sydney asked, recalling Lord Danforth mentioning the same thing. "Why is that?"

"All he needs is clean clothes, edible food, and a discreet household," Tanner said as if reciting a much-heard mantra. "He's also a private man, Miss Hunt, and doesn't care to be tripping over servants day and night."

"Does he employ a valet?"

"No, miss. If his lordship needs assistance with his wardrobe, he calls on either the footman or myself."

"I see." Sydney shared a glance with her assistant, who made a note. "Will his lordship's butler be required to attend him during all hours of the evening, then?"

"Not at all. His lordship insists on using his own key at night."

"That's right," a new voice added. "I don't need a servant to open the damned door for me, even if I'm stumbling across the threshold."

Sydney's heart kicked against the wall of her chest. She glanced up to find Lord Danforth making his way down the grand staircase. Dressed in buckskin breeches, riding boots, and a wine-colored coat tailored to embrace his broad shoulders and sculpted midsection, he made her forget how to breathe. Especially when she noticed how his damp sable locks curled roguishly at the tips. The sight conjured an image of him rising from his bath, water cascading over the hard planes of his stomach, his lean hips, his rigid—

"Good morning, ladies," Lord Danforth said.

Sydney's blood ran hotly through her veins, a flush covered her skin from head to toe. Never had she wanted anything more—to see Ethan deBeau in the nude, wet, aroused. For her.

"Lord Danforth." Amelia bumped her elbow into Sydney's.

Blinking, Sydney forced the erotic image from her mind and steadied her breathing. "Good morning, sir. I did not expect to see you."

"My schedule opened up." He halted a hand's width away. "So I thought I'd check on Tanner to make sure you haven't sent him into a swoon with your interrogation."

Tanner sniffed. "I haven't needed the salts since '91, sir."

"Sounds like you're due, old boy."

Sydney glanced between the two men. "I assure you, my lord. It is not my intention to distress Tanner, only gather enough information to recommend an appropriate replacement."

The viscount winked at his butler before closing the

minuscule distance separating their bodies. "You don't have brothers, do you?"

"As a matter of fact, I do."

"Younger brother, right?"

"What does my having a younger brother got to do with our present discussion?"

"The mothering sort." He chucked her under the chin. "No humor in your bones." Clasping his hands behind his back, he straightened. "We'll have to work on that, won't we, Tanner?"

"Indeed, sir."

Rubbing the area beneath her chin, she glanced at Amelia and noted her assistant's wide, shocked eyes. What had brought on his lordship's playful mood? Especially since he hadn't wanted her to come in the first place. If she didn't know any better, she would suspect him of flirting.

When she shifted her attention back, his blue-green eyes twinkled down at her. Gentlemen more handsome and dangerous than this man had tried to woo her into their beds. Only once before had she experienced the pull of attraction. *Philip.* Even now, two years later, her stomach clenched with regret. For a time, she had contemplated marriage to the young physician—until she'd offered the darkest piece of her soul to him, and he'd turned away.

"Well, Mrs. Cartwright," Sydney said in a brisk tone. "Do we have what we need to get started?"

"Yes, Miss Hunt. I can always call on Mr. Tanner later if I have additional questions."

"Very well. Tanner, thank you for your candid answers. Your lordship," she dipped into a curtsy before turning toward the door, "always a pleasure."

"What great timing," Lord Danforth said. "Perhaps

you would care to join me for a ride in the park, Miss Hunt. Your assistant is welcome to come along as chaperone, of course."

His invitation stopped her mid-stride, and Amelia swerved to avoid a collision. "Pardon?"

"A ride," he said, with a rogue's smile. "In a carriage. Through the park. Amidst curious gossips."

"I understood what you meant," she bit out. "What I'm wondering is why? Noblemen do not drive, ride, or stroll with commoners."

"Perhaps not." His eyes lowered in that heavy-lidded way that bespoke of a man's interest. "But I do."

"Not with me, you don't. I'm not interested in being the *ton*'s newest *on dit*."

"How very strange." He sent her a considering look. "Most ladies would vie for the position."

"Then you will have no trouble filling my spot on your seat. Good day, Lord Danforth. We will send our recommendation on Monday."

She had taken no more than two steps when he said, "What about my new footman?"

Sydney pivoted in time to see Tanner's look of askance. "What are you talking about now?"

"After more consideration, I've decided to add another footman to my staff." He brushed at invisible dirt specks on first one coat sleeve and then the other. "A viscount can never have too many footmen, or so I'm told."

Unable to stop herself, she slid her gaze down his body, taking in every inch of his attire. "A valet might be a better use of your coin."

He peered down at his clothes. "What's wrong with the way I'm dressed? Tanner assured me that the cut of my coat would cause much vaporing among the ladies."

"Hmm," Sydney mused, indulging in another slow

perusal. "I suppose I can see why they would faint." Of course, there was nothing wrong with his sense of fashion. He was impeccably dressed, from the tips of his polished Hessians to the intricate folds of his neckcloth. The only area that could use a valet's touch was his tousled hair. The soft waves seemed to be forever winking this way and that, as if he tunneled his fingers through the thick strands on a regular basis. On further consideration, she was glad he didn't use pomade or any other taming salve on those handsome curls. Somehow, the chaos suited him.

"Then I shall require a valet, too. There, you see? Tanner is all but jumping with joy at the prospect. Perhaps Mrs. Tanner is in need of a maid to help with the household chores."

The butler's lips creaked into a smile.

"Lord Danforth," she said. "Surely, you understood that I spoke in jest."

He looked to Tanner. "Did you think her comments were in earnest?"

"Quite, sir."

"There you have it, Miss Hunt," he said. "Perhaps you and I should adjourn to my study to discuss the specifics of the additional staff, and I would also like to discuss additional remunerations for my current staff."

Tanner's mouth dropped open.

Sydney was undecided. This blatant attempt of his to get her alone did not bode well. He would once again try to seduce information from her with his charm and rawboned handsomeness. And she would refuse, this time with a great deal more conviction.

Assuming he hadn't yet uncovered where they had met before, she could think of no reason for his persistence—other than his belief that they had met before. Could it be it? He'd detected something familiar about her and now wouldn't leave her be until he figured out why? Only one way to find out, but first, she wanted to test his level of need.

"Very well, my lord." She motioned to her assistant. "Come along, Mrs. Cartwright. You can record the details of our conversation."

"Um," Lord Danforth said. "Perhaps Mrs. Cartwright would prefer to inspect the butler's quarters and where my new valet will be located."

He thought quickly on his feet, she would give him that.

"Some other time, perhaps. I would rather Amelia act as secretary at our meeting."

"But then Mrs. Cartwright would have to make a return trip to view the butler's and valet's apartments," he said. "I took you for a businesswoman who did not knowingly waste her clients' time."

When charm failed to achieve the expected result, his lordship changed tactics and attacked his opponent's vital organs. A stratagem she would not soon forget. "It was not my intention to waste anyone's time. I'm simply trying to ensure that all your requirements are documented."

"I shall play secretary, while you listen raptly, Miss Hunt," he said. "My services will leave your assistant free to join Tanner on a tour."

How had he maneuvered her into such an inescapable corner? Squirming against the constraints of her new position, Sydney barely managed a civil reply. "How can I turn down such a generous offer? Mrs. Cartwright, do you mind?"

"Not at all, Miss Hunt. Tanner, would you please show me your quarters?"

"It would be my pleasure, ma'am."

Sydney splayed her arms wide. "I am at your disposal, my lord."

Something dark flared behind his unusual eyes, and Sydney felt the strike of it all the way to her toes. Then he blinked, breaking the disturbing connection as if it had never been.

"This way, then," he said.

Once they entered his study, he closed the door and motioned her toward the sapphire sofa. "May I offer you a refreshment?"

"No, thank you." She perched on the edge, angling her body toward the adjacent chair. But the irritating man sat next to her and reclined in a manner that put her erect posture in direct contrast with his informal one. With his long arm stretched across the back of the sofa and his legs spread wide, he reeked of arrogance and a complete lack of regard for propriety.

He also warmed the air around her.

"Tell me, Miss Hunt," he said. "What business do you have with Abbingale Home?"

Shock gripped her body, turning her poker-straight spine into a rod of cold steel. "Pardon?"

"The home for orphans. On White Horse Lane," he said. "I'm curious about your interest."

She had been wrong. About him and his reason for insisting on this private meeting. He'd lured her here, not for a warm kiss, but for a frigid slap to the face. By changing his tactic from seduction to a full-frontal attack, he no doubt hoped to throw her off-balance, shatter her nerves, and make her careless.

His ploy had worked—to a point. He'd cracked her armor but bolstered her resolve.

"I can hear your thoughts groping for the right response," he said. "Why don't you spare us both the time and energy of a verbal fencing match and simply answer my question?"

"How is it you know about my visits to Abbingale?"

"I happened to be in the area," he said with a shrug, "and saw you leaving."

"What were you doing in the area?"

"Taking in the scenery, of course."

"Of course." Had Lord Somerton sent one of his agents to investigate the boys' home? She wouldn't be surprised. Her contact with the Nexus had mentioned the possibility of a connection between Abbingale and Latymer, but he hadn't asked her to probe into the home's operation, only to find the baron.

Since Lord Danforth knew nothing about her underground ring of spies, he would rightly be curious about her and her interest in Abbingale. *If* she had done something to spark his curiosity. Her visit to the establishment didn't seem enough to warrant such focused attention.

"When might that have been, my lord?" she asked. "When did you see me leave Abbingale?"

His eyes narrowed the slightest bit. "I don't recall the exact day."

"Not today, then."

"No."

"Yesterday, perhaps?"

"Perhaps."

"Not likely, as I did not visit Abbingale yesterday."

"I told you," he said between thin lips. "I couldn't recall the exact day."

"Come now," she said in a teasing tone. "Are you so busy that you cannot even recall your schedule from one day ago?"

"Since my memory is so faulty, we might have more success if you list the days you were there. Your superior recall might trigger a memory in my poor mind."

"I heard once that exercise keeps us young in body

and keen of wit. Could it be that your aristocratic indulgences have turned your mind to mush?"

The corner of his mouth quirked upward. "Entirely possible."

"I take it that my association with Abbingale, and not the details involved with adding more servants to your staff, is the true impetus behind your wish for our tête-à-tête."

"Is this your way of avoiding my question?"

"I am merely looking for clarification." She eased herself back to match his indolent pose. "What does my visiting a home for orphans have to do with our discussion regarding your staff?"

His fingers brushed against the sofa near her shoulder. "Absolutely nothing."

"Do you even need the extra staff?"

"I've come to realize the maid, footman, and valet would be welcome additions. So I'll still need your agency's services."

"And what of a new butler?"

"No," he said with shocking honesty. "Tanner will still be ruling this household from his deathbed, and when he does eventually kick up his toes, he'll probably be entombed next to the silver, so that his ghostly presence can continue plaguing me for years to come."

"And the remuneration for your present staff?"

"I should like to make sure I'm paying them an adequate wage and would like to discuss providing them with more time off. It's my understanding that your services extend to these areas."

"Indeed, they do. Why make all these changes now?"

"Let's say my eyes have been recently opened to the deplorable conditions of those in service."

"I applaud your actions." She leveled her gaze on him. "But I'm curious about your original request for my agency's services. Do you always take such extreme measures after seeing a stranger leave an establishment you have an interest in?"

"I do not."

"An impulsive act, then?"

All levity disappeared from his features. "Strategy can oftentimes be confused with impulsivity, Miss Hunt." His gaze shifted to the small vee of space between her shoulder and the sofa. "Don't make the same mistake others have."

She knew better than to underestimate this man. Everything he did, he did with purpose. "Strategy? A rather interesting choice of words."

"We live in an interesting world."

Lifting a brow, she asked, "Why the ruse? Why did you not ask your rather direct question at the agency yesterday?"

He tilted his head to the side. "I didn't think you would answer the question, at the time."

"What makes you think I'll answer it now?"

"*Touché.*" He considered her for a long moment. "You presented me with a mystery. One I felt deserved a slightly more covert approach to solving, Miss Hunt, or perhaps you prefer Mrs. Henshaw."

Her earlier shock was nothing compared to her reaction at hearing him use the name of her alternate identity. Not only had he noticed her leaving the boys' home, he must have been close enough to overhear her conversations with Abbingale's staff. But when? How? If he had been anywhere near the building, she would have noticed him.

Except for today. She hadn't been aware of anything but the open doorway leading out to her carriage. Her previous visit was another matter, however. She turned her mind back to her brief tour on Wednesday. There had been a small exchange just outside the entrance door, but she could not recall the specifics.

If he hadn't been nearby, perhaps someone within the boys' home had contacted him about her. For what purpose? Sydney discarded the possibility. If that had been the case, his informant would have shared the reason behind her visits. No one at Abbingale had any cause to believe she was anything other than a potential benefactress.

She was not the only one harboring secrets. "Miss Hunt will do."

They shared a long look, an unspoken challenge between two individuals used to maintaining a high level of privacy. Neither gave in to the temptation to fill the silence or bare their soul. An impasse.

He must have realized it, too. His full lips stretched into an appreciative grin. A genuine smile. The first she'd witnessed. All the others had been manufactured to elicit a specific response from her. This one, however, was pure Ethan deBeau, and it was magnificent.

"You find something amusing, my lord?"

"No, Miss Hunt. I am merely overwhelmed with my good fortune."

The seductive timbre of his voice whispered along the rim of her ear and caressed down the ridge of her spine. And that's when she felt the first gentle tug. Then another... and another. He was toying with her hair. The furtive act was so innocent, yet heartbreakingly intimate. Her chest grew tight and her breaths shuddered between her lips.

She could not bring herself to scold him, for she did not want him to stop. "Did this good fortune befall you while we were speaking?"

He barked out a laugh. "Indeed, it did." He resumed his gentle manipulation of her hair. "I am going to enjoy unraveling you, Miss Hunt. I'm going to enjoy it immensely."

Rather than ignore his masculine boast—as she would any other gentleman of her acquaintance—she took heart. Somehow she had managed to either pique his curiosity or provoke his competitive nature. Either way, when one needed to engage in covert activities, one did not want a spy hanging about, especially a handsome, charming spy.

Changing the topic seemed a good idea, so she did. "You appear to enjoy an easy relationship with your staff."

His grin broadened, letting her know he understood her ploy. "We've been together a long time. The Tanners and my sister, Cora, were my one constant after my parents were murdered."

Feigning surprise, she exclaimed, "Murdered?"

"It happened many years ago."

"Not so many for one to easily forget, I'm sure," she said. "I'm so sorry for your loss."

"Thank you."

"Did the authorities find the man responsible?"

His jaw tautened. "Yes."

Sydney had witnessed the uglier side of man many times over the last few years and had learned to numb herself to its presence. So the chill that etched its way down her spine after Lord Danforth's terse response surprised her far more than his revelation about her dual identity.

"That is good news, my lord." Her own curiosity prompted her to ask, "How does your sister fare?"

"Quite well these days." He angled his head around to peer out the window for a long, contemplative moment. When he turned back, his affable features were back in place. "Enough about me. I'm more interested in your association with Abbingale Home."

She was not the only one who knew how to turn a topic. "I don't understand why you care. It makes no sense."

"Are you working with the matron to find apprenticeships for the young men?"

Joy rushed through her like a waterfall plunging down the face of a mountain. Had he just come up with a solution to her underlying dilemma? More than once, she had wondered what she would do if she found nothing linking Abbingale to Latymer. Leaving the boys to face such cheerless odds would have been nearly impossible. As often happened when she involved herself in the affairs of others, she became emotionally attached to the situation and sought to remedy the injustice.

Sometimes the solution was as heartbreaking as the offense.

But Lord Danforth's intrusive query might be her answer to avoiding weeks of sorrow. For that, she would give him a truth. "No, my lord. I haven't discussed apprenticeships with Mrs. Kingston, though your suggestion has a great deal of merit." Perhaps other establishments like Abbingale, or even the Foundling Hospital, could use her employment services.

"Care to share the true reason for your interest?" he asked. "Or shall this be one of those mysterious, unresolved topics in our relationship?"

Given the extent of his resources and background, she doubted her interest in Abbingale would stay a mystery. What bothered her more was that he now considered their staid professional arrangement as something… more.

"Nothing mysterious about my reasons for visiting Abbingale Home," she said. "I'm simply not accustomed to sharing my business plans with strangers."

"Business?"

She released an exaggerated sigh. "You are rather determined, aren't you?"

He released her hair and lounged deeper into the sofa, his pose more indolent than ever. "You have discovered my secret, Miss Hunt. Now will you share yours?"

Despite his body's relaxed pose, the intensity captured in his expressive eyes indicated her answer was of great importance.

"If you must know," she said, tucking a lock of hair that refused to stay pinned behind her ear, "I'm considering a donation, or possibly an annual subscription."

His face blanked, and he stared at her. After what seemed like an eternity, his slackened features firmed and his gaze glinted with a peculiar light. He sat forward, breaking the invisible barrier of what polite society would consider one's intimate space. Those beautiful eyes of his roamed her face, hair, body with a thoroughness that made her stomach clench and her throat ache. Cold sweat coated her body. She veered back until the sofa stopped her retreat.

"What is it?" She hated hearing the small tremor in her voice. "Did I say something amiss?"

Her query cut through his razor-edged study, and his features shifted into their former affable mien. "No, Miss Hunt," he said, settling back. "I applaud your charitable endeavor. In fact, I have an interest in Abbingale Home for a similar reason."

"Do you?"

"Your shocked expression does not bode well. Do I appear an uncaring person?"

"My surprise has nothing to do with the fiber of your character, sir. I simply find it amazing that, of all the boys' homes in the city, you've selected the one that's caught my interest."

"'Selected' might not be the most appropriate term. Abbingale is one of six I'll be reviewing for my largesse."

"Six?" Sydney searched his eyes, looking for the merest twitch that would disprove his statement.

He returned her inspection with a steady, unflinching gaze. "That's correct."

"Let us hope you find one that meets your criteria, whatever they might be."

"Perhaps you would like to join me," he said in a low tone. "I have yet to begin my search."

"Thank you, no," she said. "Scheduling time for numerous visits to Abbingale has taxed Mrs. Cartwright's rather enviable skill of keeping me organized. Six might lead to her resignation, and that I cannot afford."

His gaze caressed her mouth. "Then allow me to accompany you to Abbingale."

Whatever it was he wanted from her, he wanted it badly. Although the logical part of her mind screamed for her to sever any future association with him, the inquisitive faction of her mind encouraged her to plow forward.

"Why do I get the feeling you're trying to manipulate me?"

He molded his expression into a respectable imitation of affront. If she hadn't known of his work with the Nexus, his wounded display would have caused her some remorse.

"I don't know."

"I hope you understand that I'm here to assist with your staffing needs, nothing more."

"Why use an assumed name?" he asked. "You've built a good reputation around your agency, and ladies have always been encouraged to pursue charitable endeavors. Why not be yourself?"

Sydney's mind raced like lightning shooting across

the sky. What plausible excuse could she give him for concealing her identity from Abbingale's staff? Then she hit upon a possible solution, one that held a deep kernel of truth. "At the Hunt Agency, I'm in a position to help many people. Some have come to see me as a savior, of sorts, and because of this they bring an assortment of concerns to my door." She paused to organize her thoughts.

"Interesting," he said, "but how do your clients' disturbances relate to your use of an alias?"

"One of Abbingale's former maids is cousin to a client of mine. After witnessing some rather harsh disciplinary treatment of the boys, the maid gave notice, even though she could ill-afford to lose her position."

"I suspect you were able to assist in that area."

"Thankfully, yes."

"Miss Hunt, what is your true purpose for touring Abbingale Home? I take it Mrs. Henshaw, the wealthy benefactress, is nothing more than a means for entrée?"

"Yes and no."

"You do not intend to leave it that way, do you? Not after I admitted to not needing a new butler."

Because of her unconventional means of gathering information, she had become cautious in her actions and her speech. This particular part of her ruse did not require such secrecy, however. "*Yes*, occupying the feather-brained demeanor of a wealthy merchant's wife provided me with the perfect excuse for viewing the inner workings of Abbingale. *No*, because I do not intend to simply walk away after satisfying my investigation. I will provide assistance to Abbingale—whether it will be financial or operational still remains to be seen."

He began toying with her hair again. "I find the complexity of your mind as stimulating as your beautiful figure."

Heat rippled through her veins and pooled in her womb. Her inner muscles clenched around tiny arrows of pleasure. She shot to her feet, unwilling to give his declaration any more power. "My lord, it is not necessary, nor even advisable, to spout out whatever comes to one's mind."

He sighed. "So I've been told."

"Perhaps it would be best for us to reconvene our meeting tomorrow. Or, better yet, Mrs. Cartwright might be a more suitable liaison for you from this point forward."

Her new vantage point provided her with a modicum of relief from his nearness, until he unwound his large frame to tower above her, crowding her even more than before.

"I'm sure it would be no hardship to work with Mrs. Cartwright." He cradled her face between his palms, and Sydney's breath caught. "But I would prefer that we continue on as before." His thumbs brushed over her cheeks. "Well, perhaps not exactly as before."

Warm, humid air fanned over her skin a moment before his mouth covered hers. Without thought, her lips molded with the soft contours of his, allowing him to guide her into each hungry nip and taste, while her brilliant mind scrambled to gather up its loose wits.

But it was no use. Desire forced all her logic and will into a far alcove of her mind, protected by thick bars of long-suppressed need. All she could think of was the decadence of his kiss, the delight of his scent, and the joy of his attraction. He was a master at this, she thought. Making women feel special and desirable. A gentleman like him would know all about a female's pleasure points and how to use them to his advantage. A means to an end.

His kiss changed, deepened. A sense of urgency now tinged his breaths. Then he changed. Releasing her face, he slid one arm around her waist and the other into the valley between her shoulder blades until his fingers cupped the base of her skull.

A burst of lush heat blanketed her, followed swiftly by a keen sense of vulnerability. Her back stiffened, and he halted their kiss. Flattening her palms against his inconceivably massive chest, she gently, but firmly, applied pressure until he uncoiled his body from around hers.

She stepped back. His breaths seesawed with hers in an oddly rhythmic dance. Until finally, her passions cooled enough for her logic to reemerge. And her humiliation.

Dear God, she wanted nothing more than to cover her flushed face and run, long and hard, to the safety of her private apartment above the Hunt Agency. She could do none of this, not without enduring even more mortification beneath the viscount's avid regard.

"Did I frighten you?"

How could she explain the volatile mix of emotions paralyzing her? "I'm not afraid of intimacy, my lord. But I'm not comfortable with being… crowded." She cringed. *Crowded* wasn't the right word, though it was the only one that came to her muddled mind.

"My apologies. I'm quite aware that my size can be overwhelming to women. However, with you in my arms, everything felt right."

Sydney reached out to touch his arm, then thought better of it. "Your size had nothing to do with my reaction. It's more a matter of control." *So I don't feel backed in a corner, held against my will, unable to escape.*

"I see."

From the tone of his voice, Sydney worried he saw too much from her simple explanation.

He waved his finger toward her head. "Your coiffure is in need of mending."

Sydney's gaze shifted to the lock of hair dangling near the corner of her left eye. "Drat it." She grabbed the irritating skein with one hand and searched for a pin with the other.

"Allow me." He batted her hands away and lowered them to her sides. Loosely clasping one of her hands in his, he brushed the wisp of black hair behind her ear. "As soft as the finest silk," he murmured. "As dark as the purest obsidian."

His featherlight touch sent a delicious, racking shiver along every one of her nerve endings. She tried to absorb the dangerous beauty of the moment, even while she slowly leaned out of his reach. No gentleman had ever touched her with such familiarity since Philip. Handsome, attentive Philip. Her angel, her savior. The talented physician had made her forget, for a time, the cruelty of men. Their three-month-long courtship had been rich with adventure and filled with laughter. Never had she felt so free from her devastating past.

So, on one lovely spring day, when Philip whispered words of love in between drugging kisses, Sydney knew the time had come to tell him the truth. A truth, as it happens, that even an angel could not forgive.

"My lord," she said in a voice she didn't recognize. "I've made it a practice not to become intimately involved with my clients."

"I adore your unusual height. Never will I develop a stooped posture with you around. I feel more youthful already."

His attempt to make her smile almost worked. Before he succeeded, she retreated two more steps. "You are talking nonsense, sir. It is time for me to go."

"Very well." He gave her hand a squeeze of assurance before releasing it. "I look forward to our trip to Abbingale. When do you plan to return?"

"I told you—"

"That you did not have time to visit all six. You presented no objection to Abbingale."

Sydney knew debating the point with him would be senseless. He would merely lurk outside Abbingale until she arrived and then attach himself to her side. Besides, until she fully understood his motive for contacting her, she thought it best to keep him near her side. "If you insist, my lord. We will collect you at eleven on Sunday. Please be ready."

He bowed. "I will take special care with my toilette, so as not to embarrass you." When he straightened, his eyes twinkled with mischief.

Sydney's smile broke free. His playfulness poked at a deep-seated need she didn't fully comprehend but yearned to explore. "Good day, Lord Danforth." When she made to open the door, a large hand swooped in to grasp the latch. She glanced at him with an inquiring brow.

"One more thing, Miss Hunt."

"Yes?" Annoyance crackled her tone.

"Thank you for taking care of me in the warehouse."

The study and all its furnishings disappeared, as if a large hole had opened beneath their feet and everything tumbled over the edge into a great abyss. Everything, but her and the viscount.

This was the moment Sydney had dreaded since Mac had first uttered Lord Danforth's name yesterday. All she had worked for now teetered toward the same crevasse that had swallowed Sydney's world seconds ago.

"Warehouse? I'm afraid I don't know what you mean."

I won't be this helpless forever, little maid.

A sharp rap on the door startled Sydney, and she choked back a scream.

"Yes?" Lord Danforth called, not taking his disturbing gaze from Sydney's face.

"Mrs. Cartwright and I have concluded our business, sir," came the butler's muffled reply.

"A minute, Tanner."

"Yes, sir."

Relief spread into Sydney's every pore, and the interruption gave Sydney enough time to shake off her devastating paralysis and retrieve her composure. "Lord Danforth." She nodded toward his hand on the latch. "Do you mind?"

He studied her features as if looking upon a precious gift. Brushing a finger along her jawline he said, "Keep your secrets. For now."

Tanner's voice carried through the wooden panels. "My lord, there is a rather large gentleman here to see Miss Hunt."

"Thank you, Tanner." To her, he asked, "One of your shadows?"

"Most likely." More softly, she said, "Mac won't wait long."

He bent forward and pressed a devastating kiss to her cheek before moving away.

Emotion clogged Sydney's throat, and she raked her hand down her skirts to keep from reaching for him. Squaring her shoulders, she opened the door. Mac took one look at her face and motioned to someone in the corridor before putting his body between Sydney's and the viscount's.

Mick appeared. "Come, Miss Hunt." He held out a hand, and Sydney slid hers into his, taking comfort from the warmth of his palm and the strength of his grip. He coaxed her from his lordship's study.

"I will see you Sunday, Miss Hunt," Lord Danforth said.

Sydney did not stop, glance back, nor reply. Her body quaked with desire, humiliation, vulnerability, and a repulsive weakness she had not had to face in many years. Not even during her courtship with Philip. She allowed Mick to guide her away, leaning on him the slightest bit for the first time in their short acquaintance.

At the end of the corridor, Mick handed her over to Amelia and then fell in behind them. Once they were settled in the carriage, her assistant asked, "Did I do right by calling for Mac and Mick?"

Sydney met the other woman's worried gaze and nodded. Words were beyond her. Everything—breath, tears, bile, her voice—seemed to be lodged in a bitter knot in the center of her chest. The year her mother had spent in Ridgway's employ was the darkest of Sydney's life. In many ways, those weeks of living in dread and terror had molded her into the independent, careful, and strong-willed woman she was today. Those days also had laid the foundation for unexpected bouts of anxiety, hours of melancholy, and periods of intense self-hatred.

She never, ever allowed her mind to return to those bleak days. How had her six-year-old thoughts slipped by her immovable shields? Today? Why with this man? Her mind remained too rattled to form an answer.

But that did not stop her from trying to piece together her conversation with Ethan deBeau. He had recalled something from his recuperative stay in the dockside warehouse. She had taken special care with her maid's disguise to prevent future discovery—worn, dirty clothing; ash smeared on her face and hands; hair in need of several more pins and covered by a threadbare cap; and a voice soft and submissive. What had she said or done to give herself away?

Sydney clenched her hands together in her lap and squeezed. She would have to face him again in a few days, with the knowledge that he knew a dangerous part of her secret and that he had witnessed her crumble beneath the weight of her insidious past. The situation sickened her even more. Besides the O'Donnells, she allowed no man to observe her in such a weakened state. Men preyed on vulnerability. She would be no one's prey again.

Somehow she must rid herself of the viscount. She no longer wished to keep him close at hand. His reasons for seeking her out were no longer a mystery. Too much damage could be done by him poking around in her business for no other reason than to assuage his gentleman's honor.

Amelia brushed a lock of Sydney's hair away from her downcast face. The gesture elicited an awful thought, followed rapidly by full realization. Every time Sydney had tucked the same troublesome lock of hair behind her ear, Lord Danforth's features had slackened for a moment before his gaze sharpened. With each thoughtless action, she had sparked a memory of his recovery, until he finally patched it all together. Or, at least, a good portion of the mystery.

She closed her eyes, cursing herself for a fool and vowing to cut her errant hair.

Eight

"Fine afternoon to you, Amelia. These are for you."

Mac O'Donnell swiveled his head toward his brother's voice. As with many of the rooms at the Hunt Agency, the library had been converted into twin workspaces, separated by a seven-foot, double-sided bookshelf and private doors leading from the corridor to each area. One end of the bookshelf connected with the wall, leaving a three-foot gap on the other end for easy passage from one domain to the other.

Currently, his brother was on one side with Mrs. Cartwright while Mac sat alone on the other, brooding.

"And to you, Mick," Mrs. Cartwright said. "The flowers are lovely. Thank you."

"They're not much, but the old woman selling them assured me a bit of water would bring them back to life."

The assistant's side of the library could use some cheering up. While the O'Donnell side housed a desk and two chairs, a map of London affixed to the wall containing numerous markings, a small table holding two half-full decanters, a chessboard on another table, and an empty gold-wire birdcage standing in the corner, the Cartwright side held a desk and chair, a cabinet with multiple drawers, and a small stepladder in front of the wall of books. That was it.

The O'Donnell side bespoke of comfort and home, while the Cartwright side denoted a rather discomfiting lack of commitment. Even after four years. Only in the last twelve months or so had Mac noticed the stark difference in their workspaces, about the same time Mick joined the agency. Before that, Mac had spent most of his time avoiding his area, thereby avoiding his employer's assistant. When they did share the same breathing space, he tapped into every bitter memory he possessed, keeping his anger and disappointment alive. The tactic ensured they developed no greater bond than a thrice-removed acquaintance.

"You're a kind man, Mick O'Donnell," she said. "I'm sure your patronage saved the woman from going hungry today."

Mac's jaw set. His kind brother's patronage was nothing more than a cover to retrieve information, though Mac suspected the scapegrace paid more than he should have.

"How is it you never confuse me with my brother?"

Mac had often wondered the same. He leaned closer. "Quite easily."

"It's the scar, isn't it?"

"What scar?"

A moment of silence. "You're telling me that you haven't noticed the scar on the blighter's face and you can still tell us apart?"

"Of course."

"How?"

Silence again; longer this time. Then a sigh. "You wished me a good afternoon."

"I wished you a good afternoon," his brother repeated, as if doing so would make more sense of her answer.

Mac heard paper shuffling and then her chair made a high-pitched squeak, as it normally did, when she rose. On occasion, he had considered fixing the telltale sign of her departure but always decided against it. He liked being able to track her movements. He liked knowing when she was near.

"I told you," she said. "Quite easily." More shuffling. "I'm ready to continue interviewing our clients when you are. Shall I meet you downstairs in ten minutes?"

"Aye," Mick said. "Remind me to share with you what I learned from Gabby-the-flower-girl."

Feminine heels pattered across the floor, and Mac tried to envision what Mrs. Cartwright might be wearing today. A soft green to match her eyes or a somber blue to reflect her mood?

"Do you not even exchange pleasantries with the woman?" Mick asked, striding through the opening between the bookshelf and wall.

A muscle jumped in Mac's jaw. "We discuss what we need to, when we need to."

"So, no. What do you do when you pass her in the corridor or see her for the first time in the morning?"

Mac said nothing, for no words could explain the complicated emotions he experienced every time he came into contact with Mrs. Cartwright.

"Dammit, man. Have you forgotten all your manners?"

"How I communicate with Mrs. Cartwright is none of your concern. Leave it be."

"Take your own advice." His brother waved his hand toward Mrs. Cartwright's side. "Whatever you found in the girl's background is just that—in her past. She's done nothing to hurt you or anyone at the agency."

"Nothing we know of."

Disappointment trod over his brother's righteous anger. "In all our years, I have never seen you treat the fairer sex the way you do the assistant. Does this have something to do with our no-good mother?"

A rapid arrangement of scenes flashed before Mac's eyes. He tried to stop them, but somehow they always found a crack in his mental barriers. Raw fury burned through him like the glowing tip of a new sword. "Fine, she's an angel."

"Yet you will still treat her like she's the devil."

"I'll do no such thing." Mac shot up out of his chair and paced the small confines of their shared workspace. "I can respect her dedication to the agency without being her damned friend."

Mick moved to the door. "What are you afraid of, brother? That you might come to care for her? A young, beautiful woman who made a horrible blunder and is now working diligently to correct the mistake?" Mick shook his head and turned the latch. "If I didn't know you any better, I would think you had traipsed through the last twenty-six years on a golden cloud of fairy dust."

Mac slashed his hand through the air, ending the conversation. "Make sure Sydney knows about your conversation with Gabby-the-flower-girl."

Mick sent him a mocking salute. "At once, Admiral O'Donnell." He stepped into the shadow-ridden corridor. "Know this, brother. If you won't have her, I will."

Blood pounded behind Mac's eyes. He pressed his thumb and forefinger into the burning sockets, rubbing. How had it come to this? He could think of a dozen more qualified individuals to deliver a lecture on manners than his guttersnipe brother. But the bastard had found a raw nerve and then proceeded to draw a knife over it, again and again.

Mac wasn't discourteous to Mrs. Cartwright. *Amelia.* He simply avoided her until he could not. His need to evade her company had increased in the last few months, as had his awareness of her every move.

He let his hand fall to his side and strode to the opening. He studied Amelia's workspace for several minutes. Such a dismal space—stark, cold, utilitarian. By no means was this an appropriate environment for a young woman to spend hours at a time, alone and without companionship. No wonder she never smiled. His mood darkened just standing here.

The only spot of color in the whole room was the sad arrangement of yellow flowers Mick had given her. His brother knew her well, for he even brought her a small vase of water to stow them in.

Glancing over his shoulder, he located the empty birdcage. The large wire-framed cage once held an armada of warbling canaries of various colors. He had toted the birds from one apartment to the next, where they provided him with hours of company and beautiful music. His neighbors had rarely appreciated their symphony, but Mac had. So much of his early life had been scarred by the sights and sounds of greed and poverty that he never knew such beauty existed.

And then his avian friends began dying, one after the other, until there were none left. For two years, the cage had sat empty. Mac simply didn't have the heart to replace his birds, nor could he discard their cage.

He swiveled his gaze back to Amelia's workspace. His was not the only life lacking beauty.

Nine

Dear Ethan,

Teddy said I could ride with you in Hyde Park. Bastian brought Guinevere to London. Mama said to ask when you are available. Guinevere and I thought this morning at ten would be a brilliant time.

Your forever friend,
Sophie Ashcroft

PS—Bastian thought you might still be sleeping at ten. If so, I'm available at ten thirty.

ETHAN STARED AT THE MISSIVE, KNOWING INSTINCTIVELY that Somerton, also known as Bastian, was behind this miracle turnaround of Teddy's response. He dropped the small square of paper on his desk and glanced up at the clock. Nine thirty. Contrary to what Somerton supposed, Ethan had been up since seven contemplating his next reconnaissance of Abbingale.

Now that he had a feel for Abbingale's daytime activities, it was time to see what they were about at night. He mentally catalogued his repertoire of disguises and decided on black. Simple, uncomplicated black attire.

By being himself, he could move about more freely—something he was quite keen on given his faux pas yesterday. He could not recall the last time he had made such a telling mistake. Mistakes like that got people killed. But the haunted expression Miss Hunt wore when she'd exited the boys' home made him forget all of his training and experience. He had reacted with a swiftness that hadn't stopped to consider logic or reasoning. His only thought—to protect. A laughable notion, considering Miss Hunt traveled nowhere without her two strapping footmen in tow.

Then he recalled the odd episode in his study yesterday. Not the shock and dismay she had displayed when he'd thanked her for caring for him. Though her dismay seemed a little out of proportion for such a revelation. No, the moment that returned to his mind again and again was the way she'd recoiled from him. Her face, white and frozen with trepidation. It was not his size she had feared, but his taking control, his caging her within his embrace. His stomach roiled with thoughts of what her reaction might mean.

He could not even allow himself to enjoy the euphoria of discovery. He'd found her. His mousy little nursemaid, who wasn't so little after all. When the time was right, he would thank her more properly for taking care of him and then set about annoying her every minute of the day until she revealed her cloaked companion's identity. Although she would like to think so, she was not completely immune to his charm. He had only to relive their kiss to know the truth of it.

Dear God, she had the sweetest mouth. He could have kissed her for hours and have not tired of her response. And her body. Never had a woman fit so perfectly against his large frame. Most times, he worried he would crush his lover, which forced him to hold back his passions—if there had been any to begin with. In the last couple years, there had been none. With Sydney, he sensed that she would be as demanding as he in bed. And she would have been, he was sure of it, if not for the fear. A breath shuddered from between his lips.

The last thing he wanted to do was take Sydney Hunt to his bed to coax information from her. No, when they met skin to skin, he would not have espionage on his mind. The only thing on his mind would be Sydney. Only Sydney, and how he could make her forget the fear.

He checked the clock again and gritted his teeth. Nine forty. Enough time to collect his horse and make it to Somerton House at the appointed hour. Why Sophie Ashcroft had taken a liking to him, he didn't know. But he had already disappointed her once this week. He couldn't bear doing so again.

As for Miss Hunt's past, he stored away that particular mystery for later. Now, he must entertain a miniature banshee who was determined to treat him like an uncle, of sorts. He rotated his head to the left, enjoying the satisfying crackle of vertebrae. Then did the same to the right before rising.

Horses. In the next twenty minutes, he had to come up with enough questions about horses to fill an hour's worth of time. If he were conversing with an adult, the task would not be too onerous. But a seven-year-old girl? He groaned. No doubt they would spend the entire time chatting about pretty colors and perfect names.

Somehow he would make Somerton pay for his interference. Well, he would once he started speaking to the man again. His mentor's lack of faith in his abilities still boiled in his gut like sour stew.

When he entered the entry hall, he found Tanner hovering in his usual spot. "I'm off to Somerton House now."

"Of course, my lord. Your mount's out front."

"How did you know I'd need my horse?"

Tanner smiled. "We're paid to anticipate your needs."

"Or Rucker enclosed a note along with Sophie's."

"That too, my lord."

As his butler strode away, Ethan experienced a pang of guilt. Why had it taken a ruse for him to realize Tanner needed help? The old retainer had served the deBeaus well over the years, and how had Ethan repaid his faithful service? He had reduced his staff to the point where Tanner acted the butler, footman, valet, and who knew what else. With Miss Hunt's help, he'd be able to rectify his mistake, and soon.

The moment he closed the door, a familiar voice said, "Going somewhere, Danforth?"

Ethan glanced around to find the Marquess of Shevington alighting from his carriage. Seeing his friend during the day—again—shocked him so badly that all he could manage was a disbelieving stare.

"Your mouth is agape, Danforth. It's not complimentary."

"What induced you to venture out mid-morning? Must be something dire for you to brave running into nannies and babies."

"You should never try to be humorous before the midday meal," Shev said. "It doesn't take hold." He paused while a stable lad delivered Ethan's mount. "Do you have a social engagement?"

"Yes. I am to meet a young lady for a ride in the park."

"Anyone I know?"

"Doubtful. She's seven."

A look of horror crossed Shev's face. "My condolences, old man."

"You would like her," Ethan said, feeling protective. "As a matter of fact, she reminds me a lot of you. Care to walk with me to Somerton House?"

"Walk?" Shev asked as if the act were a foreign notion. "Why don't you tie your mount to the back of my carriage and then we can avoid such exertions."

"Come. The exercise will do you good, and you can astonish me with the reason for your visit as we stroll."

The marquess released a groan of resignation. "Taylor," he said to his coachman. "Drive on to Somerton House. I'll trudge along behind."

"Yes, sir."

A snap of the reins sent the marquess's carriage lurching forward. Ethan motioned to the stable lad holding his horse to follow. In order to make his appointment with Sophie Ashcroft, he would have to set a brisk pace. Knowing Sophie, she'd probably had her pixie face plastered against the front window since dispatching her invitation. It hadn't taken long for him to realize that patience was not one of the girl's virtues. A characteristic they both shared.

"What can I do for you, Shev?"

"Perhaps I am here to help you."

"Are you?"

The marquess smiled. "Yes and no. I have both a favor to ask of you and an invitation. Which would you like to hear first?"

"I have a feeling neither is going to be enjoyable. Let us start with the worst of it."

"Your dear sister Cora is in France, is she not?"

Ethan's humor drained away. "Not any longer. She returned to England not long ago."

"I see." A note of disappointment tinged the marquess's words. "Then you may forget the favor."

"Do you need to contact someone there?" Ethan asked, despite his better judgment. After what they went through to bring Cora home, he had an aversion to all things French.

Shev waved a negligent hand in the air. "It's nothing. An idle curiosity that will be forgotten within the hour."

"You're sure?" Ethan studied the pensive expression his friend could not quite mask.

"Quite. Now let us get on with the excessively bad news."

"I thought we had decided to save the best for last."

"And have you dread our entire conversation?" Shev asked in mock indignation. "I am not so callous as that, Danforth."

"Spill it."

"Mother is having a dinner party tonight, and one of her gentlemen guests can no longer attend. Her table now has an uneven number of ladies versus gentlemen. You have come through for her before, and she's hoping you would be willing to do so again."

Ethan adored Shev's mother. Spending time in Lady Shevington's company was both a blessing and a curse. In many ways, she reminded him of the mother he had lost years ago. A strong, intelligent woman dedicated to her family and generous to others. "You know I would do anything for your mother," Ethan said. "But the timing is not convenient."

"I was afraid that might be the case. Normally, I would not press the issue, but this evening is special to her and I would like to ease her mind."

"What is so special about this dinner?"

"You might recall that my mother did not come from aristocratic stock," Shev said. "She has invited many of her childhood friends and their families to dine tonight. Some of them she has not seen in years."

"Is there no one else you can ask?" The question was irrelevant, for Ethan could never say no to Lady Shevington. She had been far too good to him over the years, asking nothing in return—except the occasional evening of the numbers.

"No one other than Helsford, and I have not seen him about town for some time."

That's because he's too busy assuming his new role as Chief of the Nexus. "I'll be there, Shev. What time?"

"Eight."

Ethan glanced ahead and noted that they were only a few houses away from his destination. A familiar churning began in the pit of his stomach. What were the odds of him striding inside, snatching up Sophie, and escaping to the park without coming face-to-face with Somerton?

Zero. None. Naught.

They paused beside Shev's carriage. "See there." Ethan strove for a bit of levity. "You walked briskly for nearly a quarter hour and didn't have to stop once because of a stitch in your side."

A footman jumped off the back of the marquess's carriage, scrambling to open the door and set the steps down. Shev placed a foot on the bottom step. "I bravely ignored the horrible cramp in my right calf." His brows drew together. "What the devil is that atrocious noise?"

Ethan cocked his head and listened. "It's a bird, Shev."

"Well, make it stop." His friend rubbed his temple. "All this walking and squinting against the sun has given me a megrim. One more piercing tweet from that feathered beast and my head will splinter in two."

Waving the marquess inside, Ethan said, "You've been upright too long. Go home and get some sleep before your mother's dinner party. She won't be pleased if you arrive looking like a dissipated sot."

After Ethan closed the carriage door, Shev nodded toward Somerton House. "There's a ginger-haired creature bouncing in the window. Good day, Danforth."

Sure enough, Ethan turned his back on his departing friend and found Sophie Ashcroft jumping up and down and waving at him. Before he knew what was happening, his lips curled into an answering smile and he waved back, which then prompted her to dash off. His smile faded and he glanced around to see if anyone had noticed him acting the fool. The moment his gaze completed its sweep of the area, shame crept into his cheeks. What did he care if Somerton's neighbors saw him waving like a schoolboy to the girl? Few could withstand such an enthusiastic welcome.

Despite her father's frequent and long absences prior to his murder, Sophie appeared to be a joyful child, always nattering on about inconsequential things and flitting from one interesting object to the next. She reminded him of a butterfly, but without the delicacy. Ethan wondered if she would ever learn the reason behind her deceased father's sacrifices and, as a consequence, her sacrifices. He shrugged off the thought. Whatever Catherine Ashcroft and Somerton decided to tell the child about her father's role in the conflict with France would no doubt be the right thing for Sophie.

The entrance door swept open. "Ethan, you made it." Sophie barreled into him, wrapping her arms around his waist. She tilted her head up, revealing pretty blue eyes. "Guinevere will be so happy."

He tapped her nose. "And what of you?"

She sent him a broad grin. "Mama said the park will be full of horses."

"Yes, indeed. In all the various shades and sizes."

Ethan motioned to the entrance hall. "Shall we collect your nurse?"

"I need a new one."

Ethan blinked. "A new what?"

"Nurse," Sophie said. "Mrs. Denton retired. Mama said it's time for me to have a governess, anyway."

"Good morning, Lord Danforth," Catherine Ashcroft said. "You received Sophie's invitation, I see." Her warm smile broadened in much the same way as her daughter's.

"She could not have timed its arrival any better," he said. The girl in question beamed with delight at his praise. "Sophie mentioned that she has no nurse to join us."

"True," Catherine said. "Now that things have settled down into a normal rhythm, I'll begin the search for a governess." She hugged her daughter to her side. "My little girl is growing up."

Unbidden, an image of Miss Hunt materialized in his mind. He wondered if her services extended to governesses.

"If you're amenable, my lord," Catherine said, "I thought I would join you and Sophie."

"What of Somerton?"

"He left a little while ago to attend some business at the Foreign Office."

Relief swept through Ethan. Not only would he not have to entertain Sophie for an hour by himself, he was saved from an awkward meeting with Somerton. His mood improved by volumes. He glanced down at Sophie, who vibrated with the need to be off. Not unlike a thoroughbred at the starting gate.

"Then let us dally no longer," Ethan said. "I'm sure Guinevere is more than ready to stretch her legs."

"Splendid!" Sophie bolted for the door, leaving her mama and Ethan to follow at a more sedate pace.

"Thank you, Ethan," Catherine said, pulling on her gloves.

"You're welcome. I think. What have I done to deserve your thanks?"

Catherine paused on the entrance landing. "Sophie adores all the attention you and Sebastian shower on her, and I appreciate the patience you've shown her. But you must tell me when she becomes too much."

"She's a sweet, good-natured child, Catherine, and deserves all the happiness we can provide. I only wish my experience with children was greater. Perhaps I might be able to do more if I understood them better."

"One would never know you lack experience. You appear quite natural in her company."

"Hmm. I wonder what that says about my manhood."

She smiled. "An indicator of great talent and depth of character, sir."

Every moment he spent in Catherine's presence helped solidify how this widow from the country stole Somerton's well-protected heart. He leaned close to her ear. "You're too kind, madam. If I had no care for my present good health, I would attempt to snatch you away from Somerton. Since I like my head attached to my shoulders, I will have to content myself with longing for you from afar."

Catherine laughed. "I think you enjoy your bachelorhood far more than your good health."

He winked at her. "You may be right. Shall we?"

"Indeed. I'm surprised Sophie allowed us to linger so long. She appears quite ready."

Ethan led their small group to Hyde Park without incident. Sophie was so awestruck by the various sights he pointed out that she did little more than stare and make excited noises. He found himself enjoying his role as guide and set out to make the girl's first promenade memorable. Much to his surprise, Sophie's equestrian knowledge far surpassed his own on the subject. She knew all the various breeds and their history. From deep in her mind's well, she plucked unusual bits of trivia to share. Ethan even learned another way to treat colic.

When they reached the halfway point of their circuit, a familiar face caught Ethan's attention. Miss Hunt, along with her assistant, Mrs. Cartwright, sat in an open carriage at the side of the gravel walk. Her ever-present footmen were also in attendance—one acting as driver and the other sitting astride a horse at the back of the carriage.

The sight of his black-haired beauty sent tingling warmth shooting through his veins, brightening his day even more. As he neared her location, he realized with some astonishment that he had missed her, even though he had seen her only yesterday.

Then his gaze moved to the quartet of well-dressed gentlemen surrounding her and the murderous expression on Mac's face. The tingling warmth became scalding and altogether unpleasant. What were the men doing in the park at this hour? A time normally reserved for children and servants.

"Is something wrong, Ethan?" Catherine asked, halting a few feet ahead of him.

During his study of the proprietress and her entourage, his grip on his reins had slackened and his mount decided to indulge in a short respite—in the middle of the walk. He grasped the reins tighter and squeezed his knees, forcing his mount into motion again. "No," he said. "I merely caught sight of a new acquaintance. Allow me to introduce you."

Ethan did not wait for Catherine's consent, for it suddenly seemed imperative that he reach Miss Hunt's side. More specifically, insert himself between her and the young bucks staring at her bosom. "Good morning, Miss Hunt. Mrs. Cartwright. Gentlemen."

The proprietress angled her head to the side for a better view of him. "Lord Danforth," she said. "This is a pleasant surprise." Her gaze settled on Catherine and then Sophie, whose attention darted from one person to the next, as if she would miss something exciting.

"May I introduce Mrs. Ashcroft and her daughter, Sophie. Catherine, Sophie, this is Miss Hunt and her assistant, Mrs. Cartwright."

"It's a pleasure to meet you, Miss Hunt."

"Hello," Sophie chirped.

Miss Hunt swept her hand in a wide arc. "And these gentlemen are known as Mr. Buckley, Mr. Kirby, Mr. Talman, and Mr. Pyne."

Each man tipped their hats in Ethan and Catherine's direction, murmuring their greeting.

Pyne's assessing gaze swept over Ethan.

"Well, gentlemen," Mr. Buckley said, "shall we leave Miss Hunt to her new visitors?"

"Seems a shame," Mr. Talman said. "But I have an appointment to view a prime bit of horseflesh in a half hour."

"Good day, Sydney. Mrs. Cartwright," Pyne said, nodding to Catherine and holding Ethan's gaze for a challenging moment before following his friends.

Ethan turned back to the proprietress's carriage in time to see Mrs. Cartwright slide a comforting hand over Miss Hunt's. The proprietress patted her assistant's arm and lifted her chin.

"Miss Sophie," Miss Hunt said, "that's a fine horse you have there."

Sophie beamed. "Thank you. Her name is Guinevere. Bastian brought her to town for me."

"Lord Somerton, dear," Catherine admonished her daughter.

"Sorry, Mama." Sophie turned her big blue eyes on Miss Hunt. "I'm only supposed to call him Bastian at home."

Miss Hunt smiled at the girl's conspiratorial tone. "You must be a very special girl if the fierce Lord Somerton gave you leave to call him Bastian."

Sophie nodded her head at a rate of speed that made Ethan dizzy. "He's going to be my new papa," she whispered.

Miss Hunt's gaze swept over Catherine's mourning attire, prompting Catherine to add, "When I'm out of mourning, of course."

Not an ounce of judgment crossed the proprietress's face. To Sophie, she said, "Then we have something in common. When I was about your age, I got a new papa, too."

"Truly?"

"Truly, Sophie," Miss Hunt said. "And I grew to love him more than any words could ever express."

"Brilliant," Sophie said, wiggling in her saddle. "Did you hear that, Mama? I can love Bastian the same as Papa."

"Of course, you can," Catherine said, concerned. "Whatever gave you the impression you could not?" No sooner were the words out of her mouth, than she brushed a hand over her daughter's mop of curls. "Never mind, dear. We can discuss this later."

Ethan interjected, "Miss Hunt owns and operates an employment agency, Catherine. Perhaps she can help you locate a new governess for Sophie."

"Do you, indeed?" Catherine asked.

Miss Hunt sent Ethan a warm look before answering. "Yes, ma'am."

"I confess to dreading the process. Sophie deserves the best, and I have no notion of where to start in London."

"Mrs. Cartwright, do you have an agency card for Mrs. Ashcroft?" Miss Hunt asked.

"Certainly." The assistant fished out a white card from her reticule and stood to descend from the carriage. Only Mac dismounted in time to pluck the card from Amelia's hand and then offered it to Catherine.

"Thank you—"

"Mac, ma'am."

"Feel free to contact us whenever you're ready, Mrs. Ashcroft," Amelia said. "We would be happy to discuss the depth of our services at whatever time is convenient for you."

Catherine tucked the card into a pocket of her voluminous riding habit. "You will hear from me very soon."

Out of the corner of his eye, Ethan saw Sophie lean forward in her saddle, staring hard at Mac, who had returned to the rear of the carriage, before transferring her attention to Mick in the driver's seat. "If he's Mac, who are you?"

"Sophia Adele," her mother scolded, "you are being rude."

"Sorry, Mama," Sophie said, though her gaze did not falter.

The merry footman's lips turned up into a broad rogue's smile. He pointed his thumb at his chest. "I'm Mick."

"How do I know you're not Mac and he's Mick?" Sophie asked.

Catherine started to admonish Sophie again, but Mick shook his head, apparently delighted by the girl's question. "That's an easy question, pet. You see, I'm the more handsome brother. Mac there, he has a terrible scar on the left side of his chin. The ladies take one look at his hideous disfigurement and run straight into my arms."

Sophie's eyes narrowed on Mac, suspicion marring her smooth brow. "I don't see a scar."

Mac angled his head a little and tapped his chin. Coming from the footman who never smiled, the playful gesture was one part menacing and one part charming. Like Sophie, Ethan tried to locate the disfigurement but could only discern a small pale line about an inch in length. Hardly hideous. If anything, the old wound gave the footman an air of danger, making him even more attractive to the ladies. He wondered if Sydney found the scar appealing.

"That's not scary at all," Sophie proclaimed. "The scar on my knee is far uglier."

Laughing, Mick slapped his leg and shook his head, conceding defeat.

"Come along, Sophie," Catherine said. "I believe you have tortured our new friends more than enough for one day."

In nearly an exact replica of Mick's rogue's grin, Sophie's toothy smile revealed her delight in having tortured someone. She waved her hand. "Good-bye."

While everyone murmured their farewells, Ethan caught Miss Hunt's eye. "I will see you tomorrow."

She sent him a bland, resigned smile. "Of course, my lord."

As he and the two Ashcroft ladies guided their horses away from the carriage, Ethan could feel Catherine's frequent glances. He understood her curiosity, but he had no desire to assuage it. Because he didn't know how. His reaction to the gentlemen's attention to Miss Hunt, especially Pyne's, had felt a great deal like jealousy, an emotion he had thus far avoided.

Until today.

Until Sydney.

Ten

AS HE DID MOST NIGHTS, WILLIAM TOWNSEND observed the illuminated windows of Abbingale Home from the shadows of a rented room across the street. Searching. Always searching.

His fingers curled into the faded, mud-colored drapery. Fury, helplessness, and recrimination warred inside him. None would free him from this untenable situation.

Inside Abbingale's walls brewed a nightmare he'd helped create and was now incapable of stopping. And it did not end there. More homes like Abbingale had been enfolded into LaRouche's new scheme. The thought nauseated him. How had this happened? For months, he had strategized and then executed a plan that would garner him enormous wealth. Enough to leave England and his heritage behind and start afresh in America, where they did not look down on certain choices a man made.

But the foreigners he aided were no longer content to communicate from afar. They had invaded England's shores one threat at a time, with no one the wiser. *Emigrés* they called themselves; wealthy noblemen and merchants fleeing Bonaparte's wrath. A decade before, during the great Revolution, such immigration had happened *en masse*, and the government had been forced to put protective measures in place, such as the Foreign Letter Office, to ensure England was not harboring enemies within.

A dozen years ago, the government established the Foreign Letter Office to open correspondence to foreign embassies from their governments. The office got so good at opening, copying, and resealing the letters that evidence of their tampering went unnoticed. Within a year, this secret operation was absorbed into the Alien Office, another office known only to a trusted few.

William had been one of the few for many years. But now he was trusted by no one, and his plan to secure his own future had transformed into a monstrous enterprise that sickened him to the core. How had he lost all control to LaRouche?

Some would think the Frenchman insane, but William knew better. The man was ten times more intelligent than anyone of his acquaintance. Yes, it was true that many a genius descended into madness. LaRouche would never forfeit so much control, however. He loved power and money far too much.

A knock sounded at the door, and William whirled around, grabbing his pistol from a nearby table. No one knew he was staying here, not even LaRouche. He'd been careful not to stay in the same location for more than two days. Any more than that and his enemies were sure to find him.

William had failed his foreign partners one too many times, and he had no doubt they were now seeking his death. He was a loose end they needed to snip off. William understood, for he would have done the same had their roles been reversed.

Another knock, this one more insistent. William crept across the darkened room. He never lit candles for fear of drawing undue attention to himself. Leaning close, he pressed his ear near the door at the same time a boot slammed into the other side. Streaks of white light exploded before his eyes, and wind whipped past his ears as he sailed backward.

Unable to catch his footing, he crashed into the bed frame and the side of his head struck the sharp corner. Bone cracked, and he lost vision in his right eye. He hit the floor with enough force to drive out what little air he had left in his lungs.

A large, filthy boot stepped on the side of his throat. Pain ripped through William's neck as tendons and ligaments ground together. He grappled for his weapon while thrusting the heel of his palm to the inside of his assailant's knee. The man grunted but the pressure on William's throat did not ease. With his impaired vision and limited movement, his pistol could be inches away but it might as well be miles, for he could not locate it.

"Do that again, guv'nor," his assailant said, "and I'll break your wee privileged neck."

William squeezed his eyes shut and blinked them open again, trying to regain focus. The action proved little use, especially when his assailant rotated his boot forward, shoving William's face in the opposite direction. With his nose a mere inch from the wooden floorboards, his world narrowed down to a blurry image of a year's worth of dust and dead insects beneath the bed.

Behind him, a door creaked. "You should have answered the door on the first knock, monsieur," a newcomer said.

The sound of LaRouche's refined voice caused his fingers to reflexively dig into his assailant's ankle. A worrisome pressure began to build in William's head.

"You are looking quite unkempt, monsieur." The

Frenchman moved farther into the room until William could see the tips of his polished shoes. "I think it might be time to replace your valet. Oh, that is right. You no longer have a valet. How insensitive of me to forget."

LaRouche's not-so-subtle reminder of William's reduced circumstances did nothing to discompose him. Everything he had lost he would replace it tenfold in America. Everything but one item, he amended, with a mixture of fury and regret. Lydia, he would never be able to replace.

"What do you want, LaRouche?"

He tsked. "Surely, you know."

"The list?" Black spots now dotted his vision.

"*Oui*, monsieur. You failed to deliver."

"My man established a list of agents did not exist. Had you not ordered his death, he might have gleaned other useful intelligence about the Nexus members." He had also ordered Lydia's death, but LaRouche would never know how much that decision affected him. Never would he hand over that kind of power.

"Cochran's usefulness had come to an end," LaRouche said.

William was losing consciousness. His hand dropped away from his assailant's ankle, and his lids fluttered like a trapped butterfly in a losing battle.

"Mr. Jones, I do believe you're killing him. Now is not the time."

Before the ruffian obeyed, he thrust his boot deeper into William's throat. Sucking in a lung full of air, William somehow found enough strength and presence of mind to roll away from the two men. Like a child who had whirled around in a circle too long, he could not command his equilibrium. Instead, he crouched on one knee, his hands braced on the floor before him. "What is the point of this meeting, LaRouche?" His voice was raw, broken. "I am well aware of what you want and am working on a solution."

"How can you solve something that does not exist?"

William lifted his head and noted the hard line framing the Frenchman's mouth. "I warned you that Somerton would never betray his agents, even under duress."

"So you did," LaRouche said in a conciliatory tone that raised the hairs on William's arms. "Since you were unable to bring me a list of the Nexus secret service agents, my superiors have devised a new plan."

Rolling to his feet, William faced this new threat on limbs that quivered like a newborn fawn's. "A plan that requires my assistance?"

LaRouche sent him a knowing smile. "Call this new request an opportunity for redemption, if you will. You have much to make up for."

So, he wouldn't die today. Relief steadied his trembling legs, though he knew it to be a temporary condition. Whatever task LaRouche had in store for him, William sensed it would violate what few morals he had left. If nothing else, Bonaparte was determined to squash England beneath his rule and would order all manner of savagery to make his greatest wish come true. William could not be here when that happened. He should not even be here now. Traitors were tolerated but never accepted. Not by their home country, nor by the enemy they aided. William's plan had always been to collect his blood-fortune and then disappear. With Lydia and...

LaRouche said, "You are familiar with the new Viscount Melville?"

William nodded carefully, while his mind searched for a possible connection. "Henry Dundas, the former War Secretary."

"The very same." LaRouche began to pace a wide circle around him. "He has a grandson of the same name, if I'm not mistaken."

"I'll have to take your word for it." William's stomach coiled into a knot when he recalled Melville's current position within the government. "I try to avoid such intimate discussions."

"You surprise me," LaRouche said from behind him. "I would think an intelligence gatherer would be interested in all manner of discussions. One never knows what morsels might prove useful. Like now."

"Lord Melville?" William pressed.

"Bring me his grandson."

William concentrated on keeping his breathing even. "How old is the boy?"

LaRouche stopped before him. "*Petit* Henry will celebrate his fourth birthday in February." He tilted his head to the side. "Please do not tell me you are being plagued by scruples, monsieur."

Most had vanished from his life two years ago when he'd made his first exchange with the French. He had not been unhappy with that fact until a few weeks ago, when his euphoric state disintegrated into a pile of bone-crushing loss.

"You would ask that of me?" William infused as much scorn into his tone as he could manage. "After all the crimes I've committed against my countrymen?"

"Yes, I see your point." LaRouche pivoted to leave.

Heart pounding, William demanded, "We will make an exchange when I deliver the Dundas boy."

LaRouche paused, then glanced over his shoulder. "Of course. However, should you disappoint me again, I will be forced to destroy what is yours."

Eleven

"LORD DANFORTH, I'M SO HAPPY YOU COULD JOIN OUR little gathering." The Marchioness of Shevington crossed the drawing room, extending her hands in greeting.

Ethan obediently kissed her powdered cheek. "And miss an opportunity to spend time with one of my favorite women?"

She squeezed his hands then linked her arm with his. "Save your pretty compliments for the young ladies. They have more need for them than me."

He winked at her. "Who am I to entertain tonight?"

"I'm sure you'll understand, but I have saved the best partner for my son." Her eyes twinkled. "I am quite determined to find him a wife before year's end."

At times, Ethan both envied and empathized with his friend. Shev had a mother who adored and fawned over him like any proud mama would. But, if it were her son, her very fawning would cause Ethan to bolt any time she approached. "I will have to console myself with second best."

"As with my son, I have taken good care of you. You will not be disappointed with your dinner partner."

The smile she sent him was not one of reassurance,

but one of nefarious intent. A sudden need for masculine support hit him. "Where might I find your scapegrace son?"

"He should be here any moment. Allow me to introduce you to my friends." For the next ten minutes, Ethan met an interesting assortment of businessmen, shopkeepers, craftsmen, and even a servant or two. They all knew the marchioness from when she was a small child dashing around their neighborhood until her newly prosperous father sent her off to an exclusive boarding school for young ladies. Unlike many who were born commoners and then married into the aristocracy, the marchioness never lost touch with her childhood friends.

Of course, there were those of the *ton* who did not approve of Shev's mother mingling with the lower classes. To her credit, she paid them no mind. She had once admitted to Ethan that remembering the challenges her family faced all those years ago helped her to appreciate her good fortune today. And staying in touch with her old friends kept her from becoming a snooty aristocrat.

Ethan thought she was merely a rebel. She took an inordinate amount of glee in flouting society's customs and tweaking a few pompous noses. All this she did with only the slightest of repercussions. She paid them gladly, though, making her one of the most genuine and kind-hearted people he knew.

The marchioness halted a few feet away from the last of her guests. "Good evening, ladies and gentlemen."

Facing them stood an attractive woman in her forties, whose once beautiful blond hair had begun to dull with time. Next to her idled a younger, slimmer version of herself, with eyes bluer than Sophie Ashcroft's and a smile that would catch the notice of any masculine gaze. To her right fidgeted an even more youthful male replica. Ethan guessed the two younger guests, probably brother and sister, were still two or three years from reaching their majority.

Then Ethan's attention moved to the couple, who shifted to the left to make room for Lady Shevington. Ethan barely took notice of the older gentleman, for his entire focus centered on the tall, dark-haired beauty wrapped around the man's arm.

Miss Sydney Hunt. The maid who'd helped nurse him back to health after he'd received the worst beating of his life. He still couldn't believe he'd finally found her. If not for an unruly lock of hair, he might still be searching. Something about the simple action of tucking a strand of hair behind her ear had brought a blurry memory of her sitting at the edge of his makeshift bed into sharp focus.

Draped in rose silk, Miss Hunt outshone all the other young ladies present. Refined, confident, accessible— qualities most gentlemen would seek in a lover. Unfortunately, most of London's ballrooms were populated by debutantes taught to suppress the very qualities that would make them most appealing. Ethan had learned much about beauty and its many disguises—and uses. Although he could still admire a woman for her svelte figure and feline eyes, it was not those qualities that would make him linger in her presence for more than an hour or two.

Anticipation pulsed inside Ethan's veins. The day before, his concern for her had overridden any thoughts of the dockside maid or her cloaked partner. But now, his mind was overwhelmed with his good fortune. Hours of searching had finally born fruit, and he was one giant step closer to finding his savior. Once that long-sought occasion occurred, he would be free of this blasted debt of honor.

Why would she risk her life to care for a stranger? How did she come to know the cloaked figure? How many other disguises did she have in her repertoire? An endless stream of questions ran through his mind, but no answers surfaced. Those would have to wait until he got her alone again.

Miss Hunt's eyes rounded in recognition, and Ethan did not miss the slight shift in her posture that brought her closer to her gentleman friend. Now that Ethan's shock had dissipated, he studied the man standing protectively at her side. The term *distinguished* came to mind as he took in the man's sharp jawline, silver-dusted brown hair, respectable height, and aging, yet Corinthian build.

Lady Shevington said, "Please allow me to introduce Viscount Danforth, a good friend of my son's. Lord Danforth, it is my pleasure for you to meet one of my oldest and dearest friends, Mrs. Pratt." She indicated the blond-haired woman and then nodded toward the older gentleman at Miss Hunt's side. "And her husband, Mr. Pratt."

The pressure building around Ethan's heart eased, and he bowed over Mrs. Pratt's hand before shaking her husband's. So, this was Sydney's mother and her step-father, the man she called father and the one who helped her establish the Hunt Agency.

"And their children—Miss Hunt, Miss Pratt, and the youngest, Mr. Pratt," the marchioness said.

After the appropriate curtseys, handshakes, and bows, Mrs. Pratt said, "This is your white knight, Una?"

"Indeed, it is, Charlotte," the marchioness said. "Lord Danforth has saved me from embarrassment more than once."

Ethan placed his hand over Lady Shevington's, where it rested on his arm. "It is nothing compared to the many kindnesses you have shown me over the years."

"Yes, yes, yes, Danforth's a saint," a new voice interrupted. "When might we eat? I'm starved." Lord Shevington bent to kiss the crown of her mother's head.

She rolled her eyes in the manner of long-suffering mothers around the world. "You are always starving. Stop acting the bored aristocrat and make your hellos."

"Yes, Mother," Shev said, his lips twitching. He shook the men's hands and kissed each lady's cheek.

"Pratt," Shev said. "How is the banking business?"

"Lucrative as always, Shevington. And the House of Lords?"

"Tedious as ever, I'm afraid."

"Mr. Pratt has been charged with the difficult task of combating forgery at the Bank of England," Lady Shevington informed Ethan.

"A difficult task, indeed," Ethan said. "I suspect the Ann Hurle incident last winter caused quite the fracas within the bank."

"That poor dear," Mrs. Pratt said. "Hanged at two and twenty."

"Your 'poor dear' nearly cost the bank five hundred pounds," Mr. Pratt said. "If my clerk had not noticed the dissimilarities in Mr. Allin's signatures, she would be living quite well in America, or some other faraway country, at the moment."

"Well," Mrs. Pratt huffed, "you know the young woman could not have concocted such a scheme on her own. I still maintain the rascal who accompanied her to the bank put the girl up to forging Mr. Allin's signature and trying to sell his stocks."

"You are no doubt correct, Mother," Miss Hunt said,

breaking her silence. "Such grand schemes are rarely formulated by one intellect. But you, of all people, should know better than to underestimate the strength of the female mind."

Mrs. Pratt's fierce gaze gentled. "Quite right, dear."

"Pardon, Lady Shevington," the butler said.

"Are you ready for us to assemble in the dining room, Stafford?"

"Yes, ma'am."

"This evening, we shall not concern ourselves with precedence," she said to the group. "Lord Danforth, I have paired you with the lovely Miss Pratt. Shevington, you shall escort Miss Hunt, and I am absconding with your handsome husband, Charlotte." She smiled at Mr. Pratt. "No need to worry, Jonathan. I have the perfect dinner partner for your wife and your son."

"My concern was not for my wife, but for me."

The marchioness humphed before guiding her two remaining victims away.

"Well, Syd," Shev said with a familiarity that made Ethan's eyes narrow. "My dear mama is attempting to reform me again. Are you up for it?"

Miss Hunt smiled. "Marcus, you know how I adore challenges." She placed her hand on his proffered arm, sending Ethan a quick glance.

Ethan could do little more than stare at the striking couple in stony silence. Why hadn't Shev mentioned his close relationship with Miss Hunt when Ethan had asked him about her agency? It made no sense. Then he recalled his friend's comment about everything being a secret with him. Maybe Shev figured Ethan would refuse to answer any return questions, and he would have been right. Or, perhaps, his friend liked to see Ethan squirm.

After several conflicting seconds, he recalled his duty to her sister. "Miss Pratt, shall we join the others?"

"Yes, my lord," she said in a shy voice.

He nodded to her father. "Pratt." The older man nodded back but said nothing, simply gazed at him with a speculative gleam in his gray eyes.

Once the guests were seated, the footmen stationed around the dining room swarmed the table to ensure each guest had a serving of mock turtle soup, macaroni and chicken, braised ham, sweetbread, and an assortment of other dishes Ethan could not name. Through the first three courses, Ethan forced himself to give Miss Pratt his full attention. He had to admit, under different circumstances, he would have enjoyed his dinner partner's conversation.

Quite unlike her sister, Miss Pratt did not guard her every word. She spoke of her father's position at the bank and her mother's many charitable endeavors. She touched on her intimates' marital prospects and the museums she loved to visit. And she also bemoaned her brother's unforgivable behavior around her friends. But when she spoke of her sister, her tone wavered between awe, envy, and the slightest bit of resentment.

He understood the contrary nature of her position. She lived in the shadow of her beautiful, accomplished sister, someone she loved very much but would forever be compared to. Everything she did, her parents would weigh it against what Miss Hunt had done or not done. And she would be judged. Not on her own merit, but on how well she followed her sister's example.

A bark of laughter erupted from the opposite end of the table, drawing his attention away from Miss Pratt. Shev was grinning down at his dinner companion, who appeared equally amused by Shev. Then his friend's gaze dipped down to Miss Hunt's mouth before bending close to whisper something near her ear. Her smile broadened and was followed by a quick shake of her head.

Something hot and dangerous flowed beneath the surface of Ethan's reserve. He couldn't stop his sudden and intense dislike of the cozy scene they made. How could she encourage Shev's attentions after the stunning kiss they had shared the day before? His hands tightened around the knife and fork he held.

"You admire my sister?" Miss Pratt asked, though her inquiry held only a small questioning note.

"She is a remarkable young lady."

"And quite beautiful."

Ethan forced a smile. "As is her sister."

"Please, my lord," she said in a voice that sounded much older than her years. "I was not digging for a compliment but merely stating a fact. Men are captivated by Sydney's beauty, yet they flee when confronted with her intelligence. Lord Shevington has always been the one exception."

"But not the only exception. Weak minds can often easily feel threatened."

"It's just as well."

"I don't understand."

Miss Pratt peered down at her sister for a long time, sadness in her eyes. "Sydney's association with men will never go beyond friendship. So, you need not send your friend dagger looks for making her smile. She enjoys his company, but Lord Shevington could never provide the depth of happiness Sydney deserves. They both understand this on some level and, because of this understanding, they do not allow their parents' machinations to affect their friendship."

"Please do not stop your tale there, Miss Pratt. You have aroused my curiosity. Why will your sister's association with men never go beyond friendship?"

She sent him an apologetic glance. "I have told you all that I can. The rest you must pull from Sydney. If she will allow it."

Ethan's gaze drifted down the table again. Instead of looking at the striking couple and their shared smiles, he focused on Sydney, and Sydney alone. He noted her proud posture, strong jaw, flawless skin, and her alert, intelligent eyes. When he looked beyond her proprietress's mask, he also glimpsed an unmistakable aura of sadness hanging about her. The thought that she struggled with the same compulsion to hide—her feelings, a past hurt, a difficult decision—from her intimate circle, as he had in recent months, made him seethe with anger and ache to come to her aid.

When the time came for the ladies to retire to the drawing room and the gentlemen to settle in for a glass of port, Shevington kept the separation to a quarter hour. Once everyone was in the drawing room again, small groups gathered together to play games or to discuss anything from the weather to William Pitt's return to the premiership.

Ethan prowled around the edge of the crowd, stopping at different intervals to speak with the marchioness's guests. He did not fool himself, though. His destination was clear. It probably had been from the moment he first saw her, two hours ago.

Miss Hunt stood with her sister in front of an open door that led out to a small terrace. The proprietress bent her dark head toward her sister's lighter one. He hesitated to interrupt their private conversation, but as with most things concerning his nemesis, he could no more stop his

progression toward her than he could stop the sudden
rush of heated awareness.

"Ladies, do you mind if I join you?"

"Not at all, my lord," Miss Hunt said. "Miranda
was mentioning how much she enjoyed your company
at dinner."

"Do not sound so surprised. I'm quite capable of
pleasant conversation."

"Perhaps my surprise comes from never having
witnessed such an event."

Miss Pratt sent her sister a sidelong glance. "You are
acquainted with Lord Danforth?"

"Did he not tell you? The Hunt Agency is to locate
several new servants for his lordship."

"Is that so?"

"My butler and housekeeper are aging and could
use additional help," Ethan said. "As for the valet, I'm
not convinced of the need, but your sister believes my
wardrobe is in need of attention. Who am I to argue with
one so fashionable?"

Eyeing his clothing, Miss Pratt said, "Sydney, did you
truly criticize Lord Danforth's attire?"

Miss Hunt's gaze followed the same line down his
body, though his reaction to her scrutiny was quite
different from her younger sister's.

The corner of Miss Hunt's mouth curled. "His
lordship was not put together quite so nicely when last
we met."

Sensing she was missing something important, Miss
Pratt decided to retreat. "Jules looks to be on the verge
of revolt. If you'll excuse me, my lord?"

"Of course."

Once Miss Pratt was no longer within earshot, he
asked, "Jules?"

"My *younger* brother." Her eyes narrowed briefly, no doubt recalling his comment about her not having any humor in her bones. "He detests such sedate gatherings, especially when there are no young men his age present."

"Quite understandable." He caught and held her gaze. "It's a shame our conversation was cut short yesterday."

"That's a matter of opinion, I suppose."

"Indeed." After his parting words on Friday, he knew she expected him to ask her about the warehouse incident. But he had no intention of doing so tonight, even though the delay might kill him. He preferred to leave her suspended in a state of anticipation, always wondering when he would pounce. Not very noble of him, of course. But there you have it. He changed the subject. "How are your selection efforts progressing?"

She studied him warily for a long while before answering. "They would be much further along had we not spent valuable time searching for an unnecessary butler."

"Time you will be well compensated for, I assure you."

"There was never any doubt in my mind." She glanced around the room. "I don't recall ever seeing you at one of Lady Shevington's dinners before."

"I've only attended a few others, where she needed me to fill a chair," he said. "You were not among her guests."

"You sound quite sure of that fact."

He dropped his voice. "I am."

"To answer your previous question." All humor drained from her features. "We are on schedule. Amelia will bring the candidates on Monday for your and Tanner's approval."

"And where will you be Monday?"

"Working, my lord."

He stepped closer. "Have I finally managed to scare you away, Miss Hunt?"

"My not coming to your residence has nothing to do with you. On any given day, there are dozens of tasks to accomplish at the agency. I simply cannot do them all."

Even though her gaze remained unflinching, Ethan detected the small note of deception in her voice. "Ah, but I'm not just any client. I'm your partner."

Her mask slipped. "Pardon?"

"Partner. We both have money to give away and tomorrow we embark on our journey to find the most appropriate recipient."

"A single-stop journey. I have already chosen Abbingale as the beneficiary of my charitable donation. You, on the other hand, have only just begun the process. After our tour at Abbingale, I will wish you luck on the rest."

The more she wanted to be quit of him, the more determined he was to discover everything about her. Never in his life had he worked so hard to keep a woman's attention. Thankfully, he was not opposed to the use of blackmail. "I do hope I remember to refer to you as Mrs. Henshaw, rather than Miss Hunt, during our tour tomorrow. A slip like that would cause quite the stir, wouldn't you say?"

Her pretty eyes narrowed; calculation sparkled in their depths.

"And if, by chance, you happen to forget to collect me tomorrow at eleven, I'm more than happy to meet you at Abbingale's. To tour the facility with you is a rare opportunity I would not want to miss."

A rather unfortunate and wholly dishonorable side of his character enjoyed following the play of emotions on her face—triumphant to calculating to cornered. Somehow she managed to remain lovely during each stage of her transformation.

The direction of his thoughts made him cringe. He was becoming a damned romantic like the poet William Blake, spouting lyrical nonsense about a woman who would rather shuffle paperwork than spend time in his company.

"You could save us both a good deal of trouble," she said, "if you would state clearly what it is you want from me. I have no patience for such mental manipulation."

Mental manipulation? Why was it that he could not seduce her with words in the same manner he could other women? Her resistance challenged him. Incited him to slither beneath her skin until she could no longer recall the stack of paperwork needing her attention. Until she thought of nothing but the warmth of his breath and the caress of his hand and the glide of his flesh against hers.

William Blake be damned.

Twelve

"Are you ready, my lord?" Mick asked the next morning, with a broad, unfootman-like smile.

Ethan collected his hat and gloves from Tanner and then led the way to the waiting carriage. "Is one ever ready for sparring with Miss Hunt?"

Mick chuckled. "You got me there, sir. At least you figured out that bit early on."

Once he reached the foot pavement, his gaze swept over the carriage. "What have you done with your hideously disfigured partner?"

Mick produced another large grin. "Fighting for his life, I expect."

"Are you always this happy?"

"Nah." Mick opened the carriage door. "Sometimes, I'm happier."

Shaking his head at the audacious footman, Ethan bounded up into the carriage and sat in the back-facing seat, surprised to find only Miss Hunt inside. "You seem to be losing your staff today."

"Good afternoon to you, too, my lord." She fidgeted with the handles of a small traveling bag draped across her lap. "Mac and Amelia are working together on another task."

He considered Mick's comment about his brother fighting for his life and briefly wondered how Mrs. Cartwright fit into the equation. "So, it's just the two of us."

"And Mick."

"Oh, yes. Let us not forget the jolly twin."

"Pardon?"

"A bit of humor at your footman's expense." Ethan dropped his hat and gloves on the seat beside him. "If my sister were here, she would tell you that I often speak before I think."

"What would you tell me?"

Ethan curled his lips into a self-deprecating smile. "She's probably right."

"Then I will have to learn to ignore you."

"That might be difficult. I have a way of burrowing beneath the skin."

Amusement lit her eyes. "We'll see."

Ah, he should have warned her against making such challenges. Another failing of his, for he could never walk away from a thrown gauntlet. Especially not one so achingly lovely. "What do you have there?" He nodded toward her portmanteau.

"Nothing of importance. A little something for the boys."

Given her love of keeping secrets, she would have made an excellent agent for the Nexus. Then again, she might already be one. He wondered if Somerton had passed all his knowledge on to his replacement yet. Jealousy ripped into his stomach.

Ethan forced his mind away from the painful topic. "So, what should we talk about, I wonder?"

Instead of the wariness he'd expected, her jaw firmed. "You've had your fun, my lord," she said, with uncanny insight. "Now spit out your questions and let's be done with this farce."

"I wouldn't call it fun. More like a lesson. Living in a state of anticipation is not enjoyable, is it?"

"Not particularly."

"Why did you hide from me? All I wanted to do was thank the two of you."

"And now you have. Let that be the end of it."

"It's not that simple now. Tell me your cloaked friend's name."

"I cannot."

"Why?"

Her lips stretched into a thin line. "It's not that simple."

"You do understand how very *focused* I can be when I want something, don't you?"

"So I've come to discover." Her gaze did not waver.

A challenge. Ethan held back a smile and changed tactics. "Why don't you share with me what you've learned about Abbingale Home so far?"

She scrutinized him for a moment. "It might be best for you to see the facility's operation yourself, so you can make your own assessment."

"Or I could save myself a great deal of trouble and rely on your keen observations."

"You would trust my opinions, when you don't even know me?"

"I know you well enough."

Recollection of their kiss flickered in her eyes, and Ethan detected the same yearning in their depths that simmered in his body. But rather than reach across the carriage and take what she wanted, she sagged deeper into the cushion of her seat. Her relaxed pose did not fool him. He used the same calming device to shield his inner turmoil.

"Abbingale supports only abandoned boys, no girls or foundling infants," she said. "The home appears to be well-staffed and properly maintained."

When she lapsed into silence, Ethan asked, "That's all you have to share?"

"Is that not enough?"

"No. Like you, I have reason to believe something besides caring for abandoned boys is going on within Abbingale's walls."

"Something other than abuse, I take it, or I assume you would have mentioned it Friday."

Ethan paused to consider how much to tell her. "By my observations, the boys have a great deal of freedom."

"Freedom, as in…"

"Coming and going at will." He spread his legs wide, his knee touching hers. "Such liberty does not seem fitting with what I know of such establishments."

"Yes, I agree."

He cocked his head to the side, assessing the utter stillness of her body, the tightening of her delicate jaw. "What is it that you're not telling me, Miss Hunt?"

Her attention drifted to the window, contemplating. When she turned back, her green eyes flared with conviction, but she said nothing, merely folded her hands over her reticule.

"What do you plan to do if you uncover something undesirable?" he asked.

"Set about destroying it."

His gut cramped, and an unexpected wave of fear burned across his flesh. She answered his question with a harsh air of authority, as though she had commanded the demise of countless others. He leaned forward, bracing his forearms on his thighs. "By alerting the authorities, I presume."

"Of course."

"I don't believe you."

"What else would I do?"

"Contact your cloaked friend?"

She simply stared at him. Somehow he had to convince her that he was worth her trust. But how? How could he persuade her? His gaze dropped to her bulging bag while he stopped to consider the situation more carefully. "What if I told you I was looking for a boy thought to be staying at Abbingale Home?"

Alarm widened her eyes the slightest bit. "I would recommend that you retrieve him, my lord."

"It is a little more complicated than that. I don't know what he looks like."

"You must find a way."

"If he's there, you may be certain I will."

"Where are his parents?" she asked.

"His mother is dead. I know nothing of his father."

"Why are you searching for him?"

"A promise to his dying mother." Ethan attempted to regain control of the discussion. "What else do you know, Miss Hunt? Given the fact we're dealing with innocents, I think it's imperative we trust each other in this."

"You will doubtless not like my answer."

"That is always a possibility."

Eyes narrowing, she persisted. "My uneasiness about Abbingale stems more from instinct than anything I've observed."

"You may find this shocking, but I have a great deal of respect for women's intuition."

He sensed, rather than saw or heard, her draw in an anchoring breath. "Abbingale's matron, Mrs. Kingston, is pleasant and appears to be a steadying force. On the other hand, the nurse, Mrs. Drummond, has a sour disposition and watches me as if I'll pilfer their last meal."

"Anything else?" There had to be more.

"The place was awash in eerie silence. Had I not seen the boys for myself, I would doubt their existence."

"How many boys are living there?"

"Not quite thirty."

Before tragedy struck his family, Ethan recalled being scolded on several occasions by his tutor to be quiet or sit still or not leap over the furniture. Add his sister and Guy to the mix and a great deal of mayhem had ensued at the deBeau residence. "And you saw no signs of abuse?"

"No, but I daresay I wouldn't, would I?"

Marks from canes and leather straps would likely be hidden beneath layers of clothing and fathoms of silence. "You have a point."

"I did sense an element of fear while visiting the schoolroom."

"Fear?"

"The boys had obviously been drilled on how to act when visitors were present. Other than chanting a greeting to me on command, they spoke not a word, nor looked me in the eye."

"When dealing with so many boys, it's sometimes necessary to keep a tight rein on them."

"I understand the necessity of maintaining a certain amount of order. What I'm unable to come to terms with was the lack of laughter and male mischief. No elbowing, no sly glances, not even a single snicker the whole time I was there."

"Sounds like you are well-acquainted with the nature of boys."

"Eight years separate my brother Jules and me. He and his friends terrorized our home on more than one occasion."

Despite the seriousness of their discussion, Ethan felt one corner of his mouth tug upward. "As the eldest, I suppose you were the mothering sort."

"To a degree. No humor in my bones, remember?"
She dropped her gaze to her fingers, where they toyed
with the leather handles on her portmanteau. "Mostly I
allowed them the freedom of their youth. The shackles
of adulthood could wait." She lifted her chin, caught his
eye, then she quickly focused on the blur of buildings
through the window.

The brief visual contact struck him in the chest like
the head of a gale-force wind. Confused by the pain she
had inadvertently revealed, he tried to find the cause by
studying the smooth contours of her face—contours that
were quickly solidifying into the porcelain planes of a
Venetian mask, beautiful and cold.

He reviewed what he knew of her past. Little, he
found. Her mother married her stepfather when Sydney
was young, and the union produced a half sister and
brother. But how had she and her mother survived
during the early years? Sydney's natural father didn't
appear to be a part of her life, especially given the fact
she's using her mother's family name.

Had they stayed with relatives, or struggled on their
own? An odd sense of urgency to learn the answer
twisted his heart. "What of you, Miss Hunt? Did you
enjoy a carefree childhood?"

Slowly, her gaze slid to his. "I have many joyful
memories of my four and twenty years, but none stem
from the first years of my youth."

He sat back, smoothing his hand over his coat front,
pressing hard against his stomach to settle the churning
inside. "I am sorry to hear that. Pratt had a hand in
changing the course of your happiness, I take it."

At the mention of her stepfather, the stark edges of her
features softened and a smile, full of love, transformed her
face into a portrait of pure radiance. "Indeed, he did."

The roiling mass in his stomach cramped to an unbearable level. Ethan steered the conversation back to Abbingale. "Is there anything else about Abbingale that I should know before we arrive?"

His question severed the link to her fond memories, and in an instant, her businesslike mien was back in place. "Only the schoolmaster."

"What is your impression of him?"

"Intelligent, cultured, calm. Watchful. Perhaps too watchful."

"I'm not sure I understand."

"That makes two of us." When he started to ask another question, she flicked her hand, as if impatient with her own lack of articulation. "At times, I got the impression that he could see right through my disguise."

"Then I am glad you invited me to act as escort. I can observe the staff with a fresh set of eyes while searching for the missing boy."

"Invited?" she asked, with an uplifted brow.

Ethan winked.

Her lips twitched, then firmed. "What is the boy's name?"

Once again, he hesitated.

"Come now, Lord Danforth. I have shared a number of confidences with you this afternoon. You may trust that I will not jeopardize whatever it is you're protecting."

She had been refreshingly forthcoming—with only a bit of prodding on his part. What would it hurt to divulge the boy's name? Revealing his identity couldn't lead her, or anyone for that matter, back to the Nexus. Until a short time ago, the connection never existed and, even now, the link was too fine to contemplate. "Giles Clarke."

"A good, strong name." The carriage rolled to a stop. Gathering her possessions, she said, "Let us see if he's inside, shall we?"

Thirteen

TRANSFERRING HER PORTMANTEAU TO HER OPPOSITE hand, Sydney stepped across the threshold of Abbingale Home and felt the weight of oppression envelop her. Bare walls, thick silence, musty air. They built on top of one another to create an atmosphere more in keeping with a crypt than a boys' home. Little had changed since her last visit.

"Good afternoon, Mrs. Henshaw," Matron said the moment the entrance door closed behind Lord Danforth. She nodded. "Sir."

"Lord Danforth," Sydney said with a bright smile. "Allow me to introduce Mrs. Kingston, Abbingale Home's matron."

He stepped forward and inclined his head. "Mrs. Kingston, forgive my intrusion. When Mrs. Henshaw mentioned she was paying Abbingale a visit, I invited myself along. I hope you don't mind."

The short, redheaded woman dipped into a curtsy. "Not at all, my lord. Did you have a particular interest in coming here, or do you merely act as escort?"

"Every year I sponsor a new charity," Lord Danforth

said in an enthusiastic voice. "I'm on the lookout for next year's needy endeavor."

"Well," Matron's gaze shifted from the viscount to Sydney back to the viscount. "I hope Abbingale proves needy enough."

"From what I've heard so far, your little establishment is definitely a contender, Mrs. Kingston." He glanced around, rubbing his hands together. "Let's see some orphans."

Sydney stared up at the viscount, though she was careful to keep her brilliant smile in place. What was he doing, acting the nincompoop? Surely, the matron would be able to see through his ruse and then she would toss them both out. She couldn't let that happen. Too many questions about this place remained unanswered.

She opened her mouth to distract the matron's attention away, when the woman said, "Of course, my lord. Please follow me."

Red blotches marred Mrs. Kingston's face before she pivoted and headed up the stairs. Lord Danforth clasped his hands behind his back and followed in her wake. The jauntiness in his step almost made Sydney smile. Almost.

While on the first floor, the matron pointed out various aspects of Abbingale's operation to his lordship, and Sydney took the opportunity to lag behind long enough to peer inside closed doors and chat with passing servants. At different intervals along the way, she would toss out a chirpy, featherbrained sort of comment and the matron would patiently reply. As with before, everything was in perfect order, eliciting no reason for complaints or concerns—until they reached the landing between the first and second floors.

Instead of continuing upward, Mrs. Kingston paused and opened a door to her right. Peering up the narrowing staircase and then down from whence they came, Sydney reassessed her location. Yes, this was the landing holding her secret chamber. When it became clear that the viscount would be joining her today, she had sketched out a plan to investigate the mysterious source of light she had noticed on her previous visit, using him as a decoy.

All her planning was for naught. The door stood wide open and the matron was ushering them forward. Two steps from the landing, Sydney paused and tilted her head, listening. Her breath caught at the distinctive—and highly unexpected—sound emanating from the gaping door. *No, it couldn't be.* Drawing in a breath, she continued her ascent, her disbelief growing with each slow step she took toward the secret chamber.

Once she reached Mrs. Kingston's position, the matron moved to lead the way. They traveled down a long corridor, illuminated by four evenly spaced wall lamps. Lamplight flickered wildly, casting sinister shadows against the ceiling, floor, and anyone who walked by. The passage was so narrow that the side of her bulky portmanteau slid softly along the wall.

Over the matron's shoulder, Sydney detected another source of light. Another open door. The sound grew louder, more intense than before. It ebbed and flowed like a Drury Lane orchestra building up an audience's anticipation. Then their small group emptied into a large, cavernous chamber, and Sydney could no longer doubt her hearing; the sound of children at play surrounded them.

Sydney schooled her features into one of awe, rather than suspicion. "What is this place, Mrs. Kingston?"

Matron sent her a pleasant smile. "This is where we allow the boys to be boys."

Indeed, they did. The room was well lit by a bank of north-facing, ten-foot-high windows along the far wall, and three large chandeliers hung from above to brighten the area for evening functions. Everywhere Sydney looked, small clusters of boys were engaged in some kind of activity. Cards, jacks, blind man's bluff, and a random game of tag populated different pockets of space around the chamber. She located the ever-miserable Mrs. Drummond standing sentinel in one corner, paying the newcomers no mind. For that matter, neither did the boys. Sydney frowned.

"Oh, splendid." Lord Danforth rose up on his toes and then plopped back down on his heels. "We've located some orphans." His face reflected the same oblivious enthusiasm of a six-year-old. Remembering her own disguise, she said, "Oh, Mrs. Kingston, why have you kept this delightful sight from me?"

"Forgive me, Mrs. Henshaw," Matron said. "I wanted you to see Abbingale Home as an institution serious about its responsibility toward these young boys. However, after your last visit, I realized this side of Abbingale was as important for you to witness as its academia."

Without a word, Lord Danforth wandered off, stopping to speak with each group of boys. They were wary of him at first, but he soon had them smiling and exchanging quips.

"His lordship has a way with children," Mrs. Kingston mused.

Head bobbing in agreement, Sydney said, "Everyone loves Lord Danforth." Somehow she managed to say the words without the least bit of insincerity.

Mrs. Drummond pushed away from her corner and moved toward Danforth's position. Sydney's jaw clenched.

"You know him well, then."

Sydney patted the matron's hand. "I know what you must be thinking. What is a grand and handsome viscount doing escorting a commoner about town?"

Matron sputtered. "Oh, no—"

"You've no need to explain. Many have wondered the same thing. If not for our mothers being dear friends, I suspect I would get nothing more from him than a tip of his expensive beaver hat." She produced a tinkling laugh to show she was not put out by the prospect.

"Is there anything else you wish to see during your visit?"

The nurse was nearly upon Lord Danforth now.

Tapping her finger against her chin, Sydney pretended to give the question considerable thought, while masking her growing anxiety. She knew his lordship was attempting to locate Giles Clarke among the many boys present. Having Mrs. Drummond eavesdropping on his conversations would not do. "Lord Danforth would love to meet the schoolmaster. I've been raving about him so much that his lordship is quite eager to meet Monsieur LaRouche."

"Certainly."

Lord Danforth caught Sydney's eye and he gave his head a slight shake. No Giles Clarke yet, though there were several more boys left. He must have noticed the nurse's slow advance toward his location.

Sydney's toe nudged the portmanteau resting at her feet. They had perhaps one more opportunity to locate the missing boy. She clapped her hands together and molded her features into a sparkling smile. "I almost forgot! Are all the boys here, Mrs. Kingston?"

"All but one."

Dread tumbled like a great boulder down her torso

until it crashed in the pit of her stomach. "Oh? Is it possible to have him join us?"

"I don't think that's a wise idea. He's on bed rest, and I would hate to wake him or expose the others to his contagion."

Of all the poor luck. Sydney would have to somehow reach the boy. "Could you please assemble the boys in one long line?"

"For what purpose?"

Sydney grabbed the handles of her traveling bag. She tsked, "You'll have to wait for the surprise along with the others."

Matron peered down at the bag before moving a few feet away. "Mrs. Drummond, please line the boys up."

The nurse barked out a few commands, and Sydney glimpsed a crack in the playroom's idyllic facade. Worry shone on more than one boy's face, and none of them dawdled at the task. Within seconds a long row of boys, of varying sizes, stood before her. Eyes forward, shoulders back, arms at their sides. She felt like the commander of a small army.

"Be at ease, gentlemen," she said. "I've something for each of you."

A few brave souls sent curious looks toward her portmanteau.

"Lord Danforth, would you be so kind as to assist?"

He presented an elegant leg and bowed low. "Your servant, madam."

Giggles rippled down the line before they abruptly stopped.

Sydney glanced at the nurse. Mrs. Drummond's eyes had narrowed to murderous slits. Sydney nearly groaned with frustration. Must the woman stomp out every bit of their joy? What a miserable individual.

The viscount came to stand beside her. "What would *madame* have me do?" He winked at his audience and received a snicker in return.

"Unfortunately, one of the boys is not here. But we will make the best of it." She held out her portmanteau to him, catching his eye. "As my humble assistant, you will hold open my bag."

He started to do just that. "Not yet!" She smacked it closed and sent the boys her most dramatic, secretive look. "I have but one request before revealing the contents of my portmanteau." She paused for effect. Feet shifted, throats cleared, hands trembled. "I'll tell you my name, if you tell me yours. Every young man who shares his name may reach into the bag Lord Danforth's holding for a special prize."

His lordship presented the bag as if he were holding a golden chalice.

"Share their names?" Mrs. Drummond asked. "We can't allow such a thing."

"Whyever not?" Sydney asked.

"Well, because," the nurse stammered, her eyes flashed to the matron. "We must protect them."

"From what?" Lord Danforth asked.

The nurse's face darkened into an ugly shade of red.

"Mrs. Drummond," Matron said, "I think we can bend the rules for Mrs. Henshaw's game."

"Thank you, Mrs. Kingston." Sydney sent the woman a brilliant smile before turning back to the boys. "Does everyone understand the rules?"

Wary nods answered. They were no doubt waiting for a catch, an unseen revelation that would rip their prize away.

"Who would like to go first?"

Eyes shifted from side to side, then they touched on

the looming presence of Mrs. Drummond and the less forbidding Mrs. Kingston.

Their lack of response heightened Sydney's anxiety. What if her last-minute scheme failed? When collecting items for her bag, she had only thought to enliven the children's day. But Lord Danforth's revelation about his inability to identify the missing boy had spurred her mind into action. The solution to his problem emerged almost immediately. However, she dared not share her plan with him until she knew for certain she could deliver. Having all the boys—except the one—in the playroom was nothing short of a miracle, given her previous encounters.

Lord Danforth shook the bag, eliciting a plethora of tuneless clanging. The boys perked up, but still no hands rose into the air. "Methinks they do not believe us, Mrs. Henshaw. Perhaps a peek at a prize?"

"Wonderful idea, Lord Danforth."

The viscount made a great show of searching for an item, stopping every so often to gauge their reaction. The more animated the boys became, the closer his lordship got to finding the perfect prize. Then, with great and slow deliberation, he drew out one of the three bandilores inside. This one, painted a deep ocean blue, with specks of silver and white, was the most eye-catching. Breaths hitched and words of awe echoed around the room. Still no hands.

Their resistance to such an innocent game perplexed Sydney, but more than that, it worried her. That kind of willpower at such a young age could only come from sharp and swift discipline. The realization hurt her heart and fired her blood.

"My lord," Sydney said, "Would you mind demonstrating the bandilore?"

"I would be delighted to." Sitting the portmanteau on the floor, Lord Danforth held out the toy for all to see. A length of string was attached to a spool between the two blue discs. Holding one end of the string, his lordship wound it around the spool until the grove was nearly filled. Then he let the bandilore drop—eliciting gasps from the boys. The sparkling discs sped toward the floor and, at the last second, his lordship jerked his hand upward, reversing the discs' rotation. Up and down, up and down the bandilore traveled, captivating its young onlookers.

Three hands shot into the air.

Sydney smiled, delighted by the first sign of joy on the boys' faces. When one of the three orphans wagged his hand to gain their attention, she asked, "Your name?" The two other boys emitted groans of discontent.

The winning boy lowered his hand. "Jacob, ma'am."

"Congratulations, Jacob," she said, with a clap of her hands. "Step forward and receive your reward."

He skidded to a halt in front of Lord Danforth and wrapped his fingers around the bandilore.

"Jacob." Mrs. Drummond's commanding voice boomed out.

The boy froze. So did Sydney.

"Manners, Mr. Buckley," Mrs. Kingston said, her tone gentle but firm.

Jacob's hand fell and he swallowed hard. "Thank you, m'lord."

"You're welcome, young man. But I'm not the one to thank." Lord Danforth nodded toward Sydney. "I'm only Mrs. Henshaw's humble assistant."

The boy's gaze slashed to Sydney. "Thank you, ma'am."

Unexpected pinpricks stung the back of Sydney's eyes. "Enjoy, Jacob."

He dashed back in line, a look of wonder on his youthful face as he stared at his new treasure.

Sydney glanced down the line of boys and wondered how long each of them had been here. How long had they been deprived of such simple pleasures?

"Who's next?" Lord Danforth asked, pulling Sydney from her unpleasant musings.

More hands this time.

Somehow Sydney managed to slip back into her lighthearted persona. She smiled at a boy who had more freckles than a strawberry. "Your name?"

"A-arthur, ma'am."

She waved her hand toward the bulging bag. "You may select your own prize."

"Truly?"

The boy's eyes rounded so wide, Sydney feared they might actually pop out of his head. "Truly. Go on."

Unlike Jacob, Arthur strode up to his lordship with careful, slow steps. He held his right elbow with his left hand, almost as if he were hugging himself. Halting, he peered up at Lord Danforth.

"Nothing in there will bite you, lad," Lord Danforth said so low that Sydney barely caught his words.

Arthur took in a heaping lungful of air before thrusting his hand inside the bag—and immediately yanked it out. Clutched between his bony fingers was a linen bag, cinched at the top. "Can I open it, sir?"

Again, Lord Danforth deferred to Sydney. Given what she knew of his background, his consideration of her role in their charade surprised her. She had always assumed he cared little for women, in general. He used their bodies until he pulled every morsel of intelligence from their minds. Then he moved on to the next bountiful bed.

Red satin sheets. A masculine calf entwined with a

sleek feminine one. The image came to her with such force and heat that her heart bounded into her throat. She couldn't breathe. Couldn't see beyond the fading shadow of the erotic image. Whose calves had she just witnessed in such a compromising position? His lordship's? Hers?

"Mrs. Henshaw," Arthur said. "Can I open the bag now?"

Once more, she had to dig deep into her acting repertoire. She wiggled a finger at him. "I will be quite cross if you don't, Arthur."

She was rewarded with his big, toothy smile. "Thank you." He pulled the top open and let out a whoop. Glancing behind him, he said to his friends, "Marbles." His fingers dug inside until he retrieved a piece. "Look at how white this alley is." He rolled the large alabaster marble between his fingers. "I can barely see the pink streaks."

"Back in line," Mrs. Drummond barked out as if he were a soldier.

Arthur's joy dimmed but did not disappear. Pivoting, he returned to his position, examining each precious sphere.

"You did well," Lord Danforth murmured near Sydney's ear. "In case you couldn't tell by his reaction, the whiter the marble, the better."

Before he moved away, Sydney caught a whiff of his warm, musky scent. She drew in a long, deep breath. "I'm glad." To the boys, she asked, "Who would like to try their hand next?"

Arms razored into the air. This time, with no hesitancy. They spent the next hour learning names and giving away gifts. For Sydney, it was one of the best hours of her life. The boys were sparkling with enthusiasm, and she and Lord Danforth worked in perfect accord. Every so often, his arm would brush up against hers, sending waves of awareness tingling through her body. The idyllic setting would not have been complete, however, without Mrs. Drummond making her presence known on occasion. But Sydney did not allow the nurse's black mood to ruin the moment.

What did slowly extinguish Sydney's good cheer was the fact they were running out of boys. With only two more left, she worried Giles Clarke might be the child in the infirmary. If that turned out to be the case, she had no brilliant plan of how to reach him.

She glanced at Lord Danforth and wondered if he had come to the same conclusion. The tight set to his jaw and the narrowing of his eyes told her he had. Of course, he had. He would never have survived this long in the Nexus without the ability to detect an oncoming disaster.

Her mission faced failure. Other than a perpetually unhappy nurse and a schoolmaster's uncomfortable scrutiny, she had nothing to indicate inappropriate behavior within Abbingale Home or a link to Lord Latymer. Her last hope of finding something tangible died when she entered this secret chamber, which wasn't secret at all, and gazed upon a room full of playing children.

She had, perhaps, one more means of uncovering a connection to the baron. But that would have to wait until tonight.

Fourteen

GILES CLARKE WAS NOT HERE. ETHAN'S FRUSTRATION seethed beneath the surface of his pleasant facade. Had the intelligence the Nexus received been wrong? He doubted it. Ned Ashcroft had gone to great pains to relay the information to Somerton before he was murdered.

That left Ethan with two options to consider—one, the boy had been moved to a new location, or two, Giles was the sick one upstairs. Neither option improved his mood.

"Now that I know all your names," Miss Hunt, or rather Mrs. Henshaw, said, "it's time to share mine."

"What about him, ma'am?" one of the boys— Noah—asked.

"The game was mine to play, Noah," she said. "I did not ask Lord Danforth ahead of time if he'd like to participate."

Ethan dropped the portmanteau on the floor, beside his feet. Wood clattered together. "What is a bit of familiarity among friends? I'm Ethan."

"Thank you, sir," Noah said, "but I was talking about *him*." He pointed down the row.

After sharing a glance with Miss Hunt, Ethan strode

down to where Noah was pointing. Every boy his gaze touched on held a toy to his chest, as if they were afraid Ethan would pluck them away. And then, he caught a glimpse of a head pressed close to the shoulder blades of one of the older residents.

Craning his neck, Ethan tried to see the boy's face, but his protector shifted ever so slightly to block his line of sight. Not that it mattered, for Ethan had never seen Giles Clarke, nor did he have a description.

"Mark, right?"

Scars from a childhood illness marred the older boy's face, giving his countenance a rough look. One only had to examine the innocence around his eyes to know the truth.

"Yes, sir. Mark Snell."

"Who do you have back there?"

"He doesn't wish to play, m'lord."

In full ridiculous regalia, Ethan said, "Come now. What lad doesn't want a ball or whip-top or water-cutter?"

"All the same, sir. He passes."

Ethan heard the whoosh of skirts behind him but dared not disengage the boy's protector to discern who approached. "Have you any notion why he has no wish to accept Mrs. Henshaw's generosity?"

"He meant no disrespect."

"That's good to know. Excuse me, Mark." Ethan reached around and tapped the boy on the shoulder. When the boy tilted his head back, Ethan experienced an instant of recognition, but nothing solidified in his mind. He shook off the strange sensation that he knew this child. "Might I have a word with you, lad?"

A shudder tracked down the boy's small frame before he gathered himself and stepped around Mark. Eyes downcast, he said nothing.

Ethan peered over his shoulder and found the nurse a

few feet behind. He smiled his most dazzling smile. Then he caught Sydney's eye. "Would you mind it very much if the lads made use of your presents?"

Sydney took in the scene, and he saw understanding light her beautiful face. And something else, something deeper. Something dangerous.

"Not at all." Then the something dangerous shifted into a shallow veil of deception. "Brilliant suggestion, my lord. I'm anxious to see all their toys at work."

The boys didn't so much as move a toe over the invisible line on which they stood until Mrs. Kingston gave them a nod. Then the ensuing cacophony was nearly deafening.

"If you'll excuse us for a moment," Ethan said, "I'd like to have a chat with my new friend."

Mrs. Drummond began, "Lord Danforth, I don't think—"

Ignoring the nurse, he guided the boy to the far corner of the room and then knelt on one knee so they were eye to eye. "You've no cause to fear me. Anything you tell me, I'll keep it in the strictest confidence. Understood?"

"Yes, sir."

"Why do you not wish to share your name with Mrs. Henshaw?"

"I promised I wouldn't."

"Did any of the other boys make the same promise?"

The boy nodded.

"Yet they told us their name."

"Some made up names."

Ethan stared at the boy. If many of the boys used false names during their game, he might never identify Giles Clarke and, therefore, never be able to fulfill the promise the Nexus made to the boy's mother. "Why must you keep your identity a secret, lad?"

"Someone might get hurt."

"Someone at Abbingale?"

He shook his head, then stopped to think. Finally, he shrugged. "Maybe."

Ethan rubbed his forefinger and thumb together in quick succession. His thoughts traveled at the same speed, throwing one persuasive argument away after the other. Until— "What if I guessed your name? Would that allow you to keep your promise and ensure no one gets hurt?"

The boy's forehead crinkled, weighing Ethan's offer against whatever secret he held. After almost a full minute of consideration, he gave Ethan the signal he'd been waiting for—a slow nod.

Blurting out the name that burned the tip of his tongue was likely not the best approach. Ethan did not want to make the boy any more worried than he already was. Whatever his reason was for hiding his identity, Ethan knew the stakes had to be high. No boy his age could pass up a bag full of toys without an incredible incentive.

Rubbing his chin, Ethan ventured a few guesses. "Valentine?"

The boy shook his head.

"Isaac?"

Another shake.

"Cornelius?"

A shake followed by knitted brows.

"George? Stephen? Peter? Elijah?"

The shaking continued, though his lips began to curl.

"Augustine?"

"Giles?"

At the last name, the boy's eyes rounded with a mixture of shock and terror.

As for Ethan, his elation made him light-headed.

He'd found the missing boy. He'd found Giles Clarke. Tamping down his triumph, he probed a bit further. "Giles, is it?"

"Please don't tell anyone, sir. My mama—" He dipped his head, sniffling.

Ethan hated being the cause of the boy's distress, but he had to make sure he had the right Giles. "I met a woman recently who spoke fondly of her son, Giles. Her surname was Clarke."

Huge, mournful eyes lifted to Ethan. "Mama."

Clasping the back of the boy's neck, he said, "You're a brave lad, Giles Clarke. I will protect your secret." *And return this evening to retrieve you.*

"Is s-she coming to get me now?"

A knot the size of a cannonball formed in the back of Ethan's throat. He couldn't tell the boy the truth—that his mama couldn't save him because she'd been stabbed to death. So he settled with a poor version of the truth. "You'll be out of here in no time, Giles. Stay strong a little while longer."

"Yes, sir."

"Now come. Let's see what Mrs. Henshaw has for you."

"Please, no. If I take a toy, they'll know I told you my name."

"Who is 'they'? The lads or the staff present?"

"The—" His eyes widened.

"Are you gentlemen having a good chat?" Mrs. Kingston asked.

One more minute. That's all he had needed to pry the last morsel of intelligence from the boy. Who at Abbingale was behind his silence? Mrs. Drummond? Kingston? One of the older boys? The schoolmaster? Who had placed Giles here to ensure his mother's cooperation? Latymer—the man who betrayed his country and the Nexus and tried to kill Somerton, his friend? Or was it someone he hadn't met yet?

"A one-way conversation, for the most part," Ethan said. "No matter how hard I tried, the lad wouldn't give me his name."

Matron sighed. "It's the same with us. We had to list him in our registry as Adam. Adam Smith."

"How did he come to be at Abbingale?"

"The same as many others. Dropped off at our doorstep."

"No note?"

"No, my lord."

"Well," Ethan pressed his palms together, "the name Adam Smith will do. Let us reassemble the lads, so Adam can select his gift and everyone can find out Mrs. Henshaw's name."

Five minutes later, Giles lifted a cup and ball set from the bag. Quite a few jealous moans echoed down the line. Even the ever-serious Giles couldn't keep the delight from his features. The cup consisted of a six-inch carved piece of wood, with a point on one end and a shallow cup on the other. A string attached the wooden handle to a bright red ball. The object of the game was to catch the ball in the cup. As the player's skill progressed, the game's goal changed to impaling the ball with the pointed end.

At first sight, many believed they could master the cup within seconds. A few humorous tries later, they would have to admit defeat. Ethan knew from experience the amount of dexterity one needed to catch—or impale—the ball. The trick was to balance the handle between the forefinger and thumb, rather than grip it like a bat.

Giles gave the toy a tentative try, but the ball dropped heavily to dangle from its string. A flush entered his cheeks, though he tried to cup the ball again—and got the same results.

"It takes a light touch, lad," Ethan said. "And patience. A lot of patience."

"Thank you, ma'am. M'lord," Giles said, before resuming his place near Mark.

"Now that you have shared your names with me and Ethan, it's time for me to share mine. I'm Sydney."

Some of the younger boys giggled, no doubt loving the idea of being privy to such a vast secret. The middle boys stared at her with worshipful eyes, while the older boys tried to appear unaffected by the whole event.

As for Ethan, he stopped short of lifting a brow. Since she had devised a faux surname, he assumed she would don a false Christian name. He wondered if she would always keep him guessing. "Shall we release them?"

She nodded. "Thank you, gentlemen. Enjoy your gifts, and I'll see you in a little while."

After Mrs. Kingston's nod, the boys tore away in all directions, eager to play with their games. Ethan took in the lively scene. It reminded him of his own youth, when he, Cora, and Guy would train and play together for long hours at a time. Although he would give anything to have his parents alive and happy, the chain of events that followed their murders had prepared him for this never-ending war with France in ways he'd never imagined.

The realization was both enlightening and wrenching. Would God employ such a tragic bartering system? To obtain one's dream, one must sacrifice something beloved? Rotating on his heel, he followed the women out. Why had he tainted such a pleasant moment with dreary speculation?

Mrs. Kingston and Miss Hunt awaited him in the

corridor. "Well done, Mrs. Henshaw." He rubbed his palms together. "That was a smashing hit."

She smiled. "I haven't had this much fun in ages." She turned toward the matron. "Do you think Monsieur LaRouche has returned? Lord Danforth is so eager to meet Abbingale's schoolmaster. Isn't that right, my lord?"

"Indeed, I am." Ethan's mind reeled. How had he missed that the schoolmaster was French? Had she said his name before and he'd missed the implication? He didn't think so, nor did he believe in coincidences. A French schoolmaster employed by an establishment holding a child that the Nexus believed might be linked to Latymer? "Anyone who can teach something to thirty boys in one room has my full and utter respect... and my curiosity."

The matron's gaze jumped between him and Miss Hunt. She seemed torn about something. "If you'll excuse me a moment, I'll check on Monsieur LaRouche's whereabouts."

When Mrs. Kingston turned the corner, Miss Hunt started to say something. He held up a staying finger and then counted to twenty for safe measure. "What is it?"

"Did you find him? The missing boy."

"I did. He's here under an assumed name. Not unlike someone else I know."

She waved her hand in the air. "Adam Smith, I presume?"

"Yes."

"I thought he might be the one, given your extended interest."

"It took awhile to get him to confide in me. It's as we suspected. He's being held here to ensure his mother's cooperation."

"Only she's not with us anymore." Her voice was

tinged with sadness. Sadness for a dead woman she never knew.

"Correct."

"So why are they still keeping him here? He can be of no further use to them."

"A good question." One he had been pondering for several days. "Mrs. Ashcroft gave the boy's mother a proper burial, and Somerton made sure the notice was placed in all the papers. So, whoever is behind this scheme must know she is dead."

"Perhaps he is valuable to them in some other way."

"It's the only logical explanation. Unless," Ethan paused, giving his thoughts time to formulate. "Unless the children who become true orphans, like Giles, are converted to permanent residents of Abbingale Home."

"Would they be so charitable to their enemies' children?"

"Not, I suspect, unless it benefited them. What do you—"

"My apologies for leaving you to idle away in the corridor," Mrs. Kingston said, her cheeks flushed from her exertions, though she did not seem to be out of breath.

Miss Hunt beamed. "Give it no mind. We were having the best time chatting about the boys."

"I'm afraid Monsieur LaRouche slipped away to take care of a few business matters while the boys were occupied."

"When do you expect him to return?" Ethan asked.

"He did not indicate a time, sir."

Ethan held back a curse. Now that he knew a Frenchman resided within these walls, his sense of urgency to remove Giles Clarke from the premises had trebled.

LaRouche would have to wait. Right now, Ethan needed to concentrate on removing Giles Clarke. Then he would see to the Frenchman. And God help the man if he was anything other than the boys' schoolmaster.

"Do you care to wait, my lord?" Miss Hunt asked.

He made a show of glancing at his timepiece. "I will have to beg an introduction another day."

"Monsieur will be most displeased to have missed you, my lord," Mrs. Kingston said. "Please do return soon."

Once they were safely inside Miss Hunt's carriage, Ethan resumed their prior discussion. "What do you know of Abbingale's financial situation?"

"For the last five years, their charitable donations have increased by twenty percent each year, and their annual subscriptions have doubled in that same time period. Most of their increased revenues occurred in the last six months."

Ethan expected something more along the lines of *they're flush in the pockets* or *they can barely keep their larder stocked.* "Are you this thorough on every project you undertake?"

She stilled, and he could almost see her protective barrier sliding into place.

"I can't afford to make mistakes."

"So, your answer is yes."

Her breasts rose on a deep inhalation, testing the limits of her corset. "Yes."

The urge to shake her free of all constraints over-whelmed his good sense. "My question was meant as a compliment."

"Was it, indeed?" She strummed her fingers against the brocade of her portmanteau.

He tried again. "Why is it that any time I remark upon you or your agency's procedures you take a defensive stance?"

She closed her eyes briefly. When she reopened them, they glinted like steel blades before a battle. "How do I explain my situation to a viscount? A man. A gentleman born into wealth and privilege and a secured future. How do I explain to one such as you that I must monitor my every syllable and weigh my every action? That I must do twice the work in order to fend off any small amount of criticism? Because if I fail at any one of those endeavors, I'll lose my only chance to—"

Ethan leaned forward. "Chance to what?"

Swallowing hard, she whispered, "It's nothing."

He lifted the portmanteau from her lap and set it aside. When he made to grasp her hands, she eased them closer to her body. Instead of chasing her, he placed one hand palm up on her lap, and waited. The gamble was dangerous. If he failed to win her acceptance now, when she was most vulnerable, he held little hope of ever breaching the barriers of her reserve.

Ten seconds later, he felt his chest cave with dread. What past atrocity had shaped her ugly view of men and, in particular, men of his station? He recalled the warning her sister had delivered the previous evening. *Sydney's association with men will never go beyond friendship… So, you need not send your friend dagger looks for making her smile.*

When his pride could take Sydney's reticence no more, he started to pull away. And that's when he noticed her pulse lashing against the side of her neck. So fast. Too fast. Perhaps she wanted to reach out but was inhibited by wariness of the unknown. She knew little of him, and what she did know was veiled in secrecy and suspicion.

"Nothing in there will bite you, lass," he said, hoping she would recall the enticement he used with shy Arthur Rhodes.

The corner of her sweet mouth curled into a reluctant smile. "I'm not so sure."

"You have my word." With his hand still outstretched, he waved his fingers in a coaxing motion.

Her shoulders lost some of their stiffness. Then, with aching slowness, she cupped her fingers over his and held on as if she had never felt anything so stable.

"Tell me," he said.

"You cannot understand."

"Let's say you are correct. My privileged male mind could not possibly grasp your torment." Using his free hand, he skimmed his knuckles down her jawline until he reached the underside of her chin. With gentle pressure, he nudged her head up until she met his eyes. "Would it not ease your mind somewhat to discuss what's troubling you?"

"Do not take offense, my lord. But if I wished to bare the scars of my mind, I would do so with someone whom I have known much longer than four days."

"You might find this a bold statement," he said, unable to stop the damning words behind his teeth, "but there are times when I feel as if I have known you my whole life."

He'd shocked her. He could tell by the slight lifting of her brow and by the intense way she studied his features. But soon, her shock transformed into disbelief and, perhaps, even distaste. "A statement, I'm sure, you've made to many unhappy or vulnerable women." Her grip on his hand slackened.

The sight of her disbelief, followed by her scathing comment, quashed the tempest of emotions fluttering in his chest. Never had he felt such a strong connection to a woman. Not only was she beautiful and desirable— despite her prickly nature—her strength and intelligent conversation made him want to stretch out naked with her on a fur throw and discuss all manner of topics while sipping wine and sampling an assortment of bite-size delicacies. He wanted to entwine his limbs around her long, curvaceous body and pour his soul into her waiting arms. He wanted to share everything with her, between heated kisses and soft whispers. He simply wanted to be with her.

But any time he got too close, she narrowed those discerning eyes on him as if he were a diseased whore. The thought might not have bothered him so much if it hadn't cut so close to the truth.

"That's where you're wrong, my dear." He sat back and fixed his gaze on the passing scenery.

"I cannot help but be suspicious of men who use their charm to get what they seek."

Smart girl. "Normally, I would agree with you." He appreciated her frank honesty, though it still rankled. "But in this instance, I only wanted to ease your mind, not secure a place in your bed." He slanted her a glance. "That last sentiment will not stay true for long." Why he felt the need to prod at her sensibilities, he didn't know. All he truly recognized at that moment was a masculine need for her to understand the depth of his interest.

"Then I owe you an apology."

"Save it. Given my history, I'm certain to say or do something entirely inappropriate and it will be me begging for your forgiveness." He quirked his eyebrows up and deliberately gave her his most charming rogue's smile. "Then we will be even."

She shook her head. "I haven't the slightest idea of what to do with you, my lord."

"You are not alone. How about we start off by dispensing with the formalities, shall we? I would very much like for you to call me Ethan."

"Ethan suits you."

When she did not invite him to do the same, he said, "Sydney is a strong and lovely name."

"Is it, indeed?" she asked with a knowing smile. "I suppose you are right. One shudders to think of the looks I would have received had my parents named me Poppy."

Ethan pressed his lips together, for he could not conceive of such an ill-fated pairing. Notwithstanding her unusual height and voluptuous body, the woman before him exuded confidence, strength, and a keen sense of independence—everything the name Poppy did not.

"All too well, I'm afraid."

"Beast," she scolded, though her lips quivered. "Where did your silver tongue go? You were supposed to convince me that I could carry any name with elegance."

"Ah, you see? I must apologize already." He draped an arm over the back of his seat. "Now that we have determined you're as prickly as a hedgehog and I'm a charming cad, I wonder if we might return to Abbingale's finances?"

"By all means, my lord cad."

"Careful, hedgehog." He allowed his gaze to drop to her mouth. "I shall have to polish my silver tongue again."

Instead of being overcome by desire, she chuckled. "Your danger to women—at least to some—lies in your kindness, not your glib tongue."

Since no one in memory had ever praised him for being kind, he could only assume that he would never be a danger to Sydney Hunt. A rather gloomy realization. "Did you actually see the list of donors and subscription holders?"

"No. Amelia sifted through Abbingale's annual reports."

"Did she copy down the names?"

"More than likely, or she might still have the reports. Once I return to the agency, I'll inquire. Are you looking for someone in particular?"

"Yes." Once again, he was faced with a decision of what to tell her. Based on her earlier comments, she—or her assistant—had obviously investigated him. It wouldn't have taken a lot of digging to unearth his reputation with the ladies of the *ton*. His title, his prowess in bed, and his continued bachelorhood had drawn women to him like a lighthouse beacon calling to ships in the storm. Most of the time, the beacon guided ships to safety and, other times, to death. Either time, the beacon looked the same.

"What name, Ethan?"

Despite the seriousness of their current discussion, he took a moment to enjoy the sound of his name on her lips. So few people used his Christian name. Because of that fact, her use of it made the moment seem all the more intimate.

Like before, Ethan knew he must extend to Sydney another piece of his trust. If her assistant's paperwork provided another clue to the mystery surrounding Giles Clarke, he would be that much closer to finishing this mission. Before the full implications of that thought took shape, he handed Sydney another secret. "Latymer."

"Latymer?"

"Lord Latymer, to be precise. Do you know him?" He heard the timbre of his voice deepen, not quite threatening, but menacing nonetheless.

"It is possible I've come into contact with him. The name is familiar."

He studied her face for several heartbeats, almost praying he would find a sign of deception. It would make it so much easier when the time came to walk away. But he detected nothing, not a single flicker of guile or guilt. Releasing a long, even breath, he tried to force the tension from his body, but the bastard's claws curled deeper.

Fifteen

MAC O'DONNELL GLANCED AT HIS TIMEPIECE FOR THE hundredth time. No longer did it rest in his fob pocket; now it lay dead center on his desk. *Where was she?*

Although no specific time had been set, he had expected Amelia—*Mrs. Cartwright*—a quarter hour ago. At the end of the day yesterday, she had suggested they begin compiling their bits and pieces of intelligence on Abbingale's staff and try to make some sense of it all. He had been looking forward to this moment ever since.

Where was she?

Like his timepiece, Amelia was unfailingly punctual. Every morning at eight, he would hear the soft pad of her arrival and the muffled squeak of her chair. Every morning.

Except this one.

Eight twenty.

Sweat beaded along his hairline. He stared at the bookshelf separating their two rooms, as if he could see the crimson-draped surprise he'd placed near her desk a half hour ago. Words chanted in his head—*fool, blockhead, simpleton, dolt, idiot.* They all vied for position, each one elbowing its way to the top of the list.

"Enough!" He pushed out of his chair and thundered into her work area. Halfway to the crimson-draped item, he heard a sharp intake of breath. Ice coated his skin, freezing the sweat trickling from his temples and locking his muscles. Then a searing wave of panicked heat swept up his neck and into his cheeks.

As he spun toward the sound, time slowed to an unbearable half beat. Framed in the doorway stood Amelia Cartwright, looking unbearably pretty in a serviceable blue morning dress. Her surprised gaze jumped from him to the object on the tall table near her desk to him again. "What are you doing, Mr. O'Donnell?"

"Correcting a momentary slip into lunacy." He strode to the table, intending to put this humiliating situation behind him. Quickly.

"Wait. What is this?" She skidded to a stop in front of him, her hand extended in a staying gesture. "May I take a look?"

A foot smaller than him and about half his weight, she had no chance of preventing him from removing the evidence of his weakness. But something inside him wanted to see her reaction when she uncovered his surprise, while another part of him would rather eat a sack full of splinters.

"Perhaps it would be best if you don't."

"After all the trouble you've gone through to surprise me? I think not."

She twirled around, and Mac sensed her excitement as she stared at the crimson cover. Almost lovingly, she ran her hand over the thick material before splaying her fingers wide to learn the contours beneath.

"I know what this is," she said in an awed whisper.

"You're so certain?" He stepped closer.

She nodded. "Why would you do this?"

Another step. "Because everyone needs beauty in their life." His throat closing, Mac struggled to get the words out. "Some more than others."

The crimson coverlet bunched together beneath the force of her grip. She began pulling. Faster and faster, until the coverlet slipped free. Three canaries hopped from perch to perch, canting their heads this way and that to inspect the intruders.

Seeing the abandoned cage hopping with bright life again filled him with happiness. Yesterday, after another long day of fact finding and sifting through mounds of ledgers in Amelia's stark room, he swore not to spend another minute in such a cheerless place. He strode straight to his side, pulled out the birdcage, and then set about cleaning away two years of dust and decay. An hour later, he'd found himself in a shop that specialized in the sale of exotic animals. Birds, snakes, lizards, monkeys, and an assortment of four-legged rodents that many would kill on sight had peppered the small establishment. After a great deal of deliberation and haggling over price, Mac had selected one yellow, one pied, and one cinnamon canary.

With Mrs. Cartwright's back to him, he couldn't gauge her reaction. Did she like them? Had she expected something grander like one of those talking parrots? He edged around until he stood near the metal-framed cage and could see her face. Still clutching the red coverlet to her chest, she stood there with silent tears running down her cheeks.

"Forgive me." His voice was guttural. "I did not mean to upset you. I'll relocate the cage immediately." He reached for the cover, and she stepped back, shaking her head.

"No." She stared at the birds. "Tell me about them."

"This particular type is called Border Canary." Mac kept his voice low. "After their breeding location along the English and Scottish border. Besides the yellow, cinnamon, and pied—or variegated—colors you see here, they also come in blue, green, and white." He held out a handkerchief.

The white linen seemed to snap her out of her spellbound state. She blotted her eyes and wiped her cheeks. "Do they sing?"

"Yes. They don't carry the prettiest of tunes, but they'll keep you amused with their chatter and antics."

"Thank you, Mr. O'Donnell, for the thoughtful gesture. It's been a very long time since someone surprised me with a present, especially one so lovely." She folded the handkerchief carefully and then returned the square to him, along with the coverlet. "But I cannot accept it."

The hand holding the coverlet lowered, and crimson pooled at his feet. "Why?"

After giving the birds another long look, she turned her back on them and moved to her desk. "I would like to, truly I would. But I must speak with Miss Hunt."

Unable to bear the joyous cacophony gaining momentum behind him, he tossed the cover over the cage. All went quiet, except for the stray perplexed tweet. "What has Sydney to do with any of this?"

She settled onto the edge of her chair and dragged a stack of mismatched papers closer. "Nothing. At least, not directly. Until I speak with Miss Hunt, I cannot fully explain why I'm declining your kind gift." She met his gaze. "I'm sorry, Mr. O'Donnell. I know that's not helpful, but it's the best I can do at the moment."

Her use of his surname momentarily distracted him from the hurt of her rejection. "Call me Mac, dammit.

You certainly don't have any problems using my brother's Christian name."

"Pardon?"

"Forget it." He raked his fingers through his hair. Why the hell had he made such a pathetic statement? His brother had always had an easier way with women. It was one of the characteristics that defined them as individuals. Mac had never cared before, because he had never been without female companionship when he had need of it.

Clearing her throat, she said, "This morning, I met with Lizzie Ledford."

He welcomed the change of topic, though their discussion was far from over. Grasping the back of a chair he'd brought in for their frequent conferences, he placed it near the side of her desk but found he hadn't the stomach for sitting. So he paced. "The seamstress?"

"That's correct." She followed his progress about the room. "Our conversation took longer than expected, which is why I'm late this morning."

She was out collecting information, while he sat at his desk fuming over her absence. The realization produced a sour taste in his mouth.

"Did Lizzie have anything to add to our investigation?"

"Possibly." She disengaged the small reticule from around her slender wrist. Pulling it open, she withdrew a folded sheet of paper. "Lizzie's sister is good friends with a maid at Markham's Boardinghouse. Do you know it?"

"The name is familiar, but I can't place it at the moment."

"Perhaps it's familiar because of its location. The boardinghouse sits across from Abbingale Home."

Mac searched his mind of the area surrounding Abbingale. Much to his shame, he could not recall seeing a sign or any indication of a boardinghouse, though he knew many populated the city. "I'll have to take your word for it."

"Annie, the maid, mentioned to Lizzie's sister that she was preparing one of the empty rooms on the second floor last night, when a great clatter began on the floor above."

"Clatter?"

"Fisticuffs. Annie heard a door crash open, raised voices, furniture skittering across the floor, heavy thumps against the ceiling above her, a door closing, and then a deathly silence."

"Did she hear any of their conversation?"

"Only bits and pieces, I'm afraid. She said their conversation quieted after the initial shock." She referred to her notes. "Annie thought she heard three distinct voices. One was their lodger, a Mr. William Townsend, the second was a brutish-sounding man called Jones, and the third was someone by the name of Roosh."

"Jones we can forget. The name is too common and is likely not his true surname anyway."

"Agreed."

"What did Annie have to say about Townsend?"

"Very little. He's been there only a couple days. Tall, dark-haired, handsome, keeps to himself."

"Roosh is an odd name, isn't it? Do you think it's short for something?"

"I do."

The quiet confidence in her voice drew his attention. "You have a theory."

She nodded. "Annie also mentioned one of the men spoke funny."

"As in with a lisp or an accent?"

"Based on her attempt to mimic this Roosh, I would say a cultured, foreign accent."

Mac's thoughts shot around at lightning speed. *Roosh. Roosh.* Then it hit him. "French?"

"I believe so."

"LaRouche. The schoolmaster."

"That would be my guess as well."

"From what little Annie heard, she got the impression that Roosh—or LaRouche—wanted something from Townsend."

"Of course he did," Mac said absently. "Most beatings are nothing more than a physical show of power. A way of giving one's enemy a sample of what's to come if they don't deliver—whatever it is they have failed to deliver."

"You sound as if you know this from experience."

Mac's jaw clenched. "I know a great many things from experience, Mrs. Cartwright."

"Amelia," she said in a defiant voice. "If I'm forced to use your Christian name, then you must use mine."

An unexpected warmth settled in Mac's bones. Her commanding comment was perhaps his purest glimpse of the true woman beneath all the layers of reserve. Layers he never cared to peel away until recently. Now, he was plagued with an almost maniacal need to strip them off, so he could see if the very center of her reflected her outer perfection.

She continued, "We must now discover what would induce a schoolmaster to use brute force against a neighbor of Abbingale."

Mac pried his mind away from the feminine mystery before him and refocused on their more dangerous problem. "Either Mick or I will pay the lodger a visit."

Nodding, she made a few notations, then stopped mid-stroke. Her eyes rolled up to meet his. "Has Mick mentioned his bones?"

Fury slammed into him. What did she know of his

brother's ability to sense danger? After their mother's abandonment, his brother had hid his ability from everyone but Mac. Or so Mac had believed.

Something of his inner turmoil must have registered on his face, for she said, "Please don't be upset. He did not reveal his ability." When Mac's expression did not change, she blew out a breath. "I should not have said anything."

"If my dear brother did not tell you, how do you know?"

"I'm not supposed to say."

Of their own free will, his eyes panned down to her mouth. When her lips rolled between her teeth, his gaze locked with hers. "Do not force me to do something ungentlemanly."

"You would have to have an ounce of gentleman in you first."

He stepped forward, and she held up a hand. "Stop."

"Tell me."

Her expression became murderous. "I found him."

Unease stirred deep in his center. "What do you mean, you 'found him'?"

"On the floor. Writhing in pain."

What had awakened the violent side of his brother's special ability? The ability passed down to Mick from their father's mother? Some within their family had breathed a sigh of relief when neither of the twins had shown signs of having what many termed *bad bones*.

But when the first vicious episode struck Mick at age ten, the superstitious side of their family wanted nothing more to do with him and, by extension, Mac. So, unbeknownst to their father, their mother and her two sisters made secret arrangements to send the ten-year-old twins to London, a world away.

Exhausted and scared, he and Mick found themselves

on the filthy pavement outside Lindlewood Home for Disadvantaged Children. They stayed in the hovel for exactly eleven months and fourteen days before fleeing from the constant beatings. When they fled, they changed their names and then spent the next five years surviving the streets of London. Barely.

How long had it been since he had witnessed one of his brother's violent attacks? So long ago that he had thought Mick had learned how to control the pain. But if Amelia saw one, then he'd had a fit within the last year. Shame burned in his chest like the hottest ember.

Again, she sensed his mood. "You didn't know about his attacks?"

"He used to have them when we were younger. I didn't know—" The ache in his throat became too much; he sat down. "I had no idea he still suffered them."

"I'm sorry."

"No need. My brother hid the truth well." But why? Why would Mick shield his condition from him? Mac traced back through time, to conversations they'd had, especially when they were young lads huddled together, terrified, confused, wretchedly sad. Then he remembered, and the guilt that wedged between his lungs would have buckled his knees had he been standing.

Not long after they had been dumped at Lindlewood Home, his brother had doubled over in pain in front of the biggest, meanest boy there. Believing Mick to be an invalid, the mean boy had tried to thrash his brother. Although smaller than the other boy, Mick was stronger and faster. His brother had taken control of the fight—and that's when four of the boy's mates entered. He and Mick had made a good show of it, but in the end, they both lay senseless and bleeding on the dormitory floor.

Mac had not reacted well. Within a short period of

time, they had lost their family, friends, and any chance
of living safely in their new home. He recalled yelling
at his brother, commanding him to get his bloody curse
under control or he would leave him behind when
he escaped Lindlewood. Mac swallowed back the bile
of remembrance.

From that day to this one, Mac had never seen his
brother succumb to the pain again. Not once. Knowing
now he did so in silence, and all alone, was almost more
than Mac could bear.

"If LaRouche is capable of such brutality," Amelia
said, cutting into his bout of self-recrimination, "I can't
imagine the damage he has inflicted on those boys."

"I can." Restless, Mac shot to his feet again and began
pacing. "The sooner we end this, the better."

Even though his back was to her, Mac could feel
Amelia's assessing—and, God forbid, sympathetic—gaze
traveling over him.

Before long, she said, "Let us finish assembling all
the information we've gathered from our informants.
The key to our next step lies within all these bits
of intelligence."

As if to second her motion, a chirp sounded from
beneath the red coverlet.

Sixteen

WHEN ETHAN RETURNED HOME FROM HIS TOUR OF Abbingale, he was greeted by a gaggle of spies.

Tanner took his hat and gloves. "Lord Somerton, Lord Helsford, and Miss deBeau are waiting for you in the drawing room, sir."

Dread gripped his gut. How could he face Somerton again so soon, knowing his mentor thought so little of his abilities? Could he keep the hurt and anger at bay? What of Helsford? Could Ethan set aside his pride and congratulate his friend? He didn't know, and the realization twisted his insides more.

He eyed the drawing room door. Why would three Nexus members be visiting him at the same time? The answer could not be good. Had something happened? Had they finally tracked down Latymer? Or was this a formal announcement of Helsford's appointment to the chief's position?

He finger-combed his hair. "How long have they been waiting?"

"About an hour, my lord."

His unease multiplied as he made his way to his guests. Of the three agents, Helsford was perhaps the only one with enough patience to wait so long. Somerton, of course, would appear calm, but one could always feel the coiled energy vibrating just below the surface. Cora, on the other hand, was likely tunneling her way through the nearest wall just to stay occupied.

Once the drawing room was in sight, Ethan slowed his steps and cocked his head, straining to hear the conversation within. But there was none. A solemn silence draped the chamber, and Ethan suddenly wanted nothing to do with the inhabitants inside. His pace slowed to a stop and his hands balled into fists. Indecision kept him immobile for several long seconds.

His sister's head poked through the open doorway; a frown cut deep grooves into her forehead, and the scar on her cheek glowed white. "Ethan, why are you dawdling in the corridor?"

Grief did not weigh down her words, nor were her eyes marred with sadness, concern, or fear. No, quite the contrary. His sister merely looked annoyed. "Waiting to see how long it would take you to investigate the disturbance below. You're getting slow, runt."

Her eyes narrowed into evil, retribution-filled slits. "If that is true, perhaps you will now be able to keep apace with me, brother."

As much as his pride would like to be a braggart otherwise, Ethan didn't believe he—or any man—could keep up with his sister. Though Helsford, her betrothed, would do his damnedest to try to stick to her side. "Keeping up with you is no longer my problem." He waved a hand behind her. "I pray for the day when you'll become heavy with babe."

"Why is that?"

"Because you will either be too tired or too sick to torment me."

"What a horrible thing to say."

He sent her his most winning smile. "True, nonetheless."

"I am going to enjoy the next hour," she said in a deadly voice. "Immensely." With that promise, she swept back into the drawing room, leaving him standing in an empty corridor, his smile fading.

Pulling in a bracing breath, Ethan followed, shifting his features into his normal devil-may-care mien. "Somerton. Helsford." He made his way to the crystal decanters stationed on a small sideboard. "Care for a drink?"

Both murmured a negative response. Theirs was not a social call, then. Not that he thought otherwise, but it's always good to know where one stood.

He pivoted toward his uninvited guests. Cora sat at the end of the sofa, glaring at him, while her betrothed, also his best friend, the Earl of Helsford, stood sentinel near one of the windows. Somerton, on the other hand, was turning away from his study of the cold fire grate. "Did I forget an appointment?"

"No," Somerton said. "I was on my way to see you when I came across Helsford and Cora."

So this was not to be a formal announcement regarding Helsford's appointment. "And the reason behind your visit?"

"I have two," Somerton said. "First, I'm interested in learning why it's taking you so long to retrieve Giles Clarke."

Heat flooded Ethan's ears at his mentor's soft rebuke. He hated disappointing anyone, but most especially Somerton. Despite his current grievance against the former chief, Ethan admired the man a great deal. However, in this instance, Somerton's chastisement was unfounded. Ethan had been given this mission less than a sennight ago, though he was now only hours away from completion. If not for Sydney's assistance, identifying Giles amongst all the other boys would likely have taken him far longer.

As was his wont, he sprawled out in the nearest chair. "So, this is to be a group inquisition."

Somerton's gaze slid across the room before returning to Ethan. "Not at all. I invited Helsford and Cora along to hear the other important news I have to share."

"Ahh." He bolted back a swallow of his brandy. "My heart is all aflutter with anticipation."

Cora's glare transformed into a frown. "Ethan, what is wrong with you? You are more bothersome than normal."

He didn't feel like himself either. No matter how hard he tried, he could not force his muscles to release their death grip around his bones. His mind searched, with a near frantic pace, for some great misdeed he had done to bring these three to his doorstep. But what tormented him the most was their betrayal.

Yes, he knew his mind was splintering between a world of fact-based logic and emotion-clogged illogic. He couldn't stop the swift strikes of cold fury.

Cora, who was Somerton's first choice for chief and, evidently, the best of the Nexus, wouldn't get her chance at the position because her last mission left her scarred, physically and mentally. Ethan doubted she would have accepted the position, anyway. She had tracked down and destroyed the man who killed their parents. That was all she had ever really wanted from the Nexus, though he knew she believed in their cause.

Helsford, Somerton's second choice, might be too distracted to lead the group, but Somerton was willing to give him a chance, because he had no other alternatives. Like Cora, Helsford had joined the Nexus for personal reasons—not for love of country or any other altruistic purpose.

Somerton. A father figure, a mentor, and, at times, a friend. Ethan had killed for him, had lied for him. Had risked his life over and over to cross enemy lines to save a diplomat or a gentleman's innocent daughter for him. Somerton. One of the few people who could slash his heart in half with nothing more than a disappointed look.

No longer able to hold his indolent pose, Ethan shot out of his chair. "You're right, Cora. I'm not myself. The past few weeks haven't been what I'd call enjoyable."

"Not for any of us," she said. "What exactly is making you so peevish?"

He stared at her hard, trying to remember that she had not been privy to the complications of his mission, nor the heartbreak of Somerton's decision. Out of the corner of his eye, he saw Helsford moving closer to Cora. As if the bastard needed to protect his sister from him. The fury that had been skimming the surface of his control boiled over.

Tapping one index finger against the other, Ethan began ticking off the catalysts of his misery. "I was banished to London to rescue an orphaned boy—a mission more suitable for a greenhorn agent than one of my experience. Then a busybody proprietress begins nosing around my surveillance area and I'm forced to expand the focus of my mission, only to find out today that she's investigating Abbingale Home, too. And if that wasn't enough, dear sister, I learned that I'm not good enough to be—"

His brain finally caught up to his damned mouth before he said something unforgivable and utterly mortifying. No matter how much their actions felt like a betrayal, he would still throw himself in front of a bullet for every one of them.

"Not good enough for what?" Somerton asked, his voice low, intense.

Ethan's gaze shot from one pair of interested eyes to the next. He rubbed his forehead. "Never mind. None of it matters."

"It appears to matter a great deal," Somerton said.

Slashing his hand through the air, he said, "It doesn't." He released a deep sigh and plopped back down in his seat. "Thanks to the nosy proprietress, I can now identify Giles Clarke and will fetch him tonight."

Cora shared a look with Helsford. "She's nosy and a busybody. Whom, may I ask, are you speaking of?"

"You might wish to detour your mind from its current path." Ethan did not want his sister practicing her new matchmaking skills on him like she did on Somerton and Catherine. "Although I would not mind spending some time in her bed, I have no intention of doing so. She reeks of innocence."

"Well," Cora said. "That's rather plain speaking, even for you."

"Whatever it takes to throw you off the scent, runt."

"Why is the proprietress investigating Abbingale?" Helsford asked, bringing order back to the conversation.

"Her name is Miss Sydney Hunt. She owns and operates the Hunt Agency."

"I've heard of it," Somerton said. "My housekeeper used the agency a few years ago and was pleased with their services."

"Yes," Ethan said. "From what I can tell, the agency has an unblemished reputation."

"How did Abbingale Home come to her notice?" Somerton persisted.

"An ugly rumor had reached her ear."

"What sort of ugly rumor?" Cora asked.

"A former servant made allegations of abuse. We saw no physical evidence of it, but none of the boys appeared enamored of the place either."

"Few orphans take to the restraints of such a place," Somerton said.

"What would she have done had she witnessed said abuse?" Cora asked.

"I asked her a similar question, once I realized what she was about."

"And her answer?"

"She said something about destroying those responsible."

Cora glanced at the other two men before returning her gaze to him, or rather to his mouth. Her focus was more than a little unnerving until he realized he was smiling like a fool. He wiped his face of expression. "Something unusual did surface during my surveillance," Ethan said, redirecting them.

This time Cora smiled, not fooled by his tactic at all.

"I noticed some of the boys leaving the establishment."

"Why is that unusual?" Helsford asked.

"It's my understanding that orphans rarely leave the home once they've become a resident and, if they do, they're in groups and always escorted."

They were all silent for a while, then Cora asked, "How did Miss Hunt help you identify Giles Clarke?"

To his astonishment, Ethan balked at sharing Sydney's secret. There were no three other people on this earth that he trusted more, but he could not get the words past the protective barrier.

"I take it her investigative methods were somewhat different than yours," Helsford said.

Seeing his struggle, Somerton offered, "Every agent here understands the compelling need to safeguard the privacy of someone important to us. Through her exploration, Miss Hunt might have come across information we need. All I ask you to consider is if the privacy of one individual outweighs the protection of a nation."

Torn in a way he had never been before, Ethan reviewed what he knew of Sydney and her mission of justice. What would it hurt for them to know the lengths Sydney would go to in order to save a child? The likelihood that she would cross paths with any one of them was minimal. Even if she did, Ethan knew the agents would say nothing. Not to her, or anyone else.

"You're right, of course," Ethan said. "Miss Hunt, also known as Mrs. Henshaw, is posing as a wealthy merchant's wife in search of her next charitable endeavor."

"Quite brilliant," Cora said. "As a potential benefactress, she would gain access to the entire facility, under the guise of assessing its level of need. I can't wait to meet your Miss Hunt."

"She's not mine, and you're not meeting her."

"Whyever not?"

"Cora."

She opened her mouth to say something more, but Helsford laid a hand on her shoulder, and she clamped her lips together. Ethan shook his head at her easy acquiescence.

"Did she see anything out of the ordinary on the inside?" Somerton asked.

"Yes and no. Abbingale is well maintained and the staff ensures that the boys are schooled on various subjects. Though we saw no signs of abuse, the boys have a healthy fear of their caretakers."

"We?" Helsford asked.

"I accompanied her today."

His friend's eyebrows rose.

"Come back to that later," Somerton said. "What else?"

"Something about Miss Hunt's initial visits to Abbingale made her wary of one of the nurses and the schoolmaster." Ethan glanced around the room and noticed their closed expressions. "I know what you're thinking. That her imagination might be conjuring villains where none exist. She's not prone to overreaction, and from what I've seen, she's a good judge of character."

"Have you met them?" Somerton asked.

"I met the nurse today and would agree with Miss Hunt's assessment. She's suspicious to the point of ridiculous. The schoolmaster left before I could manage an introduction."

"What are their names?" Somerton asked.

"Mrs. Drummond and Monsieur LaRouche."

"LaRouche," Helsford repeated.

Ethan smiled, but it was not one of amusement. "Rather too coincidental, wouldn't you say?"

"Did the staff know you were coming, or did you invite yourself along?" Helsford asked, with uncanny accuracy.

"I invited myself. However, there would have been plenty of time for someone to notify him of my arrival."

"I don't like it," Somerton said. "A Frenchman's presence at the same boys' home that is holding the son of a woman forced to watch over Catherine while she's made to search my home for a nonexistent list of agents?"

"Latymer is connected to all this," Cora said. "He must be."

"I agree." Helsford kneaded her shoulder. "But how?"

"You mentioned that the boys were coming and going at odd times," Somerton said. "Did you notice if they were carrying anything as they left?"

"You're thinking of some type of courier system,"

Ethan said. "I had considered that, but the few boys I saw carried nothing."

"Maybe they're hiding something beneath their clothes," Cora said. "Or perhaps Abbingale is only their starting location. What if the boys pick up the package at their next stop?"

"Excellent point," Helsford said. "Is there any way of confirming either of these possibilities?"

"Searching one of the boys shouldn't be a problem." Ethan had done far worse in the service of his country. "And I can certainly try following them again." He paused a moment, his gaze sweeping between Somerton and Helsford, not knowing to whom he should direct his next comment. "Anything else?"

Cora cut in. "Now that you've found Giles Clarke, what are your plans?"

"I'm going to retrieve him tonight."

"Without assistance?"

Ethan stopped short of snorting. Breaking into Abbingale would require little more than stealth on his part. Quite unlike other retrieval missions he'd participated in over the last two years. She had no way of knowing his experience with such things, because she had been away in France. But she had benefited from his expertise not long ago, when he and Helsford had crossed the Channel and rescued her from an active French dungeon.

Instead of snorting, he settled with a shrug. "It's fairly straightforward."

"Is it now." She peered over her shoulder at Helsford, who also shrugged.

"The boys looked unharmed?" Somerton asked again.

Deep in the darkest pit of Ethan's stomach, dread stirred. As much as he admired Somerton, his former guardian and mentor was a ruthless bastard. Ethan's instincts screamed that he was about to feel the merciless edge of Somerton's implacable resolve. Again.

"Yes," Ethan said. "However, there's a hundred different ways of hurting a child without it being visible."

Somerton's gaze did not waver, though his jaw appeared to be carved from raw granite. "Follow the boys tonight and report back. If nothing appears amiss, finish your original mission and remove Giles Clarke from Abbingale tomorrow night."

Ethan's muscles went taut, an attempt to repulse the unsavory command. He would not stop to consider that he'd thought along similar lines after learning LaRouche had left the building. Perhaps he was no better than Somerton in this regard. Even then, he had not stopped to think about the fate of the other orphans. If it turned out that Abbingale was harboring French spies, the boys' home would have to be shut down.

Thirty homeless orphans. Some might be in a similar circumstance as Giles Clarke—forced to be there, but not without family. Others would abandon the system and strike out on their own—with no relatives or friends to help them navigate the perils of the city. And the rest? He supposed they would have to be relocated to another home for orphans.

Sweet Jesus. This was worse than crossing into enemy territory and facing capture around every corner. He prayed Somerton had a plan for Giles Clarke. Shuffling him from home to home would only serve to increase the boy's anxiety and awful loss. As for the rest of the orphans, he would speak with Sydney and see if she had any suggestions. She was good at finding new situations for people. Surely, such a skill could be applied to a bunch of orphaned orphans.

"Danforth, do you understand?" Somerton asked, his expression no less uncompromising.

Always a good soldier, Ethan capitulated, though he was certain he could already feel the fires of hell consuming him. "One more night." He did not cage the statement as a question.

"One more," Somerton agreed.

"As for Latymer's role in this possible courier scheme," Ethan said, changing the subject, "Miss Hunt's assistant has copies of Abbingale's annual reports for the last five years."

"How will those help us?" Cora's voice was rough with emotion.

"The reports list the names of Abbingale's donors and subscription holders."

"Do you think Latymer's name will show up in the register?" Helsford asked.

"Honestly, no." Ethan sighed. "He's much too careful to leave any type of trail for us to follow. All the same, I want to look at this from every angle."

"Thorough is always good," Somerton said. "Now, on to the second reason for my visit." He nodded toward Cora and Helsford. "And their primary reason for accompanying me."

Ethan had forgotten there was another reason. He had also somehow forgotten the drink in his hand. He bolted back the rest of the amber liquid and set the crystal on a nearby table. "I'm listening."

"Someone broke into my home last night and destroyed my study and library."

"Is everyone well?" Cora asked.

"No one was harmed."

"Anything missing?" Helsford asked.

"Not that I found. My personal papers were strewn everywhere, and the intruder seemed particularly interested in my file on the First Lord of the Admiralty, Lord Melville. Rather untidy to leave the file out for me to see."

"Please don't tell me we're back to the damned list," Ethan said. Sophie Ashcroft nearly lost her life because one of the Nexus's enemies believed Somerton had written the names of all his secret service agents on a very dangerous square of paper. Anyone who knew the former chief would know he would take his own life before placing his agents in danger.

"Either the list," Somerton said, "or something else entirely."

Ethan sent him an exasperated look. "Well, that narrows things down."

"If the intruder was searching for the nonexistent list," Cora said quickly, "we must assume Lord Latymer is still in the area."

"Yes," Helsford said. "Finding the former under-superintendent's weakness is of vital importance now."

"Weakness?" Cora asked.

"Helsford's right," Ethan said. "Latymer is an intelligent man. He must know by now that, if there ever had been a list, Somerton would have destroyed it the moment he sensed his enemy's interest."

"If he knows there is no list, then why the search?" Cora asked.

"A very good question." Somerton glanced between each of them. "One thing I do know is that Latymer is running out of time."

"Why do you say that?" Ethan asked, though he suspected he knew the answer.

"Twice, he has failed to deliver for the French," Somerton said. "The first time involved my assassination and the second was the agent list. Rather than achieving his goals, he lost his associates in the battle and disappointed the French. Whoever is manipulating his strings won't tolerate a third failure."

"Where do we go from here?" Helsford asked.

Somerton straightened. "Danforth continues his investigation. Follow a few boys, check for packages, and see what the annual reports uncover."

"What about us?" Cora asked.

"There is no *us*." Somerton's features hardened. "As I mentioned at the end of our last mission, you're on leave."

"But—"

"Helsford," Somerton cut in, "on the other hand, can look into Sophie's former governess's background. I want to know how Lydia Clarke got caught up in Latymer's scheme, which resulted in the boy's stay at Abbingale."

The mutinous look on Cora's face did not bode well for her ability to follow Somerton's directive. Ethan lifted an eyebrow in Helsford's direction. His friend's lips thinned in resignation.

"Send me updates as they occur." Somerton nodded and then left.

Cora made an irritated noise in the back of her throat. "Does he not realize that keeping my mind active is far better for my recovery than sitting for hours, with nothing to do but remember?"

Distracted by his own thoughts, Ethan said, "He feels a fair amount of guilt over your imprisonment. Keeping you out of harm's way is as much for his sanity as it is for your safety."

Ethan caught the astonished look on his sister's face, but he paid it no mind. She would do as she pleased, with or without Somerton's approval. As for him, his focus had shifted to the chief, or rather former chief.

Even though Somerton's new position gave him ultimate authority over the Nexus's activities, Somerton respected the chain of command, and he would want Helsford to be successful in his new role. Instead of deferring to Helsford, he had handed out orders as if he were still leading the Nexus. Why?

"As much as I appreciate the gesture," Cora said, interrupting his internal debate, "I cannot sit at home and do nothing." She glanced behind her. "Guy, you must take me with you."

Helsford smoothed his knuckle along Cora's jawline. "I hadn't planned on doing anything else."

"Shall we reassemble tomorrow?" Ethan asked.

Cora stood. "Yes, I look forward to hearing about what you discover tonight."

"Do you need assistance?" Helsford asked.

Ethan shook his head. "I don't foresee any problems."

Striding forward, Cora laid her hand on his forearm. "Invite your nosy proprietress to join us tomorrow."

"She knows nothing of the Nexus."

"Nor should she," Cora said. "She knows you're investigating a missing boy, right?"

He nodded.

"Then there is no problem." She stepped away and Helsford offered her his arm. "You can simply tell her we're helping with the search."

"You will find there is nothing *simple* about Miss Hunt."

Her smile was slow and knowing. "I'm glad to hear it."

"Cora—"

"Come along, Guy. We mustn't keep my brother any longer."

Helsford murmured, "Showed your hand, old man."

Ethan gritted his teeth as he followed the couple from the room. Helsford's pronouncement clattered inside his head like a badly tuned violin. One question surfaced, again and again.

What exactly had he shown?

Seventeen

Dear Madam,

The bearer hereof, Miss Lucy Prickett, is a young lady of honesty and obedience and has a strong sense of duty. She has served our family well for the last three years. It is with great confidence that I recommend Miss Prickett to you.

Madam, your most humble servant,
Diana Pinthorpe

SYDNEY READ OVER THE FALSE LETTER OF RECOMMEN-dation once more before passing it on to Amelia for distribution. No matter how many times she scripted recommendations, she always experienced a certain amount of angst. The same mantra filled her mind upon completion—did she manage the right tone? Provide enough information? Select the best words? She knew each recipient would read the letter with a certain amount of prejudice and expectation, making the whole process subjective and highly volatile.

So much depended on her getting it right. Livelihoods

hung in the balance and hope teetered on the edge. She rubbed her tired eyes. "Any more?"

Amelia shook her head, folding the letter. "This was the last one."

"I admit to being relieved by your answer."

"You've been at this for two hours, and the shadows are moving in." Amelia stood. "Shall I light another candle?"

Nodding, Sydney said, "Please summon Mac and Mick. We need to discuss our plans for this evening."

"Are you sure that's wise?" Her assistant sent her a wary glance. "Why not wait until tomorrow night, when you're better rested?"

Sydney dropped her pen in its holder. "Finding the link between Latymer and Abbingale has taken too long already. Every day that goes by feels like an eternity. Tonight, I will have an answer, one way or another."

Amelia was silent for a long second. "Perhaps a swift resolution is best. I fear we will not be able to fool Lord Danforth much longer."

"Nor I." Amelia started to walk away, then paused. "Do you have a moment? There's something I need to speak with you about."

"Of course. Please sit so I can see you better."

Her assistant strode around the desk and perched on the edge of a guest chair, with her hands clasped in her lap. "Four years ago, you gave me an opportunity, even after Mac uncovered my dark past."

"Mac never revealed what he found. And he assured me that whatever it was would have no negative impact on your duties here."

Amelia glanced down at her hands. "That was kind of him—and you. I shall never forget it."

Not liking the direction of their conversation, Sydney

leaned back in her chair and strove for calm. "What is it you're trying to tell me, Amelia?"

"I must go."

Sydney closed her eyes for a brief, heartbreaking second. "Why?"

"After all you've done for me, you deserve to know."

"But you won't—or can't—tell me."

A battalion of conflicting emotions swirled in Amelia's eyes. "I couldn't bear your hatred, too."

"Hate you? What do you mean?" Sydney asked, confused. Then it hit her. "Mac does not hate you."

"He does. And I can't blame him. What I did in my youth is too much of a bitter reminder to what he endured as a boy."

Mac never spoke of his youth. In fact, he avoided it like a disease. "I can assure you that my good opinion of you will not change—no matter what you reveal."

"How can you be so certain?"

Sydney sent her a gentle smile. "Because I know you, Amelia. Whatever you did, you did it for the right reasons or because it was the best option you had at the time."

A tear tracked down Amelia's pale face, and Sydney's throat prickled in reaction.

"I bore a son and then gave him away."

"Oh, Amelia." Sydney's throat tightened. "I'm so very sorry."

Clearing her throat, Amelia said, "I never lost track of him, despite the Foundling Hospital's protocol for changing the foundling's name upon arrival and then fostering the babies out to families in the country. My son will celebrate his fifth birthday next week. After which, his foster family must return him to the Hospital for the remainder of his care. When that day comes, I will reclaim him."

"How wonderful." Sydney had always thought Amelia was an extraordinary woman and amazingly talented. But this tale left her stunned and awed. "I'm so happy for you both. This is the reason you must go? Because you have a child?"

Amelia nodded. "This is a place of business. You cannot have a five-year-old running about, disrupting your meetings."

"We could hire a nurse to help watch over him."

"Thank you, Miss Hunt. Yours is a kind offer."

"You're still leaving me."

"I must. The disruption my son would cause is only one reason I must sever my employment."

"The other?"

Sydney watched the other woman's chest rise on a deep inhalation.

"I have developed inappropriate feelings for Mr. O'Donnell."

"Mac?" Sydney clarified.

"Yes," Amelia whispered. "After hearing about how their mother, without warning, shipped them to a home for orphans in London, my heart opened to him."

"Dear God. Why would she do such a thing?"

"You didn't know?" Amelia asked, her eyes rounding.

"No. Mac has never spoken of his childhood."

"Do you know about Mick's bones?"

Sydney nodded. "They're something of a precursor to danger, I believe."

"Yes, but they do much more than ache, at times. One morning, I found him writhing on the floor and that's when he told me their story."

She was missing something, and she knew it. Sydney stopped to consider the O'Donnells' mother and why she would abandon her children. That line of thought led her to their Irish heritage and how they would react to a boy who could forecast danger. "Please do not tell me that their mother sent them away because of some ridiculous superstition."

"Their mother's side of the family called it a curse."

"Of all the stupid, ignorant—" Sydney stopped her unladylike rant. It was pointless at this juncture in time. Somehow the O'Donnell brothers had survived their mother's betrayal and had become fine men in the process.

"Because of my past, Mac will never love me as I love him."

"Do not underestimate him, Amelia. I see how he looks at you."

Amelia bit her bottom lip. "Even if you are right, his attraction could never transform into love. How could it?"

"Tell him what you're planning to do."

"It will not change the decision I made in the past."

Sydney stared at her assistant, unable to come up with the persuasive words to change her mind.

"You have been kind enough to allow me to stay here without contributing to my room and board. Because of your generosity, I've managed to save most of my wages for the last four years."

"It won't be enough to live on your own and raise a child."

"Your statement would be true if I had not managed to invest a portion of my savings."

"Investments? Who is assisting you?"

"Your father." Amelia's pale face regained some of its color. "Not long after I started, you asked me to sit in on a meeting, where your father advised you on money matters. After several days of thought, I approached Mr. Pratt and asked for a recommendation on who I might speak to about investing my meager savings."

"He never said a word to me."

"You are surprised? Was it not your father from whom you learned the art of keeping confidences?"

Sydney's head was spinning. "Where will you go?"

"I found a little house just outside London, far enough away for my son to play with abandon and close enough for me to visit regularly."

"I should have known you would have it all worked out before you approached me." Sydney swallowed around a building lump in her throat. "I miss you already."

"And I you." Amelia swiped her fingers over her cheek. "I have much to do before next week, including finishing my research on Abbingale. Perhaps now would be a good time to collect the O'Donnells."

"Yes, thank you."

Once the door closed behind Amelia, Sydney buried her face in her hands. What would she do without the sure, anchoring presence of her assistant? They had worked together perfectly in every way, and Amelia had been with her since opening the agency's doors, as had Mac. It wouldn't be the same without her. Not only would she be losing her assistant, but in some way she would lose Mac, too. Despite what Amelia said, Mac had come to care for her—albeit it reluctantly—but he did care and was likely trying to figure out what to do about it.

Now she had this to worry about on top of managing Lord Danforth. She lifted her head and stared at the ceiling. Every conversation, every lingering look, every tangled feeling circled through her mind like the water-wheel of a gristmill. Images, words, and a vibrant, pulsing need to kiss the man senseless made her tired eyes grow heavier. Not with fatigue, but with a mixture of yearning and helplessness.

Earlier today, they had worked well together. Very

well. While searching for Giles Clarke, they had communicated with little more than a brush of their gazes. Each time his beautiful eyes had settled on hers, lightning arrowed straight into her core and quivered upon impact.

Now that he had found the boy, she wondered if she would see him again. The possibility that she would not did ghastly things to her body. Not the least of which, a blinding headache. Sydney squeezed the bridge of her nose, trying to stifle the oncoming pressure.

She recalled Amelia's prediction, and her faithful assistant's logic sawed through the pain of her loss. The more she was around Ethan, the more he might learn about her operation. She could not afford such exposure. She could *not*.

But a tiny seed of the forbidden had nestled itself in the depths of her heart. Would it be so bad if he discovered what truly happened at the docks? Given his work with the Nexus, did she honestly believe he would jeopardize her agency's more covert affairs?

A resounding no blared between her ears, and Sydney was warmed by the revelation. But, within seconds, her mind shied away of putting so much faith in someone she barely knew, someone who used people to obtain information. Someone who could so easily tempt her into setting aside years of caution and an obsessive need to protect her privacy.

The sound of approaching footsteps forced her to redirect her energies. She squeezed her eyes once, as if to blast away her dangerous musings. Releasing the bridge of her nose, she rolled her shoulders back and lifted her chin.

Amelia entered first, followed closely by Mac and then Mick.

Restless, Sydney stood and strode around her desk, being careful to keep her inner disquiet hidden from her companions. "Amelia, do you still have Abbingale's annual reports?"

"Yes."

"Did you come across Lord Latymer's name on the donor or subscription registers?"

"No. Latymer does not appear anywhere."

"What about his family name?"

"I did not think to search for his surname." Amelia frowned. "My apologies. That's an inexcusable oversight."

"Don't apologize. We cannot each of us think of everything. We're in this together. If you would, please scan the lists again, searching for any variation of his title and family name. Something tells me he's there, merely hidden beneath our noses."

"Of course." Her assistant made a note. "I'll locate our copy of *Debrett's Peerage and Baronetage* and look up Latymer's surname as well as other familial connections he might have used."

Sydney glanced between Mac and Amelia. "Have you uncovered anything on the staff at Abbingale?"

Mac deferred to Amelia. She said, "I met with one of our informants today—Lizzie Ledford."

"The seamstress?" Sydney clarified.

Amelia nodded. "Evidently, her sister is good friends with a maid at the Markham Boardinghouse."

A number of boardinghouses came to mind, but no Markham. "What is Markham's relevance?"

"It sits across the street from Abbingale," Mac said.

"Go on."

"The maid, Annie, witnessed an altercation there not long ago." Amelia's fingers clenched the stack of papers to her bosom. "The skirmish occurred between their tenant William Townsend and someone named Roosh."

"Roosh?"

Amelia shared a look with Mac. "After some discussion, Mac and I believe the name she heard was LaRouche, rather than Roosh. She was listening through the ceiling of the room below Mr. Townsend's."

Excitement stirred in Sydney's chest. "You're sure?"

"Not as much as we would like, but enough to recommend that we turn our attention to the schoolmaster."

"Anything else?" Sydney asked.

"Only that LaRouche wants something from Townsend," Amelia said. "But, as Mac pointed out, that's a given, considering the type of visit he paid the lodger."

Amelia's use of Mac's name for the second time distracted her for a moment. Could it be the two had formed a sort of truce over the last few days? A truce could lead to friendship, and friendship to love.

Mick spoke up. "While waiting for you today, I spied a gentleman slipping inside the same boardinghouse. I couldn't see his face, but the sight of him set my bones on fire."

Sydney sensed, rather than saw, Mac go rigid.

"William Townsend, do you think?" Sydney asked.

"Possibly."

Her gaze touched on Mick. "See if you can track down Cameron Adair. He might know of Townsend."

"The thief-taker's information won't come cheap." Mick's tone was grim.

"I'm well aware of the price of Mr. Adair's cooperation. But since my tour of Abbingale has proven mostly fruitless, I fear our options are rather limited."

Sydney understood Mick's distaste about working with Cameron Adair. The government paid the thief-taker a handsome reward for apprehending the city's most heinous criminals. In addition, theft victims—and no doubt victims of other lesser crimes—paid him a fee to locate their stolen property. She had also heard whispers that Adair wasn't opposed to charging an anti-prosecution fee to some of London's petty criminals so they could stay on the streets.

"What if he doesn't have intelligence on Townsend?"

"Then hire him to amend the deficiency."

Mick's handsome face scrunched up, as if he were trying to swallow a foul-tasting insect, only the insect was clinging to the back of his tongue.

"You don't have to befriend him. Simply get what information you can and bid him *adieu*. The more we can learn about Townsend, the better we'll understand LaRouche's position."

"If it were for anyone but you…" He allowed the thought to trail off.

His gruff sentiment made her smile. Mick could be serious when he needed to be, but most of the time, he swept through life with a wink and a grin. So, his reaction to working with Cameron Adair surprised her a little.

To Amelia and Mac, she said, "Focus your efforts on LaRouche. Who are his people? Why is he here? How long has he been in the country?"

They both nodded.

"It's time to enlist Specter's help, I think." Sydney's announcement produced three pairs of intent and expectant eyes. She understood their reaction. Her own anticipation shot through her like small, fiery arrows.

She peered at the clock—not quite noon. Specter never emerged before dark.

Eighteen

ETHAN BACKED INTO THE SHADOW OF THE TOWN house, allowing the darkness to shield him from too curious eyes. Then he waited. And waited. He waited for nearly two hours before the first boy climbed up from Abbingale's lower-level servant's entrance, or the *area*, as many were wont to call it.

He squinted into the gloom, scanning the boy's scrawny body for signs of a package. Nothing. The same as before. Though, to be certain, he would have to search the child.

Once the boy reached street level, he became a blur of movement. Even though Ethan's mind urged him to race after the boy, his instincts cautioned him to proceed with care. He held back a full five seconds before stepping into the betraying lamplight.

Rather than donning one of his many disguises, Ethan chose an uninterrupted black ensemble, from his well-worn Hessians to his borrowed wide-brimmed hat to his whiskered face. As he jogged down the pavement, he wondered which boy he tracked. Jacob? Noah? Arthur? Giles Clarke? Based on his quarry's size, Ethan narrowed it down to one of the younger residents of Abbingale.

A full street ahead of him, the boy darted to the right,

moving out of Ethan's line of sight. He increased his speed, no longer caring about the attention he drew. If questioned, the few individuals loitering the neighborhood would only recall a tall man dressed in black. A chap in a great hurry.

Several minutes later, the boy skirted across the next intersection and then barreled down a side street. Ethan followed, exertion burning low in his chest. It had been a long while since he'd given chase.

Minutes later, he became aware of the slow degradation of his surroundings. Tidy shops and corniced town houses gave way to ramshackle buildings. Clean paved streets turned into filth-strewn dirt roads. Pavements peppered with modestly dressed shopkeepers were reduced to bedraggled men and half-clad women. And London's normally odiferous air was clogged with a stench beyond anything Ethan had ever inhaled.

All this eased its way into his consciousness, and he slowed his pace in order to take better stock of his situation. Unlike the previous street, this one was teeming with people. Many sent him wary glances, others stared at him with territorial anger, and the rest paid him no mind, for they were otherwise *engaged*.

Focusing his attention ahead again, Ethan found the boy winding his way through the unsavory crowd as if he were dodging pesky vendors at market. A little before the next intersection, the boy veered toward one of the buildings on his left.

Lungs straining against the fetid air, Ethan slowed once again. The multistory stone structure sat alone, stark and gray-white, on a small parcel of land. Not a tree or shrub occupied a square inch of space. The moonlight seemed to favor the building, though. The ghostly facade pulsed with a strange glowing light.

Stuffing his hands in his pockets, he hunched his shoulders and continued past. Beneath the cover of his wide brim, he searched the area for a surveillance location he could use until the boy emerged again. A spot large enough to conceal his big frame and close enough to view the comings and goings of the glowing building.

He crossed to the other side of the hard-packed road, ignoring high-pitched feminine calls and an unnerving masculine whistle. Up ahead, he noticed about six feet of empty space separating two crumbling buildings. Having never been to this part of the city before, Ethan had no way of knowing what lurked beyond the darkness.

But his options were few. Actually, he had none. Too many people populated the area. Even the space between the buildings was questionable due to a group of older boys loitering on the steps of one of the structures.

Seeing no other alternative, Ethan tugged his hat lower and strolled toward the ruffians with slow menace. Their conversation halted at his approach. "Lads." He infused a smattering of East End into his voice.

"What you want?" the largest of the four young men asked.

"To get rid of you."

Three pairs of wary eyes glanced between Ethan and the gang's leader.

"This is our area," the leader said. "My brother won't like you causing us trouble."

"Your brother?"

"Jonas White. He owns this street."

"Owns it, does he? I suppose I could give Jonas my blunt."

"You didn't say nothing about any blunt."

"What will it take for the four of you to give up your perch for an hour?"

"Ten bob," the leader said without hesitation.

A small fortune for some. Ethan reassessed his opponent. The moment the young man mentioned his older brother, Ethan had assumed he was dealing with someone who rode on the coattails of his more dangerous brother. But the youngest White would be an enterprising—and lethal—member of this community in a few short years.

"I would be a fool to carry so much on me." Ethan lowered his voice. "You know I'm no fool, right?"

It was difficult to tell in the dark, but Ethan thought the young man paled. "Two bob. Take it or leave it." He lifted his chin.

Still a good deal of money, but he didn't have time to negotiate. "Half now." He bent to rub out a nonexistent smudge on his boot and deposited the coins on the step, then straightened. "Half later."

The leader began to protest. "Now wait a minute—"

"You've already made more in five minutes than you would in a year," Ethan said. "I'll add a sixpence to the second half if you're out of my sight in the next ten seconds."

The other three scrabbled up. "That's a half crown, Marty."

"I know what it is." Seeing he was outnumbered, the leader scooped up the coins and stood. "One hour, mister."

Once the quartet reached the pavement, they took off. Ethan followed their retreat, wondering if the leader would share the spoils with his comrades or not. Feeling the weight of time ticking by, Ethan glanced at the building where the Abbingale boy had disappeared. An unnatural stillness met his regard.

With measured steps, he inched his way toward the cavernous space separating the two buildings. Fragments of glass, stone, and only God knew what else cluttered his path, forcing him to alter his even gait. Soon enough, he reached the yawning chasm and peered around the edge. His eyes had adjusted somewhat to the lack of light, but no amount of squinting could penetrate the complete and utter darkness staring back at him.

Cocking his head, he listened for signs of disturbance from within. Nothing. Not even the scurry of tiny feet, though it was difficult to hear anything around the drum of his heart. He slid his fingers inside the left sleeve of his coat and drew a long, slender blade from the sheath attached to his forearm.

He inhaled a calming breath and then another one for good measure, all the while mentally bracing himself for a swift and violent impact. Exhaling, he crossed from one plane to the next. Once the shadows engulfed him, his heart dropped—right over the edge.

He wasn't alone.

Later, he would ponder what might have prompted his sure knowledge that something or someone occupied the space with him. Now, however, his mind was engaged in more lethal musings.

"Who's there?" Ethan pressed closer to the building, hoping his black garb would shield his exact location from the intruder. Given the level of darkness, he didn't think it would be a problem. As long as he stayed still. The moment he moved, a keen eye might discern the subtle shift of shadow within shadow.

Time suspended around absolute silence. Then something shuffled in the distance. Ethan's grip tightened around his weapon a second before the whisper of fabric reached his ears. Close. Too close. He crouched low and sliced his blade through the air, striking his target.

Air hissed between the intruder's teeth.

"Dammit," another roared, right before his fist connected with the underside of Ethan's jaw.

The power behind his assailant's blow catapulted Ethan onto his back, onto something sharp and hard. He clambered to his feet. Thankfully, he hadn't released his blade during his fall.

"Easy, my lord," a voice rasped. "You have no enemies here."

Surprise rippled through his pain-filled mind. "Who are you?" He sidestepped several paces until he blended into the building's brick wall again.

Cloth ripped. "It matters not. We were both unfortunate enough to happen upon the same hiding place."

A vague memory bumped against the barrier of his awareness. He tried to break through the membrane from the other side, to no avail. "How many are with you?" He sensed at least one other presence.

Another hiss of fractured air. "Enough to overtake you, if necessary."

"Perhaps not, if you're injured." He moved deeper into what must be some type of alleyway. Why could he not see dim light at the other end? If he could get behind the raspy-voiced stranger, he might be able to make out a silhouette or two or three.

"Danforth, I suggest you stop."

He had thought little of the intruder's use of "my lord," for Ethan had not attempted to mask his voice. Most individuals could be pinpointed to the region of England they're from by accent alone. Same goes for portions of the city and for one's access to wealth. But his alleyway companion knew him, which put Ethan at a disadvantage. A position he detested.

"We are acquainted?" he asked.

"I have a casual business arrangement with the cryptographer."

Helsford. Again, a memory pressed against his awareness like the point of a knife tenting a supple square of leather. If only he could see the stranger's face. Perhaps then, his memory might finally pierce the barrier.

"What sort of business arrangement?"

"The private kind."

Ethan's jaw clenched. "The two of you speak of me?"

"Only when the occasion warrants it. What brings you to the shadows, my lord?"

The stranger's question held only mild curiosity, a sign that his companion either did not care or did not need an answer. If the latter, the stranger must have been following him and already knew his reason for being here. Heat rose up the back of his neck and curled around the tips of his ears. His voice hardened. "I suspect you know why. Shall we dispense with the fencing match, or would you prefer to dance around all evening?"

A harsh sound, followed by more shuffling, echoed off the stone walls.

"Perhaps we can finish our round another time." The stranger's voice carried the same unruffled tone, but weaker somehow.

"You may count on it. Shall I exit first?" There was no sense in staying to watch the building across the way. No telling what had occurred in the last ten minutes. For all he knew, the boy was long gone.

"By all means, my lord."

Ethan used the same care leaving his hiding spot as he had entering it. He paused briefly to toss some coins on the step before backtracking his way to familiar territory. For a moment, he considered concealment again but discarded the notion almost instantly. Something told him that his alleyway companions wouldn't be so careless, or so bold, as to emerge from the gloom-filled cavern after him. And by the time Ethan found their hidden exit, they would be long gone.

Rather than waste any more of his time here, he tucked tail and made his way back to Abbingale to await the emergence of another child. Tomorrow, he would track down Helsford and find out who the hell was in that alley with him tonight—right after he pummeled the new chief for discussing Nexus business outside the Alien Office.

Nineteen

SWEAT DRIPPED IN SYDNEY'S EYE, THE SALTY LIQUID burning with a vengeance. But she dared not move. Not yet.

Across the alleyway where Ethan had skulked, Mac moved with lethal grace to the opening, his pistol at the ready. He peered around the corner. "He's gone." Releasing the hammer on his pistol, he stowed it away before reaching her side.

Only then did she allow her harsh breaths to shudder free. Unable to help herself, she leaned into Mick a little more. Thank God for the darkness. It had always been her friend. Tonight more so than any other. Not only had the gloom-filled alleyway protected her secret from Ethan, it had also shielded her from the sight of her own blood.

"How bad is it?" Mac asked.

"It's hard to tell in this damn cave," his brother answered. "A slash to the thigh. Her cloak might have protected the main artery, but I'm not sure. There's a lot of blood."

"Don't talk about the blood," she said through clenched teeth.

"Sorry, Syd."

"Dammit, Sydney, what were you thinking?" Mac demanded.

"The same as you." Sweat coated her body now and her face felt as if all the warmth had drained away. "M-mick did a good job of bandaging the wound."

"Grab her other side." Mick's voice sounded miles away. "We're losing her."

Sydney's eyes fluttered once, then she was gone.

❧

Someone with a gentle touch placed a cool wet cloth on Sydney's throbbing forehead. Relief was instant. "Mmm," she hummed. "Thank you, Amelia."

"You're welcome, even though I'm not Amelia."

Sydney's eyes didn't exactly fly open, for they were heavy with sleep, but she blinked them wide several times until Ethan came into view. "What are you doing here?" Her voice was crusty with disuse.

"Watching over you."

She took in her surroundings, recognizing the rich blue bed hangings, her mahogany writing box, and her small stack of travel guides. "I don't understand. Where are Amelia and Mac?"

"Amelia is sleeping and Mac is waiting unhappily in the corridor."

Lifting her head, she located Mac standing outside her bedchamber, with his arms crossed, watching them. He nodded but made no move to enter.

She melted back into the sheets. "What is going on? Why do I feel so leaden?"

"Blood loss from a knife wound."

A blast of memories flooded her vision. Following a boy from Abbingale. Hiding in an alleyway. Hearing Ethan bribing a group of ruffians. Holding her breath when he slid into the darkness with them. Scorching pain in her thigh. Fear of Mac shooting Ethan. The blood. Then nothing.

"Had you not been wearing such a voluminous cloak," he said in a low, gravelly voice, "I would have caused you a great deal more damage."

Panic shot through her veins. Had he pieced it together? Did he now know she had been both the maid and the cloaked figure at the dockside warehouse? Her gaze sought Mac's comforting presence, but Ethan's broad chest blocked her view. When she tried to scoot into a sitting position, pain lanced down her leg, stealing her breath.

"Easy," he said in a softer tone. "We'll discuss the alleyway incident later. For now, you must allow your body more rest."

"May I have some water?"

He moved to cradle her shoulders and head and then tipped a glass to her lips. "Slowly."

The cool liquid flowed into her parched mouth like the fresh burst of a spring breeze over a frozen meadow. She drank greedily until he eased the glass away. The effort left her panting with exhaustion.

He continued holding her, gently kneading her shoulders, running his hand over her hair, caressing her cheek, her neck, her arm. Sydney closed her eyes. It felt so good to be harbored within the cradle of his arms. But she couldn't be at ease.

"How long have I been in this state?" she asked.

His amazing fingers paused. "We crossed swords, so to speak, last night. It's now approaching breakfast."

"I feel as if I've slept the month away."

"Your assistant spent the better part of the night by your side. She only left an hour ago, after O'Donnell insisted."

"I don't know what I'm going to do without her." The words slipped out unbidden, and her gaze shot to Mac's. His face turned thunderous.

"Perhaps you might try for a little less excitement," Ethan said, missing the foregone nuance of her statement. "For her sake, if not for yours."

"Thank you." She gathered her strength and sat forward. "I believe I can manage on my own now." What she wouldn't do for a hairbrush and bathwater.

He rose from the bed and moved to the end, propping his shoulder against the bedpost.

The burning sensation in her thigh urged her to lie back, but she refused. Instead, she began to comb her fingers through her hair, while he rudely stared. She tolerated his behavior for all of three deep breaths before rolling her gaze up to his. "As you can see, I will survive. Please don't feel as though you need to stay."

"You don't think I will let you go that easily. Not after I've finally found you... both."

Sydney closed her eyes. So he knew. Not that she'd thought any differently, though a morsel of hope had stubbornly attached itself to her heart. All her careful planning and manipulation were for naught. If he hadn't already, he would soon learn the rest and then everything would change.

"Mind telling me how all this"—she twirled her finger around the room—"came about?"

"How I came to uncover your third identity, you mean?"

She set her jaw and narrowed her eyes, refusing to confirm the obvious.

He jerked his head toward Mac. "Perhaps your shadow can find something better to do than watch us talk."

Sydney hesitated. Having Mac or Mick nearby when

she was with a man had become second nature. She rarely registered their presence, because she knew they would always be there should she need them. But another part of her did not want Mac—her dearest friend—to witness what she was about to do.

"Mac." The large Irishman unwound his arms and strode forward. "Please escort Lord Danforth to my sitting room and then go get some rest."

Mac glanced between her and the viscount, his brows coiled in concern. "I'll get Mick to take my place."

"His lordship and I have some things to discuss." She paused meaningfully. "I'll be fine."

"I'm not so sure," Mac said. "You didn't see how angry he was last night when he followed us home."

Ethan pushed away from the bedpost. "My anger was directed at you for putting her in danger."

"Then your anger was misplaced, my lord," she said. "I do not answer to Mac or to any man." She peered at her friend. "Mac, please."

His lips firmed, pulling against his teeth until they lost color. Then he bent and whispered in her ear, "I'll be at the end of the corridor. Take the bell. It's on your bedside table."

He pivoted and took two long strides, placing his face mere inches from Ethan's. "One raised voice," Mac said. "That's all it will take for me to rip you apart."

"You think so?" Ethan brushed an invisible speck off the shoulder of Mac's coat. "I assure you, I am not so easily dismembered."

Mac knocked the viscount's hand away. "Follow me."

"Ten minutes?" Ethan asked her, though his query was more of a command.

"Of course."

When the door closed, Sydney flipped back the covers

to assess the damage to her leg. A large bandage wrapped around the middle of her thigh. Gingerly, she probed the outer edge of the linen, working her way toward the center until the pain became too much. She smoothed her fingers over a small three-inch ridge, guessing Ethan's blade had cut deep enough to require a few stitches.

She blew out a disgusted breath. This mishap would sorely limit her movements for a couple days and further delay her investigation of Abbingale Home. Now was not the time to dwell on her newest complication, though. First, she must prepare herself for the onslaught of questions and confessions she would soon face.

Easing her legs over the edge of the bed, Sydney hesitated. When she didn't break out into a sweat and the bedchamber didn't swim before her eyes, she pushed on, gaining her feet. She took her first tentative step and felt the skin around her stitches pull tight. She tested them a few more times and everything seemed to stay in place. On her way to the basin, she gave the bellpull two hard yanks. She would definitely need some help getting dressed today.

A quarter hour later, she limped into the sitting room, not caring a whit that she was late. The mother-of-pearl–handled cane her maid found thumped against the wooden planks. Rather than go through the torture of a corset and dress, she settled for a quick rinse and brush, clean chemise, and long wrap.

Ethan rushed to her side the moment he saw her. "Put your arms around my neck." He crouched down a little.

"Excuse me?"

He hooked one arm under her knees and the other around her back.

"Ethan, no!" Good God, she was too large to tote around like a babe.

Her protest went unheeded, and he lifted her against his chest. Sydney's arms clung to his neck. "Ethan, this is unnecessary. The cane was working fine." She would never admit to him that she found it difficult to balance her weight on such a narrow object.

"You should enjoy this rare glimpse of my gallantry."

Sydney studied his profile, noting the sharp edge of his cheekbone and the hard cast to his eyes. Anger seethed beneath every handsome angle, though she would never have known from the gentle care he employed while settling her into a cushioned chair. He even fluffed a pillow before wedging it behind her. She frowned, wondering at his solicitude when he was so furious with her.

"Thank you." She steadied her cane against the chair and straightened her clothes.

He began pacing. Every few seconds, he would halt and shoot his fiery gaze at her. This went on for nearly a minute. Long enough to tie Sydney's nerves into a hard knot.

Finally, he snapped. "Do you know how close I came to killing you?"

She stared at him, uncomprehending.

"Do you?" He advanced toward her.

"Ethan, I—"

He braced his hands on the chair's arms, caging her. "Another inch or two and I could have hit the artery. You would have died in that goddamned alleyway and I would never have known."

Remorse gnawed at her throat. His eyes burned with something far worse than anger. What she saw in those blue-green depths had nothing to do with her hiding the cloaked specter from him. No, what she saw raging in his eyes was fear.

She laid her hand on his forearm, felt the bone-deep tremor. "But you didn't. The wound will heal in a matter of days."

His chest rose and then he released a long breath. "I am not fond of you, at the moment."

"I know." His peevish tone made her want to smile. "This is probably not a good time to bring up the fact that I was in the alleyway first."

"No, it is not."

"Perhaps then, you might enlighten me on what happened after I blacked out."

"Fainted." He pushed away and plopped in a chair.

She snorted. "I have never done so in my life."

"Well, now you have. According to Mick, all he did was mention blood a few times, and out you went."

Sydney recalled the warm liquid seeping down her leg and the metallic scent that filled her nose and coated her tongue. A shudder rippled through her. "Let's change the subject, shall we? Please tell me what happened."

He smirked, though it did not last long. "When I left you, I had no intention of trying to locate the other entrance. I figured by the time I did, you would be long gone."

"Something changed your mind, or a stroke of good luck?"

"I suppose you could say both." His gaze dropped to her leg. "Instinct prevailed over logic, and your injury curbed my hasty retreat."

"So, you caught us leaving, recognized the twins, and followed us home?"

"Not at first," he said. "You and Mac were already in the carriage, and Mick's ragged clothing and hat concealed his features."

"Then you followed."

He nodded. "Imagine my surprise when the carriage I was tracking rocked to a halt outside your agency?"

Somehow she could picture the moment with perfect clarity. Probably because she'd had nightmares about him discovering her secret identity for days.

"Still, I had not yet put the one with the other." He rubbed the pad of his forefinger over his bottom lip, back and forth. Back and forth. "The lock of unruly hair was a perfect bit of misdirection, Sydney."

She had never heard her name spoken in such admirable tones. Not even from her parents. And yet, admiration wasn't the only emotion she heard tucked between the syllables. Her chest muscles squeezed tighter. "I suspect you are giving me credit for something I am not capable of masterminding, Ethan."

"There now," he said. "We are fast friends. It does not normally take me a sennight to persuade a beautiful woman to emphasize my name in such a fetching way."

"I suspect your women are too busy moaning their husband's secrets in your ear to say your name at all."

The roguish grin he had been casting her way dimmed, and something stormy took its place. "What do you know of it?"

"Enough."

His handsome face darkened. Instead of defending his actions, he went on the offensive. "Why did you hide the truth?"

"For the same reason you concealed your motives for seducing women," she hedged. "To protect."

"What truth are you talking about?"

She had gone too far. He only wanted to know why she had avoided his detection when all he wanted to do was thank her. But her mind had been on an even greater deception—the reasons behind her wearing the cloak.

"You do not trust me, I see. No matter—in time, you will." Leaning forward, he rested his forearms on his knees. "Let us continue down your previous train of thought. Why would I need to coax information from women?"

"To protect England, of course."

He canted his head to the side, more alert than ever. "What are you protecting?"

"Its people."

"From whom or what?"

"Men like you."

He exploded out of his seat. "What the hell is that supposed to mean?"

The hotheaded viscount finally made an appearance. This was the side of him that had led many, including his family and superiors, on one merry chase after another.

"Men of privilege and wealth," she said in her calmest voice. "Men who care for nothing but their own comforts and desires. Men who abuse their staff and then abandon them to a miserable fate. In sum, the aristocracy, my lord, of which you are a member."

Folding his arms over his chest, he started pacing again. "Do not think to lump me in with the profligates of my class."

"Tell me, when was the last time you took up a cause within the House of Lords?"

"You appear to know about a great many things you shouldn't. Perhaps you already have an answer for the question."

Sydney did not allow herself to be baited by his petulant comment. She let her silence unfold into an unspoken reprimand.

"I have been somewhat preoccupied of late," he said, when the silence stretched. "I haven't had much time for political squabbling."

"Ah, but effective political debate, or squabbling as you term it, is the backbone, the very marrow, of this great country. Without it, without you, the people have no voice."

He stared at her long and hard, his eyes burning with thoughts of an inner demon. Angling his head away, he transferred his tortured gaze to the window. "I rarely win an argument with my sister, and I don't seem to be faring any better with you," he said with unexpected candor. "How persuasive do you think I'd be in a chamber full of seasoned debaters?"

"Are you implying Cora and I are less fearsome than the House of Lords?"

"Less fearsome? No. More heart, yes."

Despite the voice of caution echoing between her ears, she said, "Ethan, you're passionate about everything you do. Passion paired with charm and persistence is a winning, or, if you'd prefer, a deadly, combination."

With aching slowness, he transferred his attention from the window to her. "Is it, indeed?"

Years of carnal knowledge entered his gaze, transforming his tortured countenance to one of warmth and hunger. She felt the power of his need, all the way to her feminine center. Anticipation. Fear. Unadulterated desire wove its tantalizing tentacles between every muscle, every nerve ending, every dream she possessed.

"Do not think to try to seduce me," she said. "My life is complicated enough."

"It doesn't have to be complicated. Only pleasurable."

"I see you consider the two exclusive of each other." She poured every ounce of conviction into her next words. "They are not."

"I assure you, they can be. With the proper guidance."

"Are you offering your services?"

"If I were?"

Sydney's toes hung over the precipice of a very bad decision. The businesswoman in her recognized the danger he presented. She did not share her affections often, and never on the level he was suggesting. Despite his assurances, she could lose her heart to this man, especially if she became intimate with him.

On the other hand, she was so tired of being alone. If spending an evening or two in the arms of an accomplished lover could assuage the burdensome emotion, why not learn from one so experienced?

She slid her toes toward the edge another inch. "I would want to know the rules."

The darkness behind his eyes swirled into a storm. Unfolding his arms, he strode to her. His brawny frame seemed to grow larger and more formidable with each step. She found herself pressing her spine deeper into the chair's cushioned back. Even while her mind grew annoyed with her body's subtle act of submission, she gathered herself to do far worse.

"The rules?" he asked. "As in a numbered list?"

Her shoulders squared the slightest bit. "Perhaps not something so formal, but there must be some type of code you mentally tick off."

He knelt in front of her, his muscular legs spread into a wide vee, cradling her. "Do you take nothing for chance?"

"No."

He skimmed the back of one finger along her cheek. "My rules were formed by habit, which have now settled into instinct."

"How many do you have?"

"Perhaps five."

Five. She opened her mouth to speak, but had to

draw in a breath of much-needed air first. "Instinct Rule Number One?"

The corner of his mouth curled up into a roguish smile. "Never feel with your mind, only your body."

"My mind?"

"Yes." He braced his free hand on her chair. "Do not think about the warmth of your lover's skin against yours, nor the tenderness of his touch. Feel it, enjoy it, but do not think on it. If you do, the memory will soon be etched on your mind and will grow life. And then you will yearn for it, yearn for your lover." His fingers began an erotic journey. They skimmed down her neck. "Yearning begets need." Traced over her throat. "Need begets emotion." And slid up the other side, cupping her cheek. "Emotion begets complication."

The more he told her not to think about the beauty he designed against her flesh, the more she concentrated on his seductive path. "Number two?" she asked through a shuddering breath.

"Lean forward."

Heart pounding, she angled toward him, feeling the skin around her stitches stretch. At that precise moment, she would have ripped them all out if that's what it took to hear his next words.

His thumb swept a caress over her cheek. "Kiss to stimulate your lover's arousal, not his affections."

The moment his lush, warm lips nuzzled the underside of her jaw, Sydney's eyes fluttered shut. She wanted this so badly. Had probably wanted it since the morning he opened his eyes inside the dockside warehouse.

Even then, with his swollen face, split lip, and bruised ribs, she had experienced an unnerving attraction to this man. He seemed broken in more ways than just his body. In the depths of his beautiful eyes, she saw resilience combined with vulnerability, determination with disappointment, and fear with murderous intent. The volatile mix had made her ache to take him into her arms and soothe it all away.

So, when Ethan's magical lips descended to the hollow of her throat, she could no longer recount the reasons to refuse herself this small moment of ecstasy.

"Arouse, my lord?" she asked in a voice not her own. "Is that what you're trying to do, or is this merely a lesson?"

"Perhaps it is both. Shall I proceed?"

Twenty

TIME NARROWED TO A SINGLE PULSE POINT ON THE proprietress's throat while Ethan awaited her answer. The rhythmic thrust beneath her flesh kept him transfixed long past what was appropriate. He knew he should lift his gaze to hers, but something primal would not allow him to shift his focus from the truth pounding against the curve of her graceful neck.

After weeks of searching, he had finally found his cloaked savior—and his determined nurse. Never once had he considered them one and the same. His pain-induced mind had created a larger-than-life, godlike figure lurking beneath the black cloak. At least now he knew how his savior managed to haul him from the alleyway to the warehouse. Her two hulking footmen could move a small building if they set their minds to it.

He still didn't know how he felt about the discovery. Last night, his overriding emotion was fear. When he saw Mac carrying her from the carriage into the agency, he was out of his mind with terror. He had struck a friend, not a foe. A woman, no less. A woman who had saved his life. A woman he was growing fonder of by the minute.

Then came the anger at her protectors, the betrayal

over her silence, and finally a sense of wonder at her bravery. In the darkness, she had mentioned a business arrangement with Helsford, or, rather, the cryptographer. Did that mean she knew of the Nexus, or did her knowledge stop at Helsford's special skill? One thing was for certain. If he found out that his friend had known his rescuer's identity all along, he would rip off the cryptographer's limbs one by one.

"Please do," Sydney whispered, wrenching him from his contemplative silence.

When Ethan had thrown out the challenge of engaging in an uncomplicated affair, he never expected the staid and careful proprietress to accept. But she had, and her every act of surrender tore at his heart.

Could he take her to his bed, as he had countless others, and simply walk away? He feared he knew the answer and still could not bring himself to stop. Because he wanted to feel her flesh sliding against his with an almost unbearable need.

He cupped her other cheek. Soft and delicate. Courageous and intelligent. Humble and caring. He held it all in the palm of his hand.

"Shall we make this unforgettable?" He kissed the corner of her mouth.

Opening her wrap, she said, "It already is." She turned her head until their lips slid into a union so perfect that the backs of his eyes stung with an unfamiliar emotion.

Groaning his approval, he increased the pressure of his lips and then softened them again. Over and over, he built her anticipation and, in return, his. He broke free to sample the vulnerable softness of her long, beautiful neck. The erratic pulse beneath his lips urged him lower and lower until he met the diaphanous barrier of her chemise. The backs of his fingers trailed along the same path as his mouth, not stopping at the fine linen barrier. They trailed over her generous bosom, pausing just before her straining peak.

He ached to take her breast in his mouth, twirl his tongue around her sensitive bud, and draw hard on it until she keened her pleasure. The need to taste her delicate flesh pounded between his ears, deafening him to reason. In less than three seconds, he could have his placard open, her chemise lifted, and his cock inside the slick warmth of her passage. A shudder of repressed passion racked his body, and Ethan nearly spilled right then and there.

Swallowing, he peered up at her. "Not only am I a cad, but I'm also a fool."

She tunneled her fingers into the hair above his left ear. "No, Ethan. Never." Arching her back, she brought the object of his torment ever closer to his mouth.

"You don't understand. My c-control," his voice cracked, "eludes me with you."

"Then set it free." She hooked her fingers over the neckline of her chemise and pulled it low until one perfect mound was exposed. Her fingers curled into the back of his head, and Ethan was lost.

His hand traveled up her rib cage to the underside of her breast, pleased with how she overflowed his large palm. Then his mouth covered her engorged nub, and they both groaned their satisfaction. Her skin was spun from the most exquisite silk, a cool layer of perfection covering molten desire. He inhaled her feminine scent, memorized the texture of her unblemished skin, and trembled against the telling sounds of her passion.

"I have longed to feel you in my arms," she whispered around harsh breaths.

"As have I." He retraced his path back up to her lips.

Hours. He could spend hours learning every curve and valley of her body, locating every unexplored nook of her mouth.

She skimmed her hands up his arms and over his shoulders. The gesture was equal parts intimate and innocent, and Ethan found himself on the verge of consuming her entirely.

But, in that one simple motion, something reached into the haze of his desire and grasped the last cord of rational thought. She was an innocent. He knew it to the depths of his debauched soul. How she had managed to protect something so precious, given her predilection for dangerous activities and unsavory people, he knew not. She had, though, and she was handing the invaluable gift to him. The realization encased his body in a slab of ice.

He did not deserve such a rich offering. For more years than he wished to count, he had used his body to swindle information from wives and mistresses of powerful men. Good God, did he even know how to make love for pleasure, and pleasure alone? Even if he did, he could not do so with this woman. She deserved far better than the likes of him. A boudoir spy.

And, if all of that wasn't reason enough to halt this madness, she had sustained a nearly life-ending injury. One delivered by his hand.

With an almost crushing reluctance, he ended the kiss, removed his shaking hands, and sat back on his heels. His nails bit into his palms. After a moment, she opened her eyes, languid and filled with unspent desire. The sight nearly sent him back into her arms. Instead, he managed a smile. "You're lovely, Sydney. Truly lovely."

The compliment seemed to shake the languorous hunger from her features. She fixed her chemise, pulled her wrap closed, and folded her hands together in her lap. "A rather vapid c-commentary," she said, with a slight catch in her throat, "on my ability to stimulate your arousal."

He wanted to touch her, to reassure her, though he feared making matters worse. "Vapid? My words were not meant to diminish your effect on me. You did quite well in stimulating my interest, I assure you."

Her attention flicked downward, causing his gut to clench. "Don't believe me, sweet Sydney? Allow me to show you."

Rising up on his knees, he watched her expression and knew the exact moment the material of his buckskin breeches grew taut over his painful erection. Her eyes widened and her cheeks flushed.

To make sure she never doubted her power over him, he caressed his pulsing manhood with one long upward stroke and then squeezed. "This is all you, Sydney. All you."

"If you want me, why did you stop?"

"And run the risk of hurting you more?" He laid his hand on the knee of her injured leg. "I couldn't."

The hard click of her swallow reached his ears. He glanced at her and noted tears shimmering in her eyes. "I've upset you. My sister was right. I have the finesse of a battering ram." Even though he knew he shouldn't, he once again cradled her cheek within his palm. "Do not cry, I beg you."

Shaking her head, she closed her eyes and pressed into his warmth. Tears filled her lowered lashes until they became too heavy and a fall of liquid pearls dripped onto her cheeks.

"No, Ethan. You did not upset me. Quite the opposite." She lifted her lids. "You've begun to heal my soul."

Twenty-one

ETHAN LOCATED HELSFORD AT THEIR CLUB ON ST. James Street.

As he meandered his way through Brooks's, he searched the exclusive gentlemen's club for his friend's familiar queue of long, dark hair. Leave it to Helsford to retain the old ways when men all around him were favoring a shorter, more elegant cut.

He still hadn't decided how he would broach the subject of Sydney's connection to Helsford without it looking like she had betrayed a confidence. In the dark alleyway, she had used her partnership with Helsford as a means of keeping everyone calm. She couldn't have known Ethan would identify her minutes later. After his aborted seduction in her sitting room this morning and her astounding revelation, he hadn't had the heart to press her on the subject of why she had kept her alternate identity from him.

Though, with a cooler mind, it didn't take him long to guess at her reasoning. She had no way of knowing how he would react to the news of a woman aiding the Nexus. Would he reveal her secret? Force her to stop? Tell her father? Kill her for knowing too much?

Set about destroying her business? He suspected her reticence had something to do with the latter.

The Hunt Agency was everything to her. She had gained independence through her business and provided a much-needed safe haven for her service clients. If she lost the agency, she would not be the only one affected. Something in her past drove her efforts. Drove her to help those who had been wronged by wealthy, narcissistic men.

Ethan's stride slowed. Could that be what happened to her mother all those years ago? Something awful must have occurred for Sydney not to carry her natural father's surname. Then he recalled the reason behind her family's attendance at the Marchioness of Shevington's dinner party. Sydney's mother had been a childhood friend of the marchioness's, a woman born of humble beginnings.

Had Mrs. Pratt been in service? The connection—all the connections—made perfect sense. Sydney's damning words returned.

Men who care for nothing but their own comforts and desires. Men who abuse their staff and then abandon them to a miserable fate. In sum, the aristocracy, my lord, of which you are a member.

How had her mother been wronged? He focused his attention on Sydney's one comment—*Men who abuse their staff and then abandon them to a miserable fate.* Ethan's growing elation of piecing together Sydney's past deflated as the answer became all too clear.

As with so many domestic female servants, Mrs. Pratt must have been the victim of her employer's lust. Hadn't Sydney referred to herself as a bastard spinster during their first meeting? Uncovering her mother's awful secret answered another one of his questions. He now had an idea of what Sydney had survived during the first years of her life. Poverty, ridicule, hopelessness, and a host of other conditions too terrible to contemplate.

No wonder she felt compelled to help others. She remembered. Remembered what it was like to have nothing. Nothing until an act of kindness from one caring individual changed everything. In Sydney and her mother's case, the act of kindness arrived in the form of Jonathan Pratt.

"Danforth, why are you standing in the middle of the room, looking equal parts murderous and miserable?"

Ethan glanced around Brooks's drawing room to find it empty except for Helsford, who peered at him above the morning paper. "I was contemplating what I'm going to do to our missing baron when we find him."

"And the misery?"

"Somerton probably won't allow it."

"Ahh, that would explain it. Were you looking for me or someone else?"

Ethan sagged into an adjacent chair, picking up the yellow-and-white-veined marble paperweight. "You."

Helsford folded the paper and tossed it on a table before leveling his black, unfathomable eyes on him.

"What can you tell me about your informant?"

If anything, Helsford's face became even more inscrutable.

"An interesting question. Especially since we make it a rule not to discuss our informants."

"Yes, in most circumstances. I agree it is best not to reveal the details about them. Once we break an informant's confidence, their trust is lost to us forever."

"I predict that you're going to ask me to make an exception."

Ethan nodded. "For the one who knows you as a cryptographer."

"You have met, then."

"The individual I met mentioned a casual business arrangement, so I could only guess as to what that meant."

"A rather one-sided arrangement, I'm afraid. Specter occasionally solicited news about Somerton, but that's been the extent of our sharing."

"Somerton? You did not find that odd?"

"Of course I did. However, the questions ventured no deeper than inquiring about his health."

Ethan tucked that bit of information away. "Specter, you say?"

"It's the name I use to summon him," Helsford said. "I write *Specter* on a piece of paper and place it in any one of a dozen locations throughout the city. A few hours later would find us standing in a dark alcove, one of his choosing."

"Can you give me the barest of descriptions?"

"Tall, raspy yet menacing voice, hooded cloak."

Lifting his brow, Ethan asked, "Have you never seen Specter?"

One corner of his friend's mouth quirked up. "No."

"How do you know it's a *him*, then?"

Helsford thought about it for a second. "I suppose I don't, though I was never given a reason to suspect he was a she."

"Nor she a he."

His friend released a wry smile. "True. What do you know?"

This time, it was Ethan's turn to hesitate.

"Danforth, I've given you details about my most valuable spy." Helsford's tone was laced with a subtle warning. "I expect the favor to be returned."

For the first time in days, Ethan allowed himself to view his friend as something other than an adversary for the Chief of the Nexus position. Helsford had the same strength of will and implacable resolve as Somerton. He did not allow his temper, nor his emotions, to guide his decision or actions. The only difference he could see between the two agents was Helsford had a line he would not cross and, as far as Ethan could determine, Somerton had none. Is that what it took to be an effective chief? The ability to command anything—for the greater good? If so, few he knew could live up to Somerton's standard, but Helsford came closer to the ideal than Ethan.

"You will make a good chief," Ethan said, surprising himself.

Helsford blinked, uncomprehending. "Are you privy to information I am not?"

Ethan frowned. "Somerton has not asked you to assume the chief's position yet?"

"No, why would he?"

"Because you are his chosen replacement." Ethan said the words with care, even though Helsford's reaction indicated that Somerton had not approached his friend yet about the position. Why was Somerton waiting? The sooner Somerton appointed a replacement, the faster everyone would settle in to the new routine.

"He told you this?" Helsford asked.

"Yes, last Thursday."

"So long ago," Helsford mused. "Is that why you've been in such a foul mood?"

"You make me sound petulant."

"Or very disappointed."

"I had waited a long time for the opportunity." Ethan heard the defeated tone in his voice. "And then it was gone. My reaction to the news had nothing to do with you."

"News that never materialized." His friend's voice held a new intensity. "I wonder why?"

Ethan waved off the question. "He's waiting for the right time. Latymer still eludes us, and this issue with Abbingale complicates everything."

"Why discuss my appointment with you? Do not take offense, but I would think it would be more appropriate to discuss the issue of my appointment with Superintendent Reeves."

He knew Helsford was right and that his irritation over the comment was unreasonable. But rational thought did not stop him from biting back. "Once he received my blessing, he was going to speak with the head of the Alien Office next."

"Dammit, Danforth. Did Somerton know how badly you wanted the chief's position?"

"How could he not? I've spent the last decade proving to him that I could step into the position."

"But did you *tell* him?"

"Of course not. How would I have gone about informing him of my interest? *Say, Chief, when you're ready to move on, I'd like your position.*"

Helsford's eyes narrowed. "What did you say to him when he asked for your blessing?"

Ethan glanced away, not wanting to relive the painful memory. "I told him you would not disappoint him."

"You told him—" Helsford leaned forward in his seat, propping his forearms on his knees. "Did you not think to challenge him on his decision? Did you not try to fight for what you wanted?"

Angry now, Ethan said, "At the expense of my friend? No. Never."

"And that's why you'll never be chief."

The verbal blow struck with a vehemence that knocked Ethan off-balance. "What did you say?"

"He was testing you, Danforth."

Ethan blinked, fighting back the strange layer of fog that had settled on his mind. "Testing me?"

"To see how badly you wanted the position."

"What about you?"

"Somerton knows where I stand on the subject. After his promotion, I made it clear that I had no desire to lead the Nexus."

"So, it was all a damned lie? How he preferred Cora, but she was too damaged, so he picked you. Though he thought you might be too distracted by your concern for my sister. That's why he wanted to discuss your appointment with me. I knew you best, he said. Did I think you'd be a liability to the Nexus? he asked." Ethan shot to his feet and threw the paperweight as hard as he could against the far wall. The heavy marble sank deep. "Who the hell does the bastard think he is to meddle with our minds in this way?"

Rising, Helsford said, "Someone who knows what it takes to lead the Nexus and retain a modicum of his humanity. You have too much heart, my friend. Be glad you escaped."

Ethan barely heard Helsford's words. His mind was stuck in a web of humiliation and despair. What would he do now? Knowing the extent of Somerton's duplicity changed everything. He wished he could purge the last quarter hour from existence, for he could no longer blame Somerton for losing the position. That honor belonged to him, and him alone.

"I must go." Ethan swung around and made for the exit.

Helsford said, "I haven't forgotten about Specter. You owe me details."

"Tomorrow." It was the only answer he could manage. He needed to clear his head, escape the painful reminders. What he wouldn't give to sink inside a willing body right now. A woman who didn't mind it rough and without pleasantries. An image surfaced, with Sydney beneath him, her legs splayed wide and her body rocking with each of his powerful thrusts.

If only she were ready for such an invasion. He wouldn't stop there, though. Once their bodies had recovered, he would love her again. The next time slow and purposeful. He would make her come first with his mouth and then with his cock, but not until she begged for release.

"Danforth." A new, familiar voice intruded. "I'm glad to have caught up with you."

Halting mid-stride, Ethan peered into hard, crystalline eyes. Eyes he'd hoped not to see for a long while.

"Somerton."

Twenty-two

LEANING AGAINST A LARGE OAK TREE TRUNK, WILLIAM Townsend watched the woman with the shocking red hair make her way along the park's footpath. He checked his timepiece—precisely half past eleven. Punctual, habitual, and female, a perfect combination.

He followed her progress as she made her way toward his location. The redhead was not an attractive woman, nor was she difficult to look upon. No, Margaret Finley was average in every way—features, intelligence, height, bosom. Every way except her feet, he amended. Her feet were small and attached to the prettiest ankles he'd ever seen. And William had seen quite a few.

When she drew close enough for him to see her eyes, he was pleased to note the glint of excitement reflected in their depths. "Fine morning to you, Margaret."

She halted at the sound of his voice and her gaze searched the area. The moment she located him by the tree, her lips curled into a sunny smile of welcome. "Will, you came."

For some time, he'd understood the impact his countenance had on women, especially females who were not accustomed to focused male attention. He found their vulnerability rather pathetic, though he had used it often to his advantage. As he would now.

"Of course I did, love." He straightened but did not leave the shelter of the tree. Instead, he motioned for her to come to him, infusing as much desire as he could into his dark gaze.

An unflattering shade of crimson blossomed along her throat and into her spotted cheeks. As many would in her situation, she glanced left and right in a pitiful show of modesty. Satisfied no one would witness her clandestine meeting, she plodded across the length of lawn until she stopped beside him, breathless.

He skimmed the back of his knuckle down the length of her cheek. Soft and smooth. Like Lydia's. "You're looking quite fetching today, Margaret."

"Thank you." She rolled her bottom lip between her teeth. "Not as fetching as you, Will. I swear you'd be the handsomest gentleman in Hyde Park, wearing nothing but a potato sack."

Stepping closer, he said, "Perhaps we might test a portion of your theory later."

"Let's go, nurse," a small, petulant voice demanded.

Margaret's shy smile dimmed, and she turned to the toddler sitting in a sturdy wooden carriage. With his chubby fingers clutched around the rim, he made emphatic go-motions with his upper body.

"Now, Master Henry, you must be patient," Margaret-the-nurse said. "We'll be off in a moment."

"Want to see ducks." His go-motions rocked the carriage forward an inch or two.

Margaret sent William an apologetic smile. "He's in a demanding mood today."

"Another Great Tyrant in the making," William said, referencing the toddler's illustrious grandfather's sobriquet.

"Pardon?" Margaret's confusion clearly stated her awareness of political affairs.

William smiled. "Nothing, my dear. Shall I show you a shortcut to the Serpentine?"

A look of uncertainty crossed her spotted face. "Will you show me the way back to this footpath? I'm so easily lost in this big park and all its various walks and paths."

"Of course. We will take the footpath behind us, which will bisect the main carriage route and lead us straight to the Serpentine."

Her dull blue gaze tried to follow his verbal directions, though she appeared to lose track at the word *bisect*.

"Nurse, I want ducks."

Margaret glanced between the demanding toddler and William.

"Trust me." William smoothed a strand of flaming hair behind her ear. "I won't lose you."

"Then I would love to see your shortcut, sir." She grasped the carriage handle and began to pull it across the bumpy lawn with some difficulty.

William ignored her struggle until other pedestrians came into view. He peered down at her in feigned surprise. "Allow me, my dear. Master Henry's carriage must be quite burdensome to draw across such uneven ground."

"Oh, no, sir," she said in horror. "It is only a little ways more."

"I insist." William gave her no more opportunity to argue. He towed the toddler over the lawn and down the footpath, while maintaining a constant chatter with the nurse. Once they crossed the main carriage route, the woodlands thickened, providing a natural shield.

Even though the blood in his veins pumped more wildly, William kept his gait even and his voice calm. His gaze was another matter. With systematic precision, he scanned his surroundings for anything out of the ordinary and for familiar faces.

Soon, he would have the means to satisfy LaRouche's newest ultimatum. Regret shot through his chest. He found his current course distasteful, but no more than any of the other directives LaRouche had given him in recent weeks. This would be the last time he bent to the Frenchman's demands. He had already booked passage for two to America. In twenty-four hours, England would be nothing more than a speck of dirt at his back.

They came to the intersection where their footpath crossed one of the main routes. Outside of a couple carriages, a stray rider, and a small group of uniformed children, the wider gravel walk was fairly deserted at this time of day. Such would not be the case this afternoon. Once the fashionable hour approached, the children would disappear and this part of Hyde Park would teem with gleaming carriages and elegant riders.

"Ready?" William asked the nurse, who nodded in return. "We'll cross after this carriage passes."

But they had idled too long for the toddler. "I want ducks!" the future Viscount Melville screamed at the top of his lungs.

Heads swiveled toward them. William jerked his chin downward to protect his features from curious onlookers. Furious, he threw his leather coin purse in the child's lap to shut him up.

"Oh, Will," Margaret cried, making the situation worse. "Your purse." She bent to retrieve it.

He grabbed her arm, halting her interference. "Leave it. The sound will keep the child entertained until we reach the du—waterfowl."

She peered up at him with wary eyes. "You're hurting me."

He released her and then smoothed the backs of his

fingers over her upper arm. "My apologies, love. I'm not used to such squealing and fear I overreacted."

The nurse smiled, though the beam seemed weaker than before.

Movement to the right caught his eye. An open-top carriage pulled to the side to speak with two women and a child on horseback. A ribbon of unease skipped down his spine. One of the riders sparked a faint sense of familiarity. He narrowed his concentration on the equestrienne with the yellow bonnet. Her seat was accomplished and her figure slender. Beneath the bonnet, he could see that her sable-colored hair was styled in a close-cropped fashion. It wasn't until she tilted her head just so that he noticed the scar.

His chest rose on a harsh intake of breath. He knew of only one woman whose beauty was marred by such an unfortunate disfigurement.

Cora deBeau. Raven. One of the Nexus's most valuable secret service agents. Once his comrade, now his enemy.

William spared a glance around the area to make sure no other agents lurked nearby. He detected none, but with the Nexus, one could never be certain. Sweat pebbled on his upper lip. He was torn between retreating to a safe distance and finishing his task. When he glanced back at the group of women, he found a footman on horseback staring right at him.

The toddler jangled the coin pouch. "Ducks, ducks, ducks."

William grabbed the toddler from the carriage.

"What are you doing?" Margaret asked.

"Making it easy for us to cross," he said. "Come along."

With long strides, he set out for the other side. He heard a *plop-ping* sound, but paid it no mind. Master Henry started to fuss.

"Will, wait," Margaret said. "He dropped your coins."

He did not slow his pace.

"Go back," the toddler said, stretching his body over William's shoulder.

William smacked the boy's bottom. "Hold still. We're almost to the ducks."

The swat rendered the child silent for all of three seconds and then he released a blood-curdling scream.

"Will, stop!" Margaret's voice grew more distant. "Someone, help me. Please."

Cursing, he half walked, half ran toward the dense tree line. About twenty feet away, he chanced a glance at the Raven and her group. Raven and the footman wheeled their mounts in his direction.

"Let me go!" the toddler yelled, wiggling in earnest. "Nurse!"

"Master Henry!"

The shadows from the canopy closed in around William, and the brush grew thicker. Another quick check behind him revealed he was no longer visible, though he could hear the distinctive sound of horse's hooves bearing down on him.

He tossed the toddler over his shoulder, like a side of beef, and ran.

Twenty-three

A WOMAN'S SCREAM OF TERROR PIERCED THE SERENITY of Sydney's outing. Craning her neck, she noticed a distraught woman standing at the edge of the gravel path and a gentleman carrying a child, walking quickly toward the woodlands. "What's going on?" She rose to her feet for a better look.

"Stay here," Mac commanded, with a severe look in her and Amelia's direction. He kicked his horse into motion.

"Sophie," Catherine Ashcroft said, "come to me."

Sydney watched as the seven-year-old did as her mother bid, though her gaze kept slashing back to the unfolding tableau ahead. "What's happening, Mama?"

"A minor family squabble," Catherine said. "Nothing for you to worry about, but I want you to stay by my side, understood?"

"Uh-huh."

"Rigby," Sydney said to her driver, feigning nonchalance for Sophie's sake, "I'm stepping down."

"I'll hold them steady, miss."

Amelia laid a restraining hand on her arm. "You're injured."

Sydney patted her friend's hand. "I'm not going far, I promise." Using her walking stick, she thumped her way toward Cora, who sat on her horse, tense and ready, staring at the spot where Mac disappeared into the woodlands.

After Ethan had left that morning, Sydney had removed the bandage and noted the damage wasn't as bad as she had feared. The knife wound was raw and tender, but barely deep enough to need stitches. She gave the area another thorough cleaning, lathered it with a foul-smelling salve left by Amelia's apothecary and then she insisted on a drive through the park. Her decision was met with much tsking by her assistant and scowling by her bodyguard. With Mick gone to meet the thief-taker Cameron Adair, she was spared his opinion.

In the end, she won the row, reasoning they could use the opportunity to touch base with any of their service clients who might be in the park. Although they had not run across any clients, their paths had crossed with these three interesting young ladies.

Sydney sidled up next to Cora's horse and noticed the agent's right hand rested on something at her waist. Standing there calmly was one of the hardest things Sydney had ever done. Had Mick been with them, she would not have felt quite so anxious.

"I don't like the feeling of this," Cora said in a low voice.

"Nor do I." Sydney couldn't take her eyes off the place where Mac had disappeared. "That wasn't a domestic issue."

"No. How skilled is your footman under difficult situations?"

"Very. Though the child might complicate things." Sydney peered up at Cora. "All appears to be well here. Perhaps, you might check on Mac while I speak with the child's chaperone."

The agent met her gaze; a wealth of understanding passed between them. Cora nodded and kicked her horse into motion.

Over her shoulder, Sydney said to Amelia and Catherine, "I'm going to go speak with the child's—" she glanced at Sophie, "mother."

In an uneven gait, she hurried to where the woman paced at the edge of the tree line. Given her attire and the way she referred to the child, Sydney doubted the woman was the child's mother. More like his nurse. "Hello, I'm Sydney Hunt. Are you harmed?"

"I'm fine." The woman paused. "What's happening? Why would Will steal Henry?"

"I don't know." Sydney settled her hand on the woman's back. "But my friends will bring back your child." She prayed she was telling the truth.

"He's not my boy. I'm Margaret Finley, his nurse. Was his nurse. Once Mr. Saunders-Dundas finds out I lost his heir, I'll be sacked for sure."

"Saunders-Dundas," Sydney repeated, stunned. "Robert Saunders-Dundas?"

"Yes, ma'am," the nurse said. "Do you know him?"

"Only by reputation." Sydney's mind raced. "Did you know the gentleman who ran off with your charge?"

Margaret's face crumpled. "Not well. I met Will yesterday. He was so gallant and charming. Said he wanted to see me again today." She blew her nose in a handkerchief. "What could he want with Master Henry?"

"What's Will's surname?"

Margaret's gaze dropped to the ground, her eyes frantically shifting from side to side. "He never told me," she whispered.

Sydney rubbed the nurse's back, feeling an odd kinship with the woman. Movement near the tree line caught her attention. Cora guided her mount out, her expression murderous. The hope Sydney had been carrying in her heart plunged into her stomach. Then she caught a glimpse of Mac's dark head.

Relief washed away the dread. They were both safe. But the child—her throat closed.

"Ducks," a small voice cried. "Want to see ducks!"

Margaret's head whipped up. "Master Henry." She ran toward the trio.

The plump-cheeked child sat in front of Mac, waving his arms in frustration. She smiled and followed the nurse at a more sedate pace.

"Thank you, sir." Margaret pulled the child from the saddle and hugged him close. "Thank you so much."

Sydney stepped closer to Mac and Cora, while the nurse cooed nonsensical words into her charge's ear. "What happened?"

"He was not able to lose us in the woodlands like he thought," Mac said in a quiet, dangerous tone. "So he dropped the child to distract us."

Cora said, "When the kidnapper broke free of the underbrush, he knocked a gentleman off his horse and took off."

"Everyone is all right?" Sydney asked.

"Yes."

Sydney checked the nurse's location before asking, "Who was it?"

"I don't know for certain," Mac said.

"But you have a guess."

A muscle in Mac's jaw jumped. "A loose one."

"Mine is better than loose," Cora said.

"Who then?"

"Lord Latymer."

Twenty-four

ETHAN SAT IN SOMERTON'S DRAWING ROOM, LISTENING with half an ear to the conversation around him. Anger, humiliation, frustration, and a heightened sense of expectation spiraled inside his mind like a child's top spinning out of control. He'd said little since Somerton had retrieved him and Helsford from Brooks's a half hour ago.

For the first time in his life, he hadn't the faintest idea of what to say or how to act around his former mentor. Part of him wanted to apologize for being a damned fool and throwing away his chance at the chief's position. Another part of him wanted to beat the manipulating bastard to a bloody, unrecognizable stump. Both notions turned his stomach sour and his heart cold.

Besides all that, the waiting scored his nerves raw. Cora and Catherine would be here any moment and then the group would discuss the latest regarding the Clarke-Latymer situation. Hours would pass before he could go to Sydney. He had so many questions. Was she Specter? Why did she become the elusive underworld spy? Who else knew? Why had she saved him and then disappeared?

Most of all, he simply wanted to be with her. Wanted

to discuss Somerton's test and how he'd failed it. Wanted to touch her, kiss her, hold her in his arms.

Sweet Jesus, forgive him. He wanted to bury every ounce of regret and disappointment in her warm body and have her soothe it all away.

"They're here," Somerton said from his position by the window.

Ethan rubbed his hands over his face and sat up a little straighter. Perhaps, if he could hurry their meeting along, he might still be able to see Sydney before going to White Horse Street and plucking Giles Clarke from Abbingale Home. Which reminded him that he still didn't know why Sydney had been traipsing around the other night. So many questions.

A minute later, Catherine Ashcroft burst into the drawing room and went straight to Somerton at the window. "Good afternoon, Lord Helsford. Lord Danforth." She peered up at her soon-to-be-betrothed. "Lord Somerton."

The ever-serious spymaster's lips stretched into a smile, and he dutifully bussed her proffered cheek. "Mrs. Ashcroft."

"Ethan!" Sophie Ashcroft exclaimed, running into the room. She climbed onto his lap and wrapped her bony arms around his neck. "Wait until you hear what happened at the park. Oh! And I have a guillotine for Dragonthorpe."

"Such a bloodthirsty banshee."

She pressed closer, and Ethan felt his eyes go out of focus. "We have a surprise for you."

"Do you, indeed."

Her red-gold curls bounced excitedly. "Yes, but Mama said I must hold my tongue."

"And how will you do that? With a pair of forceps?"

He smacked his thumb and forefinger in front of her face, making her squeal. "Or with your fingers?" He moved his pinching fingers toward her mouth and then dove toward her rib cage.

Sophie let out a shrill laugh. "No, Ethan." More giggles. "No. S-sstop."

When she doubled over, trying to fight off his attack, he saw Sydney standing in the doorway of the drawing room, smiling faintly at their antics. He froze, his own tongue refusing to work.

The little she-devil in his lap yelled, "Surprise!" Sophie clapped her hands together. "We found them in the park."

Sophie's use of the word *them* snapped him out of his trance. He noted Cora joining Helsford near the sideboard and Amelia Cartwright moving to stand by a red-and-orange-striped chair against the wall.

"Miss Hunt and Mrs. Cartwright consented to join us for luncheon," Catherine Ashcroft said.

Ethan rose, tucking the scrap of a girl in the corner of one arm. When he reached Sydney's side, he glanced down at her cane. "Should you be up and about?"

"I could not have borne another hour of idleness." She flipped a ruffle on Sophie's dress back in place, garnering her a grateful smile. "The wound is not as bad as someone led me to believe."

He had seen the bloody mess that was her leg before the apothecary had cleaned her up. No matter how superficial the cut had turned out, Ethan would always remember how she looked when Mac had first set her down on the bed. He recalled the suffocating constriction in his chest and the bleakness blanketing his mind. Never did he want to experience those feelings again.

Sophie cupped a hand around her mouth and whispered loudly in his ear. "Ask her to sit."

The blood drained from his face at his thoughtlessness. He'd suffered knife wounds before and knew how they could pulse with fiery pain when upright too long. "Yes, of course." Ethan offered Sydney his arm. "Miss Banshee has reminded me of my manners. We have a seat for you over here."

Smiling at his helper, Sydney slid her hand into the crook of his free arm and allowed him to lead her to the chair he'd vacated.

"A moment." Ethan lifted his arm away and then lowered Sophie until her feet touched the floor. Feeling charitable, he kissed the crown of her red-gold head. When she started to scamper off, he dug his fingers into her sides. She shrieked before bursting into giggles and breaking free.

He turned back to Sydney. "Now, where were we?"

"You are not to be trusted, I see."

Ethan's smile faded. "No." He offered a hand of support while she eased into the chair.

"Miss Hunt might need this." Somerton held out a small poppy-colored stool.

Nodding his thanks, Ethan placed the stool at Sydney's feet. "May I?" He pointed toward her leg.

In answer, she jerked her head once. Her hand curled around the handle of her walking stick until her knuckle-bones were outlined in vivid detail beneath her taut skin. With as much gentleness as he could manage, he grasped the lower edge of her calf and settled the stool beneath her foot. By the time he finished, the back of his neck was damp.

With great reluctance, he lifted his attention to Sydney's face to see what kind of damage he had reaped with his clumsy efforts.

Her eyes twinkled back. "Thank you, my lord.

Perhaps you might encourage Mrs. Cartwright to join us over here."

Thankful to have another task, Ethan located the assistant still standing against the wall. He marched over and lifted the red-and-orange-striped chair. "Follow me, if you will." He set the chair next to Sydney's and waved his hand toward it. "Mrs. Cartwright?"

Shoulders back, the small blond assistant strode forward and perched on the edge. "Thank you, my lord."

Watching Sydney's face carefully, Ethan asked, "Have you met the Earl of Somerton or Earl of Helsford?"

Features even, she shook her head. "I don't believe we've ever been formally introduced."

Ethan nearly smiled his admiration. She tiptoed along neutral ground by not being completely dishonest, nor completely truthful. "Lord Somerton, Lord Helsford. May I present Miss Hunt and her assistant, Mrs. Cartwright?" The gentlemen bowed and the ladies nodded.

"If you'll excuse us," Catherine Ashcroft said, towing Sophie from the room. "We're going to freshen up a bit before we sit down at the table. You have much to discuss while I'm gone."

Ethan glanced between Sydney and Mrs. Cartwright, who were staring at Cora. "What happened at the park?"

"We interrupted a kidnapping," Cora said.

Both Ethan and Helsford moaned. Even Somerton released a long, hissing breath.

"Do not glare at me, Ethan," Sydney said. "Mac chased the man down. I merely spoke to the child's nurse."

"And what did you do, my dear?" Helsford asked Cora.

"I picked up the child after the kidnapper flung him to the ground." Her eyes narrowed on the silent man across the room. "Do not even try to use this against me. I'm perfectly fine."

Somerton raised an eyebrow at her rebuke. "Can I assume Catherine behaved herself?"

"Yes. She had Sophie to corral."

When the three women exchanged glances again, Ethan demanded, "What are you not telling us?"

Cora nodded to Sydney. "The child is the grandson of Henry Dundas, Viscount Melville."

This time, it was Ethan's turn to silently communicate with the three other Nexus agents.

"First Lord of the Admiralty," Somerton said.

"After the intruder ransacked your study, didn't he leave Melville's file lying out?" Ethan asked.

"Yes," Somerton said. "A fact that seemed rather careless at the time. Did you identify the kidnapper?"

"Lord Latymer, sir," Cora said.

Ethan realized no one knew how to react to the news. Because of him, his family—especially Cora and Catherine—was drawing Sydney into the fold. Their acceptance, however, did not extend to Nexus business. What they didn't understand—and Ethan was reluctant to share her secret until he learned more—was that Sydney probably knew as much as they did about Latymer's betrayal.

On top of that maze of logic, Sydney would never reveal her role as Specter, assuming she was Helsford's informant. That secret would force her to remain cautious about her level of questioning.

Quite the muck.

"A warning?" Helsford asked.

"From whom?" Cora asked, incredulous. "Latymer?"

Helsford shrugged. "Perhaps he suffered a bout of conscience."

"He has none."

"The child is unharmed, I hope," Somerton said,

covering the awkward silence that followed Cora's vehement remark.

Sydney nodded. "We gave the nurse and child a ride partway home. She insisted on strolling him the rest of the distance for fear of drawing unwanted attention. From the sound of it, she met William—or Lord Latymer— yesterday and he coaxed her to return this morning."

"Well," Somerton said, "all turned out well, thanks to—"

"Mac," Sydney said, filling in the blank. "He works for me. As does his brother."

After a contemplative silence, Cora ventured, "Miss Hunt, I understand you have an interest in Abbingale, as we do."

"Oh?" Sydney sent Ethan a hard look. "How's that?"

"I mentioned to them that I could not have identified Giles Clarke without your assistance yesterday." Ethan had learned so much more about her since their temporary partnership at Abbingale and his subsequent discussion with Cora and the others yesterday.

"Ethan also told us that you were investigating allegations of abuse at the Home, in the guise of a rich benefactress," Cora added.

This time it was Ethan's turn to glare. Cora could have left out that particular detail. Why was his sister purposefully putting him and Sydney in conflict with each other?

Sydney appeared ill at ease with the conversation. "That's correct."

"I recall Ethan also mentioning a client of yours leaving Abbingale after she witnessed some disturbing sights," Cora said. "Do I have the right of it?"

Mrs. Cartwright sent Sydney a curious look.

"Yes, Miss deBeau."

"Did you take the servant's story to the authorities?"

"No."

"Might I ask why?"

"Cora," Ethan interrupted. "I thought you invited Miss Hunt here to dine with us, not to suffer an interrogation."

"My apologies, Miss Hunt," Cora said. "I did not mean to make you feel uncomfortable. Your story is fascinating and more than a little heroic."

The explanation Cora provided eased the tension sharpening Sydney's shoulders into perfect squares.

"Hardly heroic, Miss deBeau," Sydney said. "I found nothing that would support the maid's allegations."

"But your instincts warned otherwise," Ethan said.

She leaned more fully back into her chair. "My instincts accounted for nothing in this situation."

"Perhaps not the abuse itself," Ethan conceded, "but you suspected that a few of the staff were not as they appeared."

"Although our promise extended only to retrieving young Giles Clarke," Somerton said, "I should like to know what caliber of people we're leaving the rest of the boys with."

The former chief's comment gave her a start. Ethan couldn't determine if it was the content of his question that had alarmed her or if it was the messenger himself that caused her body to jolt.

"Mrs. Drummond's dour attitude and suspicious nature seemed disproportionate for the occasion, and Monsieur LaRouche, the schoolmaster." She paused, searching for the right words. "With one long examination the schoolmaster managed to see through my pretense. And the children clearly fear them both." She gave herself a shake as if shrugging off an unpleasant memory. "No matter how hard I try to convince myself otherwise, I cannot feel right about their presence at Abbingale."

"Sometimes we have nothing more than our gut to guide us," Helsford said.

She nodded. "Indeed, my lord."

"I couldn't help but notice your footman outside," Somerton said to Sydney. "Catherine mentioned to me before she left that he has a twin."

Sydney sank deeper into the cushion of her chair, and Mrs. Cartwright perched straighter in her seat. "Mrs. Ashcroft is correct, my lord. As I mentioned earlier, both brothers work for me. What do my footmen have to do with the nature of our current discussion?"

Ethan wondered the same thing. He moved closer to Sydney's chair.

Catherine reentered the drawing room. "Mother is entertaining Sophie until we're ready to eat." She moved to Somerton's side, twining her arm around his.

Resting his long fingers over Catherine's, Somerton refocused on Sydney. "Not long ago, an attempt was made to take Sophie from us."

Sydney's eyes flared briefly, and Ethan's insides contracted against the first pang of understanding.

"At a most crucial moment," Somerton continued, "a stranger in a black-hooded cloak, accompanied by two identical-looking men, intervened and helped us avert the kidnapping."

"H-how—" Sydney stopped to clear her throat. "How fortuitous, my lord. I am happy to hear the villains were thwarted."

"We were quite fortunate to have garnered such a friend, though we have not been afforded an opportunity to express our appreciation."

The moment Ethan had discerned Somerton's

intentions, a knot formed at the base of his stomach and had grown to such a degree that he now found it difficult to breathe. He peered at Helsford to see if his friend was following where Somerton led. The normally unflappable cryptographer was staring at Sydney with wide, disbelieving eyes. Ethan almost felt sorry for the man. After two years, he'd finally come face-to-face with his informant. Specter.

Cora seemed less surprised than her betrothed. Given her line of questioning, she must have suspected there was much more to Sydney and had determined to ferret it out. Well, she had.

Only one question remained now—who would break their silence first?

Twenty-five

Every fine hair on Sydney's back and arms rose to attention. Lord Somerton knew—or at least strongly suspected—that it was she who had helped them save Sophie. How? How was it possible that he had linked the O'Donnell brothers to the aborted kidnapping? Among other things, the evening sky had been overcast, painting the countryside in an even, thick stroke of impenetrable black.

Then she recalled how the clouds had parted and Somerton and the others had burst upon the volatile scene. Somerton had been in front of the pack, the perfect position to catch a glimpse of the O'Donnells before they slipped from sight.

She couldn't dispute Somerton's subtle claim, for Ethan would recognize the lie. Disappointing any of these people was the last thing she wanted to do, but she had no idea how to talk about Specter. A secret she had guarded for so long—and for good reason.

She glanced around the room and found everyone's gaze on her. They did not try to hide their admiration, and the realization caused an insistent prickle behind her eyes. She was about to break down in front of all these incredibly strong, gifted people whom she admired. Panic set in.

Amelia stood abruptly. "My stomach has taken a turn," she announced. "I'm sorry, but I fear I must decline your invitation for luncheon."

Catherine rushed forward. "May we offer you a place to rest or call for a physician?"

Grateful for Amelia's quick thinking, Sydney rose. "Thank you, Mrs. Ashcroft," she said in a low, hoarse voice. "You are most kind, but perhaps it is best if I escorted Mrs. Cartwright home."

"I hate the thought of you being jounced around while struggling with a putrid stomach."

"Rigby will drive slowly." Sydney hated the subterfuge, especially since she was certain everyone—even Catherine, though she was new to the Nexus and far more merciful—saw through Amelia's thin veil of pretense. Sydney hardened her heart against the guilt. Everything was crumbling around her, and she had no notion of how to stop it.

"Of course." Catherine touched her sleeve, and Sydney caught the sparkle of tears in the other woman's eyes. "Please, let us try again. Dinner, perhaps."

"You are too kind, Mrs. Ashcroft." Sydney made to leave and came face-to-face with a large male chest. Tilting her head back, she peered into the black, penetrating eyes of Lord Helsford.

"The same stranger who helped rescue Sophie also helped save my betrothed and my closest friend," Helsford said, protecting her informant status. "As Somerton said, we have a deep and profound wish to thank our cloaked defender. We will forever be in our new friend's debt."

Then, to Sydney's amazement and horror, Lord

Helsford lifted her hand to his mouth and gallantly kissed her knuckles. Stepping back, he handed her off to Ethan, who silently guided her from the room. The door closed behind them, and the sob she had been battling to quash broke free.

Ethan's comforting arms wrapped around her and held tight. "We'll be there in a moment, Mrs. Cartwright."

Sydney heard the soft patter of Amelia's retreating feet and the quiet click of the entry door. Her tears would not stop. Over and over, her mind relived the scene in the drawing room. People she had admired for so long thanking her for the small part she had played in foiling the scheming French. She had done so little, and yet they treated her like a war hero. Like one of them.

"Sydney. Sweet Sydney." Ethan kissed her forehead. "Please don't cry." He kneaded her neck and rubbed gentle circles on her back.

"I'm s-sorry," she whispered. "What they said," she sniffed, "I don't deserve—"

"Shhh. Let me take you away from here. Some place where we may talk in private."

At that moment, Sydney would have consented to anything. All she wanted was to curl up in a tight ball and hide from the world. If Ethan happened to be holding her at the same time, all the better.

"Yes, please," she said.

He handed her a handkerchief and gave her a moment to repair some of the damage. Once she nodded her readiness, he whisked her out of the house, to his waiting carriage.

Mac surged forward to stop him, but Amelia stepped into his path. "Let her go." He made to cut around her, and she boldly placed her hand in the center of his chest. "She will be safe with him, Mac. I swear it."

Sydney sent her bodyguard a reassuring smile and then a grateful one to Amelia before entering Ethan's carriage.

"Danforth," Mac called, his voice low and urgent.

At the door, Ethan slashed a level look at the footman. "If she rings the bell, you had bloody well better stop."

Mortification heated Sydney's cheeks. "Oh, dear God."

Instead of taking offense to Mac's demanding tone, Ethan said, "You have my word." With that, he jumped into the carriage and signaled for his driver to move on. The moment they were under way, he drew her against his chest and pressed his lips to her hair.

"Where are we going?" she asked after several minutes of silence.

"Home." He tipped his head to the side to look at her face. "Unless you would rather go somewhere else."

"Home—I mean—your home is fine. As long as my presence won't scandalize Tanner too badly."

"Tanner cannot be scandalized. I've dedicated years to the task and have finally given up."

Despite the emotional turmoil battering at her, she smiled at his attempt at levity. "I have no doubt." She thought back to the exchange in the drawing room. "Why would Latymer attempt to kidnap Melville's grandson?"

"What is the one and only thing standing in the way of Bonaparte invading England's shores?"

"The Nexus?"

A slow smile curled his lips, and his arm around her waist tightened, drawing her close. Until then, she hadn't realized how much she'd needed to be in his arms.

He kissed her temple. "Besides the Nexus."

With his masculine scent filling her nose, she found it hard to focus on his question. Finally, she ventured, "His Majesty's Navy."

He gave her a gentle squeeze. "Precisely."

"You think taking the child would force the First Lord of the Admiralty to do their bidding?"

"The French did it before. With Lydia Clarke and her son Giles."

"Dear Lord."

They said no more, each contemplating the significance of the French scheme. Sydney soon found herself in his study, wrapped in a burgundy throw and tucked in the corner of the sofa. Though tension pulsed inside her every nerve and muscle, his tender care made her feel precious and loved. Not since Philip had she felt this way, and she missed the craving warmth that only a man's attention could engender.

He settled on the sofa, bare inches away, angling his big body toward her. "Are you certain I can't offer you some refreshment—tea, biscuits, sandwiches, anything?"

The mere thought of food did nasty things to her stomach. "No, thank you. I'm quite content as I am."

"No food, no drink." He studied her face as if he were gazing upon a piece of treasured artwork. "We are left with only two other choices with which to occupy ourselves."

"Only two?" The query came out far more breathlessly than she had intended.

He nodded. "The most obvious option," his gaze flicked down to her mouth and lingered there for a heart-stuttering moment, "is a rousing game of chess."

"Chess?"

"With the right opponent, the game can be quite invigorating."

The tension gripping her body eased its hold. "Since I have never played the game, the only person who would be invigorated by the experience would be you."

He grinned. "I do enjoy delivering a sound trouncing from time to time."

"Somehow that fact does not shock me."

"If you will not allow me to trounce you in chess," he covered her hand with his, "we are left with only one other option."

She had not realized how cold her fingers were until his warm palm penetrated the icy layer. "What might that be?"

"Conversation, of course."

Conversation. The very last thing she wanted to do, though she knew when she had agreed to escape with him this moment would arrive. Terror, regret, and an odd kind of embarrassment filled her heart. Over the last several years, her life had settled into a comfortable, fulfilling routine. She found good situations for her service clients and dependable staff for her hiring clients. On occasion, she assisted other servants who had been wronged by their employers and left to fend for themselves. She had also provided valuable information to a group of spies charged with safeguarding her country.

What would her life look like after she spewed everything she held precious to this man? For the first time ever, she had no clear vision of the consequences of her actions. And that unwelcome realization paralyzed her tongue and scrambled all logical thought.

After giving her fingers an encouraging squeeze, he placed her hand on his leg and smoothed her fingers flat. Angled toward her as he was, her hand rested on the inside of his thigh, just above the back of his knee. The location was both comforting and highly intimate. Her fingers were no longer cold.

"Shall I go first?" he asked.

"Please do."

"Complete honesty?"

Sydney glanced down at their clasped hands, at the

unspoken promise in their touch. Nodding, she added, "Without judgment or interference?"

Leaning close, he spoke near her ear. "The former I can promise." He pressed his lips to her cheek and pulled in a long breath. "The interference I cannot."

She had closed her eyes while he spoke, absorbing his soft baritone like one does a long-anticipated summer breeze. When she finally raised her lids, he was studying her again. This time, his look did not cherish her; it devoured her. No woman, young or old, innocent or well-trod, could mistake the sensual hunger pulsing off him.

"Ethan?"

"Yes?"

"Can we talk later?" she asked on an unsteady breath. "I should like to hear about number three."

"Three?" No sooner than he asked the question, the lines on his forehead melted away and a deep, sultry smile appeared. "You wish to hear more rules for the bedchamber?"

"How many Instinct Rules do you have?"

"Enough to keep you occupied for a while." He flipped the burgundy throw off her legs. "What of your injury?"

She edged forward, bracing her hand against the back of the sofa. Where she got the courage to do and say what she did next, she would never know. But she would come to cherish the memory forever.

Using her free hand, she feathered her fingers up his arm, along his shoulder, and over the folds of his neck-cloth until she cupped his strong, square jaw. "There is one way to spare my leg from overexertion." She caressed his lower lip with the pad of her thumb.

He parted his lips and slowly, carefully drew her

thumb inside the warm, moist cavern of his mouth. His tongue played against the soft flesh before sliding away to make way for the raw scrape of his teeth. The shock of the dueling sensations left her reeling for air.

Covering her hand with his, he released her thumb. "Number three: Never, ever sup from your lover's hand; utensils are infinitely safer."

Sydney stared at her glistening thumb, aching for something she couldn't put into words. "And infinitely more boring."

"Indeed." His smile faded. "Tell me how to spare your leg." His voice was rough, no longer playful.

She inhaled a bracing breath. "I know I am much larger than your other women—"

"Stop." He tilted her chin up. "Never speak of them, because I will never think of them."

"How is that possible?" she asked. "You've known so many."

"Do you want the honest answer, Sydney?"

"Of course." Though his fierce expression made her question the veracity of her reply.

"I stopped thinking of them the moment I left their bed."

She stared at him. "Every one of them?"

"I did not... care for my assigned tasks."

Assigned? She had not thought of his actions in those terms. "Have I become a task?"

"No," he said harshly. "Good God, no. You are—" He drove his fingers into his hair and squeezed his eyes shut.

She caught his wrist. "I'm what?"

He clamped his lips together.

"I'm what, Ethan?"

"*Mine.*" His eyes blazed and his breaths blew out in

ragged gasps. "And you are not too damn large. You're perfect. Your body is the most glorious thing I have ever beheld, and I'm reluctant to taint it with my touch. In all my years, I have never wanted another woman like you, and I have wanted you from the beginning."

Tears of the most profound happiness burned her eyes.

He averted his gaze, as if he had said something wrong. She placed two fingers on his rigid jaw and exerted gentle pressure until their gazes locked. "Carry me to your bed, my lord."

His eyes widened and then they grew fierce. "Sweet heaven, I don't deserve you. But I'm not strong enough to warn you away." With that declaration, he scooped her up into his arms and carried her upstairs.

Although her attention never strayed from his gorgeous profile, she was keenly aware of the lack of servants on the way to their destination. Had he sent them away? In the middle of the day? Or was Tanner so well attuned to his master's needs? Then another violent thought struck her in the chest. "Ethan?"

His long strides slowed. "Yes, sweet."

She toyed with the ends of his hair, feeling ridiculous and gauche. "Did you bring the others here?" She would not refer to them as his women again.

"Never."

The bite of jealousy faded, and she laid her head against his shoulder, kissing the side of his neck. "Thank you."

His strides lengthened, and Sydney kissed him again. And again.

Twenty-six

ETHAN VIBRATED WITH THE NEED TO RIP AWAY EVERY layer of civility and take Sydney against the hard panels of his bedchamber door. The soft, tentative pressure of her lips against his oversensitized flesh hardened his body to the point of pleasure-pain.

Easy, Danforth. Easy. She's an innocent. He continued the chant all the way to his chamber, intensifying the reminder when his bed came into view. With as much care as he could manage, he lowered her legs until her feet touched the floor. He kept his arm behind her back while she tested her wounded leg.

She grabbed the end bed poster for additional support, and Ethan worried he had somehow aggravated her injury during his rapid flight up the stairs. He brushed the backs of his fingers along the delicate rim of her jawline and said the hardest words he'd ever uttered. "Shall we talk instead?"

"Afraid I'll hurt you, my lord?" Her lips twitched.

Yes. Rounding in front of her, he said, "Hold on." He grasped her beneath the arms and settled her on the edge of the bed. "Make yourself comfortable while I fight with these damned boots."

The smile she sent him was both impish and seductive. "As you wish." She kicked off her pale blue shoes.

A sense of urgency infused Ethan's struggle to remove his boots, especially when she lifted the hem of her dress to remove her stockings. "Do not touch, Miss Hunt."

One raven-colored brow lifted at his commanding tone. She said nothing, though. Rather, she leaned back, bracing her weight on her forearms. Then she slid one stockinged foot over the counterpane, toward her bum. With the hem of her dress already gathered above her knee, the lightweight fabric skimmed down her long, curvaceous limb, pooling at the juncture of her legs.

His foot picked that moment to *pop* free of his fitted boot. The unexpected give forced him off-balance, and he nearly plunged face-first to the carpet below. Sydney's muffled laugh reached him. Righting himself in the chair again, he threw his expensive leather Hessian to the side and went to work on the other. "You will not find the situation quite so amusing once I'm free of these blasted boots."

She chuckled low. "Until then, I'm going to enjoy the moment with abandon."

Ethan threw everything he had into the next tug and was rewarded with the *whoofing* sound of his foot sliding free. He dropped the boot, and the amused vixen quieted.

Rising, he began working on his cravat while prowling toward the delectable woman reclining on his bed. He halted between her legs, his neckcloth hanging limply down his chest. Neither of them was smiling now. The simple gesture would have taken far too much concentration. Concentration Ethan needed so he would not bungle this experience for her.

Easy, Danforth. Easy. She's an innocent.

"Where is your reticule?" he asked.

She blinked. "My reticule?"

"I promised your watchdog that I would listen for the damn bell," he said, with more surliness than he'd intended. "You are carrying it in your bag, I presume?"

Chagrin stained her cheeks. "Mac worries if I do not keep it nearby."

"Is there a particular reason why?"

"Yes, but I do not care to discuss it now." Sadness imbued her features that only moments ago were glowing with laughter.

"Where's the bell, Sydney?"

"I dropped it on the floor." She pointed to the corner of the bed.

Ethan bent down to retrieve the embroidered reticule that was a shade darker than her blue dress. He placed the bag in her lap and turned his hand palm up. "If you will, please."

She loosened the ribbons and drew out a small object wrapped in linen. Spreading open the handkerchief, she offered him the bell.

"Thank you." He carried the tinkling silver to the bedside table. He caught her troubled gaze. "I will listen for it… and obey."

He heard her swallow and caught the quiver in her delicate chin before she swiped her knuckles across the trembling area. His stomach knotted at the sight, and he swore then and there that she would never have to use the bell again.

Resuming his place between her legs, he asked, "Now, where were we, hedgehog?"

As he'd hoped, his query was met with a wobbly smile. "I think you were about to punish me for my amusement at your expense, my lord cad."

And just like that, the air thickened with a fragrance that no man could ignore. "I'm going to make love to you, sweet Sydney."

Her breathing deepened. "Would that be now, or sometime in the not-too-distant future?"

"Being gentle won't be easy for me, especially the first time," he said through clenched teeth. "I will try my damnedest, but the moment my skin touches yours, I—"

Grasping the ends of his neckcloth, she exerted slow but sure pressure until he could see flecks of emerald intermingled with a calmer jade in the outer rings of her eyes.

"Ethan," she whispered, "let us, this once, be ourselves."

"Gladly." He moved in to kiss her.

"Except my hair," she clarified, her lips brushing his as she spoke. "I'll never be able to repair it and don't wish to leave here looking completely ravished."

He nuzzled the side of her nose. "Only slightly ravished?"

"Yes," she said, smiling. "That sounds perfect." And then she lifted her mouth to his, and Ethan freed his mind of everything but how to please the woman in his arms.

Sydney had never felt so decadent in all her life. Her skirts were bunched at her hips, her fingers were clamped in a man's skin-warmed cravat, and her tongue tangled with Ethan deBeau's. Dear God, she couldn't believe she was doing this, but she would not—could not—stop now.

In the next instant, he was gone. Sydney blinked to clear the haze of desire. He stood at the side of the bed, removing his coat, waistcoat, and finally his shirt. The muscles of his stomach rippled with each harsh breath, and his massive chest expanded before her eyes. "Oh, Ethan," she said in a shaky voice. "You are stunning."

"When you look at me that way," he said in a guttural

voice, "I feel as though I could stop Bonaparte with nothing more than my bare hands."

She shifted closer, and he hurried to assist. When she stood before him, she lifted his hand between them and set her palm against his, marveling at the size difference, for she did not have small hands. "Yes. I believe you could."

"Turn for me." He twined his fingers with hers and then kissed each one of her knuckles. "I need to see you now."

His quiet request swept over her in a luxuriant wave, and a tremor of anticipation formed deep in her body's center. She presented her back to him and followed the progress of his expert fingers. Another wave of insecurity struck her hard. She could not change his past, nor could she alter the future. All she had was the here and now. And she hoped with all her heart that her large frame would not be a disappointment.

Even if it was, she would likely never know. He had made any number of women feel as though they were the most precious beings while sharing a bed. He was an experienced seducer, a rogue without equal. And he was hers for the next hour.

Soon, she stood in nothing more than her chemise and stockings. She shivered, though she was not cold. She trembled, though she was not scared. She ached, though she was not injured. At least, not *there*.

Warm lips danced along her right shoulder, nipping and licking their way toward the curve of her throat. When he reached the sensitive valley beneath her lobe, the tips of her breasts hardened into painful, desperate peaks. She grasped the backs of his thighs, more for support than any attempt to bring their bodies closer. But closer they came.

Not realizing her intent, he pressed his hardness into the crease of her bottom. Without thought, she thrust back and heard air hiss between his teeth. The sound made her stomach quiver and her thighs clench.

He drew her arms up and locked them around his neck, then his hands explored her body like the most exacting Italian sculptor. Catching her earlobe with his hot mouth, he drew hard on it and then soothed the tender flesh with his tongue. All the while, one attentive hand covered her aching peak and the other sought her lower stomach. He kneaded her breast and laid his palm on her mound, curling his long finger over the damp center.

The invasion of her cleft sent her heart humming with excitement and her blood hardened into crystals of ice. The contradictory sensations confused her until long-repressed, dark memories crawled their way to the surface, shredding her euphoria. Sydney squeezed her eyes shut.

Sensing her withdrawal, Ethan removed his hands and drew her arms down. He smoothed his thumbs over her upper arms. "Too fast?"

The contrition in his voice made her throat ache. "No, Ethan. Everything was perfect." *Except me.* She could not think of how to right the situation, so they could resume their lovemaking. She wanted to be with him so badly. But the past was lodged in her mind now and would not budge. Like a beacon, she searched for her bell. The twinkle of silver on the bedside table brought her a measure of comfort, but not enough to stop the shiver.

He draped his coat over her shoulders, and his musky scent billowed up to fill her nose.

"Perhaps now would be a good time to tell me the

story behind your tiny weapon." Folding back the bed covers, he plumped the pillows into an upright position. "In with you."

She hesitated. "Ethan, I—"

"No need to worry, Sydney. I've postponed your ravishment until later." He lifted her fingers to his lips, kissing them with an unexpected reverence. "Anticipation is almost as sweet as the ravishment." Then he waved his hand toward the small cocoon he'd created. "Please."

Still wearing his coat, she slid between the covers and settled against the soft pillows. Ethan tucked the counterpane around her legs and waist and then walked around to the other side. After making the same preparations, he joined her on the bed. They sat there, motionless, staring into the distance. If she hadn't been so worried about the questions he would ask, she would have enjoyed their companionable silence, the comfort of having Ethan next to her. What was he thinking? How much did he understand about her reticence?

Her thoughts eventually led her to Philip, her first and only love. To this day, she didn't know why she had felt compelled to share this difficult piece of her past with him. But she had, and he had walked away. Walked away with regret in his voice and disgust in his eyes. Never in her lifetime would she forget that moment, nor the one following a month later when she saw him help a beautiful woman alight from his carriage.

She knew the precise moment when Ethan turned his attention to studying her profile. Warmth kindled in her chest and blazed into her limbs. All of a sudden, she felt desolate and alone. She craved the security of his embrace and the heat of his kiss.

Would he leave her as Philip had? Would the beautiful blue-green rims of his eyes dull with disgust, too?

When the answers remained stubbornly out of reach, she pressed her forearm against her churning stomach.

"Sydney." His voice was quiet, the sweetest she had ever heard. "Will you share with me why O'Donnell insists you keep the bell nearby?"

Nodding, she lifted her gaze to his. "If you will kiss me one last time."

"One last time?" Understanding dawned, and his features darkened. "You believe whatever it is that you're about to tell me will scare me away."

"It is not comfortable news for a man to hear."

"Then I can't imagine the courage it will take for you to convey it."

When he ceased being an irredeemable rogue, he was quite dangerous to her heart.

"Yes, well, I have had many years to come to terms with my past," she said. "You, on the other hand, will have mere seconds to absorb the information and set your mind's course."

"A past that haunts you still?"

"Not particularly. I have an amazing ability to block out unpleasant moments in my life. Though in recent days, I've discovered there are certain… situations that can swiftly draw forth a painful time."

He offered his hand, palm up, between them. "I'm ready when you are."

Instead of sliding her hand into his, she twisted around and kissed him. He might not believe it would be their last, but Sydney knew if not their last, it was near to it. Given the vast differences in their stations, any intimacy between them could never be considered anything more than a pleasurable dalliance. Soon, he would have to consider a suitable wife and begin a family. The relent-less, age-old pursuit of protecting one's empire, by marrying well and fathering a brood of children to carry on the line and to strengthen one's position in society, would be upon him soon.

Within seconds of claiming his mouth, she realized her mistake. The tenor of this kiss was far different from the last, or perhaps she was different. Instead of focusing on how her body reacted to his touch, her thoughts centered on him. On the saltiness of his flesh, the rasp of his tongue, and the ripple of his muscle. She learned what he liked and didn't like by listening to the subtle—and sometimes not so subtle—fluctuations in his breathing and the firmness of his grip on her face.

Then she felt the first jolt of the fall. The first give of her heart. How had she let this man—of all the men in England—scurry beneath her defenses and become so important to her? The terrifying sensation forced her to pull back and stare at him.

"I'm not opposed to postponing our discussion," he said, his voice husky.

She allowed a small smile. "Why am I not surprised?" Finding his hand, she twined her fingers with his and filled her lungs with courage.

"My mother came from a good, hardworking family, but a poor one. She's the eldest of six children and felt the weight of responsibility to contribute to the family's coffers at an early age." Sydney kept her attention on the far wall. "The day after she turned twelve, she took a maid's position at a nearby estate."

He carefully transferred her hand to his right one and then curled his arm around her shoulders. At first, she tensed until he pressed his lips to her temple. The comforting gesture was so reminiscent of how her mother used to soothe her nicks and heartaches that she melted against him.

"She survived long days of backbreaking labor, all the while sending her earnings home. My mother did this for years, slowly rising through the ranks of domestic service until she attained the position of housekeeper."

"Now I know where you get your resiliency."

His quiet praise pushed back the chill creeping into her heart. "Not long after she became the housekeeper, the old earl died and his handsome *ton*-polished son removed to the estate." She burrowed deeper into his side. "The new earl wooed my mother into forgetting every bit of common sense she had attained since leaving the cradle. He made her feel beautiful and special. Made her believe their class difference meant nothing to him."

"Allow me to guess. Your mother became enceinte—with you."

"Yes."

"Then he sacked her."

"Actually, no. His mother did."

"But he did not overrule his mother and allowed his mistress to leave with no means to care for his daughter." He spat the words out as if they were bitter on his tongue.

"Something like that, yes."

"No wonder you despise *my kind*." He left the bed and stalked the chamber like a caged animal, shirtless.

Every agitated step surged through his powerful body. Muscle shifted beneath flesh in an oddly graceful rhythm that was both mesmerizing and enticing. His thick brows were clenched together and his thumb and forefinger pinched the bridge of his nose.

Sydney felt his fury, even with a dozen feet separating them. She sat forward. "Ethan, please do not take my earlier comments to heart. You are stronger and more honorable than my father—the earl. And I am not so naïve at this age as was my mother."

His gaze slashed to hers. "Where did she go? Home?"

Tears collected in the back of her throat. "She does not speak of those first few years."

"Christ." He prowled to the foot of the bed and braced his hands against the counterpane.

Violence chiseled his handsome features into a framework she did not recognize. A fleeting thought entered her mind, and she wondered if his value to the Nexus went beyond a lady's bedchamber.

"What happened next?" he asked.

Sitting in her chemise, in the middle of his bed, she could not share the rest of her story while under such fierce scrutiny. She averted her attention to find more neutral territory, but found none. The contours of his upper chest and arms drew her gaze and would not let go. She pulled his coat closer.

"Do not lose your courage now." A muscle flexed in his chest. "Tell me how the two of you survived."

She broke free of her trance and bolstered her nerves. "From what I've gathered, my mother did go home until I was born. But my grandfather did not approve of her bastard child, and we were soon forced to leave." Her gaze dropped to her hands. Hands she could not seem to keep warm. "That's when she brought me to London and did only God-knows-what to keep us alive."

"Your mother got you through those hellish first years and then something changed—for the better, I gather."

Nodding, Sydney said, "Somehow she managed to obtain another housekeeper position. By then, my uncle and one of my aunts had come to London. Through their combined efforts, everyone got on well enough. When I turned six, my mother placed me under the supervision of the kindly cook in the household where she worked. I rather liked cleaning vegetables while listening to Cook's outrageous stories."

"No wonder the Hunt Agency is so successful. You have firsthand knowledge of the positions you're filling."

Wanting nothing more than to be finished with her story, she ignored his observation and trudged on. "Within the year, I came to the attention of the master's fifteen-year-old son."

The image that had shattered their precious intimacy earlier resurfaced.

"Be quiet, little one," the master's son said, the tip of his finger trailed down the length of her cheek to the side of her neck. "Or I will be forced to have your dear mama sacked. You wouldn't want that, would you? Seeing your mama begging on the streets again, hungry and cold?"

Sydney glanced at the closed door of the scullery. Tears welled, blurring her vision. "N-no, sir."

His finger continued its descent, and Sydney bit her bottom lip, holding back her scream.

Ridgway's son's perversions had occurred almost two decades ago. A lifetime. But even after years of repression, the image materialized, sharp and clear and just as frightening.

A low animallike sound erupted from the foot of the bed. Ethan pushed away and resumed his pacing. He said nothing, though his agitation was clear. His strong fingers rubbed his forehead and raked through his wavy hair. He stared at the floor as if he could summon the answers he sought from the boards themselves.

"One day, Cook saw him follow me inside the scullery, and she notified my mother."

She noticed Ethan halted, listening.

"Mother picked up one of the dirty pans and bashed the master's son in the head, saving me, I think, from the worst of his depravity." A smile quivered on her lips, recalling her mother's courage. "One second he was pawing at my skirts and, the next, he was on the floor, sniveling like a baby." Her amusement faded. "Of course, his father did not like the turn of events. He blamed me for tempting his son and then released my mother."

"It's always so convenient to blame brutish behavior on the victim," he said.

With the exception of the one memory, all the others leading up to her last encounter with the son in the scullery had trickled away with the passage of time... and a great determination not to allow fearful thoughts to take root.

"Out of desperation, my mother sought out Una Wimberly, her childhood friend and the Marchioness of Shevington, who wrote her a faux letter of recommendation for another housekeeper position." She smiled a little. "At the Pratt residence."

"And so began Pratt's courtship of your mother?"

She nodded. "Mother resisted for a time, but my father can be rather persuasive."

"This is why you keep the bell?"

"Not directly, though I believe my father might have confided some of my story to Mac after I hired him. Within a couple days of opening the agency, a groomsman came to us, seeking a position. We looked into his background and found that he had been released from his past three employers for his abusive behavior toward their animals. I told the groomsman that the agency would not be able to help him, and he did not take the news well."

"Is there anything about your life not fraught with danger?"

Where was his revulsion? And the downward pull of his features as he gazed upon her with his newfound knowledge? "One could say the same of you."

"Jesus, you're going to make my hair turn gray before I reach the age of thirty." He strode to the opposite side of the bed. His beautiful eyes focused on her with a vulnerable intensity. "I'm still here, Sydney."

"Why?" She wanted to pull back the revealing question, but it was too late.

He lifted one knee and settled it on the edge of the bed. "Because I'm not like the weakling coxcomb you entrusted the story to before. Who was he? That Pyne chap I met in the park?"

"How did you know?"

"In case I haven't said it plainly before," he lowered his chin, "I'm a spy. I observe and gather information. And I'm good at it."

Her throat grew tight. "The vile boy compromised my innocence."

The bed dipped beneath his weight. "In the not-too-distant future, I will wrench the bloody bastard's name from you and finish what your mother started."

"You'll do no such thing. He must have children by now."

"Even more reason."

He crawled across the bed and then angled his body toward hers, trapping her in place by anchoring one large hand near her waist. They reclined nose-to-nose, hip-to-hip. If not for the combined heat of their bodies and the shivers nesting in her lower stomach, the moment would have felt deeply poignant. Instead, all she wanted to do was skim her fingers down the hard planes of his torso. So she did.

At first contact, the smooth flesh beneath her fingertips

contracted as if her touch burned. Her gaze shifted from his glorious chest to his stormy eyes. Rather than encourage her with words, he leaned back to rest on his elbow, opening himself up for her full exploration.

A wave of inadequacy washed over her. Had he been with so many sophisticated women that her tentative caresses felt more like an annoying gnat, rather than a precursor to making love? The thought grew life, and she made to remove her hand. And that's when, out of the corner of her eye, she caught an infinitesimal movement to her right.

Shifting her attention, she noticed he strained against the confines of his breeches. Like a heartbeat, his erection pulsed at regular intervals beneath the buttoned placard. Her lips parted, and she drew in a shuddering breath. Her hand drifted lower.

No longer content with a mere brush of her fingers, she flattened her palm and learned the contours of his hard abdomen. Silk and steel. Vulnerable and dangerous. Tempting and taunting. They were all there, hidden in the ridges and valleys. And she wanted to taste every single rise and fall.

"Sweet Sydney, do you know what you're doing?"

Dipping her fingers below his waistline, she said, "Haven't the faintest idea."

His voice was low, menacing. "You have possibly five more minutes to figure it out, then I'm taking control before you do me permanent damage."

She paused, with her two middle fingers barely touching the peak of his erection. "Damage?"

"Four minutes," he said through clenched teeth.

Her confidence returned, and she slipped her fingers free. A soft oath reached her ears. "Patience, my lord."

"Three minutes."

Heart pounding, she freed the buttons holding his placard closed. Then, as if opening a much-anticipated present, she peeled back the soft leather and her eyes widened with both horror and wonder. She tried to relax her posture, to call forth the calm that had never failed her. But it remained stubbornly absent.

So, she did the next thing that came to mind. She attacked the threat.

Bending forward, she kissed his chest and stomach, exploring his upper body while her hand ventured lower. He was incredibly warm down there, almost humid damp. And then she curled her fingers around the breadth of him, and the area between her legs contracted, as if trying to hold something close.

"Sydney, good God," he hissed. "O-one minute."

She lifted her head to watch while she tested his hard length. He thrust his hips, and her hand glided upward with remarkable ease, even though she never moved a single muscle. Shock and a sense of self-preservation compelled her to look at the man. Ethan. Her lover.

"Your time is up."

One hand clamped around the back of her neck, holding her, while his mouth devoured her lips. She made to release his length, so she could embrace him.

"Keep those wicked fingers where they are."

He kissed her again, this time with his tongue. The act emboldened her. She gripped him tighter and glided her hand all the way up his length and back down.

"You are," he whispered harshly against her lips, "so good at that."

It was all the encouragement she needed. Again and again, she manipulated his erection until a drop of moisture slipped from the engorged tip and eased over her knuckle. She swept her thumb in a wide arc, spreading the droplet. Soon, his musky scent filled her nose, causing saliva to drench her mouth.

He swallowed thickly. "Time's up for us both, I'm afraid." Rearing up on his knees, he grasped himself. "What I'm about to do, I'm doing so that I don't hurt you in my haste. Understand?"

His earnest face and his moving hand divided her attention. "No."

"You will." Then his hand and hips set about a rhythm that made her cheeks flush with heat. On his last thrust, his face took on a pained look and he whipped the sheet over his hand. A groan ripped from his throat; its guttural syllables tangled to form a single word. *Sydney.*

Throwing off her covers, she rose on her knees before him, ignoring the ache in her leg. He wiped himself with the sheet and tossed it away. His staff looked so different now, less intimidating somehow. She had a rudimentary understanding of how this worked, but now, with his flaccid... appendage, she wondered about the mechanics of the act.

His thumb smoothed up the center of her brow. "So serious. Do not worry, hedgehog. I will take care of your needs in but a few minutes."

She sent him a cross look and waved her hand toward his uncooperative appendage. "Is there anything I can do to—um—encourage it?"

The grin he sent her was designed to either melt the receiver's heart or rub her nerves raw. "You might try removing your chemise."

Panic gripped her chest. "I want to encourage its attention, not frighten it away."

He scowled. "What are you talking about?"

"Do not pretend with me, Ethan. Please, not now."

She inhaled a bracing breath. "I'm sure you're used to more svelte figures."

Hooking his finger beneath her chin, he lifted and leaned close. "Never, ever compare yourself to another woman. Never."

Tears bit into the backs of her eyes. She nodded.

"Promise me."

She had to swallow to get the words out. "I promise, Ethan."

The words barely crossed her lips before he sealed them with a kiss. When she made to wrap her arms around his neck and press her aching breasts against him, he released her. The abrupt action and her off-center position forced her to scurry for balance.

Annoyance caused her eyes to narrow on him, which he countered with a rogue's grin.

"Now about that chemise."

Even though she had given her promise, her mind rebelled at the thought of revealing herself to his practiced eye.

"Arms up, Hunt." He grasped the bottom edge of her undergarment.

She grabbed his wrists. "*I'll* do it." Somehow she had to gain command of this situation and, right now, she felt at a distinct disadvantage. Over the years, she had learned how to use her height as a means of bolstering her confidence, especially around men. Perhaps she could use it now, but how? Then she knew.

"If you would be so kind as to offer me a hand up, sir?"

"Up?"

"That's right."

Brow furrowed, he held out his hand.

She slid her fingers into his and propped her other hand on his shoulder for extra balance, then clambered to her feet. A few seconds later she released his hand and shoulder and peered down at him. Power rushed through her when she found his hungry gaze devouring her body.

"How is your leg holding up?"

"It's fine." She ran her fingers along the side of his face. "Do not worry."

Sitting back on his heels, he burrowed his hands under her chemise to clasp her legs, right above the knees, and waited.

Her recently recovered courage began to evaporate. She gathered two handfuls of linen together, intending to rip the blasted thing off and be done with it.

"Slowly," he ordered.

Closing her eyes, she again searched for the calm she could always count on—and finally found a small measure. It was enough. She lifted her lids and followed his every expression as she pulled her chemise over her head in one deliberate and fluid motion.

His hands tightened around her knees. "Sweet Sydney, what were you so worried about?"

When she opened her mouth to explain, he interrupted, "Never mind. Just remember what I said earlier." He smoothed his lips around the edges of her bandage. "I'm sorry," he murmured after every other medicinal press of his mouth. Then he followed the way of her discarded chemise, edging closer and closer to the apex of her legs.

An uncontrollable shiver shook her to the marrow. He reached her bushy mound and inhaled a long, deep breath, and his palms skimmed up the back of her legs to squeeze her bottom.

"Your scent," he whispered, nuzzling her curls, "is so intoxicating."

The shiver moved down to her legs, and she clasped his head loosely. Whatever he intended, she did not want to disturb him. She wanted to experience every second of his lovemaking. Especially all the small nuances like the way his harsh breaths tunneled through her curls, making her squirm with excitement. She had an almost violent urge to thrust her hips forward and wrap her leg around his shoulder to help him penetrate deeper. Her body was weeping for want of him.

"Ethan." Her fingers convulsed around his skull. "I ache."

"Where, my sweet?"

She tried to pinpoint an exact location, but every facet of her body screamed for attention. "Everywhere?"

"Ahhh." He slid his tongue into her navel. "I am a happy man."

Confused, she tugged on his hair until he lifted his gaze to hers. "Why does my suffering make you happy?"

He smiled. "Sweet, innocent Sydney." He covered one needy peak with his hot mouth. Sydney's back arched, forcing him to take more.

When he trailed toward her other breast, he said, "Because I must make every"—he flicked his tongue against her ruched nub—"single place"—he teased the delicate pink aureole—"on your lovely body"—he blew cool air against her damp flesh—"feel better." Cupping both of her breasts in his hands, he plumped them together until he could slide easily from one throbbing tip to the next.

"Oh." She tilted her head back and gave herself over into his keeping.

As promised, he eased the aches of her body, from the delicate hollow of her neck to the pulsing, hot slit between her legs. Every caress, every kiss soothed her and drove her toward an unknown destination. She tried to reciprocate, to give him the same pleasure, but he turned her away with a gentle murmur. "Next time."

Changing position, he sat back on his heels. "Hold on to the bedpost, love."

She glanced over her shoulder to find the tall, stout oak column. After grasping it, she sent him a quizzical look.

"Just for a moment." With that, he rolled onto his back, slipped free of his buckskin breeches, and returned to his former position. "Now, we are evenly matched." He held out his hand. "Come to me."

His appendage no longer needed encouragement. Long and thick, his staff jutted out from a nest of curly hair similar to hers. But all resemblance stopped there. Taking his hand, she allowed him to guide her forward. Instinct took over, and she positioned her knees to the outside of his thighs, effectively straddling his lap. With his hands clamped around her waist, he eased her down, watching her face—she assumed—for any signs of discomfort. Then she was seated on his lap, with her legs angled protectively around his hips.

Wrapping his arms about her waist, he drew her into his body. The heat of his flesh pressing against her tender breasts felt incredibly decadent and his hard length against her wet heat drove her mad with wanting. To take her mind off the area between her legs, she threw all her passions into her kiss. It was then she realized there was one ache he'd missed, an ache so deep and so demanding that she worried he would not be able to give her relief.

She had miscalculated. Rather than assuage her craving, their kiss magnified her need. Before she knew what she was doing, she stroked her damp cleft sinuously along his erection, the action both bliss and torture. Ethan must have felt the same, for he groaned deep in his throat and met her demand with one of his own.

"Syd," he said against her throat. "It's time."

"Thank God."

"Hold on."

He barely gave her time to react to his order. In a whirl of movement, she went from sitting on his lap to staring up into his handsome face. She rose onto her elbows and kissed the hard edge of his jaw. Musk and sweat mingled together on his flesh, creating a tantalizing scent she would forever associate with this one man.

"Ethan, I don't know what to do," she whispered. "Tell me how to please you."

Easing her back down, he said, "You already have, love." He kissed her brow, her eyes, the corner of her mouth. "I understand there is pain the first time." He stared at her expectantly.

Sydney nodded, having heard as much.

"Brace your feet on the bed like this." He angled one of her legs into an upright position. "Try to relax and let me know if I become... too much."

Then he dipped his head to trace a beguiling path down her torso, stopping to give attention to each breast before moving to her navel. By the time he made the journey upward again, tremors racked her body and her hands would not be still.

When he reached the base of her neck, she felt the first soft, yet firm probe at her opening.

"You're so tight, so ready for me," he breathed against her throat. "Bear with me, love. Bear with me."

He inched inside, then eased out a little. The next time he pushed in farther and eased away again. He did this twice more, but a thin barrier blocked his next venture forward.

Lifting his head, he said, "Last chance to change your mind."

His determination to be gentle had cost him much. Sweat dampened his body. The muscles in his arms shook. It was then Sydney fully comprehended the emotion that had revealed itself in their earlier kiss. A disquieting fact, one she hoped would not lead to foolish expectations, as it had her mother.

She loved him. Good God, she was in love with Ethan deBeau. An aristocrat. A spy. A gentleman who cared for his servants. A rogue who patiently won a boy's trust.

He fit his cheek next to hers and whispered, "Don't fret, sweet. It's all right." His body began to slide free of hers, and she clamped her legs around his bottom, holding him in place.

"No, please," she said. "I want this."

"Be sure. We're about to do something irreparable."

"Can you protect me?" she asked. "From having a babe?"

His nostrils widened. "Yes."

"Then don't stop." She squeezed her legs and curled her hips at the same time, but she only managed to cause herself more discomfort.

"On the count of three." He stroked her passage once, twice, and on the third stroke he broke through her barrier.

A pent-up breath burst from Sydney's lungs, and her inner muscles squeezed his staff. Air hissed between his teeth.

"Oh, sweet," he said. "Don't. Do that. Right now."

She didn't understand what he was talking about. When he pulsed inside her, her muscles responded in kind.

"Christ," he groaned. "I'm done for." He braced his weight on his forearms and thrust inside her with startling determination.

Remembering her own pleasure earlier, she rocked against him, picking up his rhythm. Their pace increased and their breaths heaved. Then a new sensation deep in her channel emerged, and she instinctively grasped for it. Clawed her way toward it until she touched the edge. And before she could smile her triumph, she was floating on the other side.

She cried out, pushing into Ethan with all her might. He jerked out of her, burying his own cries into her pillow.

The silence that followed was almost as shattering as the strength of their combined releases. They lingered in each other's heat, absorbing the poignancy of the moment.

Then he placed a soft kiss on her neck before moving to her side. "How is your leg?"

After testing it a little, she said, "All is well."

His attention moved to between her legs. "And here?" He skimmed his knuckles over her curls.

Her muscles clenched and her spine arched. "I'll live, my lord."

Bending forward, he nuzzled her cheek. "I have no doubt." He bounded from the bed and filled the basin with water. Finding a square of linen, he brought everything back and set it on the bedside table.

Sydney sat up while she watched him submerge the cloth and ring it out. Then he turned to her.

"May I do the honors?" he asked.

She glanced down at her body and noticed her stomach was wet with his seed.

"There might also be a little blood." He nodded to a small red smear on the sheet.

"You want to cleanse me?"

He nodded, holding the cloth between his two big hands. "Very much."

The thought of a man, a viscount no less, washing her body like a babe was more than a little discomfiting. All the same, she reclined back and lifted one leg. "As you wish."

"This might still be a little cold."

That he would even think to try to warm the wet cloth for her made her heart lurch. "It will be more tolerable than it was straight from the basin."

With gentle brushes, he cleaned the moisture from her stomach and from between her legs. She tried not to flinch, but the combination of having a man take care of her in such a way and the tenderness of her flesh caused her to twitch a time or two. He rinsed the cloth and then placed the cold compress against her burning flesh.

"Better?"

"Yes, thank you."

He rinsed the cloth one more time and cleaned himself with efficient swipes. When he was done, he turned back to her. "I must return you to the agency shortly, but I should like to hold you for a while."

An image of their naked bodies snuggled together warmed her from the inside out. Even though she had much to do, spending another ten minutes in Ethan's arms was too much temptation to pass up. She started to accept, then noticed his closed expression and rigid posture—both so at odds with his enchanting request.

What had happened in so short a time? An unpleasant thought struck. "What is it?" She tried for a teasing tone, but heard the strain in her own voice. "Are you not acting in accordance with one of your Instinct Rules?"

His hard gaze flickered, and the small hope that she'd read him wrong died. Feeling more vulnerable than she had while disrobing, she folded her arms around her knees. "Which one?"

"Do not tarry in your lover's bed after the act; go home."

The trouble with unwise decisions is that one cannot blame others for them. And in her case, she knew what they both were and were not and still chose to share his bed. Oddly, she wasn't angry or regretful; she merely longed for more time with him. She wanted to idle in her love for him, in the amazing feelings that even now refused to be stifled. For however long time would allow. But her idle had already come to a heart-aching end. Still, she considered accepting his request to hold her for a while, but the tension now surrounding them would suck any pleasure from the moment.

Unfolding her body, she reached for her discarded chemise and slipped it over her head. She padded to where he sat frozen and silent, staring off into the distance. Leaning her hip against the side of the bed, she said, "Then I should go."

Twenty-seven

"HOW LONG HAVE YOU BEEN TRAIPSING ABOUT THE city in your cloaked disguise?" Ethan asked.

Sydney finished sipping her tea and then set her cup down in its saucer. After their bout of extraordinary love-making and subsequent row, Ethan had insisted she stay for a light meal before he escorted her back to the agency.

So, they had removed to a small dining room downstairs, decorated in cheery hues of yellow, white, sage, and lavender. The room's happy demeanor did not match her companion's, though he tried to hide the fact.

Inside that brilliant mind of his waged a silent war. One she did not fully understand, but suspected he battled unfamiliar feelings. What they were exactly, she couldn't be sure. She only knew that he'd wanted to hold her, and his need had put him into conflict against his Instinct Rules. Rules he'd developed years ago to protect himself.

Since her brush with evil in Ridgway's scullery, she had established her own protective barriers and knew they could not be so easily set aside. Having had her fill of cold ham, boiled eggs, and cheese, she pushed her plate away. "A little over three years."

"What prompted you to take such dangerous chances with your life?"

"Before I answer your question, I must extract a promise."

He nodded. "If I can."

"With a few exceptions, my forays in the cloak have all been in support of the Hunt Agency's operations." She paused, searching for the right words. "If my clandestine activities become widely known, my agency could be at risk. I won't allow that to happen. My work there is important—for many reasons you do not yet recognize."

"So, my promise," he said, easing back into his chair, "is to protect your secret, or secrets, as it were."

"Yes."

His lips thinned into a displeased line, matching the stormy current riding the rest of his features. "I've already been safeguarding them, Sydney. You have my promise, all the same."

"Thank you, Ethan. I hope you understand why I couldn't take the chance."

"Of course." Some of the tension left his body, though his expectant glare remained. "I thought you were one of us, you know."

"Us?"

"The Nexus."

Warmth curled in her stomach. "Truly? Why?" She couldn't imagine being welcomed into such an elite group.

"Might have had something to do with your penchant for disguises and keeping secrets."

"Since the moment I learned of the Nexus's main objective, I have long admired your work and sacrifices."

"Is that why you became Helsford's informant?"

Heat trailed up her neck. She nodded.

"How many of us do you know?"

She studied his features and found only curiosity. "Just the four of you."

He sagged deeper into his chair. "Now, about those confidences I must keep…"

She released a long breath. "What many do not realize is that the Hunt Agency is, in fact, three separate operations dependent on one another."

"Three?"

Nodding, she said, "On one side, we provide a service to our clients to either hire new or replacement servants for their household. This section sustains the agency financially."

"A viscount in need of a replacement butler would fall under this area?"

"Indeed." A smile inched across her face. "And if the viscount only gives us a fortnight to find a replacement, we charge him double our normal fee."

"A smart businesswoman."

"We offer similar assistance to our service clients who are seeking employment." She lifted her chin. "For them, our payment comes in the form of information."

"What type of information?"

"Any and all. Mostly, we're hoping to gain knowledge of their employer and his or her inner circle. The more we know about them, the better we can place servants in their household. Should a future need arise, of course."

"You're using servants to spy on their employers in order to protect future hires?"

"That about sums it up."

"And you're not charging the out-of-work servants for your service?"

"No," she said, feeling uncomfortable. "But most of

the time, the two needs go hand-in-hand and I don't have far to look for a willing employer."

He sent her an I-don't-believe-it's-that-easy look. "The third area of the agency?"

She cleared her throat. "The final service we offer is a bit more unconventional."

"More unconventional than having servants spy on their employers?"

"Much more."

He laid his serviette onto the table and crossed one leg over the other. "Then I cannot wait to hear it."

During their conversation, his anger had slowly dissipated and was replaced by his normal provoking manner. "On occasion, one of our service clients will bring a friend of theirs to our attention. In these instances, the servant has been unfairly mistreated and turned out with no recommendation to take to another employer. The Hunt Agency remedies the loss."

He tapped the side of his forefinger against his lower lip. "You're writing false letters of recommendation."

"Only for those individuals who find themselves without employment through no fault of their own."

"Such as?"

The muscles in her neck went taut. "A sixteen-year-old maid who submitted to the master of the house and became heavy with child. A kitchen maid who had been beaten by a chef because she did not cut a carrot right. A footman who rebuffed the advances of a male houseguest. A lady's maid who laid out the wrong color dress for the occasion." Sydney paused to slow the hard rise and fall of her chest. "Shall I go on, my lord? There are a hundred others I could name."

"Not necessary. I see what you mean. Why did you start using the cloak?"

She couldn't tell if her falsifying references had offended his aristocratic sensibilities or if he was merely taking it all in. "One evening, we received word that a former client, retired and without family, was quite ill and could not afford medical treatment. He lived in an unsavory area of the city, and Mac was being quite difficult about me going."

"A sensible man. I'm starting to warm up to him."

"Our compromise was that I would dress less like a woman. The cloak was Mac's idea. The breeches mine."

"Much to his later regret, I'm sure."

Sydney still recalled the incredible feeling of freedom and safety she'd found that first time, walking the streets of London and hiding behind the dark folds of Mac's cloak. To this day, she felt more centered, more herself when in the Specter guise.

"You're likely right," she said.

"Please tell me that you take Mac or Mick with you any time you don the cloak."

"Of course I do. Both, actually. The people I meet with are not even aware that the brothers are lurking in the shadows." She narrowed her eyes on him. "Please tell *me* you didn't think I was so reckless as to do otherwise."

He grinned. "I admit, the possibility had crossed my mind."

She tried to share his amusement, but she couldn't manage it. Not yet. Not until she told him everything. "While I'm baring my soul," she slid her damp palms over her serviette, "I should make sure you're fully aware of the last of it. So there's no misunderstanding."

"I'm listening."

"I know a good deal about the Nexus and your primary objective."

A heartbeat passed, and he said nothing. Two. Three.

Then finally, "After your cryptographer comment in the alleyway, I surmised as much, though I wasn't certain of the extent of your knowledge."

"And of your role in the organization."

He glanced away then, his jaw set in granite. "Yes, you mentioned as much this morning, and yet you still shared my bed." He shot to his feet and strode to the window. "Or, perhaps, you were not referring to my skill in the boudoir, but my talent for extracting prisoners from foreign lands." When he turned back to her, his eyes carried the burden of a thousand years of sorrow. "With whatever means necessary. Which role were you referring to, sweet Sydney?"

She ignored his mocking tone and focused on the moral struggle he tried to hide. "Would you do any of it differently?"

"No. I'm honored to serve my country in whatever capacity she demands."

"Somehow your admirable words don't match the resentment I heard in your tone earlier."

"I resent people casting judgment on actions they could never comprehend."

"You think I was judging you?"

His silence was emphasized by a steely-eyed glare. Sydney placed her serviette on the table and stood. "No, Ethan. I merely mentioned that I was aware of your bedchamber activities. The other, I knew nothing about and would certainly not judge." He turned away again, and pain sliced through her stomach.

"You're a hero, Ethan. Same as any decorated general who must order a thousand men into battle, knowing many might not return. War—even the behind-the-scenes kind—is filled with honorable men making intolerable decisions, or, in your case, intolerable actions. My only regret is that more of my countrymen won't learn of the sacrifices you've made to ensure our safety. So, for them, and me, I thank you."

Slowly, he swiveled his head toward her, and Sydney saw tears glistening in his eyes.

"Oh, Ethan."

She made to go to him, but a rap on the door stopped her cold.

"Pardon, my lord," Tanner said, stepping inside. "Mrs. Cartwright is here to see Miss Hunt. The young lady claims the matter is urgent."

Sydney hadn't taken her eyes off Ethan, though he'd averted his face at the butler's knock. "Thank you, Tanner. I'll be there in half a minute."

"Very well, miss." Tanner backed out and closed the door.

With slow, careful strides, she approached the silent man by the window. "Ethan. After knowing all that I do about you, I'm still here."

A muscle in his jaw worked furiously, but he refused to look at her. She ran her hand down his arm until she reached his clenched fist. Bringing his hand to her lips, she kissed the hair-dusted back and then laid her cheek against the only part of him accessible to her.

"I must go see what has happened. Amelia isn't one for theatrics. If she said something's urgent, it no doubt is." She pressed her lips against his skin once more and stepped away.

Long fingers halted her retreat and twirled her around. His warm, insistent mouth claimed hers as if it would be a hundred years before the next time. Then he slowed their pace, and the kiss transformed into a lush, hot sharing. A yearning and a promise.

He pulled back enough to whisper, "You're late."

Glancing up, she saw something in his eyes that made her heart skip its next beat. Then he nodded to the door. "Go."

She planted her palms on his cheeks and rose up on her toes, kissing him swiftly. Before he could draw her close, she backed away, a smile playing on her lips.

He took a threatening step closer. "Never toy with a spy, hedgehog."

"I shall try to heed your warning, my lord cad." She swiveled around and rushed out to find Amelia pacing the entry hall. Dread wiped clean the dazzling sensations peppering her body. "What's wrong?"

Tears gathered in Amelia's eyes. "Mick's been shot."

Twenty-eight

SYDNEY STORMED INTO THE AGENCY'S DRAWING ROOM where her clients normally waited to be escorted up to her study. Rather than carry Mick up three flights of stairs and risk further injury, Amelia had assembled a makeshift bed for him down here before coming to get her.

The scene that greeted her was far worse than she'd expected. Bloody rags were strewn about the floor, filling the room with a caustic, rusty scent that made her head spin and stomach roil.

On the pallet lay an ashen-faced Mick, with his brother steadying his upper body and the thief-taker Cameron Adair securing his lower. Standing at the patient's side was Charlotte Fielding, a good friend of Amelia's and a brilliant apothecary.

A large hand settled on Sydney's lower back, and she took instant comfort from having Ethan at her side. Her breaths were coming faster and her skin had turned clammy. Soon, she would have to leave so she didn't make matters worse by blacking out. But not yet.

"Help me out of this coat," Ethan said, already working on the buttons.

When he'd heard Amelia's announcement, he'd taken

control and hurried them out to the awaiting carriage, pausing only long enough to bark an order at Tanner to summon Lord Somerton. Once under way, he'd questioned Amelia relentlessly until she had no more answers. Unfortunately, she'd had little to share because she'd left almost immediately to fetch Sydney.

It took her several hard yanks to break him free of the fitted garment. His silver waistcoat followed.

Tilting her chin up, he spoke quickly. "Somerton and the others will be here soon. I need you to fill them in on everything." He must have felt her stiffen. "Everything, Sydney, please. You and Amelia might have knowledge we do not, and likewise for us. When we get a break here, we'll question the thief-taker about Mick." He kissed her forehead. "You know you can trust them."

She nodded, glancing over his shoulder. Mac caught her gaze and she detected no hope in his eyes. She swallowed back her fear and infused enough determination for them both in her return gaze. Then Ethan ushered her and a protesting Amelia out, closing the door behind them. Arm in arm, she and Amelia ascended the stairs. Away from the blood and Mac's hopeless expression.

A half hour later, Ethan entered her private study, where she kept company with Lords Somerton and Helsford, Cora deBeau, and Amelia. Fatigue scarred his handsome features, and she could see a spray of blood he tried to hide beneath his waistcoat. Leaning against the closed door, he sent the Nexus trio a meaningful look. Cora rose and joined the two men near the window, their backs to the room.

Sydney and Amelia stood, too. Their hands clasped together in silent support. "What news, Ethan?"

"I'm sorry, Sydney. We couldn't save him."

Sydney closed her eyes and felt her heart slowly caving in on itself. Mick in various stages of mischief flashed through her mind—him laughing, winking, slapping his knee. For the past year, his good cheer had echoed off the Agency's walls, bringing a smile to her face again and again. So much sadness. She couldn't breathe, couldn't think. Couldn't begin to imagine how this terrible loss would change her life forever.

She opened her eyes and stared at Ethan's watery image. "How?"

"Mrs. Fielding managed to remove the bullet, but she believes the ball shattered one of Mick's ribs. One of the bone fragments must have punctured his right lung."

Amelia dropped her face in her hands, and Sydney pulled her assistant against her shoulder. Then Ethan gathered them both in the curve of his strong arms, and Sydney finally allowed the tears to fall.

She wasn't sure how much time had passed before Ethan squeezed her shoulder and eased back.

"Mac's still in shock," he said, "but I don't think it will last long."

Amelia swiped her fingers beneath her eyes. "I'll go. He might try something stupid, like murdering Mr. Adair."

"Perhaps you would be kind enough to send Adair up to us," Ethan suggested.

Nodding, she hurried from the room. Somerton jerked his head toward the door, and the two agents—Lord Helsford and Cora—followed.

Ethan guided her to the chair behind her desk and then waited by her side until Adair arrived with his Nexus escort.

"Mr. Adair," Sydney said in a quivery voice. "Please allow me to introduce you to Lord Somerton, Lord

Helsford, Lord Danforth, and Miss deBeau." Everyone made their nods. "Please sit and tell us what transpired prior to Mick O'Donnell getting sh-shot."

Ethan squeezed her shoulder, the action giving her much-needed strength.

Adair didn't move from his place by the door. His sharp gaze assessed every individual in the room, and she got the impression they all came up lacking somehow.

"You may trust these people," she said, though she could not say the same for him. "They are my friends."

The thief-taker continued to assess them as though they were a menagerie of exotic animals.

"Adair, this is important," Ethan said. "More lives might be lost if we don't get to the bottom of what happened today."

"I don't see how that is my concern," Adair said. "I completed my contractual obligation." He held up his bloody hands. "More so, actually."

Ethan stepped forward, and Sydney sensed his explosive anger. Grasping his hand, she burrowed her fingers between his and used her thumb to rub soothing circles over his palm. He eased back to her side.

"Then I shall hire you to tell us what happened to Mr. O'Donnell," Somerton said.

"And you are again?"

"Earl of Somerton. You may call upon me at 35 Charles Street tomorrow to collect payment."

"I accept."

Sydney had always known Adair was highly motivated by money, but his ransoming information regarding Mick's murder made her stomach revolt. To the Nexus, she said, "I asked Mick to contact Mr. Adair to locate a gentleman by the name of William Townsend."

Everyone's energy shifted from Adair to her. Cora and

Lord Helsford shared a look, Somerton fixed his hard crystalline eyes on her, and Ethan squatted down beside her. He started to ask her a question, but Lord Somerton cut in. "Later, Danforth. Let's hear what Mr. Adair has to say first."

"Townsend was no longer at the boardinghouse O'Donnell mentioned," Adair said. "I tracked him down at an establishment near the London Docks and sent for O'Donnell."

"What time did you send for Mick?" she asked.

"Around noon, I believe."

"What happened next?" Ethan asked.

"O'Donnell went inside to get a better look at Townsend, so he could confirm some suspicion he had about the gentleman."

"Where were you, Mr. Adair?" the silent, dark-eyed Lord Helsford asked.

"I followed, naturally."

"Naturally," Ethan scoffed.

"Had I not, *my lord*"—steel coated Adair's words— "your friend would have died alone and rotting away at the dockyard inn, as we speak."

"Mind your damn tongue, Adair," Ethan warned.

The thief-taker's gaze flicked to Sydney. "My apologies, Miss Hunt."

She nodded, though she thought her teeth would crack from the pressure of holding back the tears.

"Do you recall the name of the establishment?" Helsford asked.

"An inn called the Elephant Tusk."

Mac appeared, filling the doorframe. Amelia hovered behind.

"Come in, please," Sydney said.

Mac moved inside, though only a little. His grief and

anger evident in the deep grooves surrounding his eyes. Amelia slipped in next to him, supportive yet wary.

"You followed O'Donnell inside," Somerton prompted.

"Not immediately." Adair angled his body toward Mac, keeping him in view. "After a half hour, O'Donnell gave up waiting for Townsend and made his way upstairs." He glanced around the room, showing his first sign of uneasiness. "At the same time he pressed his ear against Townsend's door, the bloody thing opened."

Amelia clasped her hands together and held them against her mouth. Sydney longed to do the same, but she kept her hands locked in her lap. Hearing about Mick's final hour was both a blessing and a horror. Though she wanted this nightmarish tale to be over, she sat on tenterhooks, eating up the thief-taker's every word.

"Get on with it, Adair," Mac said in a hoarse voice. "The worst has already happened."

Adair's lips thinned. "Even from my position at the far end of the corridor, I saw recognition light in O'Donnell's eyes. Then he said, 'It is you,' right before he forced his way inside. I heard nothing amiss, so I started back down the stairs. That's when I heard gunfire." He stared down at his bloody hands. "By the time I reached O'Donnell, Townsend was gone, using a second set of stairs at the opposite end of the corridor." Dropping his arms back to his sides, Adair directed his last words to Mac. "He insisted I bring him here so he could share whatever information he'd discovered in Townsend's room."

The two men stared at each other for what seemed like an eternity. Finally, Mac broke the silence. "Thank you for bringing my brother home. If you need anything, come find me."

Adair nodded.

"Anything else?" Sydney asked. "Anything at all?"

"Considering I found Townsend at the docks, I doubt he'll be in England for much longer."

"I suspect you're right," Somerton said. "Thank you for your assistance this afternoon."

Amelia stepped forward. "Mr. Adair, if you'll follow me, I'll show you where you can rinse off before heading out."

After the door closed behind them, Somerton spoke to Mac in a careful voice. "Mr. O'Donnell, did your brother share anything with you before he passed away?"

"No." His closed expression did not allow for further questioning.

Ethan knelt next to Sydney and folded her ice-cold fingers between his warm hands. "Why did you seek William Townsend?"

Heart pounding, she said, "Townsend lodged at a boardinghouse across the street from Abbingale. We received word that an altercation had occurred between Townsend and a man whom we believed was LaRouche, the schoolmaster. I asked Mick to contact Mr. Adair to see what he knew about Townsend."

Ethan glanced at the other Nexus.

Knowing she had missed something important, she said, "You know who William Townsend is, don't you?"

Somerton spoke, "Someone who has plagued us for weeks, though we've been unable to track him down."

"Someone who allowed the French to use his country estate as a trap and execution site," Helsford said.

"Someone who slipped between our fingers today," Cora finished.

The horrible name materialized, and Sydney's attention slashed to Ethan. "Latymer."

He nodded, confirming the link to Abbingale she'd

been looking for. All that time she had spent inside the home searching for a connection, the bastard had been lounging in the boardinghouse across the street.

"How did I not tie the two together?" she asked, appalled by her incompetence.

Ethan frowned. "Latymer has eluded us all, Sydney. He did not attain his position as Under-Superintendent of the Alien Office by political appointment. He earned the right."

"He's correct, Miss Hunt," Somerton said. "Latymer was not only my colleague—he was my friend. Never once did I suspect him of such duplicity or evil."

Although she appreciated their reassuring words, they did nothing to assuage the hollow ache in her heart. Whirling around, she faced her friend. "Mac," she said in a voice sounding nothing like her own. "I'm so sorry." She rose to go to him.

He held up a staying hand. "You're not to blame. I—" Emotion closed off his words. "Pardon me." He disappeared down the corridor, never once looking her in the eyes.

Ethan settled his hand on the back of her neck and kissed her temple. Unlike before, his warmth did not penetrate the thick layer of ice coating her blood.

"It'll be all right," Ethan murmured. "He needs time."

Perhaps. She also knew, no matter what else happened, the Mac she knew was lost to her forever.

Twenty-nine

ETHAN PAUSED ON THE LANDING TO LISTEN FOR approaching footsteps. Tonight, he would complete his mission and remove Giles Clarke from this questionable place and tomorrow he would... what? Locate and kill Latymer, certainly. But beyond that? His jaw clenched. For the first time in many years, he could not see his future, only an endless black chasm. One thing he knew for certain: he would never return to the boudoir.

Thoughts of the bedchamber inevitably led him to Sydney. To her generous nature and selfless acts. To her beautiful body and the incredible hour they'd spent together this afternoon. And, of course, to the catastrophe he'd created at the end.

Why had he ever started sharing those damned rules with her? They did nothing more than remind them both of his unsavory past. He didn't want her thinking about his previous lovers. With a few exceptions, they had used him as much as he'd used them. It was the handful who sought something more enduring from their liaison that haunted his conscience. None of the others.

When Sydney had shyly admitted to her feelings of inadequacy, he feared his head would explode with anguish. No woman such as she should ever experience those kinds of doubts. If he had the ability to sculpt the perfect woman, he could think of no better model—in face or form—than Sydney Hunt.

Like many other things recently, he had botched it with her. After their lovemaking, he'd wanted to crawl in bed beside her and stay for days. A first for him, and surprisingly the thought of eternity in her arms hadn't scared him. No, what brought on his momentary paralysis was his complete and utter inexperience of what to do next.

Before Sydney, he knew the exact minute he would leave a woman's bed. Not so this afternoon, and in his confusion, he had failed to mask his struggle. And his failure had cost them both.

Afterward, she had attempted to recapture their pre-lovemaking relationship, asking him about rescuing Giles and what he thought about LaRouche. She no longer pretended ignorance of the Nexus, nor tried to protect her Specter identity. The moment would have been monumental had it not been followed by so much crushing loss.

The news about Mick O'Donnell had devastated her, but she somehow summoned her brave face. Not for herself, but for her staff. She instinctively understood how to offer her support and still maintain an aura of quiet strength.

Once arrangements had been made for Mick, Somerton had dispatched Ethan and Helsford to Abbingale to rescue the Clarke boy. The moment he and Helsford reached Abbingale, his friend broke off to do a bit of reconnaissance of the lower level, leaving Ethan to retrieve the boy.

A sound from below jarred him back to the present.

He climbed to the floor that held the three large sleeping chambers. After checking to make sure the corridor was clear, he hurried to the entrance of the first chamber. Once inside, he crept from bed to bed with the aid of a candle he'd brought along and examined each boy for Giles Clarke's familiar features. What he didn't expect was the rush of guilt he felt every time he recognized a face and then continued on, abandoning each of them to an uncertain fate.

Halfway through the third chamber and no sign of Giles, his gut twisted with anxiety. The boy had to be here, because if he wasn't that meant Ethan should have gone against Somerton's order and retrieved him last night. When the uneasy thought began to take root, he quickened his pace to the next bed.

He bent to examine the next boy's features.

His eyes popped open, and he held his hand up to block the candlelight. "My lord, is that you?"

Ethan stared down at the pockmarked boy, his jaw clenching in frustration. "Yes, Mark," he whispered. "It is I, Lord Danforth."

"What are you doing here, sir?" He sat up, rubbing the sleep from his eyes.

"Can you keep a secret?"

"Yes, sir."

"I'm looking for Giles Clarke."

The boy's gaze shifted to the bed across the aisle. "Why?"

"Because I want to take him to his new family." The lie fell easily from his lips. He hoped it would become the truth, eventually.

Mark's face scrunched in confusion. "But, sir. Giles's papa fetched him about an hour ago."

"What?" his harsh voice rose above a whisper. One hour. He'd missed rescuing Giles Clarke by one hour.

The boy flinched, and several disheveled heads rose from narrow beds to investigate the disturbance.

"I'm sorry," Ethan said, twisting around to stare at the empty bed. "You caught me by surprise, is all."

"Caught Giles by surprise, too. He thought his papa was dead."

"Quickly, can you tell me what the gentleman looked like?"

The boy shook his head. "Giles sleeps across the way, and the man kept his back to me."

Ethan straightened, staring at the empty bed.

"Arthur Rhodes might have seen something." Mark threw back his covers. "He's in the bed next to Giles's."

Mark and another sleepy-eyed boy led him to Arthur, who remained huddled beneath thin covers.

Everyone in the dormitory was awake now and they padded over on bare feet. They formed a semicircle around Ethan, waiting. Getting out of this place without alerting their keepers was all but impossible now. He might as well make the best of it and work on coming up with a plausible excuse for his presence.

Ethan set his candle on the bedside table. "Mr. Rhodes, do you have a moment, please?"

No reply came, but from the motion under the covers, Ethan guessed he'd just been told no.

"I'm concerned for Giles," he said. "Do you have a description of the gentleman he left with an hour ago?"

More silence.

"Artie," Mark said, jabbing the boy in the shoulder, "I think you should answer his lordship. Giles was your friend."

The covers slowly lowered, and Ethan recalled the freckle-faced boy, who was afraid to stick his hand in

Sydney's bag. Brilliant. He had to pull vital information from the most timid orphan in residence.

Ethan knelt beside the bed. "What is upsetting you?"

"I can't tell you, sir." Tears clogged his voice.

"Gentlemen," Ethan glanced at the small crowd, "give us a moment, please."

"You heard him, lads. Let's give Artie some space." Mark shooed them all back to their beds.

Even though his body vibrated with tension, Ethan produced a calm, confidential tone. "Arthur, you and I are friends now. Yes?"

"I-I suppose so."

"As my friend, you are under my protection. Understand?"

The boy nodded.

"If a certain gentleman, who took your friend Giles, threatened you in any way, I want you to know that I would kill him if he ever tried to harm you." He chucked the boy under the chin to take the sting out of his words.

"You would?"

"Of course. Friends watch out for each other. Always."

"He's going to hurt Giles?"

Ethan squeezed the boy's shoulder. "Let's focus on finding them. Mind if I ask you a few questions?"

The boy shook his head.

"Do you think the man was as tall as me?"

"Maybe even taller, sir."

"Did he have brown hair?"

"No. His was as black as I've ever seen."

"How about his build? Was he stocky like me or lean like your schoolmaster?"

He thought for a second. "More like Monsieur."

"Can you think of anything else that would help me identify him? Anything at all?"

Arthur swiped his nose. "The way you talk. You sound a lot like each other."

"You mean my accent?"

"Yes, sir."

"Did he happen to mention anything about their destination? A city or foreign country? A boardinghouse or seaside cottage? A carriage or ship?"

"Yes!"

Ethan's heart smacked against the wall of his chest. "Which one?"

"Ship," Arthur said with excitement. "He promised Giles that he'd get to travel on a ship."

"A ship, not a boat. Is that right?"

He nodded. "Lots of sails."

Ethan's mind buzzed with possibilities. The boy's description of Giles's father sounded an awful lot like Lord Latymer. From the beginning, they had suspected the baron of having a connection to Abbingale, but at no time had anyone conceived of this situation. Could Latymer truly be the Clarke boy's father? If so, what was Giles doing here and why did Latymer have to secret the boy away? Or was this an attempt at redirection?

Then he recalled Cameron Adair's prediction about Latymer leaving the country.

"Did the gentleman mention the name of the ship, or when it might set sail?"

The boy searched his mind. "No, sir."

Ethan pushed to his feet. "You have my deepest gratitude for your bravery." To mark the solemnness of the occasion, Ethan presented a leg and bowed lower than he'd bowed in a very long time. "Now, I must be off."

Pivoting on his heel, he turned to leave and was met by a group of hopeful young faces.

"Can we go with you, sir?" one boy asked. "To help save Giles?"

Ethan's heart dropped into his stomach. "I'm not sure that's a good idea—"

"Please, sir," another said. "We're tired of losing our friends during the night."

"What do you mean?"

"They disappear in the middle of the night and never return."

"How many have disappeared?"

Mark spoke up. "One every few weeks or so. Just the gifted ones, though."

"Gifted ones?"

Everyone's attention swiveled back to Mark. The boy's pockmarked face reddened. "Like me, sir."

"How are you gifted?"

"It's just a title Monsieur uses." He closed the distance between them and whispered in Ethan's ear. "Monsieur uses the term to distinguish those of us who shouldn't be here."

"And why is that?"

The boy hesitated.

"Your secret is safe with me. I swear it."

Clearing his throat, Mark said, "Because we're not orphans."

Before Ethan could question him further, a shrill voice cut through the chamber.

"What's going on here?" Mrs. Drummond marched down the center aisle.

Ethan whispered to Mark, "Where might I find the schoolmaster?"

"I don't know, sir," Mark whispered back. "We haven't seen him since your visit yesterday."

Elbowing her way through the last of the boys, Mrs.

Drummond's eyes widened when she noticed Ethan in their center. "Lord Danforth," she glanced around, her expression anxious, "what are you doing here?"

The plausible excuse he needed failed to materialize. When faced with an impossible situation, especially one involving a woman, Ethan reverted to his tried-and-true weapon—charm and a seductive smile.

"Good evening, Mrs. Drummond. How nice to see you again."

She waved the boys away. "Back to bed with you. Now."

Dejected, they shuffled away, glancing back several times before climbing into their narrow beds.

The nurse leveled her steely eyes on him. "Explain your business here, my lord."

Not wanting the boys to see the lengths he would go to in order to win the nurse's silence, Ethan indicated a nearby exit. "Shall we?"

She hesitated a moment before nodding. Once they were away from young ears, Ethan began weaving his spell.

"I know my visit this evening might seem a little unorthodox."

She sent him a confused look. "What do you mean unorthodox?"

"Irregular. But, I assure you," he set his hand to the center of her lower back and deepened his voice, "my reason for being here is a very good one."

His nearness unsettled her, and she took a small step away but did not completely break contact. "And what reason would that be?"

They were nearing the staircase. He reduced the gap between their bodies. "You recall that I'm considering making a donation to Abbingale."

The nurse glanced at him out of the corner of her eye and then nodded. She didn't move away.

"It's been my experience to tour an establishment during the day to get a sense of the operation. Then make a clandestine visit at night to see behind the curtains, so to speak."

"Sounds as if you're spying on us."

"In a way, I am." He produced a warm, conspiratorial smile. "We're talking about a good deal of money, Mrs. Drummond."

The rigid line of her lips loosened, not into a smile but something infinitely more friendly. Again, she scanned the area with a nervous eye. "You should not be here, my lord."

"You're right, of course." Pausing near the staircase, he stood close enough to smell the starch in her clothing. "But one can never be too careful. I'm sure you understand."

"If you leave now, I won't inform Matron about your visit. Dither around here any longer and I'll be forced to say something." Her steely command was edged with breathless anticipation.

He leaned forward, his stomach muscles tightened and his throat clenched to hold down the bile. The hand at her back urged her forward. He pressed his lips against her cheek and produced a long, flesh-prickling breath. Then he lingered two seconds longer than was appropriate. When he lifted his head, slowly, he made sure his most intimate smile was in place. "Thank you, Mrs. Drummond. I shall not forget your kindness."

She swallowed hard, moving away. "Good night, Lord Danforth."

"Good night—" Pain sliced into Ethan's skull, and his legs buckled.

The nurse gasped, staggered back, and then crumbled to the floor.

Ethan shook his head to clear his vision and managed not only to make it worse, but to send another shooting pain into his left eye and down his spine. He sensed a forbidding presence next to him and attempted to get to his feet. Another mistake that made him drunkenly fall to his backside.

"Up with you, guv'nor." A large pair of hands seized his arm. "We'll take you some place nice so you can rest. A lo-o-ong rest." The man chuckled.

Ethan struggled, though his half-blinded attempt was pathetic. His attacker decided to take the easier route, and he slammed his massive boot into Ethan's side, hurling him down the stairs. His right shoulder connected with a corner of a stair, and he heard a sickening pop—then nothing but his body thudding down the remaining stairs, followed by a *thwack* when he bounced off the landing wall. Unable to break his momentum, he started rolling down the next set of stairs. As luck would have it, he managed to grab a sturdy baluster, bringing his headlong flight to a violent halt.

Footsteps pounded down after him. Closing his eyes against his swirling surroundings, he made to grasp the hidden knife inside his boot. His right arm wouldn't move. He tried again. Nothing. The bastard's fingers clawed into his hair, forcing Ethan's head back at an unnatural angle. The swirling increased.

Jaw clenched, he grappled for the knife with his left hand. Twisting his body, he lashed out three times in quick succession. A loud bellow accompanied by several curses rent the air. The man's grip on Ethan's hair disappeared.

Opening his eyes, he blinked several times. His focus slowly returned and the first thing he noticed was the blood spurting from his attacker's thigh. A good sign for

Ethan, a very bad sign for the injured footpad. Within a few short minutes, there would be no more blood left to eject from the wound. He shuddered. This could have been Sydney's fate last evening.

Backing down the stairs, Ethan said, "I would suggest you have that looked at. Now." Though he knew the man would never make it to a surgeon in time.

His attacker glared at him, with shocked, faintly glazed eyes. "You bloody well killed me."

"I do believe I was provoked." Ethan stumbled down the last two stairs; pain sliced through his arm.

Sweat streamed over the other man's temples, giving his colorless face a waxy sheen. "I'm going to crush your scrawny neck." He charged after Ethan, but the amount of blood he'd already lost made him clumsy and his aim off.

Ethan moved out of the way at the last moment, and the big man went hurtling to the floor. He did not get back up.

Nausea surged into Ethan's throat, and he pressed the back of his hand to his mouth. For several seconds, he fought a silent battle and slowly the bile receded, leaving a raw, burning trail behind. The bastard had hit his head hard enough to give him a damn concussion. On top of that unpleasant realization, his right arm hung uselessly at his side and hurt like hell. Then a muscle in his crippled arm spasmed, and Ethan nearly blacked out.

Good God, he didn't need this now. With Giles Clarke missing and talk of ships, Ethan suspected he had minutes to locate the boy, rather than days. He bent to sheathe his knife and pain splintered in his head and arm. Clenching his teeth, he cupped the elbow of his injured arm with his hand and felt a modicum of relief.

"Lord Danforth," a new voice called from above.

Careful not to make any sudden moves, he swiveled

enough to peer up the stairs and found Abbingale's matron descending. One of her hands glided along the handrail and the other was hidden behind her skirts. She stared at the macabre scene below as if it were nothing more than a spilled cup of tea.

"Mrs. Kingston." Recalling the nurse's sharp gasp, he glanced beyond the matron's shoulder for signs of the other woman.

"Mrs. Drummond can no longer help you, my lord," she said with an amiable smile.

His muscles went taut. "Why is that?"

"The moment she set you free, she was no longer of any use to us."

"Us?" He nodded toward the dead man, knowing he was more likely a hired footpad than a mastermind. The more questions she answered, the closer he would come to unraveling the mystery surrounding this place. "You and this gentleman?"

"Don't be absurd."

She continued forward in an even, unfaltering descent. Nothing in her tone or expression matched her matter-of-fact I-kill-people-every-day words.

"Perhaps you should stop where you are, Mrs. Kingston. I should also like to see what's in your left hand."

She complied without hesitation, halting several stairs above him to point a pistol at his head.

"It is merely a precaution, my lord. I would much prefer not to have another mess to clean up tonight."

"Nor do I wish to be a mess." Precious minutes were slipping away. "Mrs. Kingston, I hate to cut our reunion short, but I have a missing boy to find." He eyed her calm facade. "You wouldn't happen to know where I might find him. Giles Clarke? Or, if you prefer, Adam Smith?"

"Your skill at prevarication should be commended, my lord." She waved him back against the wall before continuing her descent. "During your visit yesterday, I detected nothing amiss with your performance as an overindulged nobleman."

"High praise from someone who knows a bit about the subject."

"Am I to assume Mrs. Henshaw was also performing?"

Ethan would love to confirm her suspicions, but there were still too many unanswered questions and unknown people involved. Until he knew more, he would minimize Sydney's exposure.

"Mrs. Henshaw was an unfortunate victim in my scheme." A wave of dizziness washed over him. He braced his shoulder blades against the wall to keep from pitching forward. "Since we are in a sharing mood, perhaps you might explain why the boys are coming and going from the property throughout the day."

One of her eyebrows rose in surprise. "Monsieur LaRouche said you were a spy. Even though I did not fully believe him, I decided to initiate my plan a few days sooner than I had scheduled."

"What sort of plan?"

"Killing him, of course," she said, without emotion. "I didn't mind him using the boys to courier government secrets to his various French contacts around the city. But he changed the rules on his gifted boys. Once they'd outserved their purpose, he began selling them like slaves." The gun in her hand trembled as a shudder tracked down her stout frame. "I found out where the last boy went, and I want no part of that kind of depravity."

Ethan stared at the woman in fascinated horror. In the time it took to snap one's fingers, the matron had explained all the mysterious goings-on at Abbingale.

"You just killed him? A French intelligence agent? Do you really think they'll let you live after tampering with their system?"

"Who would ever suspect me? If anything, you'll be the one blamed." She pointed her weapon toward the stairs leading down. "After you."

Walking meant jarring his shoulder. Jarring his shoulder meant excruciating pain. Excruciating pain meant vulnerability. Vulnerability meant death.

He carved his most charming smile across his face. "But we were getting on so well here."

"I am immune to men and their charm, my lord. I think their attempts at seduction rather disgusting." She raised her brows, waiting.

It was then he realized that pain was not his worst enemy. No, he had to face the shameful fact that, in his present condition and while she brandished a weapon, he might not be able to overpower this diminutive redheaded murderer. With his luck, he would faint the second he released his useless arm.

Gathering his strength, he pushed away from the wall in one fluid motion and took a step toward the stairs. A wave of lightheadedness hit him. He paused a moment until his equilibrium stabilized. At the far end of the corridor, another figure emerged from one of the chambers. Ethan squinted for a better look at the same time the figure faced him, taking in the chilling scene.

"No!" The figure ran toward them, cloak billowing out behind.

Time slowed. Realization blared.

Cloaked figure. Sydney.

"Stop!" But he was too late. Mrs. Kingston swung her pistol toward the new threat. Not stopping to think about the pain, he plowed into the woman. Her weapon fired, and Ethan waited for the answering feminine scream. None came, though that might be because his ears were filled with his own roar of pain as he and the matron crashed to the floor.

His stomach heaved and his sight filled with black and white spots. Unconsciousness pushed at his mind, demanding entrance. Oblivion was both a temptation and a nightmare. He couldn't give in to his body's demands. Not yet. Not until Sydney was safe.

Scuffling noises sounded behind him. He pushed away from the floor with his good arm. Ghostly images eddied in front of his face. Ignoring them, he sat back on his heels, reaching between his legs for his knife. The air shifted around him, and he whipped his head up. His eyes registered the cloaked figure before they blurred again. *Sydney.*

"Not supposed to be here," he whispered, swaying.

"And miss my opportunity to save you again?" a raspy voice asked.

He blinked several times to clear his vision, but her hooded image wavered in and out of focus. "Are you hurt?"

A gloved hand cupped his face. "All's well, my love."

He tried to shake his head. The movement was sluggish. "Giles missing," he managed before lurching forward.

Thirty

A STEEL PIKE JAMMED INTO ETHAN'S SHOULDER, thrusting him awake. "Son of a—"

Cool hands clasped his face. "Look at me, Ethan," Sydney demanded.

His gaze slashed around, not recognizing the room. "Where am I?"

Her fingers dug into his cheeks until his attention settled on her. She no longer wore the black cloak. "You're still at Abbingale. In a small parlor located on the first floor. Your shoulder is dislocated, and Mrs. Fielding is attempting to make an adjustment."

"By cutting the damned thing off?" He angled his head around to see how much was left.

"Don't be ridiculous. She's trying to help you."

"Besides, my lord," the apothecary said behind him, "severing the limb is only necessary if the patient is uncooperative."

Ethan twisted in his chair to glare at the owner of the impertinent remark; Sydney held tight, but he still caught a glimpse of Helsford lurking near the apothecary.

"Now, I'm going to release you," Sydney said. "But you must relax and sit perfectly still."

"I'm not going to like this, am I?"

Mrs. Fielding cupped her hand over the top of his dislocated shoulder, positioning her thumb to the center of his shoulder blade. "The worst part is over, my lord. Removing your fitted coat likely hurt you far more than will snapping the ball back into its socket."

"I'm weak-kneed with relief, Mrs. Fielding." He clenched his teeth together, then nodded his readiness to Sydney. She released his face, though she continued kneeling in front of him.

"Lord Helsford, would you mind taking your position?"

"My pleasure." He moved to Ethan's right side.

"Helsford?" Ethan heard the double *en tendre* behind his friend's words. "If you so much as touch me—"

"His lordship has agreed to be my assistant, if necessary," Mrs. Fielding said. "Now, what I'm about to do will feel a little strange and might be uncomfortable, but you should not feel any significant pain. If you do, let me know immediately. Understood?"

"Yes, ma'am."

Sydney scowled at his militant tone.

With her hand still on his shoulder, Mrs. Fielding grasped his wrist, where it hung at his side. Slowly, she lifted his arm in a wide arc, and the bone rotating beneath his skin did, indeed, feel strange, like the moving parts of a clock not quite aligned. She reached the hundred-degree angle and stopped.

"I'm going to need your assistance after all, Lord Helsford."

His friend smirked. "Interesting to note Danforth's mind is not the only stubborn part of his body."

"Shut up, Helsford." Sweat raked down his spine, and the discomfort in his arm began to build.

The earl bent at one knee and pushed three fingers into the front of Ethan's armpit.

"Ethan, look at me."

He trained his eyes on Sydney, on the emerald sphere of her irises. Somehow staring into her eyes gave him the strength to endure their manipulations. A small twitch in his cheek was the only outward sign he felt what they were doing.

Pop!

A harsh, relieved breath escaped his nose.

"What was that?" Sydney demanded.

"His shoulder rotating back into place."

Sydney sent him a smile and squeezed his hand before climbing to her feet.

"You did well, my lord," the apothecary said.

"Are you talking to the jackanapes kneeling on the floor or me?" Ethan asked.

"Both, I suppose."

"All he did was stick his fingers in my armpit."

Helsford rose. "All you did was stare longingly into Miss Hunt's eyes."

"A difficult feat with your clumsy fingers digging around."

"Boys," Sydney scolded, carrying a small pillow and a couple torn lengths of sheet.

"Where's your walking stick?" he asked, scowling.

Helsford grinned, ear to ear. "She used it to thrash the matron."

Ethan started to share Helsford's smile and then realized he'd put her in a situation where she had to defend them both. Shifting his gaze to the floor, he tested his right shoulder. The movement hurt like hell, but at least he could use his arm again.

"Not too far," Mrs. Fielding warned.

He halted the action.

"Once a shoulder dislocates, the joint is forever

unstable and you can easily dislocate it again. Especially right now."

"Brilliant."

Sydney handed the pillow to the apothecary, who placed it between his injured arm and torso.

"My lord, please bend your arm for me." Mrs. Fielding helped guide his arm into the position she wanted.

Sydney held out one end of the torn sheet to the apothecary and together they devised a secure sling for his arm. Then they used the other length of sheet to immobilize his arm against his body.

"Is that really necessary?" he asked, feeling like an invalid.

"Yes, my lord." Mrs. Fielding tied off the strip of linen. "It's important that you not use your arm for three weeks. Once you remove the sling, you must not lift anything heavy for at least two months, for the reasons I've already mentioned."

Helsford did one of those disbelieving air snorts. He knew better than most what such confinement would do to Ethan's mental state.

"Three weeks? Are you certain?"

The apothecary's lips pressed together. "You might be able to remove it in a fortnight." Her next words were directed at Sydney. "Though I don't advise it."

Ethan's stomach roiled at the thought of going through such nauseating pain a second time.

"If you have ice available to you, I suggest you use some on the shoulder for a few days to reduce the swelling. Same for the lump on your head." The apothecary picked up a small portmanteau that acted as a medical bag and dug out a brown bottle. "I know a few exercises that will strengthen the shoulder and reduce the stiffness. I'll pay you a visit when it's time to remove the sling and share them with you." For the first time, she appeared unsure. "If it pleases you, my lord."

"It pleases him, Mrs. Fielding," Helsford said. "May I walk you out?"

Surprise widened her eyes. "Thank you, my lord. But that's not necessary. I'm used to navigating the city on my own."

"Mrs. Fielding," Ethan interrupted. Exhaustion rode heavily on his chest. "Helsford wants to pay for your services in private and ensure you get home safely." He flicked his hand toward his friend. "If you don't allow him his gentlemanly due, he becomes intolerable."

She glanced between him and Helsford, then nodded.

"Thank you, Mrs. Fielding," Ethan said. "I think."

"You're welcome, Lord Danforth. I think." She handed him the brown bottle. "For the pain."

Ethan read the label. Laudanum.

Sydney walked with the apothecary for a while, speaking to her in a low voice. At the door, she bid the healer farewell and then returned to his side. "How do you feel?"

He shifted awkwardly in the hardback chair. "Like that's the closest I ever want to come to having a limb severed."

She stared at him. "You paint quite the picture."

"What were the two of you whispering about?"

"Do you always inquire about private conversations?"

"When I believe they're about me."

She sighed. "You have a severe concussion, Ethan. Mrs. Fielding warned me to watch for certain symptoms."

"That's all?"

"Yes."

"How long was I out?" He couldn't keep the self-disgust from his voice.

"Not long." She brushed a lock of hair off his forehead; her fingers continued a featherlight trail down his cheek. "Time enough for us to send for Mrs. Fielding and wrestle you into this chair."

Rubbing his splintering forehead, he said, "I don't recall anything after seeing you running down the corridor." Except the paralyzing fear. He recalled that.

"You rammed into Mrs. Kingston, sending her gun flying," she said. "Lord Helsford was racing up the stairs at the same time and subdued the woman."

"*After* you clouted her."

She sent him a quelling look. "Matron's being interrogated by Lord Somerton at the moment. Mrs. Ashcroft, Miss deBeau, and Amelia are attending the boys."

"The bodies?"

"Removed."

"It's nice to know all I have to do is take a wee nap and everything is taken care of by the time I wake." No wonder Somerton had reservations about him for the chief's position. When Cora had needed him, he'd lain senseless in a warehouse for days. At the most critical moment tonight, he got a bump on the head and fell unconscious, leaving the woman he loved to fight for her life. Could he be anymore inept?

He almost groaned out loud. Did he truly love Sydney? He must. Why else would he put up with her stubborn, managing ways? Her kindness and selflessness. Her aching kisses and lush, warm body. A resigned breath poured from his lungs, and his hand fell away.

"Ethan," she said in a stern voice. "Nothing is taken care of. We've set some things into motion, but there's a great deal more to do. We still have no idea what's truly going on here and now Giles Clarke is missing."

"Dammit, how could I have forgotten?" He tried to

stand and a wave of dizziness struck him. He landed hard in his seat, and a cold sweat broke out on his face. "Christ."

"You didn't forget. I daresay the pain has been a bit of a distraction," she said, steadying him. "Amelia found William Townsend's name on Abbingale's subscription list."

Grasping the opportunity to do something besides sitting there and getting sick, Ethan considered this information in conjunction with what he'd learned earlier. "The boys told me that Giles's father had come to collect him."

She pulled a chair closer and sat. "You think Lord Latymer is Giles Clarke's father."

"It seems rather fantastical, but the association would explain a great deal."

"How so?"

"Latymer's career was set. He could have easily risen to Foreign Secretary. Then for no reason that we understood, he became entangled in a French plot to kill his friend, the only individual who possessed full knowledge of the Nexus. Why would an ambitious, aristocratic gentleman give up his career and heritage?"

"To protect his son."

"Precisely."

"But what was he protecting Giles from?"

"Mark Snell said one of the gifted boys disappears every few weeks. That the gifted boys are not orphans."

"There are other boys here who have families? Does that mean they're being held against their will?"

"Mark's revelation coincides with what we know of Giles Clarke and his mother. Someone was forcing Mrs. Clarke to monitor Catherine Ashcroft's every move. And that same someone was likely using Giles to coerce his father into betraying his country."

"A form of extortion?"

"Consider the attempt to kidnap Lord Melville's grandson," he said. "They kidnap the children in order to force their parent—or parents, in Giles's case—to do their bidding."

"How horrible."

Not half as horrible as what he'd learned from Mrs. Kingston.

"What?" she asked, reading his expression.

"I'm not sure I should tell you."

"Does it have to do with the children?"

He nodded, and she closed her eyes.

When she opened them again, she wore her proprietress expression. "Tell me."

"You were right to question LaRouche's generosity when it came to caring for the children of his enemies. According to Mrs. Kingston, the Frenchman began selling some of the boys." The tears glistening in her eyes proved he did not need to expound.

"And the other boys? The runners?"

"As we thought, they were part of an elaborate French intelligence scheme."

Her expression took on a faraway look as if she was trying to imagine such an awful chain of events. "I must find the boys he sold," she said in a broken whisper.

He leaned forward and kissed her trembling lips. "Yes, we must."

Gratitude shone in her beautiful green eyes. "We?"

"Yes. *We.*" He sealed the promise with another kiss. "You might like to know LaRouche is dead."

"How? When?"

"I suspect sometime yesterday. When LaRouche started trafficking the boys, he evidently crossed the matron's moral threshold. She had already planned out his death. My arrival yesterday merely sped up the process."

"What did your arrival have to do with it?"

"She didn't get around to that part, but I suspect it had something to do with him calling me a spy. She must have seen her little enterprise crumbling before her eyes."

"Good Lord. All that was happening beneath this roof, and I did not see any of it."

"Not true." He grasped her hand. "You knew something was not right here. That's more than anyone else cared to notice."

"Do you think Latymer's going to flee England?"

"There's nothing here for him anymore. One of the boys overheard him tell Giles they were traveling on a ship."

"Cameron Adair was right."

"So it would seem." He studied her face. "Earlier, you did not mention what Mac's doing."

The last dim light faded from her features. "That's because I have no idea. I haven't seen him since our discussion in my study. Amelia is sick with worry, as am I."

"He's grieving and angry. The combination of those two emotions can be blinding at first. Once he overcomes the initial shock, they will help focus him."

"On what?"

"Finding his brother's killer, of course."

She squeezed her eyes shut. "Oh, God."

Angling forward, he curled his finger under her chin, tilting her head back until she looked at him. "You didn't really think he would sit back and allow the Nexus to avenge Mick's death, did you?"

Her breath shuddered. "I didn't think that far."

"That's because you're not a man," he said softly. "Revenge is our very first consideration."

"I could not bear it if I lost him, too."

"He's angry, not stupid. Unlike his brother, he knows who he's up against."

"Won't Lord Somerton want to question Latymer before Mac," she hesitated, "avenges Mick?"

"Somerton caught up to Mac after our conversation in your study."

"And?"

"They came to an understanding."

"Oh." Worry creased her brow.

"The Nexus will watch over Mac and see to Latymer, should he falter. Perhaps you, and the other ladies, could focus your considerable talents on coming up with a plan for Abbingale's lost boys, including Giles Clarke, when we locate him."

She nodded. "I'd like that, and thank you for keeping an eye on Mac."

"You're welcome." Ethan moved his hand to the back of her neck, pulling her closer. "I'm sorry I failed you."

Her fingers curled around his forearm and her other hand gripped his nape. "You didn't fail me, Ethan. You couldn't ever."

"I left you vulnerable—"

She silenced him with a kiss, a long, comforting kiss. "Your first instinct was to safeguard me, and you did, at great cost to yourself. Had I stayed away, like you asked, you would not have suffered so."

"As much as I hate to admit this," he brushed his lips over her jaw, "you gave me the incentive—and the distraction—I needed to disarm Mrs. Kingston."

Following his lead, she dotted warm kisses along his neck. "I couldn't stand not knowing how you fared.

Amelia distracted the others long enough for me to get away."

He kissed the corner of her mouth. "Which would explain why everyone is here now."

She smiled. "All part of my master plan."

"I am a lucky man to be in love with such an intelligent woman."

She froze.

"Given my past, I'm sorry for the burden my declaration places on you. And this isn't exactly how I wanted to tell you." He blew out a breath and rested his forehead against hers. "Hell, I'm not even sure I wanted to tell you." Considering her silence, he was making a muck of things. Again.

He drew away. "I'm sorry. I can see this was not the time. Maybe never was."

"Ethan," she said in a wobbly voice. "You're such a fool."

Tears gathered in her eyes, and her features appeared... happy.

Hope slammed into his heart and, for a moment, he forgot all about the pains in his body.

A throat cleared, and in walked his friend.

"Bloody awful timing, Helsford."

Then Somerton followed. His expression grim and pale.

Cold dread seeped into Ethan's bones. Somerton's interrogation of the matron had evidently produced fruit, but nobody was going to like the taste of it.

Thirty-one

ONLY MINUTES AGO, SYDNEY COULD SEE NOT BUT THE vague outlines of her bedchamber furniture. Now, the blue-gray predawn light misted into the room, giving every object a day side and a night side. Mornings had always been her favorite time. They held such promise, such immeasurable possibilities. She glanced down and smiled. Today more so than any other.

Especially after last night's horrific revelations. Mrs. Kingston had produced a ledger used by LaRouche to log each transaction made on the gifted boys—procurement dates, names, extortion detail and resolution, and finally, the boy's bill of sale. Viewing the stark rows and columns of men using and selling children had made her physically ill.

Somerton had also come away from the interrogation with a list of homes used in LaRouche's courier system. When the spymaster had asked Mrs. Kingston what she had done with the Frenchman's body, she led them to the cellar. To the darkest, coldest corner. There, they found LaRouche's body balled into a burlap bag and shoved into a recessed area.

Today would no doubt bring more heartache as they

tackled the difficult process of identifying each boy and determining who was a true orphan and who had a family to go home to. Today also signaled the beginning of so many happy endings, and that's what Sydney would focus her mind on. But later.

Right now, all she wanted to do was to be near Ethan. With the greatest care, she brushed her fingertips over the curled ends of his sable locks. She did not want to wake him, but she could not seem to stop touching him. Or looking at him. While awake, he was more handsome than any gentleman she'd ever known. In slumber, when his features loosened their hold on worry, self-recrimination, guilt, shame, and all the other emotions that he tried to hide, his beauty could topple any mystical god's.

He loved her, and she loved him. She was too frightened to think beyond those two glorious facts.

His eyes blinked open, and Sydney cursed her selfishness. He had endured so much pain last night before she finally talked him into taking some of the laudanum. Sleep was important during the healing process, and now she'd just deprived him of precious recovery time.

"My apologies," she said. "I did not mean to disturb you. Here, I'll leave you be." She started to rise, but he grasped her hand and brought it to his lips.

"Did you get any rest?" he asked, his voice cracking with disuse. "Or did you play nursemaid all night?"

"Let me get you something to drink."

"After you answer my question."

"Lord Helsford was right. You are a stubborn man."

He raised his eyebrow, waiting.

She sighed. "I wanted to be available, should you have had need of me."

"In other words… no." Using his left arm, he levered

himself into an upright position. He caressed her cheek with the backs of his fingers. "Thank you. Now, about that glass of water."

Scrambling out of bed, she draped her rose-colored silk wrap around her shoulders and secured the sash at her waist. After pouring a glass of water, she turned to find him standing in the center of the room, in nothing but his smalls and bandages. Water splashed over the rim.

"What are you doing? I would have brought it to you."

"I'm quite capable of fetching my own water. I merely wanted to see you walk across the chamber in your chemise." He sighed, plucking at her wrap. "Alas, you thwarted my plan by donning this pretty pink confection."

"Your water, my lord."

He took the glass and carried it to his lips. The moment he tipped back his head, she shimmied out of her wrap and let it pool around her wrists. He half snorted, half choked on the water. She smiled and pulled her wrap back on.

"Vixen."

"Reprobate."

His eyes narrowed.

"How is your head?" she asked. "Any nausea? Dizziness?"

His lips twitched at her turn of topic. "It aches, but no other ill effects, at the moment."

Striding to one of the two chairs, she patted the seat. "Come here. I want to hear about your conversation with Lord Somerton."

He stiffened. "Why?"

"You're not the only one who is curious about private tête-à-têtes."

"Our discussion had nothing to do with you."

"Did it not?" She held her breath, hoping he would confide in her.

"What do you know, Sydney?" His tone was menacing.

She had gambled and lost. After her conversation with Lord Helsford, she hadn't been able to think of any other way to broach the subject of his conversation.

He tossed back the rest of his water and slammed the glass on the table. "Sydney?"

"Oh, all right. But you must sit. I won't have you towering over me like one of those mythical, foul-smelling monsters."

That caught him up short. He angled his head toward one shoulder, then the next, his nostrils flaring each time. When she realized what he was doing, she burst out laughing. He stomped over and plopped into the chair and winced. She bent down and kissed the top of his head.

Taking the other chair, she said, "Lord Helsford mentioned that Somerton was ready to appoint a new chief for the Nexus." Her body hummed with nervous excitement. "Are you the one?"

"No and yes and no."

Her jaw dropped. "Pardon?"

Tilting his head back, he rested it against the chair. "At the end of last week, Somerton gave me an opportunity to fight for the position. A position I'd been training for and working toward for over a decade."

"Who was your competition?"

"Helsford, or so I believed."

"What do you mean?"

"I saw Helsford later and congratulated him." His mouth twisted. "All right, I didn't exactly congratulate him, but I told him I thought he'd make a good chief. That's when Helsford told me he'd already informed Somerton that he wanted nothing to do with the position."

The short distance separating them seemed a great cavern. She rose and snuggled against his leg, resting her head on his lap. A second later, his fingers tunneled through her hair. Sydney removed her hair tie and unwound her braid.

"I cannot wait to feel your silky hair draped over my chest."

She smiled and kissed his knee. "Why Somerton's deception?"

"To be chief, you have to be willing to do anything in service of England," he said softly. "Because I wasn't willing to pit myself against Helsford, I revealed my weakness. My inability to put my country first."

She lifted her head. "No, Ethan. You showed him your humanity."

He bussed her forehead. "That, too, hedgehog."

"And tonight?"

"Tonight, he admitted two difficult truths. One was that he'd always hoped I would take over the chief's position."

"How wonderful."

He tucked a lock of hair behind her ear. "I admit, hearing his revelation repaired some of my damaged pride."

"The second truth?"

"That he was glad I chose loved ones over my country."

"As am I." She studied his features for any sign of regret and found none.

He brushed her cheek, and she felt cool air slide over her damp skin.

"Are you very disappointed?"

Smiling, he said, "Not in the least."

"You wanted the position so badly, though."

He nodded. "I thought being the chief would validate my work with the Nexus, make my contribution more meaningful. It wasn't until my conversation last night with Somerton that I realized a title does not imbue one's work with value. A title is nothing but letters on a sheet of paper. Compassion, integrity, principles, diligence—those are the qualities that bring honor and significance to one's work. And those qualities are controlled by me, and me alone."

Sydney rose up on her knees and nudged his legs open so she could burrow closer. "Does this mean you're no longer interested in being chief?"

Reaching out, he cupped the side of her throat, his thumb resting on her pulse point. "Not chief, not boudoir spy, and not rescuer of imprisoned damsels. Though I might still have to keep company with a few ants, on occasion."

She ignored his strange reference to ants. "What will you do instead?"

"A few things come to mind. First, I would like to offer my services to the Hunt Agency. I rather like the thought of helping those who cannot help themselves."

"What type of assistance?"

He nudged the side of his nose with hers. "Have I mentioned I'm a very good spy and can ferret out the most troublesome details?"

"Ahh," she smoothed her hands up his broad chest, "I do recall something to that effect. What else comes to mind?"

"I mean to take you to bed and allow you to ravish my poor broken body."

She swooped in to pull his plump bottom lip between her teeth; her tongue teased the soft underside. Then she let go. "Will you be breaking one of your Instinct Rules?"

Curling his lower lip inward, he ran his tongue over where hers had trailed. "As a matter of fact, I will."

"Number five?" she challenged.

"Do not take your lover to bed more than twice."

Sydney's eyes rolled to her bed, where she'd spent several peaceful hours watching over him. "Too late. I slept with you last night."

The fingers at the back of her neck were tightening, preparing. "Since the sequence has been broken, I'm saved from sharing my final, most important rule." A familiar rogue's grin played along his lips.

She tried to hold out, she really did. But her curiosity had always been one of her greatest weaknesses. Through gritted teeth, she said, "Number six?"

The gentle pressure on her neck grew until they were nose to nose. When he spoke next, his lips caressed hers. "Ignore all the rules when you find the lover of your heart."

In case you missed it, here's an
excerpt from Tracey Devlyn's debut

A Lady's Revenge

Available now from Sourcebooks Casablanca

❧

1804
Near Honfleur, France

GUY TREVELYAN, EARL OF HELSFORD, STOPPED SHORT
at the sharp smell of burning flesh. The caustic odor
melded with the dungeon's thick, moldy air, stinging his
eyes and seizing his lungs. His watery gaze slashed to the
cell's open door, and he cocked his head, listening.

There.

A sudden scrape of metal against metal. A faint sizzling
sound followed by a muffled scream.

He stepped forward to put an end to the prisoner's
obvious suffering but was yanked back and forced up
against the dungeon's cold stone wall, a solid forearm
pressed against the base of his throat.

Danforth.

Guy thrust his knee into the bastard's stomach,
enjoying the sound of air hissing between his assailant's
lips, but the man didn't release his hold. Nearly the same
size as Guy, the Viscount Danforth wasn't an easy man to
dislodge. Guy knew that fact well. For many years they
had tested each other's strength.

"What the hell is wrong with you?" the viscount

whispered near his ear. "We're here for the Raven. No one else."

Guy stared into Danforth's shadowed face, surprised and thankful for his friend's quick reflexes. What would have happened had he stormed into the cell to save a prisoner he knew nothing about, against odds he hadn't taken time to calculate? Something in the prisoner's cry of pain struck deep into his gut. His reaction had been swift and instinctual, more in line with Danforth's reckless tendencies than his own carefully considered decisions.

"Leave off," Guy hissed, furious with himself. He pushed against Danforth's hold, and the other man's arm dropped away.

He had to concentrate on their assignment, or none of them would leave this French nightmare alive. The mission: retrieve the Raven, a female spy credited with saving hundreds of British lives by infiltrating the newly appointed emperor's intimate circle and relaying information back to the Alien Office.

Guy shook his head, unable to fathom the courage needed to pull off such an ill-fated assignment. The ever-changing landscape of the French government ensured no one was safe—not the former king, the *Ancien Régime*, the bourgeoisie, or the commoner. And, most especially, not an English secret service agent.

Although Napoleon's manipulation of the weak and floundering Consulate stabilized a country on the brink of civil destruction, the revered general-turned-dictator wasn't content to reign over just one country. He wanted to rule all of Europe, possibly the entire world. And, if his enemies didn't unite under one solid coalition soon, he might achieve his goal.

Another muffled, gut-twisting cry from the cell drew his attention. He clenched his teeth, staring at the faint light spilling out of the room, alert for movement or any signs of what he might find within.

Sweet Jesus, he hoped the individual being tortured by one of Valère's henchmen wasn't the Raven. In his years with the Alien Office, he had witnessed a lot of disturbing scenes, some of his creation. But to witness the mangled countenance of a woman... The notion struck too close to the fear that had boiled in his chest for months—*years*—giving him no respite.

On second thought, he hoped the prisoner was the Raven. Then he wouldn't have to make the decision to leave the poor, unfortunate soul behind, and they could get the hell out of this underground crypt posthaste.

"Are you well?" Danforth asked, eyeing him as if he didn't recognize his oldest friend.

Guy shoved away from the stone wall, shrugging off the chill that had settled like ice in his bones. Devil take it, what did the chief of the Alien Office expect him to do? Walk up to the prisoner and say, "Hello, are you the Raven? No? What a shame. Well, have a nice evening." Only one person knew what the agent looked like, and Somerton did not offer up those details before ushering them off to France. *Why?* he wondered for the thousandth time. It was an answer he intended to find as soon as they got back to London, assuming they survived this mission.

"I'm fine." He jabbed his thumb over his shoulder. "Now cease with the mothering and get behind me."

He barely noticed the fist connecting with his arm, having already braced himself for Danforth's retaliation. Some things never change. Inching toward the cell door, he tilted his head and concentrated on the low rumble of voices until he was close enough to make out individual words.

"Why do you force me to be so cruel?" a plaintive voice from inside the chamber asked. The Frenchman spoke slowly, as if talking to a child, which allowed Guy to quickly translate the man's unctuous words. The gaoler continued, "All you have to do is provide my master with the information he seeks."

A chain rattled. "Go to the devil, Boucher," a guttural voice whispered.

Guy's jaw hardened. The prisoner's words were so low and distorted that it was impossible to distinguish the speaker's gender. Every second they spent trying to solve the prisoner's identity was a second closer to discovery.

The interrogator let out a deep, exaggerated sigh. "The branding iron seems to have lost its effect on you. Let me see if I have something more persuasive."

An animallike growl preceded the prisoner's broken whisper. "Your black soul will burn for this."

Boucher chuckled low, controlled. "But not tonight, little spy. As you have come to discover, I do not have the same aversion to seeing you suffer as my master does."

Something eerily familiar about the prisoner's voice caught Guy's attention. His gaze sliced back to Danforth to find puzzlement etched deeply between his friend's brows.

Guy turned back, the ferocity of his heartbeat pumping in his ears. His stomach churned with the certain knowledge that what he found in this room of despair would change his life forever. He steadied his hand against the rough surface of the dungeon wall, leaned forward to peer into the cell, and was struck by a sudden wave of fetid air. The smell was so foul that it sucked the breath from his lungs, and he nearly coughed to expel the sickening taste from his mouth and throat.

The cell was twice the size of the others they had

searched. Heaps of filthy straw littered the floor caked with human waste and God knew what else. Several strategically placed candles illuminated a small, circular area, leaving the room's corners steeped in darkness. In the center stood a long wooden table with a young man strapped to its surface by thick iron manacles.

A young man. Disappointment spiraled through him. He glanced at Danforth and shook his head, and then evaluated their situation. The corridor beyond the candlelit chamber loomed like a great, impenetrable abyss.

The intelligence Danforth had seduced from Valère's maid suggested the chateau's dungeon held twelve cells. If the maid's information was correct, that left four more chambers to search. Would they, like all the others, be strangely empty?

Guy narrowed his gaze, fighting to see something—anything—down the darkened passage. It yawned eerily silent. Too damned silent. The lack of movement, guards, and other prisoners scraped his nerves raw. That and the realization they would not be able to slide past the nearby cell without drawing attention from its occupants.

Dammit.

He ignored Danforth's warning tap on his shoulder and peered into the young man's cell again. The prisoner's filthy legs and arms splayed in a perfect X across the table's bloodstained surface. A few feet away, with his back to the prisoner, stood a slender man dressed in the clothes of a gentleman, his unusual white-capped head bent in concentration over an assortment of spine-chilling instruments. *Boucher.*

Guy watched the man assess each device with the careful attention of an enraptured lover, masterfully prolonging the young man's terror. Give a victim long enough, and he'll create plenty of painful scenes in his own mind that the interrogator need only touch his weapon to the prisoner's skin to elicit a full, babbling confession.

He couldn't walk away from the poor soul struggling on the table, nor could he cold-bloodedly put an end to his misery. The young man was a countryman, not his enemy, and he would never leave one of his own in Valère's hands.

With great care, he withdrew a six-inch hunting knife from his boot. He heard Danforth curse softly, violently, behind him, and then a rustle of movement. His hand shot out to stay his friend, and a short struggle ensued. Their roles now reversed, Guy whispered in Danforth's ear, "There's no way around, and I'm not leaving him here."

"We don't have time—"

"I'm. Not. Leaving. Him."

After a moment, Danforth gave a sharp nod and settled into the rear support position once more, anger dripping off him in waves.

He couldn't blame his friend for wanting to press on. Evil penetrated every crack and hollow of this place. Even with his vast experience with the darker side of human nature, Guy felt trapped and edgy and unusually desperate.

Guy shifted his attention to the prisoner just as the young man's head swiveled toward the open doorway. Bleakness and terror etched his swollen, blood-encrusted face, but something more blazed behind the young man's steady gaze—strength, fortitude, and a hint of hope.

He was a fighter, a warrior entombed in a rapidly weakening young man's body. A rush of fury mixed with a healthy dose of respect surged through Guy. How did one so young get involved with the likes of Valère?

The prisoner's chest rose high with each deep, agonized breath. As his torturer intended, the young man knew Boucher's next attempt at pulling information from him would be far worse than the last.

Candlelight flickered over his youthful features. When the prisoner focused in on Guy's position, his terrified blue-green eyes—or eye, as one was little more than a bloated slit—opened wide.

Guy's heart jolted, fearing the young man would call out. With an index finger to his lips, he motioned for the prisoner to remain quiet.

Familiarity washed over Guy again. His gaze cleaved to the prisoner's; his focus sharpened.

Blue-green eyes. An unusual color Guy had seen only once before. His muscles contracted. A wave of frigid heat swept across every inch of his skin, and nausea twisted in his gut.

He knew those eyes.

The young man wasn't a man at all. But a goddamned woman.

Cora.